BLUE MADONNA

Billy Boyle
The First Wave
Blood Alone
Evil for Evil
Rag and Bone
A Mortal Terror
Death's Door
A Blind Goddess
The Rest Is Silence
The White Ghost
The Devouring

On Desperate Ground
Souvenir

BLUE MADONNA

A Billy Boyle World War II Mystery

James R. Benn

SOHO CRIME

Published by Soho Press, Inc.
853 Broadway
New York, NY 10003

Library of Congress Cataloging-in-Publication Data

Benn, James R.
Blue Madonna / James R. Benn.

ISBN 978-1-61695-834-3
eISBN 978-1-61695-643-1

1. Boyle, Billy (Fictitious character)—Fiction.
2. World War, 1939–1945—Fiction. 3. Undercover operations—
Fiction. 4. Murder—Investigation—Fiction. I. Title
PS3602.E6644 B67 2016 813'.6—dc23

Printed in the United States of America

10 9 8 7 6 5 4 3 2 1

For Debbie

Being everything which now thou art,
Be nothing which thou art not.
—Edgar Allan Poe

It is just as sentimental to pretend that war does not have its monstrous ugliness as it is to deny that it has its own strange and fatal beauty.

—Professor Bernard MacGregor Walker Knox,
former Jedburgh (Team Giles)

The Life That I Have

The life that I have
Is all that I have
And the life that I have
Is yours.

The love that I have
Of the life that I have
Is yours and yours and yours.

A sleep I shall have
A rest I shall have
Yet death will be but a pause.

For the peace of my years
In the long green grass
Will be yours and yours and yours.

—Leo Marks,
Special Operations
Executive cryptographer

BLUE MADONNA

PART ONE

ENGLAND • MAY 30, 1944

CHAPTER ONE

IT WAS A nice day for a drive. Late May, but warm and sunny, which you couldn't always count on in England. We sped past fields of ripening grain, sheep grazing on hillsides, and low, rolling hills, each topped with its own sunlit copse of trees. Small villages with quaint names like Lower Slaughter, Bourton-on-the-Water, Notgrove, and Sevenhampton disappeared behind us as we neared Cheltenham.

It would have been nicer without the handcuffs.

And if my companions hadn't been military police. Big, silent MPs. Both sergeants, both tight-lipped, both armed.

Unlike me. I'm a captain, I like to chew the fat, and I'd been relieved of my pistol. That left us with nothing in common except for our destination, the Services of Supply base on the outskirts of Cheltenham, a little corner of Gloucestershire that controlled all of Uncle Sam's stockpiles of food, ammunition, fuel, and whatever else American forces needed to fight this war. Which was more than you could imagine. SOS reported to Supreme Headquarters, Allied Expeditionary Force—SHAEF—which was where I worked. Not that my flaming-sword shoulder patch had impressed the MPs, far as I could tell.

In addition to running the supply chain, SOS was responsible for judicial services. The commanding general, John C. H. Lee, had been nicknamed "Court House" in some quarters for his initials and his attitude. Which had me more worried than the handcuffs. The MP in the backseat had the key and would probably want his cuffs back when we got to the base. Court House

Lee also ran the stockade, the kind of place where they tossed you in and forgot you.

"Either of you guys cops before the war?" I asked, trying one last time to start a conversation. "I was."

Silence.

"Boston PD," I continued, turning to catch the eye of the MP behind me. "Made detective right before Pearl Harbor. My dad's a homicide detective. It's kind of a family business." No response. The jeep crested a hill, the winding road leading into a valley dotted with Quonset huts, tents, and swarming vehicles.

"That's it," the MP said, tapping the shoulder of the driver and ignoring me. We pulled up to a gate where more MPs inspected the driver's paperwork. They gave me the once-over; lots of enlisted men got brought in sporting cuffs, but damn few captains in their Class A uniform did. I was a curiosity.

"What'd he do?" a sentry asked the guy in the backseat, nodding in my direction.

"Open the goddamn gate," was the only answer he got. I felt a little better knowing that my MP didn't want to talk to anyone. But not much.

We drove down the main thoroughfare of the huge base. It was like being in a city, except instead of tall buildings, crates of supplies stacked three stories high and covered with camouflage netting cast shadows across the road. There were city blocks of long Quonset huts and wooden barracks painted a uniform pond-scum green. Huge tents with their guy lines stretched taut looked like the dreariest circus imaginable had come to town and forgotten to leave. Trucks weighed down with supplies lurched by, grinding gears and straining to haul their loads of Spam, artillery shells, or scotch destined for the senior ranks.

What the hell was I doing here?

The jeep pulled over in front of a Quonset hut. The walkway was lined with whitewashed stones, a sure sign that officers here didn't like GIs with time on their hands. Signs were staked in the ground on either side of the walk. One read, OFFICE OF THE PROVOST MARSHAL GENERAL, CRIMINAL INVESTIGATION DIVISION; the sign was plain, the paint chipped and faded. No nonsense, like most CID agents I'd run into. The other was more ornate, the words US ARMY JUDGE ADVOCATE GENERAL in bold letters over a gold pen and sword crossed above a laurel wreath. Lawyers liked that kind of thing.

The driver switched off the engine. I waited for them to say something, but they both sat there, as silent as ever. I had no idea what to expect, no reason I could think of to have been rousted out of bed at dawn and driven here. From their expressions, the MPs didn't know much, either. They had one advantage over me; they didn't care.

"It's been great, fellas," I said. "See you around." I got one leg out of the jeep before they both grabbed me. I figured it was worth a shot, if only to rile them.

"Try that again, and I'll handcuff you to the steering wheel," the driver said.

"He speaks!" I said, turning to the sergeant behind me. He almost cracked a smile. Thought about it, anyway. "So, guys, spill, will ya? What's the deal? What are we doing here?"

"Hold yer horses," he said, almost friendly now that the journey was over. For him, at least. "We're waiting for a guy."

"Who?"

"Some colonel," he said, consulting his orders. "Colonel Samuel Harding. Anyone you know?"

"Yeah," I said. A figure emerged from the Quonset hut. "That's him."

I had no trouble spotting Harding. I'd worked for him since I landed in England back in '42, a shavetail second louie with vomit on his shoes after a trans-Atlantic flight in a B-17. Fortunately his opinion of me had improved some since those early days, and

I was sure he'd straighten things out. Maybe he'd had me brought here for that very purpose.

I breathed a sigh of relief as I held up manacled hands and gave my best impression of a nonchalant grin. "What gives, Colonel?" In the circumstances, I thought it best not to call him Sam.

A new MP approached the jeep and took hold of my arm. It was a practiced cop's clasp, a firm grip that let me know who was in control. A couple of GIs walking by stopped to gawk. A uniformed agent followed Harding out of the hut, the agent's shoulder brassard, lack of any rank insignia, and stocky build all advertising CID. A couple of other guys in Class As headed in, giving me nervous glances as if I might leap from the jeep and assault them. Their nerves, spectacles, and briefcases said JAG.

We were drawing quite a crowd, and I was having trouble keeping up the grin. Harding strode to the jeep, the CID agent one step behind.

"Take the cuffs off," Harding said to the MP in the jeep, who quickly obliged. The new MP pulled me out of the seat as I was rubbing my wrists to get the circulation going. Harding was giving me a grim stare, but I still felt relieved to be out of handcuffs. I figured it was time to act military, so I gave the colonel a snappy salute.

"Captain William Boyle," he said, returning the salute as if it irritated him, "you have been brought here to face a general court-martial regarding willful violation of the Articles of War. These men will escort you in to meet with your counsel."

"You're joking, aren't you? Sir?" I felt like Alice falling down the rabbit hole, finding myself in a place where nothing made sense. I looked around for someone to come to my rescue, but there was no one but Harding, his unwavering stare, the strong-arm men, and a gathering crowd.

"This is no joke, Captain. Serious charges have been brought against you, and given the gravity of the situation, it has been decided at the highest level to expedite the proceedings. You have one hour. I suggest you use it wisely." With that, he about-faced, leaving me with a stone-faced MP who made me miss the company of my two surly companions, and a CID agent who grabbed my other arm even tighter, smiling as he pulled me along.

I was going to ask what the hell was happening, but the CID guy looked like he enjoyed hauling in a captain too much to be bothered. Besides, something crazy was going on, and I knew I wouldn't get a straight answer from anyone if Sam Harding himself was pulling the wool over my eyes. So I zipped it as they dragged me down a narrow hall and let them shove me into a space that was more like a closet with aspirations to be an office. It had a metal table bolted to the floor and two folding chairs. I sat with my hands folded on the table, the feel of cold steel around my wrists still hard to shake.

I was in big trouble. And I had no idea why.

Ten minutes later, a skinny kid entered the room and took the other chair. His uniform jacket was too big for him, or he was too shrimpy for Uncle Sam's smallest size; it was hard to tell. He wore a second lieutenant's bars and the JAG gold pen and sword. "So you're the guy everyone's talking about."

"You left something out," I said.

"What?" He went wide-eyed as he opened his briefcase, glancing inside as if whatever he forgot was in there.

"Three things, actually. Two *sirs* and the fact you should still be standing at attention. As far as officers go, kid, you're the lowest of the low. Didn't they teach you anything in basic?"

"No," he said, pushing his chair back to stand. His briefcase tumbled to the floor, and a mass of papers spilled out. He knelt to retrieve them, thought better of it, and knocked over the metal chair as he tried to imitate attention. "I mean, I didn't go to basic training. Sir. We had an accelerated officer's training course, then a few weeks at JAG school, and here I am. Sir. Sorry."

"Good. Two *sirs*, and you're at a semblance of attention. Now gather your papers and tell my defense counsel I'm tired of waiting."

"Captain Boyle, sir, I *am* your defense counsel. Peter Scott. Lieutenant Scott. Sir."

"Jesus, sit down, Scott, you're making me nervous. You're it, really?"

"Yes, sir, I am," he said, placing the paperwork on the table and organizing the sheets. It looked like it calmed him. "I've been reviewing the charges, and I have to say this is serious."

"Yeah, the handcuffs and the MPs kinda gave me that idea already, Scott. What am I accused of?"

"You don't know?"

"How the hell would I know?" I was so steamed I forgot to bawl him out for missing a *sir* again.

"I mean, usually they tell you ahead of time. I think."

"You think? You're JAG; you should know. What kind of lawyer are you anyway, Scott?"

"Real estate," he said in a low voice. "Sir. Or at least that was what I was planning on. Joining my father's firm, I mean."

"It was a rhetorical question, Scott. I don't give a damn about your civilian life. They taught you rhetoric in law school, didn't they?"

"Yes, they did. I was captain of the debate team." Obviously the concept of rhetorical questions still eluded him. I studied his face, and he blinked nervously as I leaned forward.

"Hang on. You were planning on joining your father's firm? So you never actually practiced law?"

"Well, no, not exactly."

"How long have you been in the army, Scott?"

"Three months, sir."

"Officer's training, JAG school, transport over here—that doesn't leave much time for court-martial experience, does it?"

"Well, no. As a matter of fact, I arrived from the States last week. This is my first case." He smiled as if I should be honored.

"Scott, be a good kid and go get Colonel Harding, will ya?"

"No, sir. He instructed me not to let anyone see you. He sounded like he meant it. No, sir." His eyes were like saucers as he shook his head a couple of times more than he needed to. He was scared, which told me the word had in fact come direct from Sam Harding.

"Okay," I said, glancing at my watch. "We're wasting time. Tell me about these charges."

CHAPTER TWO

"THERE'S FOUR CHARGES against you," Scott began. "No, five. Make that five." He shuffled his papers, and I tried to keep my temper. If I needed a lawyer, it might be nice to have one who could count. "Here we go. Five counts of violating the Articles of War."

The first was Article 83. Willful loss or wrongful disposition of military property. No worries. Lots of guys lost equipment. Slap on the wrist, maybe restitution.

Then Article 84. Unlawful disposition or sale of military property. Slightly worse, since it involved making a profit off the army.

Article 87. Personal interest in the sale of provisions. Uh-oh. That one was usually reserved for senior officers involved in crooked dealings with suppliers. It was bad, but I had no role in what the army bought. I'd wait and see if the kid picked up on that one.

Article 93, Section G. Larceny. Now we were into the serious stuff. Loss of commission, dishonorable discharge, jail time.

Article 96. Disorder to the prejudice of good order and military discipline. The kitchen sink. If all the others fell through, they'd make this one stick.

"So what did I steal?" I asked, figuring to start with the easy stuff.

"I'm sure they'll tell us," he said. "The trial judge advocate, that is."

"Yeah, the prosecutor."

"Or you could tell me now," Scott said. "This doesn't look good, but they're not charging you with assault or anything like that, so maybe we can get the sentence reduced. What do you think?"

"Where are you from, Scott?"

"Indiana, Captain."

"Good. If I'm ever stupid enough to move to the state that produced you, I'll know who not to get for a lawyer. Now the first thing you're going to do is ask for the Article Eighty-Seven charge to be dismissed. That only applies to commanding officers who take kickbacks. Got it?"

"You're not a commanding officer?"

"Look, kid," I said, pointing to my SHAEF shoulder patch with the flaming sword. "This is where I work. Do I look like General Eisenhower to you?"

"Of course not," Scott said, jotting down a note. "What else?"

"How about I'm innocent?"

"They told us at JAG school everyone says they're innocent," he answered. It was the smartest thing out of his mouth yet.

"That's right, they do. I used to be a cop back in Boston, and I agree. You'll never hear a guy in his right mind admit his guilt. But you have to remember that doesn't mean everyone is lying when they say they didn't do it."

"You're right, Captain, sorry. This is just so new to me."

"When were you brought in on this?" I asked, trying for a gentle tone. I was starting to feel jittery at the thought of what was about to happen, but I didn't want Scott to pick up on it. If he got any more nervous, he might faint in the courtroom.

"Yesterday morning. They told me to keep myself available for a case. I got these charges about two hours ago."

"Who told you, exactly?" I asked in a whisper, leaning forward.

"Major Charles Thompson, sir. He'll be prosecuting. He claimed the evidence was solid and he had a witness. Said it would be over real quick, I'd get some experience, and not to worry about losing."

"Was Colonel Harding here yesterday?"

"Yes. He and Major Thompson were in conference most of the morning."

I didn't know what to say. Harding must have thought I did something horrible to feed me to the lions like this. I was being fitted for a frame, and I needed someone in my corner besides this legal genius from the Midwest.

"Listen, Lieutenant Scott," I said, drawing my ace in the hole, "I've got a relative at SHAEF who might be able to cut through all this. General Eisenhower. He's my uncle." Well, a distant cousin on my mother's side, but I'd always called him Uncle Ike. He was older—and a damn sight wiser—than me.

"I know," Scott said, shaking his head. "I've been warned you might bring that up. Major Thompson said if you tried to exercise undue influence, they'd prepare a list of new charges. Trying to intimidate the members of the court-martial with your family connections would not go over well, so I'd advise you to keep quiet about it."

"I can't contact SHAEF?"

"You are waiting for your court-martial to begin, Captain. There's no time for phone calls. Listen, you're in enough trouble without dragging General Eisenhower's good name into it." He glanced at his watch, gathered up his papers, and left the room.

I noticed the door wasn't locked. I waited a minute, then opened it, glancing up and down the corridor. No one in sight. I wasn't sure what I was doing, but odds were I'd be tempted by an available vehicle. I walked toward the exit, trying to look like I hadn't a care in the world as I passed a couple of officers engrossed in their own conversation. Daylight beckoned ahead, but was quickly blotted out by Colonel Harding opening the door for a civilian.

A civilian I recognized. A damn villain if there ever was one.

"Captain Boyle, is it now?" Archie Chapman croaked. "Come up in the world, haven't we?"

"Boyle, what the hell do you think you're doing?" Harding hissed, breaking up Old Home Week with Archie. "Get back in there."

"Colonel, I'm being railroaded. What's the story?" I whispered, hoping he'd whisper the secret he was keeping from me. "And what's Archie doing here?"

Harding didn't answer. He snapped his fingers as he looked over my shoulder, and I sensed a couple of MPs headed my way.

"This man is threatening a witness," he said as the MPs pinned my arms behind my back. "Take him away."

"Don't be too rough on Peaches," Archie said, a rheumy laugh escaping his lips and echoing off the curved metal walls.

Scott jumped out of an office and joined the procession, glancing back at Harding and his charge. "Is that the witness?" he asked as the MPs guided me into the courtroom: a few battered tables and a scattering of chairs, the American flag, and one exit, blocked by the MPs.

"That'd be my guess," I said. "Archie Chapman. London crime boss. Runs an outfit in Shoreditch. A bit off in the head. Drinks a lot of gin and likes to quote poetry while waving his pigsticker from the Great War."

"Pigsticker?" Scott asked, worry lines pinching his forehead tight.

"Bayonet. Big old long thing, sharp as a razor. He probably didn't bring it with him." Scott looked worried, and I immediately regretted it. "Sorry, bad joke."

"I wasn't worried," he said. "If he's mentally unstable, we can use that to impeach his testimony."

"He's not that kind of crazy," I said, glad Scott was beginning to think like a lawyer. "Crazy like a fox, prone to violence, and damn smart. If he's here, you can be sure there's something in it for him."

"How do you know him?" Scott asked, pen poised over his note-pad. That was a tough one. A lot of what went on six months ago with Archie and his pals was hush-hush. Even given my current situation, I couldn't trust Scott with that story. Except for one part.

Peaches, Canned, Syrup, Heavy.

"In the course of an investigation, it was necessary to steal a truck," I said, beginning to get uncomfortable with where this might lead.

"Hmmm," Scott said, tapping his pen against his lips. "So you commandeered a vehicle in order to carry out your assignment, right?" He was certainly trying to help.

"Yeah, sure," I said. "We also commandeered the contents of the truck. Canned peaches. A lot of them."

"So that's why he called you Peaches," Scott said. "How many cans?"

"Sixty-four crates. Six large cans per crate," I whispered.

He worked his fingers. "Three hundred and eighty-four cans?"

"Big ones."

"That's worth a small fortune on the black market, Captain. You accounted for them?"

"Well, depends what you mean by 'accounted for.' I know where they went. It just wasn't to the quartermaster."

"Jeez, Captain, my first case and my client is going to Leaven-worth." I was worried he might cry. I knew I felt like it. "You returned the truck, didn't you?"

I shrugged. I thought they did find the chassis, minus tires, engine, fuel tank, and anything else that could be sold or traded. Even the canvas flaps had been looted. It was better for Scott not to know the details.

"Listen, kid, that's old news. Harding didn't care about the truck, not much anyway. The case was solved, and everyone was happy." Well, again, the whole truth wouldn't do anyone any good at this point. "They're using Archie, or he's using them."

"Ten-hut!" The MP at the door snapped his heels and came to attention as he announced the arrival of a gaggle of brass. A colonel, two majors, and two captains sat at the main table, the lesser ranks on either end. A thickset guy with jet-black hair took the table next to ours. He slammed a thick file down on the table as he gave me a sideways glance. More officers filled the chairs behind us, some of them laughing and nodding in my direction. Seemed like I was the entertainment for the day.

Colonel Timothy Beaumont was the presiding officer. Close-cropped hair going grey at the temples, cheekbones riding high above a frown that had worn lines into his chin. The other members of the court deferred to him and avoided looking at me. He went through a lot of legal mumbo jumbo that left Scott bobbing his head in agreement as he took copious notes, eager to please the judge. It gave him something to do.

"Major Thompson, please read the charges and specifications," Beaumont finally said, leaning back in his chair.

"First charge," Thompson said, shooting to his feet and glancing at his papers. "Violation of Article Eighty-Three, in that Captain William Boyle, beginning in January 1944, willfully suffered military property belonging to the United States to be disposed of by sale to one Archibald Chapman. This activity continued until the first of April 1944. Military stores valued in excess of one hundred thousand dollars were wrongfully disposed of."

Scott looked at me, eyes wide, impressed at my supposed initiative. All I could think was that the date I ended my nefarious schemes was April Fools' Day.

"Second charge," Thompson continued, his voice a low, threatening growl. "Violation of Article Eighty-Four, in that Captain William Boyle, from January through May 1944, did unlawfully sell to Archibald Chapman military property valued as above."

The door behind me opened, and I caught a glance of Harding shepherding Archie into the back row.

"Third charge," Thompson said. "Violation of Article Eighty-Seven." Scott was half out of his seat, ready to object as I'd suggested. "We withdraw this charge due to lack of sufficient evidence." Scott fell back into his seat with a sigh. It was the only point he could have hoped to score in this kangaroo court.

Then we got to the big-ticket violation. Article 93, Larceny. Same amount, same name. Thompson withdrew the charge of violating Article 96, Disorder to the prejudice of military discipline. "Unnecessary," he said in conclusion. "We have more than enough evidence to find the defendant guilty of the three major charges."

The message was clear. They didn't need to waste time. I looked back at Colonel Harding, who kept his eyes up front. Archie looked gleeful, as if he were enjoying an outing from the old gangster's home. The audience looked ready to stand and cheer.

Thompson called Archie to the stand, and it was a delight to watch Archie swear to tell the truth so convincingly, given that he barely had a nodding acquaintance with it.

"Please tell the court of your first encounter with the accused," Thompson said.

"It was a cold night in January, I do remember that," Archie said, affecting the pose of a deep thinker and rubbing the grey stubble on his chin. "Lieutenant Boyle—that was his rank then—brought me a business proposition, in the form of a truck filled with canned peaches."

"Which he stole from me," I whispered to Scott, who wrinkled his brow and jotted a note.

"He offered to sell you these goods, which were the property of the US Army," Thompson said.

"Objection," Scott said. "Leading question. Mr. Chapman is not an authority on the provenance of peaches." I was impressed. The kid was in the game. He was sustained.

"He offered to sell you the peaches?" Thompson said, offering a slight bow in his protégé's direction.

"He did, that very night."

"How many cans?" Thompson asked.

"More than three hundred."

"Do you recall what was written on the cans?"

"I think it was 'Peaches, Canned, Syrup, Heavy.' You know, that backward way of writing the army likes? And the cans were green, I recall."

"Did you agree on a price?"

"It was two hundred and forty pounds, I believe. A good price for such a luxury item, but we never concluded the sale," Archie said, throwing a grin my way.

"Did you conclude any other business at a later date with the accused?" Thompson asked.

"Lots, lots. After we got over that first encounter, it was smooth sailing. Lieutenant Boyle brought us all sorts of things. Sugar, liquor, blankets, coffee, cigarettes, nothing but the best!"

"And you paid him?"

"Oh, indeed! Paid him well—always in cash, of course."

"I ask you to review this listing of dates, items sold, and prices paid," Thompson said, handing a sheet of paper to Archie and another to Scott. "Let the record show that the defense has also been given a copy. Is this information accurate, Mr. Chapman?"

"That it is, just as I laid it out for you," Archie said. I looked at what they said I'd sold him. If it were true, I'd be moving to Beacon Hill in Boston after the war instead of Southie.

"Very well," Thompson said. "I also submit for the record a written statement from the quartermaster's office detailing thefts of military supplies during the period in question. These thefts match the descriptions given by Mr. Chapman. No further questions."

"Redirect, Lieutenant Scott?" Colonel Beaumont said, his pen poised over his notepad. His tone suggested Scott get a move on.

"I'd like to request a recess, Colonel, to discuss this information with my client," Scott answered.

"Request denied. Proceed."

"Check these dates and write down any alibi you can think of," Scott whispered, pushing the paper my way. I scanned the dates, trying to remember where I was exactly during the last five months. Doing my job all across southern England, along with Colonel Harding some of the time. For the most part, I was always with one of two guys. Kaz, also known as Lieutenant Piotr Augustus Kazimierz of the Polish Army-in-Exile, and Staff Sergeant Mike Miecznikowski, known to all as Big Mike. The three of us made up General Eisenhower's Office of Special Investigations, which pretty well described what we did. We handled low crimes in high places, crimes that needed to be solved and kept on the QT while we did it. On most of these dates, we were working on one case or another.

I ticked off the dates, thinking it'd be a snap to get Kaz or Big Mike in here to straighten things out. Except that we all worked for Colonel Harding, and he was the one pulling the strings, I was damn sure of that much.

"Mr. Chapman," Scott began, strolling in front of the witness like he was an old country lawyer, "what is your occupation?"

"I was a soldier in the last war," Archie said, peering at Scott from under bushy eyebrows. "That was my last regular job. Killing Germans."

"Since then, how have you supported yourself?"

"Oh, a variety of ways," Archie said, shrugging. "Lately mostly buying materials from you lot. Fellows like Captain Boyle here, they don't mind doing business with me."

"Black market business, correct?"

"That's the term, boy."

"Which is illegal in Great Britain. So you are a criminal, correct?"

"If I were, wouldn't it be me on trial, and in an English court?"

"You may well be soon, Mr. Chapman," Scott said. Somehow

I doubted it. "Doing black market business must require that you are not always honest with the authorities, I'd imagine."

"Oh, and you're an expert, are you? Done some deals yourself, then?" There was a ripple of laughter in the room, cut short by Colonel Beaumont's threatening stare.

"Ask a specific question, Lieutenant," Beaumont said.

"Mr. Chapman, have you lied to the English authorities at any point during the past six months?"

"Lied?" Archie did his chin rub again, but this time I think he was stumped. It would be hard for anyone to believe he'd been honest for that long. "Yes, I've shaved a bit off the truth on occasion. For business purposes."

"Very well," Scott said, giving an approving nod. "We've established you lie to your fellow Englishmen. How about Americans? Have you lied to any Americans during the same period?"

"I like Americans," Archie said with a toothy grin. "You Yanks have brought so many good things to England, I could never lie to one of you."

Scott stood close to Archie, leaning over the witness chair. "So you are a liar, just not in this case?"

"Be careful, boy," Archie said, years of fog, gin, and cigarettes coarsening his low, vicious growl. "I might take offense."

"No more questions," Scott said.

"Do you have any other witnesses, Major Thompson?" Beaumont said. He didn't. No reason to waste time when the deck was stacked in your favor. Beaumont then told Scott it was his turn. I'd scrawled out Big Mike's name and duty station along with Kaz's information. He asked the court to make both of them available as defense witnesses and asked for an adjournment while they were brought in.

"I'm afraid that's impossible," Beaumont said. "I am advised these two men are on an assignment with a top-secret classification. They are unavailable for testimony."

"But sir," Scott began, "how—"

"I am not going to repeat myself, Lieutenant," Beaumont said. "Proceed."

"I'm going to call you as a witness," Scott whispered as he sat next to me. "We have to do something."

"No, we don't," I said. "Whatever happens next has already been decided. Let's get it over with. I'm not going to testify. We're done."

CHAPTER THREE

IT DIDN'T TAKE long. Ten minutes later, Beaumont called the court to order. Even more people had filed in to hear the verdict. JAG officers, CID men, and assorted noncoms from who knew where. Scott and I stood to hear the sentence.

"Captain William Boyle, you have been found guilty as charged under Articles of War Eighty-Three, Eighty-Four, and Ninety-Three. It is the sentence of this court that you be reduced in rank to the grade of private and confined to hard labor for three months, at such a place as the reviewing authority may direct. The business of this general court-martial is concluded."

The gavel came down.

"I'm sorry," Scott said, offering his hand. "I wish I'd done better."

"Don't worry, the fix was in. You couldn't have done anything."

Major Thompson led Scott out of the room, and I wondered how far away they'd send him. Whoever was orchestrating this charade would be covering his tracks soon, and dollars to doughnuts Scott would find himself on a slow boat to some Pacific backwater before the week was out.

Two MPs, a sergeant and a corporal, escorted me to a small room. They ordered me to remove my short-waisted Ike jacket. One of them removed my captain's bars and decorations from the jacket while the other took the bars off my shirt collar and garrison cap. I was relieved of my tie and belt; evidently for some, loss of rank was too much of a burden to bear.

"Fellas, how would I hang myself in here anyway?" I asked. The low, curved walls of the Quonset hut offered little hope for the suicidal.

"Had a guy once who strangled himself with his belt. Passed out and died on us," the corporal said. "But I don't expect we need to worry about you. Scuttlebutt is you got someone at SHAEF looking out for you."

"Yeah, well, he better show up soon. Where'd you hear that?"

"No talking with the prisoner," his more businesslike sergeant said. He tossed my Ike jacket at me, and they left me alone. I sat at the rickety wooden table, wondering what the hell had just happened.

Private Billy Boyle.

Three months of hard labor.

How much worse could it get?

The door opened, and Colonel Harding entered, followed by the CID agent who'd been at his side earlier. And Archie Chapman. I was about to find out how much worse.

Harding waited until the door was firmly shut and they were all seated. "You did well in there, Boyle."

"It's easy to be a patsy," I said. "What's he doing here?" I offered a sharp nod in Archie's direction.

"Easy, Peaches," Archie said. "We're all in this together."

"Great," I said. "So you're all pitching in on the hard labor? What the hell is happening, Colonel?"

"I'm sorry, Boyle, but we thought it best that you react as naturally as possible," Harding said. "It was part of the plan. Don't worry, the loss of rank isn't official. Beaumont and Thompson were in on it."

"I hope that goes for the confinement at hard labor as well," I said, trying to mask the emotions flooding my mind. Relief, anger, joy, all with a touch of fear about where this was headed. I didn't want them to know I'd been too concerned, so I laughed. Ha, ha, ha.

I didn't even convince myself.

"Shouldn't be a problem," the CID guy said as he introduced himself. "Agent David Hatch." I'd have preferred more certainty, but by now I was too curious to debate his choice of words. "Although the plan does require you to be put in the stockade for a while."

"Somebody back up and start from the beginning. Explain to this lowly private what the deal is."

"You know how serious theft and pilferage is," Harding began. "From the moment supplies are off-loaded from ships, they're subject to repeated plundering. Some of it is small time, but it adds up. Truck drivers, railway workers, quartermaster men, anyone who comes in contact with military supplies can be tempted to steal."

"At this point it's an epidemic," Hatch said. "Forty percent of all cases CID has involves the theft of supplies. Not petty pilferage; it's the wholesale looting of supplies being stockpiled for the invasion."

"Everything from fuel to penicillin," Harding added. "With the right black market contacts, it's easy to get rich quick."

"Sure," I said. "There's plenty of people willing to pay for what they can't get under rationing. And no shortage of those willing to sell the stuff, right, Archie?"

"No arguing with that, Peaches. But this is something different. It goes beyond providing the necessities of life to ordinary folk." I knew that wasn't all posturing. Archie and his gang were based in Shoreditch, a bombed-out and poor part of London. He spread his wealth around, keeping the neighborhood folks happy and on his side.

"Chapman's right," Harding said, setting a pack of Lucky Strikes on the table. Archie snatched one, and Harding fired up his Zippo for both of them. "We're after a major gang. They have connections to the English criminal world and the black market."

"Americans?" I asked.

"Mostly," Agent Hatch said. "They call themselves the Morgan Gang. They started small, selling pilfered supplies to the black market locally and then branched out to Oxford and Birmingham. Recently they made contact with a group of British deserters in the same line of work and joined forces."

"Makes sense," I said. "Men on the inside and the outside."

"Made sense to them, too," Hatch continued. "We've had our own problem with desertions, especially with the invasion coming anytime now. We know a dozen American deserters have recently joined them and are being used to stage armed robberies of supply trucks."

"Their inside men pass on information about routes and manifests," Harding said. "Then the deserters—Yanks and Brits—pull off the robberies, in uniform or civilian clothes. They sell the supplies off fast. That's where the English gangs come in. They have the contacts to dispose of the goods quickly, moving them into the black market in small batches. No one's the wiser."

"But the army's the poorer," I said, eyeing Archie and wondering why he was involved. The real reason, not whatever story he'd spin sooner or later.

"And the Morgan Gang gets richer," Hatch said. "Coffee is going for ten bucks a pound. A fifty-carton box of smokes brings in a cool thousand. We're talking big money."

"They've been hitting fuel shipments lately," Harding said. "Two deuce-and-a-half trucks filled with fifty-gallon drums of gasoline were hijacked last week. At gunpoint."

"Petrol's a tempting target," Archie said. "There's precious little allowed for business and none at all for private use. Those with cash will pay well to drive their fancy cars again."

"Penicillin as well," Hatch said. "Gangs need the stuff to treat their prostitutes or anyone who gets the clap and wants to be treated off the books."

"We're going to need a lot of penicillin in field hospitals once the invasion begins," Harding said. "If we don't stop these thefts, a lot of boys are going to die without the stuff."

"Okay, I understand," I said. "You've got a well-organized gang looting army supplies. What part am I playing in all this? And why is Archie here?"

"They're not only organized," Hatch said, "they're ruthless. They'll use anything from payoffs to threats to get what they want. Say they need information about what's in a boxcar on a train headed to Birmingham. They'll start with a shipping clerk and offer a bribe. If that doesn't work, the clerk gets a warning, then a beating. Either way, the poor slob is in their pocket. They'll blackmail him if he cooperates and break his legs if he doesn't."

"They're smart, too," Harding added. "Usually it's the Brit deserters who do the beatings, once the target goes off base. Impossible to trace them."

"Let me guess," I said. "I'm here because you can't trust your own men. You want me to go undercover as a crook myself."

"Exactly," Hatch said. "Besides Beaumont and Thompson, no one outside this room knows the truth."

"And it was you who spread the gossip about me?"

"Yes," said Harding. "We wanted to be sure word spread. And it has. That's why so many spectators showed up. We're betting the Morgans know all about you."

"Right now we have a couple of suspected members in the stockade on unrelated charges. There was a drunken brawl in town, and we're using that to keep them on ice," Hatch added.

"So I'm headed to the stockade for a criminal heart-to-heart with a violent thief. But I still want to know what role Archie plays."

"I found myself in a bit of trouble, Peaches," Archie explained. "Inspector Scutt of Scotland Yard, your old pal, he had me in a tough spot. When that happens, the best thing to do is put somebody else into an even worse spot."

"The English gang the Morgan crew is working with?" I asked.

"The Campbell Street Boys, they call themselves, although they were boys before the last war. Got their start on the Portsmouth docks and expanded from there. I'd picked up a few tidbits about their work with the Morgans and offered that up in exchange for Scotland Yard to leave me be. Next thing I know, your colonel brings me here and tells me to perjure myself. The nerve of the man! But it's only a Yank tribunal, so I don't care. Glad to oblige." He waved his hand as if granting us his blessing.

"Come on, Archie, there's got to be more in it for you," I said. "You're not the obliging type."

"He's a smart one, that Peaches," Archie said with a chuckle as he stabbed a finger in my direction. "Yes, I have an arrangement with a fellow who's a competitor of the Campbell Street Boys. There's a man down in Brighton who's trying to move in their direction, and he'll pay nicely if they go down. So I'm invested in the outcome, you see. Invested in your performance, like."

"You didn't say anything about this," Harding said.

"You never asked," Archie said. "Unlike Peaches. You picked the right man for the job."

"Anything else you haven't told us?" Hatch asked.

"Just that the Campbell Street Boys don't mind a dash of blood now and then. As a matter of fact, they like it. And it seems like these Morgans don't mind getting their hands dirty, either. So watch out, Peaches. Even in the nick, they're dangerous."

"We run a secure stockade, Mr. Chapman," Hatch said, his back stiffening.

"You might," Archie said. "But you know as well as me that the Morgans have someone inside. One of your MPs or any one of those soldier boys. A few seconds when the right back is turned, and Peaches'll be found with his throat slit. So take care."

"No one else knows about Billy," Harding said, studying me for any sign of panic. I was a little worried, mostly over that fact that it was Archie Chapman who seemed most concerned about my well-being.

"I believe you, Colonel," I said, struggling to sound confident. "Who is Morgan anyway?"

"It's a phony name," Hatch said. "We've questioned every guy named Morgan on this base, and not one of them looks like a criminal mastermind."

"Who are the suspects in the stockade?" I said.

"Herbert Franklin, a buck sergeant in a signals company, and Private First Class Martin Hammer, a medical orderly," Hatch said. "Far as we know, they haven't a clue we think they're part of the gang."

"But any one of your men could have been compromised," I said. "No offense."

"None taken. And you're right. That's why you're here," Hatch said.

I looked at Archie, who sighed and shook his head. Three months at hard labor didn't look so bad. "What am I after, exactly? You're not expecting a confession, are you?"

"No. We know the Morgans have at least two safe houses. One is within a half hour's drive of this base; the other is close to Birmingham. We need a location. If you can convince them of your worth, they might offer it up. If they take you to the wrong place, you'll have to sweet-talk your way to the other."

"Why would they tell me anything if I'm in the slammer with them?"

"You'll be getting out. Tomorrow an officer will visit the stockade and ask for volunteers for a dangerous mission. You can tell Hammer about it, let him think it's the work of your SHAEF contact. The story is you'll escape after they take you and need a place to hide out."

"Sounds easy. I get the location, the officer springs me, and you give me my captain's bars back. Right?"

"There's something else," Hatch said. There always was.

"We need to get someone out of that safe house. Alive. If we go storming in, they'll kill him. If a fugitive shows up, someone who's been vouched for, he stands a better chance. For right now, that's all you need to know."

"You mean there's more?"

"A lot more," Harding said. "Right now, go to jail and make new friends."

CHAPTER FOUR

I DIDN'T LIKE this setup one bit. Harding was holding out on me, Hatch was tossing me in the clink, and Archie Chapman was on my side. My world was upside down.

Two MPs who weren't clued in to the sting strong-armed me into the barbed-wire enclosure at the edge of camp. Guards opened up the double gates and signed some paperwork, and the MPs gave me one last good shove before they left.

"Welcome to Disciplinary Training Center Number Twelve," said a tech sergeant, flipping through the sheets he'd been handed. "Shut up, do as you're told, and we'll make your stay as pleasant as possible. Which ain't much. You're stuck with us until the provost marshal sends orders to transport you some-place where they got big rocks what need to be made into little rocks." The other guards, all privates, dutifully laughed, and I resisted the temptation to ask how many times they'd heard that line. But given that the tech sergeant now outranked me—and had a billy club stuck under his arm—I decided to listen to his advice. He looked disappointed as he crooked a thumb in the direction of the wooden barracks. A quick shove moved me up the steps and inside.

Two MPs drinking coffee eyed me as my escort pushed me toward a clerk pecking away at his typewriter. He gave the clerk my name.

"This is the guy everyone's talking about," the clerk said, glancing at the MPs.

"He doesn't look like much," one of them replied.

"Cut the gawking," I said, my anger at the situation Harding had put me in boiling over. Pain shot through my body as the guard behind me rammed his club into my back, a perfectly placed kidney hit. I fell forward, gasping as waves of agony rolled over me.

They all laughed.

"Get up, goddamn it," said the guard, kicking me so I toppled over. More laughter. "No speaking unless spoken to, and then call the lowest private 'sir,' understand? You are less than nothing here. You are the shit on my boot heel, get it? I'm talking to you, Boyle."

"Yes, sir," I said, struggling to stand. I was willing to say anything to spare my other kidney.

"Toes and nose, Boyle, on that wall," he said. "I'm going for a smoke."

"Yes, sir," I said, wondering what he meant and if I was allowed to ask.

"Stand over there," the clerk said, still grinning over my walloping. "Toes and nose touching the wall."

It sounded easy. It was, for the first ten minutes or so. Then the ache in my kidney worked its way up my back, my legs stiffened, and my knees began to buckle. Sweat beaded on my forehead, and I gritted my teeth as laughter rippled behind me. As soon as I thought I couldn't take another second, I felt the poke of the billy club again.

"Let's go, buttercup," the guard said. "Too bad you missed chow." Everyone thought that was hilarious.

In back of the barracks—quarters and offices for the staff, not prisoners—a barbed-wire enclosure about twelve feet high surrounded a tent city with an open parade ground in the center and a track around the perimeter. Big enough for two or three hundred guys, depending on how many they stuffed into each tent. Off to one side, a low wooden building served as the kitchen, to judge by the foul smell of rotting garbage wafting on the breeze.

I was deposited at a tent facing the parade ground and told to keep out of trouble. The advice was a bit late, but I kept that to myself. The flaps were open, and I entered my new home. Two bunk beds, a stool, a couple of footlockers, and three prisoners greeted me. The stool was the friendliest of the lot.

"That's your bunk," one of them said. He was a Private First Class, short and stocky, with wavy black hair trimmed close to the scalp on the sides. The bunk was a top, of course. It also had no blanket. I pointed this out to the PFC.

"I was cold last night," he said.

A jailhouse challenge. I could let him have the blanket and avoid a fight. It wasn't like I had anything else he'd want. But I was tired of being used and pushed around. I didn't really think about it, but I found myself charging forward, pulling him off the edge of his bunk, and throwing him to the floor.

"This hasn't been a swell day for me, so don't force me to ruin yours as well," I said, my knee pressed to his chest, my fist pulled back and ready to strike.

"Leave him alone," shouted a skinny guy, leaping up from the stool. He grabbed for my hand, but it was easy to shake him off. The third GI strolled out of the tent, unconcerned with the drama. Probably the smartest one of the bunch, me included.

"Hey now," the PFC said, his hands palms up in surrender. "Don't get your knickers in a twist, buddy. You can have your blanket. We're all in the same boat here. Now, Frankie, back off before you get yourself hurt."

Frankie did, and I followed suit, helping to hoist the PFC up. "Sorry," I said. "It's been a bad day. Court-martialed, and then they kept my toes and nose to the wall long enough to miss chow."

"Standard operating procedure around here," he said. "I'm Marty Hammer, and this is Herb Franklin, but we call him Frankie. The quiet guy who left is John Murphy. He don't talk much."

"Billy Boyle," I said, realizing that Harding must have set up my tent mates. "Recently Captain Boyle. I see you two still have your stripes."

"Have a seat, Boyle," Hammer said, pulling the stool closer. He tossed the blanket up on my bunk as Frankie rummaged around in the footlocker. He came up with a package of crackers and a chocolate bar. "It ain't much, but you're welcome to it."

"I didn't know we had PX privileges," I said. "Thanks."

"Good one," Frankie said. He was all skin and bones, with thinning hair brushed back from a high forehead. "We got our own PX right here."

"Shut up, Frankie," Hammer said. Odd for a PFC to talk to a noncom that way, but this was an odd situation. Frankie looked hurt. I ate the crackers. "We heard about you, Boyle. The whole camp's been buzzing."

"You guys must not have much excitement here," I said, brushing crumbs from the corner of my mouth. "I'm just a hard-working officer who got railroaded."

"Yeah, the fall guy, right?" Frankie said with a smile. "Somebody's patsy?"

"What's it to you? I appreciate the food and all, but that's my business, and I intend to take care of it."

"No harm meant," Hammer said, lighting up a cigarette. "We don't have much to do here but chew the fat. After dinner, that is. The rest of the time we got KP, calisthenics, close-order drill, all that crap."

"Yeah, they're trying to rehabilitate us as soldiers," Frankie said with a harsh laugh. "There's guys like us, threw a few punches in a pub, that sort of thing. Then there's guys like Murphy, waiting for their court-martial."

"What'd he do?"

"Stabbed a Brit. Husband of the gal he was shacked up with. Guy came home after a tour on a sub and found the two of them goin' at it. Murphy claims self-defense, but no one believes him," Frankie said.

"Why?"

"He done it before," Hammer said. "Knifed a husband who came home early from work, but it weren't serious, and the guy didn't want to be embarrassed, so Murphy walked. No charges. Still, he bragged about it, so there you go."

"Then there's guys like you," Frankie said. I broke off a piece of chocolate and ate it. "Guys headed for hard labor. You'll be here a few days, no more."

"I'm not planning on it. I'll be out of here two days, max, and no hard labor."

"I hear you got some pull," Hammer said. "But how's that gonna work? I mean, if you really had any juice, why'd you get court-martialed?"

"And found guilty?" Frankie said. They were both giving me the hard stare. They smelled a rat, maybe. Or wanted to know my secret. It was time to make a move, the kind of move a crooked captain with pull would make.

"I don't need the third degree," I said, tossing the rest of the chocolate bar on the wood-plank floor. "And I don't want any more of your chow. It's not worth listening to you flap your god-damn gums."

"Hey!" Hammer said, grabbing the chocolate. "You crazy? That stuff is gold in here."

"Yeah," I said, standing and kicking the stool away. "So why give it to me? You after a piece of my action, is that it?"

"Action?" Hammer said, his eyebrows shooting up. "What action? You got nothing but breakin' rocks in your future."

"Whatever you say, Hammer. Stick to your penny-ante PX operation, and I'll be out of your hair in two days, tops. Until then, stay out of my way." I climbed up onto the top bunk, feeling the pangs of hunger overwhelming the dry crackers in my gut. It had gone dark, the only light coming from a single bare bulb hanging from the center pole.

"Touchy guy," Frankie said to the empty air. Hammer shook his head, disappointment etched in his frown as he field-stripped his cigarette butt. From my perch, I watched as Murphy returned and climbed silently up into his bunk.

"You're not going to cause trouble, are you?" Murphy asked, staring at the sloping canvas about a foot from his face. Which was a strange question coming from a guy who caused a fair bit of turmoil himself.

"Not planning on it," I said. "Won't be here long enough."

"Trouble doesn't take long," Murphy said. Then the light went out, and I heard him roll over and punch his pillow. It was lights out for the entire camp. Through the half-open tent flap I saw nothing but darkness. A profound quiet settled in around us. In the midst of a few hundred men hitting the hay at nine o'clock, the only sounds were the rustling of blankets and bodies tossing back and forth. There must have been a prohibition against talk-ing, with a punishment worthy of silencing this bunch of fighters, thieves, and killers. I tried to sleep, but hunger and anger kept my mind roiling.

How was I going to get Hammer to tell me about the safe house? It was interesting that he seemed to call the shots, a PFC bossing around a buck sergeant. Maybe the Morgan Gang had its own ranks, and Hammer was a top man.

Why weren't Kaz and Big Mike in on this? I'd been so swept up in Harding's explanations that I hadn't thought to ask. Not undercover like me, but at least nearby in case of trouble.

And what was the rest of the story Harding hadn't told me? He'd said there was more to come after this. For now I didn't plan on losing sleep over things I didn't know. I had enough to keep me up as it was.

■   ■   ■

REVEILLE OVER A loudspeaker was a lousy way to wake up. Especially when it was barely light. Everybody moved quickly, so I joined in, lacing up my shoes and following at a trot to the parade ground. We lined up in rows and were counted. Twice. Then jumping jacks, push-ups, deep knee bends, all under the watchful eyes of guards walking the perimeter, slapping billy clubs into their palms. Charles Atlas had nothing on their motivational methods. Half the prisoners were sent to run the track, while the other half marched up and down the parade ground. Then we switched. Not a single prisoner said a word.

Finally the chow line formed for breakfast. It inched forward into a long, narrow wooden building attached to the guards' barracks. Low grey clouds had been threatening rain all morning, and now it began, a soft mist at first, then a pattering of raindrops, soon a downpour. A grumble rolled through the line, followed quickly by a guard in a rain poncho warning against speaking. Heads down, we shuffled inside.

Chest-high double tables ran down the center of the room. No seats. Food was served from the kitchen at one end, and prisoners ate as they moved down the line, pushing their trays forward. A bowl of porridge and a spoon. A slice of bread with jam. A cup of black coffee.

"Eat everything," Murphy whispered from behind me. I nodded, glancing ahead to see a guard check each tray. I was hungry enough that I didn't need prodding. The coffee was lukewarm, so getting it all down was easy. Not good, but easy. My tray was inspected twice, once at the end of the line to be sure I'd eaten, and again when I placed it on a clearing table, probably to be sure I hadn't swiped the spoon.

"We have thirty minutes," Murphy said as we left the building. "It's okay to talk. Best not to look at the guards; it only gives them an excuse."

"Thanks," I said, hunching my shoulders against the rain. "I appreciate the advice. Hammer and Frankie weren't all that helpful."

"That's funny," he said. "After they went through all that trouble to get you assigned to our tent, I thought you were a pal of theirs."

"No, not exactly pals," I said, trying to sound like I was in the know. "Just something I fixed up. They're operators, you know?"

"Yeah, I know. They got some deal with the clerk in the barracks office. I saw them talking a few times. Not something you usually see in here. You working an angle?"

"Yeah, I got something going. How about you?"

"I plan on telling the court-martial board they ought to put me in a combat outfit. No women and plenty of Krauts to kill. That'll keep me out of trouble."

"There's a crazy logic to that, Murphy." Might get him killed, too, but so might his romances. His knifework hadn't been fatal yet, but there was always next time.

We ran for the tent, making our way through the flap and shaking off the rain. Frankie and Hammer were changing into dry shirts and gave a half-hearted nod in my direction. Maybe they bought my tough-guy act. Now all I had to do was figure out what they wanted from me.

And if I could give it to them. Quid pro quo.

CHAPTER FIVE

"LISTEN, BOYLE," HAMMER said, sitting on the edge of his bunk. "We got off on the wrong foot yesterday. I'm sorry."

"Yeah," Frankie chimed in. "For us, being in here is no big deal. We'll be out soon as they decide we learned our lesson, and we keep our stripes. Gotta be hard for you, losing your captain's bars and all, and gettin' sent up the river. Even Murphy here has a hope of getting out, but you're done for."

"Yeah, that was so tactless of you," I said. "I feel much better now." I took off my shirt and gave a go at wringing it out, squeezing a few drops from the damp wool. The air was cold, and shivers shot through my body.

"Here," Hammer said, tossing me a towel. "Have a seat. We got a proposition for you."

"Give a listen, Boyle, okay?" Frankie said, pulling up the stool and resting his elbows on his knees.

"I got nothing else to do for now," I said, settling in next to Hammer and drying off. "What happens next?"

"You mean, in here?" Hammer asked. "More drill, running the track with a full pack, whatever those bastards think up. But we're interested in what happens next with you."

"I told you I'll be a free man soon."

"Yeah, yeah," Hammer said. "But what if that don't work out? Wouldn't you want a little nest egg waiting for you when your three months is done?"

"I know I would," Frankie said. "How you gonna get by on a private's pay? Fifty bucks a month is chump change, pal."

"You'll get no argument from me, boys," I said. "But I've got nothing to offer. Wish I had."

"You got something we want," Hammer said. "Contacts. And we'll pay for the introduction."

"You mean contacts with the criminal underworld," I said. "The kind of contacts I don't have because I'm innocent. I've been railroaded, remember?" Any crook worth his salt protested his innocence to any and all who'd listen. I needed to play that role. Plus, a smart crook would suspect every stranger of being a snitch. "Anyway, I'm getting out of here. So thanks for the offer, but no, thanks."

Hard to get, that's me.

"Hey, we'll talk some more tonight," Hammer said. "Keep an open mind, will ya?"

I shrugged. Not a worry in the world. Whistles sounded, and I threw on my shirt and Ike jacket before dashing outside after the others. I'd say one thing for this place, it taught guys how to move fast.

The rain had stopped, so at least I wasn't getting any wetter. We formed up, had roll call again, and stood around until the numbers came out right. Some of the men were taken away to clean the barracks and kitchens, while others were given packs loaded with rocks and ordered to run the track around the perimeter in formation. The rest of us did close-order drill. Quick time, double time, half step, side step, back step, flank march, all the chickenshit stuff I'd learned in basic and hoped never to have to do again. Fortunately, it all came back to me. Others not so proficient were pulled out of line and made to do push-ups as guards screamed abuse at them.

Then it was our turn to run with the packs. It wasn't that the weight was tough, it was that the straps digging into my shoulders hurt. With every step—in unison, column of fours—the rocks jolted against my back. I tried to lose myself in the rhythm of the run, thinking about my days on the track team back in Boston. Catholic school, of course. My mother counted on the nuns to keep me in line and on Dad to serve as backup. When a ruler across the knuckles didn't get the message across, Dad's belt was ready to grace my backside. I learned fast.

Which was the idea here, far as I could tell. Some guys were incorrigible; they'd be shipped home to Leavenworth. Others were redeemable and would be ready to do their part when the army needed them. With D-Day on the horizon, there would be a demand for infantry replacements. A big demand, even if they were small-time crooks.

More whistles, and we dropped our packs and fell in again. Another count, and we were dismissed for chow. Reminders to keep moving, no talking, and eat everything came from guards who were waiting for anyone to disobey, eager for a break in the routine. A good thrashing made the time go faster.

Lunch was shit on a shingle. Two pieces of toast with chipped beef in what the army called "creamy white sauce." They were right about the color. I was hungry enough to eat it all without being prompted. There was a thirty-minute break after the mid-day meal, and I looked forward to sunning myself under the clearing skies.

"Boyle," Murphy called from across the parade ground, "they want you at the guards' office." So much for relaxing.

I approached the door to the barracks hesitantly. I didn't want another kidney whack for breaking a rule I didn't know about. But the door opened, and a massive GI pulled me inside.

Big Mike.

"Move it," he yelled in my ear. "See the clerk and get back here pronto!" He pointed with his billy club, a snarl curling his lips.

Okay, I get it. We don't know each other. I hustled over to the clerk and stood at attention.

"Boyle, this is your stuff. Fatigue outfit, boots, the works. Your

Uncle Sam takes care of you. Now get out and get cleaned up. You stink." He pointed to a pile of clothes and a small box with a razor, soap, toothbrush, all the usual necessities. I grabbed everything, fumbling at the door with my hands full. Big Mike came along, cursing and yelling about what a low-life scum I was, and opened the door. He followed me into the courtyard, shoving me along with the billy club.

"How's it going, Billy?" This came in a sideways whisper.

"Got 'em right where I want 'em," I said. "Or they have me, I'm not sure. Hammer arranged for me to bunk with them. They want my black market contacts."

"Then Sam's plan worked," he said. "They bought the package. You ought to be able to parlay that."

"Tonight, I hope. Tomorrow you spring me. Now do me a favor," I said, stopping to face him. "Hit me. Knock me down."

"Aw, Billy, no."

"Come on, a good shove. Send me flying. We got a good audience."

We were on the parade ground, with dozens of guys hanging around, waiting for the next round. I was about to insult Big Mike to get him really mad, but I didn't need to. He stepped into me, billy club jabbing at my chest, calling me all sorts of names, some of them in Polish. Big Mike had been a Detroit cop before the war, and he knew his way around a billy club. Next thing I knew, I was on my back and he was strolling around me, twirling that club like a pro.

"Next time I tell you to hustle, you listen, you worthless piece of shit!"

He walked away, and I dusted myself off, glad that the biggest sergeant in the US Army was watching out for me.

"New guy?" Frankie asked as I approached the tent.

"How would I know?" I said. "Another goon as far as I'm concerned."

"You got that stuff just in time," Hammer said. "Today's wash day. Come on."

I followed my tent mates to the rear of the camp where a series of tubs and faucets were arrayed in the open air. A hut contained showers, with the mess hall approach: *Don't stop moving. In one end dirty, out the other clean. No talking, no horseplay.* Dirty clothes were hand-washed in the sinks and taken back to the tents to dry over the guy wires. Every prisoner had two sets of fatigues, one to change into and one to clean. They weren't keeping me long enough for two outfits, although I'd need a new set of Class As when all this was over. The chocolate-brown wool shirt was dirty and torn, my shoes scuffed and scraped, and my tailor-made Eisenhower jacket was in need of mending. If I'd known I was headed for a prison camp, I would have dressed for the occasion.

After washing clothes, we grabbed buckets and mops to clean the plank flooring in our tents. Guards swarmed around us, yelling at men to move at double time, then yelling again if even a drop of water was spilled. This wasn't about cleanliness; it was about obedience. Which was a good thing to learn if any of these guys were going to be in a rifle squad anytime soon. Lives would depend on it.

But not every guard understood the reasoning. Some plain enjoyed it. If I ever had anything to say about it—which was doubtful—I'd suggest putting them all in a platoon and sending them up against the Krauts once we hit the beach. Some of those tough guys would be whimpering hulks in no time.

After the buckets and mops were returned, we had another calisthenics session. The army did love jumping jacks. Some fancy close-order drill, then another roll call, and then back to our tents to take down the laundry, dry or not. Standing outside at attention, we waited for guards to inspect each tent for cleanliness.

Big Mike stomped into our tent, followed by another guard. I heard the latch on the footlocker open.

"Leave that be," the other guard said.

"Why?" Big Mike asked, sounding merely puzzled.

"Those guys are okay," the other guard said, nodding toward Frankie and Hammer. "No need to roust their stuff. They're only in for a week or so over a pub fight. Nothing to worry about."

"Sure," Big Mike said as they exited, ignoring us. "What about the other two?"

"Headed for hard time," came the answer. "Forget about them."

"See?" Hammer whispered, following me to the chow line. "We got things sewed up here. We can do you a world of good, Boyle."

"I bet," I said out of the corner of my mouth. I didn't doubt it. Hammer knew what he was doing. The guards left his footlocker alone, the clerk was his pal, and he had all the food and smokes he wanted. Only a PFC, he bossed around Frankie, who didn't seem to mind. Tonight I'd make a deal with him, one too good to pass up.

Chow was hamburger with watery mashed potatoes and limp string beans. I ate everything and could have gone for seconds, lousy as it was. I was ready to be a free man any time now.

"Hey, Murph, take a stroll, will ya?" Hammer said, back in the tent. He tossed him a four-pack of Chesterfields, the kind GIs expect to find in their K-ration meals at the front. Murphy grunted his acceptance and strolled out, indifferent to our plans and conspiracies.

"So you give our offer any thought?" Frankie asked, stretched out on his bunk, head propped up on one hand. I put my foot up on his blanket and leaned in.

"Yeah," I said. "We can make a deal."

Hammer moved closer, sitting at Frankie's feet. "You give us the names of your London contacts," Hammer said. "Whoever you wholesale stuff to. We give you twenty-five pounds. Then another hundred when it pans out."

"And if it doesn't?" I asked.

"Then we're out a C-note," Hammer said, converting the currency to dollars with shrug. "But if there's trouble, like cop trouble, then we pay somebody on the inside to put a shiv in your ribs. Sound fair?"

"That's reasonable insurance," I said. "You got that much of an organization? Or are you two it?"

"Organization we got," Frankie said. "Plenty."

"How do I get my money?"

"You get the down payment right now," Hammer said. He reached into his pocket and thumbed White Fivers off a thick roll. "Twenty-five English pounds. The other one hundred when you get out, assuming you ain't dead."

"Tell me why I should trust you," I said.

"Listen," Hammer said. "We got two ways of doin' business. One is with kid gloves. The other is with brass knuckles. Our boss doesn't flinch at the brass-knuckle approach, believe me. But he prefers the kid gloves. Money, information, you scratchin' my back while I scratch yours. Everybody comes up a winner, he says."

"You can't make money off a corpse, he says," Frankie threw in. "I like that one."

"I'll take the down payment." I gave them Archie's name and where to find him. Deep underground in a Shoreditch air-raid shelter. Archie continued to sleep down there in case the *Luftwaffe* started up the Blitz again. And because it was easy to see who was coming. "Tell him Peaches sent you. That'll clinch it."

"Good," Hammer said, handing over the bills. We shook hands.

"Now *I* have a deal for *you*," I said. "I wasn't just flapping my gums about getting out of this. Tomorrow they're going to ask for volunteers. Volunteers for a dangerous combat assignment."

"You're going get yourself killed, Boyle," Frankie said. "Take the three months and the bankroll."

"I'm not getting killed. I accept, and after I get out of here, I disappear. This pin money is nice, but I've got more stashed away.

I'm going to need identity papers and a safe place to lay low for a few days. How about you keep the hundred pounds in exchange? You've got to have the pull to make that happen."

"Maybe," Hammer said, quickly glancing at Frankie, who shrugged. "And then we can keep an eye on you, make sure this limey Chapman checks out."

"We could do some business," I said. "I know plenty of guys. All that stuff I sold, remember? Maybe your organization has an opening."

"One thing at a time," Hammer said. "A place to hide out is not a problem. Papers are easy. We got ration books, clothing coupons, anything you need. We can get you discharge papers, medical forms, Brit identity cards, driver's license, you name it."

"I like the way you fellows work," I said. "You think big."

"You got to, you wanna make a few bucks these days," Hammer said. "Uncle Sam thinks big. Why shouldn't we?"

CHAPTER SIX

IT TOOK AWHILE, but Hammer worked it out. He got a guard to pass a message to the clerk, which resulted in Hammer being hauled away not long before lights out. A lot of rough stuff, shoving, and the waving of billy clubs. A good show for the boys.

Around midnight he was returned, hardly the worse for wear. He smelled of whiskey and cigarettes. The fix was in. For the hundred pounds they'd keep, I'd get an address outside of Birmingham where I'd be expected. I was to ask for Willie Foster and do what I was told. Willie would arrange for one set of civilian duds and provide three days of meals and lodging. Anything else I needed to pay or barter for; information on crooked GIs able to provide supplies would get me documents, a longer stay, whatever I could trade for.

"What, are you running a printing press?" I asked.

"Don't need to," Hammer said with a wink. "These Brits leave their government buildings unguarded at night. All we have to do is break in to some bureaucrat's office in the Ministry of Trade and help ourselves to stacks of ration books, clothing coupons, whatever. I swear, sometimes they don't even know they've been burgled."

"All you got to worry about is getting there," Frankie said. "It's Sixty-five Goosemoor Lane, Castle Bromwich. That's on the outskirts of Birmingham. They got a big Spitfire factory there, and Goosemoor Lane is a stone's throw away on the north side. There's a bombed-out house on a corner, then number sixty-five.

Two-story brick joint. It's run-down, so no one takes much notice."

"And it's a busy street. Lots of workers at the factory rent rooms, so there's always people coming or going," Hammer said. "It's perfect."

"I know the area. Anyone else besides Willie there?" I asked.

"No one you need to worry about," Hammer said. "Don't get Willie upset; he's got a temper."

"I'll be the perfect guest," I said. It sounded like there was somebody else in residence. Voluntary or not, that was the question. If it was our man, I'd get him out and be done with this charade. If not, then Willie would have some pressure applied to reveal the location of the second safe house. "Quiet as a mouse."

"You let Willie know about any contacts you got," Hammer said, leaning close and dropping his voice. "He has 'em checked out, and if they look good, you go along and make the introductions."

"Who do I negotiate with? Willie?"

"No," Hammer said, obviously amused at the thought. "Willie will bring you to the man. That's what Willie's good at. That and breaking bones."

"I got a line on a shipment of blankets," I said. "Coming in on railway cars, right off the boat. Guys from the railway battalion are ready to unlatch the doors and look the other way."

"How many?" Frankie asked.

"Ten thousand thick wool blankets," I said. "Ready to be made into coats or sold as is. I also know some tailors who'd be glad for the work and don't ask questions."

"Interesting," Hammer said. "If all that's true, there's something in it for you. But *we're* taking the risks, remember."

"Who is 'we,' exactly?" I asked, hoping prospects of profits would get him gabby. With rationing, cloth was a rarity, and unemployed tailors were known to work on anything to bring in a few quid. Women's brown wool coats with US Army stenciled on the inside—covered by a nice lining—would bring a high price.

"Once again, no one you need to worry about," Hammer said, clamming up.

"So who's springing you?" Frankie asked.

"No one *you* need to worry about," I said, smiling at the prospect of leaving this place and these two bums. Just watch morning roll call and wave goodbye. I'd be in Castle Bromwich by teatime.

I SLEPT FITFULLY, wondering how tomorrow would go and what would happen when I drove out of here a free man. From what Harding had said, this was a setup for something else, something that sounded big. But it was nothing I could figure out, so I tried to put it out of my mind, thinking instead about a decent meal I could eat sitting down.

Reveille. Roll call, and no cavalry to the rescue. Hammer and Frankie exchanged snickers as we finished up calisthenics and headed to the kitchen for powdered eggs and cold toast. As the line exited the mess hall, guards told us to form up again and look sharp about it. That was unusual, and in any prison the unusual was greeted with equal parts fear, panic, and giddy excitement. Rumors began to swirl as guards told us to cut the chatter and stand at attention. Hammer gave me a raised eyebrow of admiration.

An MP lieutenant strode out of the barracks with two men trailing him. The first was Big Mike, a head taller than the second louie and scowling as he surveyed the ranks of prisoners. Behind him was Kaz in his resplendent best, a tailored English officer's dress uniform complete with gleaming leather Sam Browne belt and his Webley revolver sidearm. He wore double lieutenant's pips, a SHAEF flaming-arrow patch on one shoulder along with *Poland* stitched on the other. A jagged scar on one cheek began under his steel-rimmed spectacles and disappeared at the edge of his lips. He walked into the yard with an air of studied nonchalance.

"Listen up!" the lieutenant bellowed. "We have a visitor. This officer is seeking volunteers for a dangerous assignment. There can be no guarantee of safe return, but if accepted, your record will be wiped clean. *If* you survive. Anyone interested in volunteering, remain in place. The rest of you, dismissed."

With that, the parade ground emptied, survival of the fleetest the rule of the day. Besides me, only three men remained: Murphy and two others. Kaz approached each of them, asking questions, spinning some sort of plausible yarn. One by one, they were sent away. Murphy looked disappointed. Maybe he'd have a better chance for sanctioned butchery at his court-martial.

"Hello, Billy," Kaz said, his voice a whisper. The MP stood not far behind him, so we played out the scene. "It's not like you to volunteer." He smiled, but the scar that ran along the side of his cheek gave him a look that was vaguely terrifying.

"It's not like you to go slumming," I said. "What's the plan?"

"Do you have everything you need?"

"An address tucked away up here," I said, tapping my head.

"Keep it there," Kaz said. "I'd hate for Colonel Harding to detain you here any longer, although he might find it amusing."

"Well, let's go," I said. "It won't take me long to pack."

"This man will do, Lieutenant," Kaz said. "Barely."

Under Big Mike's watchful eye, I grabbed my ruined Class As and tucked the bundle under my arm, giving Hammer and Frankie a wink. They feigned disinterest, but I could tell they were impressed. Visions of wool overcoats danced before their eyes.

WE DROVE OUT the main gate, Big Mike at the wheel and Kaz in back, playing the role of the dashing, secretive British officer.

Meaning he managed to keep it zipped until the gate closed down behind us.

"That was quite exciting," he said, leaning forward from the jeep's backseat. "I think I gave a good performance, don't you? Perhaps I should take up acting after the war."

"If you're such a good actor, why didn't you volunteer for the role of the surly guard?" Big Mike said. "Giving prisoners grief would have been more of a challenge than prancing around the parade ground."

"Prance? Billy, did I prance? I think not."

"Guys, I think you're ignoring the lead role in this play. Remember the one who was court-martialed and dumped in the stockade?"

"I heard you were great, Billy," Big Mike said, giving me a gentle poke with his elbow that almost knocked me out of the jeep. "Sam was right not to spill the beans. You never could have pulled off that lost look he told us about."

"Thanks," I said, getting that the two of them had enjoyed their bit of playacting much more than I had. "You were a convincing turnkey, Big Mike. I would have been scared if I didn't know you were a cream puff at heart."

"I can still play the part," Big Mike said, grabbing a billy club from next to his seat. "I kept a souvenir."

"I may have to borrow that as a prop," I said, thinking ahead to our next move. "Where do we go from here?"

"Burton Green, a little village outside of Coventry," Kaz said. "We meet Colonel Harding there, and you can rest up and get some decent food. Or decent compared to the stockade."

"Sam said he'd brief us on the rest of this operation," Big Mike said. "He's got something else cooking, but he won't say. Top priority is to spring this guy. Without him gettin' killed."

"The guy would probably like that," I said, lifting my face to the sun. It may have only been a short-lived ruse, but barbed-wire enclosures didn't shake off easy, and I enjoyed the freedom of a ride in the country. Especially with Big Mike at the wheel. Big Mike was broad at the shoulders, all muscle. The scuttlebutt at SHAEF was that he kept a seamstress busy resewing the split seams on his uniform jacket. Uncle Sam just didn't stock khaki in his size.

We settled into the drive, negotiating winding roads and the occasional military convoy. They were all headed south, toward the coast and the ten-mile restricted area, from the Wash to Land's End. No one but authorized personnel went in, and damn few got out. The south of England was one huge armed camp, men and supplies alike stockpiled for the coming invasion. Against the flow of lethal traffic, we headed into the Midlands.

The outskirts of Coventry revealed themselves as in any city. Fields gave way to clusters of brick houses and small factories and shops strung up along the narrow road. Then we pulled into the city center.

It was a desert.

Whole blocks were cleared of rubble from the bombing raids of 1940. Nothing was left but the outlines of buildings, granite foundations standing like tombstones. Only the roofless ruins of Coventry Cathedral hinted at what had once stood here.

"Coventried," Kaz said once we'd left the vacant heart of the city behind. "The Germans invented a new word to describe the total destruction of a city with high explosives and fire-bombs. *Coventriert*."

"Lots of Kraut cities don't look half as good right now," Big Mike said. "Helluva war."

I had to agree.

THIRTY MINUTES LATER, we found Burton Green, a cross-roads town thick with half-timbered houses, their blackened oak beams cracked and fissured with age but still standing strong. The air war was hell on cities, but country life plodded on, especially this far northwest of London.

Our destination was The Butcher's Arms, a pub with a few rooms that Harding had commandeered for the night. The sign hanging over the narrow door was a picture of a man with a pig in one arm and a glass of beer in the other. That said it all.

Harding had taken all four rooms upstairs and provided me with a clean set of olive-drab clothing and a small bag of gear. I washed up as best I could, limiting myself to the four inches of water allowed for any bath. It was sufficient to sluice away the smell of the hoosegow but not enough to leave me really feeling clean. Given that I was supposed to be a criminal on the lam, it all worked out.

I laced up my combat boots and donned my Eisenhower jacket, checking myself in the mirror as I straightened my field scarf. It was strange wearing no badge of rank. Back when I was a cop in Boston, my shield was the most important part of my blues. Over here, even the lowly gold bar of a second louie got you into the officers' club and a host of other establishments off-limits to enlisted men. I had nothing, not even the single stripe of a PFC.

Billy Boyle, buck private.

I found Big Mike carrying two pints back to the table where Kaz and Harding were still working on theirs. He handed me one with a look that said they might have both been for him.

"Cheers," Harding said as I took a seat. "Here's to the ex-con."

"Escaped convict," I said, after a healthy pull on the ale.

"Like Paul Muni in the movie," Kaz said. *I Am a Fugitive From a Chain Gang.*"

"It wasn't exactly a chain gang," I said. Kaz was very enthusiastic about American gangster films. "As a matter of fact, my tent mates seemed to have the run of the place. Hammer and Frankie anyway. It looks like they bought the story, Colonel. They even arranged to have me assigned to their tent to check me out."

"Good," Harding said. "It means we're able to move quickly on this."

"Yeah, as well as me not spending more time in the stockade."

"Listen, Boyle, I'm not unsympathetic to what you've gone through," he replied, "but this is big. We're losing so much to gangs like this that it's like having half a dozen Liberty Ships torpedoed in the North Atlantic. The Morgan Gang is the biggest we've seen, and it's very well organized. This is our chance to take them down. Right now it's as dangerous as a Kraut division."

"Hammer explained their methods," I said, nodding. "If they need someone's cooperation, they offer a big payoff or a beating and broken bones."

"It works," Big Mike said. "I tried to get a line on what they were up to while I was there, but no one bit. Guys were either clearly spooked or gave me the cold shoulder. I think everyone knew what I was talking about."

"It's an open secret, but no one has been willing to spill the beans," Harding added. "Until now."

"The guy in the safe house?" I asked.

"No," Harding said. "That's Corporal Donald Blake. The Morgans recruited him because he works at the Quartermaster Market Center outside of Bristol. Blake has access to all the supplies being shipped in from the States, mostly foodstuffs. But he's small fry."

"So why do we care about him?" I asked.

"Because his cousin cares about him," Harding said. "CID finally got a guy who would talk. Sergeant Alvin Blake, radio operator and navigator on a B-26 bomber. His bomb group is based outside Southampton, and he's been diverting supplies to the Morgans. PX stuff mostly, but CID thinks he also had a hand in setting up a recent hijacking. Three trucks filled with canned food—a small fortune."

"Why does he wish to talk?" Kaz asked.

"The gang leaned hard on his cousin Donald. Apparently the two are close, and when Donald had a weekend pass, he visited his cousin and complained to him about how he was being forced to steal supplies. Not knowing, of course, that Alvin was already part of the gang."

"Let me guess," I said. "Alvin got in touch with CID and agreed to name names. Then someone snitched, and the Morgans grabbed Donald as leverage."

"Exactly. Which was one reason Agent Hatch got in touch with me. He wanted to run this operation outside of channels, to reduce the chance of the Morgans' informant picking up on it."

"Why not simply kill Alvin?" I asked.

"We're not sure," Harding said. "They could have, but then they'd lose a valuable contact. Maybe they want to see if he'll come back into the fold once he saw they could get to his cousin."

"Southampton is within the restricted coastal zone," Kaz said. "Perhaps they cannot gain access to the base."

"Hatch thinks there are other members of the gang on base," Harding said. "They're probably the ones who gave Alvin Blake the message about his cousin. He recanted everything. He's a few years older than Donald and feels protective."

"It's one thing to relay messages," Big Mike said. "But the restricted area makes rough stuff harder. They can't bring in an English gang or a deserter. Without papers, they'd never get close."

"What does Alvin have to say?" I asked. "Will he testify if his cousin Donald is safe?"

"He was ready to before," Harding said, "No reason why he wouldn't be again, especially if we promise to have Donald transferred far away to someplace safe."

I took a long pull on my ale and thought about this tale of two cousins. It made sense. Cousins could sometimes be closer than brothers. You shared family ties but not your toys and clothes, which took some of the rough edges off the lifelong relationship.

"Blake knows enough to take down the Morgan Gang?" I asked.

"He knows a lot," Harding said, draining his own glass. "We get names and make some arrests; the rest of the gang will be fighting over who gets to make a deal. It will gut the organization."

"They oughta hang," Big Mike said, gulping the last of his beer. No one argued. Thieves stealing from combat troops didn't elicit sympathy from any of us.

At that moment, four bowls of steaming hot rabbit stew arrived. Our server informed us it was the specialty of the house, since rabbit was off-ration. They were easy to raise and to hunt, so it was a popular alternative to the more highly rationed meats. I'd heard there was some resistance to the idea at first, since the little guys were so adorable with their fluffy tails and floppy ears. But as food rationing tightened, cooking pots began to fill up with Peter Rabbit, and any qualms were quickly overcome. I ate the excellent stew, wondering at the fate that had befallen my dinner. He once had been free, and now he was cooked and served up.

I felt a vague kinship.

CHAPTER SEVEN

I WALKED UP to the brick two-story, the billy club in my belt digging into my ribs. I wore a heavy stubble and civilian coat, the slightest of desperate disguises. I knocked: sharp, impatient raps, the sound of a fugitive seeking shelter. I glanced behind me, watching the flow of workmen headed for the gates at the Castle Bromwich Aeroplane Factory. They built Spitfires there, and the test pilots were already up and noisily running the latest batch through their paces from the adjoining airfield.

I knocked again. Criminals weren't the earliest of risers. No one on the sidewalk paid me any mind. This was the last residential street before the factory area, all the red-brick and slate roofs grimy from coal smoke and whatever else belched out of the nearby chimneys. Crowded and anonymous, it was the perfect spot for a hideout. The house was run-down but not yet decrepit. The paint on the window sills was peeling, and upstairs two windows were boarded over. Broken glass or a makeshift cell?

"Yeah?" A rough voice barked as the door opened a bit, still secured by the chain.

"I'm looking for Willie," I said. "Hammer sent me."

The chain rattled loose, and the door opened a few inches farther. I entered a narrow hallway with cracked linoleum, faded wallpaper, and a guy with a pencil-thin mustache. He glowered at me as if I'd interrupted him at something important. His sleeves were rolled up and his suspenders hung loose at his side. Either he'd just gotten up or come in from a hard night on the town.

"Come on," he said, waving a lazy hand my way. He walked down the hall, past the staircase and a couple of rooms.

"Are you Willie?" I asked as we entered the kitchen. Curtains were pulled over the windows, and teacups were scattered over a rough wooden table.

"No, *that's* Willie," he said, as I heard the door shut behind me and felt the barrel of a pistol against my neck. It was cold, the sharp odor of gun oil rising in my nostrils.

"Have a seat," Willie said, shoving me toward the table. "Nick, pat him down." Nick pulled off my coat roughly and went through my pockets. There was nothing but a few shillings and of course the billy club.

"Planning a bit of rough stuff, eh?" Willie said, pushing me down onto the chair. Nick rapped the table with the club, hard enough to remind me what a billy club could do to a man's bones.

"It's all I had for protection," I said. "I took it off the MP who was driving me."

"What happened to him?" Willie asked, coming around to face me. He was short and squat, thick waisted, with a set of yellow-grey teeth behind meaty lips.

"I left him by the side of the road, sleeping like a baby," I said. "I drove until I figured they'd put out an alarm, then ditched the jeep and made my way into Coventry. Caught a bus and got off with those suckers headed into the factory. No one spotted me."

"No?" Willie said, handing over his Webley Bulldog revolver to Nick. He shook a Lucky Strike from a pack and sparked a wooden match to life with his fingernail. "Pretty smart guy, aren't you?"

"Look, fellas," I said, spreading my arms wide in a friendly gesture, "no need to give me a hard time. Me and Hammer worked out a deal. He sent me here. So let's be pals, okay? Things can work out swell for everyone."

"We already got a lot of friends, ain't we, Nick?" Willie said, straddling the chair opposite me. I hadn't expected them to cook me breakfast, but I hadn't expected the third degree, either.

"Yeah, I don't think we need any more pals, not like this Yank," Nick said.

"Hey, what's your beef? I came here in good faith, ready to trade what I know."

"Good faith?" Willie said, pulling on his cigarette. "Then why'd you lie to Hammer and Frankie?"

"What lie?" I asked, feigning indignation while I scrambled to think of where I'd tripped up.

"Listen, Willie, he's told so many lies he can't figure out which one," Nick said with a laugh as he waved the Bulldog at me. It was a short-barreled piece with a small grip, perfect for stashing in a pocket.

"Hey, put that thing away," Willie said, which told me they weren't planning on plugging me, at least not right now.

"I was on the up and up with Hammer," I said. "I can put you in touch with people who will make you a lot of money."

"Those ten thousand wool blankets," Willie asked, "where are they?"

"What?" I had almost forgotten the story I'd spun for Hammer, so I stalled as best I could. "How'd you hear about that already?"

"We hear everything," Willie said, his voice low and his eyes narrowed as his fingers beat out a drumbeat for each word on the table. "Start with the blankets, and tell the truth, or Nick puts a forty-four slug into your head."

"They're in a warehouse in Bristol. They came in with a convoy about a week ago. I got a guy in a railway battalion who's setting the whole thing up. Soon as they load them, they're ours at the first stop." It sounded good to me. Wool blankets were a hot commodity.

"I said the truth," Willie said, slamming his palm on the table. Nick pulled the Bulldog back out.

"Okay, okay," I said, getting the feeling they weren't bluffing. If word got from the stockade to these guys as fast as it did, they had reliable communications and sources of information. Given that they'd already infiltrated the quartermaster corps and CID, maybe I'd underestimated them. "There are no blankets. At least, none I know of. I was trying to impress Hammer, get his attention. But that doesn't mean I don't have contacts. Valuable contacts."

"Yeah, we got someone checking on your contacts. I heard of Archie Chapman," Willie said. "If that ain't a lie as well, we might live up to our end of the bargain. But if that's another phony story, well, then you'll be sorry you ever walked through our door."

"Because you won't be walking out," Nick added, still gripping the Bulldog.

"I think he gets it," Willie said, leaving no doubt as to who was the brains and who was the muscle.

"How'd you know?" I asked. "About the blankets."

"Nick, stash the piece and brew up some tea for our guest, all right?" Nick looked disappointed but shuffled over to the stove, stuffing the pistol into his pants pocket. "You think there'd be ten thousand blankets within a hundred miles, and we wouldn't know about it? Our boys hit a train in Basingstoke last month, took off a couple thousand army blankets. That was the last of any quantity in the area. A U-boat sunk a transport in a convoy a couple of weeks ago. Guess what it carried?"

"Wool blankets," I said, impressed with their intelligence sources.

"Right. So there's a shortage of blankets right now. You overplayed your hand, Mr. Boyle."

"Listen, that was only for show. But Archie Chapman is the real deal, as are my other contacts. You'll see."

"We better, and soon," Willie said. He crushed out his cigarette and leaned back, eyeing me like a dubious banker facing a farmer asking for a loan. After a drought.

Nick set down the tea. Unlike most households, there was no shortage of sugar at 65 Goosemoor Lane. We drank, an almost domestic moment. I figured even though they were criminals, they were English, and odds were they wouldn't interrupt this ritual with gunfire.

"You're going to fix me up with identity papers, right?" I said. "Assuming everything checks out."

"Yeah." Willie nodded. "We'll make you a Canadian to confuse things a bit. Medical discharge, ration book, the works."

"Will they hold up if I get caught at a checkpoint?"

"Why not? They're the real thing. Nothing but the best for you, Boyle. We've got doctors who will sign anything, and we got stacks of all sorts of government forms stolen right out from under their noses."

"This war's the best thing that ever happened," Nick added. "There's more valuable stuff lying around than ever. I used to be a smash-and-grab man, going after jewelry and the like in store windows. Now all we have to do is a bit of burglary in the wee hours, and we can fill in the paperwork for whatever we want." Looked like Nick had some brains after all.

"And then your lot comes along." Willie chuckled. "With everything from nylon stockings to whiskey to canned hams. A man'd be a fool not to get rich these days."

"Someday," I said, "we'll look back on these as the good old days." That got a laugh. I was tempted to ask if any of their pals or family had died in this war that made them so rich, but I held back. Too much respect for the British Bulldog. "So how safe is this place anyway? I assume Hammer and Frankie don't hand out the address willy-nilly."

"It's safe, don't you worry," Willie said. "We only go out during the shift changes. That way, we blend in with the laborers and keep from drawing attention to ourselves."

"Good plan," I said. "Police don't come around much?"

"Not on this street," Willie said. "It's mostly cheap rooming houses and apartments now, for all the workers. There's a couple of pubs a few streets over, and they draw the most attention. We're well hidden in plain sight."

"I don't doubt you, but no way do I want to end up back in the clink." I already knew about the rooming houses. Kaz and Big Mike had taken up residence on the other side of the street where they could keep an eye on things. Not that they could do much if Nick took the dog for a walk, but it was still comforting to know.

I sipped my tea, keeping an eye on my new friends as Willie nodded his agreement about jail. As it grew silent in the kitchen, I listened to the background noise. The rumble of a truck headed down the road; the faint creaks of an old house. But no other footsteps, no sign of life, neither a captive rattling chains nor a gangster sharpening a blade. I stayed quiet, hoping for a hint of Donald Blake, but the only sound was the sudden roar of Spitfires overhead.

"Damn test pilots," Willie muttered. "They fly every plane that comes out from that factory. All they need do is take off, climb, do a few maneuvers, then land. No need to rattle our windows."

"Does that go on all day? I could use some shut-eye."

"Good luck with that, Boyle. They'll be at it till six o'clock tonight. Nick'll fix you some grub, and then rest up as best you can. Once we get word back about Archie Chapman, we'll get your papers. Or not," Willie said with a wink to his pal. They both chuckled.

"You'll get my papers," I said. "And if you're smart, you'll cut out the wise-guy stuff. When your boss hears about my connections, he may make me a partner. May as well start calling me 'Mr. Boyle, sir,' so you can get used to it. Now what's to eat, Nick?"

Nick hesitated, looking to Willie to see if my insolence needed to be punished. I could almost see the wheels in Willie's mind turning, calculating the consequences if I wasn't blowing smoke.

"Make us some eggs, Nick," was all he said, his eyes not leaving mine. A guy who knew how to play the angles. Nick grabbed a once-white apron, wrapping the string around his waist and knotting it. It was the kind of apron a short-order cook wore—full protection from splatters from the neck down. It was grimy and worn, but what interested me most was that it was too large for Nick. The sides covered his pockets, held down by the tied string. He'd be able to get to the Bulldog, but not quickly. I figured five to seven seconds of fumbling before he got a grip on it.

"Eggs for three?" I asked, trying to sound bored and indifferent.

"Best not to ask too many questions," Willie said. "Mr. Boyle."

"Sure. But tell me: How many people know I'm here?"

"Why?" Willie said.

"So I know who to come after if the cops show up. I'm not spending the rest of my life in Leavenworth, so I don't plan on letting them take me. But I do plan on evening the score if anyone snitches."

"That ain't the kind of operation we run," Willie said. "We reward loyalty and punish disobedience. Grassers are put down like the dogs they are."

"Smart," I said, watching Nick at work cracking eggs. "A united front."

"Exactly," Willie said, smiling. "Don't worry. Long as you're honest, you're safe with us." I almost laughed, but caught myself.

Then I heard it. A footstep. Another. The sounds came from upstairs, echoing off the ancient plaster walls. I yawned wide and loud, trying not to appear as if I'd heard. I caught a quick glance between Nick and Willie. It vanished instantly.

That was as close as I was going to come to proof Blake was being held upstairs.

Nick cracked another egg, this one thin-shelled and splintering in his hand, which ended up covered in sticky egg white. Willie caught me looking, his eyes going wide for a split second before

I grabbed the billy club from between us and cracked him over the head.

Nick swung around at the sound as I leapt on the table and lunged at him as he tried to reach for his gun, coming up with nothing but a fistful of apron before I connected. He staggered, a dull look on his face, but stayed upright, his hand reaching for a pocket he couldn't quite find. I gave him one more hit, a gentle rap, so maybe he'd wake up at some point. These guys weren't angels, but I didn't want to play the devil myself.

He fell forward on his knees. I rolled him over and took the Bulldog. I tied his hands with the apron strings and then checked on Willie. He was still breathing, but had a helluva lump on his head. I couldn't find anything to tie him with and didn't want to take the time to search. I took two chairs and set them on top of his torso, figuring he'd make a racket if he tried to get up. If Blake were here, I wouldn't need that much time anyway.

I bolted from the kitchen and took the stairs two at a time, billy club in one hand and the Bulldog in the other. I came to a wide hallway off the landing, with one door on the right and two on the left. The right side was where I'd seen the boarded windows, so I made for that door. As quiet as I tried to be, my boots seemed to thunder against the hardwood floor. One bare bulb lit the hall, casting shadows where wallpaper peeled from the plasterboard. I stuffed the club into my belt; paint chips flaked off the door where I laid my hand against it. I tried the handle. Locked.

"Donald Blake?" I heard a stumble from inside. Maybe he was tied up, trying to make for the door. I rattled the handle again, but it felt solid, probably a deadbolt. I stepped back, studying the door. It was as old as the house, the wood brittle and dry. Only rookies tried to force a door at the lock. I reared back and aimed a kick above the bottom hinge. Wood splintered, and the door caved in. I moved back and threw my shoulder against it, hoping to burst the top hinge.

It worked. I went down with the door, falling onto cracked panels and rolling free, holding onto the Bulldog's small grip as best I could. I saw a blurred figure in the darkened room, his arm extended.

It was a gun.

I rolled again and saw his hand waver. He fired, and the flash was blinding in the cramped space. I squeezed off two rounds in his direction and then two more as he collapsed into the corner. I got up on my knees and scrambled over to him, knocking the .38 revolver from his hand.

It didn't matter. Three holes in his chest had pretty much neutralized the threat.

"Who are you?"

I nearly jumped out of my skin. I spun around and aimed the Bulldog at a form huddled against the wall.

"Don't shoot!"

He'd already been shot. Blood gushed from his shoulder and decorated the wall behind him. His hands and feet were tied. His mouth was open, drawing in gasps of air, disbelief rampant on his face. Getting shot was always such a surprise.

I'd misjudged the shooter. He hadn't been going for me; he'd been trying to get a bead on Donald, who was behind me. He was going to put Donald down like a dog.

"Are you Donald Blake?" He nodded, his eyes studying the wound. It looked bad, but not the kind of bad where you end up six feet under. "Here," I said, grabbing a shirt from a pile of clothes on the floor and pressing it against his shoulder. "Hold this. Help is on the way."

CHAPTER EIGHT

THE SOUNDS OF shattering and splintering wood announced Big Mike's arrival at the front door with his sledgehammer. Footsteps pounded up the stairs, and I called out.

"In here! The other rooms haven't been checked." I doubted anybody was lying in wait; another captive was far more likely.

"All clear," Kaz announced as he entered the room, his Webley at the ready, his eyes scanning the carnage. "My God, Billy, did you have to shoot both of them?"

"Only one. He was trying to finish off Donald here." The poor guy was confused and uncertain of our intentions. He cowered against the wall, shivering in fear and numb with shock. "It's all right, we're friends," I said, trying to keep him focused. "We're going to get you out of here."

He nodded, aware enough to like the sound of that idea.

"Nobody downstairs," Big Mike said as he lumbered into the room, sledge in one hand and .45 automatic in the other. "Hey, looks like a slaughterhouse in here." He holstered his pistol and set down the sledgehammer, taking a medic's field kit from across his broad shoulders.

"Who . . . who are you guys?" Blake managed to say, looking frightened as Big Mike loomed over him.

"We're the cavalry, kid," Big Mike said, getting down on his knees. "Billy, move, will ya?" He cut away the shirt around the bloody wound and sprinkled sulfa powder front and back. "Don't worry, buddy, it's a through and through, and I think it missed the bone. You'll be fine. Coupla minutes, you won't feel a thing." He took out a morphine syrette and jabbed Blake in the thigh, squeezing the tube between his thumb and finger. Then he pinned the tube to Blake's collar to signal how much of a dose he'd been given.

"Those guys still out cold?" I asked as Big Mike wrapped a compress bandage around Blake's shoulder.

"What guys? I said the place was clear."

"I thought you meant no one was conscious," I said. "I clocked two guys with the billy club in the kitchen before I made my way up here."

"Nobody there," he said. "Give me a hand." I helped him get Blake up, and we headed for the hall.

"Kaz, check the kitchen and the back," I said. "There were two thugs down there." He scampered ahead, Webley raised and ready for business.

When we got downstairs, Kaz greeted us with, "No one here." He was definitely disappointed.

Outside, a small crowd had gathered, a few workmen, older gents resting on canes and women with grey hair tucked under their headscarves. Kaz stopped to talk to them. "Ladies and gentlemen, please be careful. Two black market criminals have escaped and may be dangerous. Please keep an eye out so they do not return to carry off the coffee and clothing stored upstairs before the police arrive."

With a smile, he stepped off and helped Big Mike guide Blake to where they had garaged the jeep. As one, the crowd looked at the broken front door and surged into the house. One gentleman cautioned the others to let the ladies go first.

"No reason to take a chance on the villains returning," Kaz said. "There were tins of ground coffee, stacks of wool shirts, and boxes of shoes. A gold mine for these poor folk." In the few minutes it took to get the jeep out of the garage and on the road, we passed an elderly couple with bulging overcoats and grins on their weathered faces.

I wasn't too worried about Willie's and Nick's return. Besides losing all the goods stashed in the house, they'd let the Morgans' get-out-of-jail-free card escape on their watch. They'd be lucky to live out the week.

"There's a small hospital attached to the airfield," Big Mike said. "I scouted it out in case we might need it. We'll get him patched up and then head out, the sooner the better."

"I don't think we need to worry about the Morgans finding us," I said.

"I ain't worried about them," Big Mike said. "Sam wants us back in London with this guy in one piece." He crooked a thumb at Blake, who gazed dully ahead.

"Let us hope he is not badly wounded," Kaz said. "This city is dreary. I'd rather dine in London tonight."

We arrived at the entrance to the airfield attached to the Spitfire factory. The guards let us in, and we followed signs marked with a red cross. They had their own fire station, in case of airplane crashes, and what was more a small clinic than a hospital. A nurse met us at the door and called for the doctor as she led Blake into an examination room.

"First gunshot wound," Dr. Raymond Jeffords said. His face was lined and his hair stark white, but his hands were steady as he removed Blake's shirt and bandage. "In this place anyway. Plenty of cuts and scrapes from the factory floor, and the occasional injury when one of the airplanes doesn't behave, but no bullet holes in my patients, thank God. I had enough of that in the last war. Now steady, lad."

He cleansed and probed the wound as Blake grimaced and groaned.

"Is it serious?" Kaz asked, probably worried about finding a decent restaurant in this neighborhood.

"Might have been, an inch or two to the left," Jeffords said. "Or if the round were a larger caliber. But it went straight through, no broken bones or debris in the wound. Back in my day, this would only call for a few days' rest and then back to the trenches." He smiled, and I had the sense that was to keep Blake's spirits up. Especially since there were no trenches in sight.

The doctor stitched up the bullet holes, telling Blake sternly each time he cried out that it was a fine thing to feel the pain. If he could focus on a bit of light needlework, it meant he hadn't been badly injured. It was an effective bedside manner; Blake even managed a smile when he was done.

Jeffords ushered the three of us out of the examining room while a nurse bandaged Blake. "The lad will be fine in no time," he said. "The young heal fast. He'll need bandages changed in another day, and that arm needs to stay in a sling. A bit of rest is what he needs."

"We have to take him to London," Big Mike said. "We have a jeep."

"That's a hundred and twenty miles or so," Jeffords said. "It would probably be all right in a car with proper seats, but I'd worry about those stitches in a jeep. Why don't you take him to the Dudley Road Hospital? It's not far, and he can rest overnight."

"No, that won't cut it. Maybe a train," Big Mike said.

"A first-class compartment," Kaz said. Now we were talking his language.

"Safe enough," Jeffords said. "I'll need your names for my report. Gunshot wounds must be reported to the police, you know."

"I'm sorry, doctor, but we can't do that," I said.

"As I cannot let you go without the proper information," Jeffords said. "And why is a mere private speaking for an officer and a sergeant? Damned odd."

"Doctor Jeffords," Kaz said, withdrawing a letter on SHAEF stationery from his jacket, "this may answer your questions."

"Hmph," Jeffords said, reading the letter. "Any and all

assistance, eh? Well, I've given you that, but I'm wary of not report-ing a gunshot wound. Can you tell me what all this is in aid of?"

"An undercover investigation into the black market," Kaz said. "We hope you can keep this quiet. We don't want the criminals to know we've been here."

"We can be discreet," Jeffords said. "It's a small staff here, enough for first aid and to stabilize any serious injuries. I should be long since retired myself, but I don't mind doing my bit."

"Thank you, Dr. Jeffords," I said. "We'll take the patient to the train station as soon as he's ready."

"Do you have any other compatriots, or is this a small opera-tion? Need to know and all that?"

"Quite small," Kaz said. "Why do you ask?"

"Well, your jeep, my lad," Jeffords said. "If there's only the four of you, and you leave it at the station, what's to become of it?"

"SMART GUY," BIG Mike said as we watched Jeffords drive off in our jeep from outside New Street Station. "He figured the odds and came up aces."

"Do you think we can trust him to keep quiet?" Kaz asked.

"Sure," I said. The jeep had convinced Jeffords to deep-six the paperwork. "He's got a jeep he can fix up to take a stretcher, and he won't have to walk to the factory when there's an injury. They probably have enough surplus fuel to keep that thing running. Why would he spoil a good thing?"

"Somebody would have stolen the jeep anyway," Big Mike said. "We couldn't call the stockade and tell them where we left it, could we? Might as well tell the Morgan Gang we're headed to London."

Kaz organized the tickets and managed to get a first-class compartment for the next train to London's Euston Station, leav-ing in an hour's time. We shepherded Blake through the crowd, keeping an eye out for MPs or police who might question our motley crew. Jeffords had given Blake a shirt and a discarded overcoat, which he wore across his shoulders. He looked shaky, but he hung onto Big Mike's arm like it was a life preserver and managed to stay upright.

We let Kaz take the lead. As an aristocrat, he could talk his way out of anything. We had the SHAEF orders, but I didn't want to flash them around unless we had to. Our best bet was to get Blake out of town quickly and quietly.

Our train was already in the station, so we found our carriage and settled into the compartment, the upholstered seats just what the doctor ordered.

"Where're we going?" Blake asked weakly, his stare darting between us, still wary of some trick.

"London, like I said," Big Mike told him. "First class all the way. You ever heard of the Dorchester Hotel? That's where these guys live. Real fancy place, room service, that sorta thing. You'll stay with them tonight. All you gotta do is answer a few questions. But not right now."

"Okay," Blake said. "Will you be there, too?" Kaz raised his eyebrow at Big Mike, who finally said he would. For the first time, the kid smiled. Then he went to sleep, his head resting against Big Mike's arm.

"You've made a friend," Kaz said.

"Yeah," Big Mike said. "But Estelle won't like it. I told her I'd take her out if we made it back tonight. Now she'll think I'm living the high life with you bums."

Estelle Gordon was a WAC corporal who'd gotten in hot water for helping us out awhile back. She'd been issued a transfer to North Africa for her good works, but Big Mike had fallen for her—hard—and used his SHAEF connections to halt the transfer and get her a posting in London. Where he, conveniently, was also posted. She was a little more than half his height in heels, a fireball in a small package.

"I would invite her to dine with us," Kaz said. "But we are under orders to keep Donald's presence in London a secret. So it will be the four of us and room service at the Dorchester, if that suits you both?"

It did. By Kaz's standards, dining in his room was roughing it. For me, after my time in the stockade, it sounded like heaven. Which it was anyway, for a kid from South Boston who thought the doorman at the Copley Square Hotel was the best-dressed guy in Beantown.

CHAPTER NINE

THE WEATHER HAD turned cold and windy as we arrived at Euston Station. Blake shivered under his jacket as we piled into a cab and headed for the Dorchester.

"We should've picked up something to eat on the train," Big Mike said. "He's weak from loss of blood and probably hasn't eaten a thing all day."

"Two days," Blake murmured. "I tried to get away, so they punished me. No food."

"Jeez," Big Mike said between his teeth. "Hang in there. How's the shoulder?"

"Not as bad as before," Blake said. "Sorry I conked out on the train. I couldn't sleep in that place. I kept worrying they'd come for me."

"No problem," I said. "We can talk at the Dorchester. It'll be an improvement."

"Fancy place, huh?" Blake asked.

"An oasis," Kaz said. "One that I am happy to call home."

The taxi pulled into the circular drive in front of the hotel. We'd decided Big Mike would head over to Norfolk House in Saint James's Square, report to Harding, pick up a new uniform for Blake, and return for dinner—after making apologies to Estelle, of course. Kaz and I helped Blake inside. He was wobbly, but the sleep seemed to have helped, and he gawked at the doormen and the senior officers strolling by. The hotel entrance was surrounded by sandbags, a reminder of the days when bombs rained down on London most nights.

As we made our way down the long marble hallway and past the reception desk, hotel staff smiled and nodded greetings to Kaz. He was rich, sure, and a baron to boot, but the sympathies of the Dorchester staff extended far beyond that. Posh aristocrats were a dime a dozen in this part of town.

We rode the lift to the top floor, where Kaz had his suite.

"Holy cow," Blake exclaimed as we entered. A chandelier lit the large, wood-paneled sitting room, which looked out over Hyde Park. The sun was setting, bathing the city in a soft amber light. Holy cow, indeed.

"Please sit," Kaz said, nodding to the couches that faced each other. "I will call room service and have some soup sent up immediately." I took Blake's coat, which had probably been discarded months ago by an injured worker. Kaz crinkled his nose as he spoke into the telephone. I left the coat in the hall to go out with the trash.

"Some place," Blake said, still starstruck. "You live here, too?"

"I do. But it's Kaz's place."

"I didn't know privates and lieutenants roomed together," Blake said. "You sure you guys are on the up and up?"

"It's a long story. I wasn't always a private." Kaz's story was even longer. It was in this very room that he and his family had spent their last Christmas together, the year before the war started. In 1938, sensing conflict on the horizon, Kaz's father had brought the family to England to visit. The ostensible purpose was to see Kaz, who was studying at Oxford. But the real reason was to plan a move for the entire extended family to the safety of England. His father had gotten his substantial fortune transferred to Swiss accounts and was searching for suitable properties for his family and business. The idea was that by the next Christmas, the Kazimierz clan would be celebrating in their new English home. But by December 1939, Poland was under the Nazi heel, and Kaz's family was wiped out, executed along with other members of the Polish intelligentsia.

Making this suite his home was Kaz's way of staying connected to a family and a time ground into dust by war and hatred. He was the last of his line, with more money than he knew what to do with, a penchant for taking chances, and delight in taking revenge whenever he could. When I'd first met him, he was a skinny, spectacle-wearing egghead, an expert at European languages and the finest wines. Two years later, he'd built up his body to serve him as well as his intellect and resolve. Now he was a wiry, tenacious, spectacle-wearing egghead who was a terror with his Webley break-top revolver.

"A beef consommé will be here shortly," Kaz said, setting down the phone. "That should restore you enough to wait for a proper dinner."

"Thanks, Lieutenant," Blake said. "I don't know how I can thank you. All of you."

"We'll talk about that in a while," I said. I wanted him stronger before we discussed his cousin and bringing down the Morgan Gang.

An hour later, we were ready for dinner, provided with a flourish by waiters who swooped in, set up a table, served the food, and were gone in minutes without so much as a whisper. Big Mike had returned with a duffel bag full of clothes and supplies for our guest, along with a summons from Harding to deliver Blake to Norfolk House by 0800 hours.

"Thanks, Big Mike," Blake said, emerging from the bedroom looking much better after a wash and a new set of khakis, his arm in a makeshift sling. "But I can't wear this shirt; it's got sergeant's stripes. I'm a corporal."

"Not anymore, you're not, kid," Big Mike said, smiling at Blake like he was a kid brother. "You've been promoted."

"Cheers," I said, raising a glass of Sémillon, one of the white Bordeaux wines Kaz favored. Blake beamed as we drank and tucked into the halibut with parsley potatoes, carrots, and new peas. Big Mike and Blake did some damage to a basket of warm rolls and a second bottle of wine before we got to the dessert of apple pudding.

We were all pleasantly sated, and Blake was a bit tipsy on the wine, so I figured it was time to nail a few things down. "Things are going well, aren't they, Sergeant? A lot better than yesterday at this time. No food, no hope, and now here you are."

"Yeah, it's been great," Blake agreed, his eyes shifting back and forth, watching warily for any hint of danger.

"So here's the deal," I said. "You got your promotion, and the army's going to transfer you to Italy, probably to Naples, nice and safe, far from the front and even farther from your troubles here."

"Okay," Blake said, clearly waiting for the other shoe to drop.

"All you have to do is tell us everything you know about the Morgan Gang. Names, what you stole for them, anything and everything."

"I could get court-martialed for that," he said.

"We don't want to arrest you, kid," Big Mike said with a smile that turned grim in two shakes. "If we did, you'd be in a deep, dark cell somewhere, a place so dismal you'd tell us anything to get out. But instead you're here in this fancy joint, enjoying a swell meal with your new pals. So relax."

"The other accommodations could be arranged," Kaz said, leaning back and giving Blake a studied, languid stare. "If you'd prefer not to talk."

"No, no," Blake said. "I owe you guys. But that Morgan bunch, they mean business."

"They do," I said. "So do we."

"You sound like them," Blake said, his body sinking into the chair. "They promised I'd get rich if I went along with them. Or crippled if I didn't. Even when I went along, they double-crossed me. Why should I trust you?"

"Like Big Mike told you," I said, "we could do anything we

want with you. We're choosing to overlook your mistakes with these people and protect you from them." Blake was nothing more than a frightened petty thief who'd gotten in over his head. He probably had a list of people to blame for his troubles, and like most small-time crooks, his own name wasn't anywhere on it.

"You don't have much of a choice, young man," Kaz said, sounding authoritative even though he was no more than a couple of years older than Blake. "Unless you count being let loose for the Morgans to find you, or being transferred to a rifle platoon, which I understand includes an all-expenses-paid trip to the beaches of France."

Blake looked to Big Mike for comfort, but all he got was a shrug. It was up to him whether he wanted to face us, the Morgans, or the Germans. We'd rescued him and given him a nice meal. Still, he hesitated, which said something about the reach of the Morgan Gang.

"I'll tell you everything," Blake finally said, fortified by another glass of wine. "Where should I start?"

"At the beginning," Kaz said. Big Mike took out a notebook, and Donald Blake spilled his guts.

It had started out small, a few damaged crates, their contents scattered over the warehouse floor. A suggestion that it wouldn't hurt to give them away, impress the girls at the pub with nylons, cigarettes, jars of jam, whatever happened to be subject to normal breakage that day. The kind of stuff you knew was wrong, but what the hell, everyone was doing it, so why not?

Then the demands came for falsified records, looking the other way as stolen trucks were filled with supplies at the loading dock. Payment was in cold cash, more money than an army corporal could make in a year. Blake got cold feet.

"I got a weekend pass and went to see a cousin of mine. He's the flight engineer on a B-26, flying out of Beaulieu airbase in Hampshire," Blake said, the story flowing like water over a breached dam. Once most guys began admitting their guilt, it was hard to get them to shut up. "I had to talk to someone—I didn't know what to do. I mean the money was great, but I was the one taking all the risks. I thought Switch would know what to do."

"Switch?" I asked.

"Well, his name's Alvin. But he's been Switch since we were little, on account of the switchblade he stole from a kid who was pushing him around. Switch Blake, sounds like *switchblade*, see?"

"Yeah, I get it. He sounds like a tough customer," Big Mike said. "What was his advice?"

"I shouldn't tell you, not now."

"Why not?" I asked, hoping he'd tell us about his cousin freely. It'd be nice to know he was being straight with us.

"Switch was going to take care of everything," Blake said, his voice beginning to waver. "He said he knew people, he could have the whole gang arrested, or at least the top men."

"Who was he going to talk to?" Big Mike asked, his tone soothing.

"It doesn't matter," Blake said.

"Let us be the judge of that," Kaz said, his voice firm. Blake remained silent, his hands clasped as if in prayer.

"We know about Alvin," I said. "We know why the Morgan Gang was holding you."

"What about Alvin?" Blake said, an echo of hope as he spoke his name.

"We know that Alvin—Switch—was deeply involved with them. And that he suffered a case of remorse when you came to him. He was high enough in the gang to know the major players, and he was ready to cooperate with CID and name names. That's why the Morgans snatched you. For leverage."

"Jesus, I almost got him killed. I had no idea," Blake said, slamming his hand on the table. "I guess it wasn't all bad luck then, huh?"

"What wasn't?" I asked, not following him.

"That he got shot down about ten days ago. I called his base, and a pal of his told me."

"Shot down?" I said, dully repeating the obvious as I tried to work out the implications.

"Yeah. Over France. All seven crewmen were spotted bailing out, so there's a good chance he's alive. Probably in a POW camp."

"Did your kidnappers know this?" Big Mike asked.

"They grabbed me a couple of days after I found out, but they never made mention of it. They couldn't have known about it any quicker than me. But I overheard the guys downstairs arguing, and they made some mention of a bomber, so I thought they might have found out. Then the next morning, you guys came along."

"Did Cousin Alvin tell you how involved he was with the Morgans?" Kaz said.

"Sure," Blake said. "When I went to see him, he told me if it was anyone else, he'd have me killed. But since I was family, he'd help. He figured the army would let us both walk if he gave evidence against the others."

"Were you surprised?" Big Mike asked.

"At first, yeah. But then Switch was always working the angles, you know? Even when we were kids, he liked to shoplift comic books and candy, small-time stuff like that. Or he'd send me into a store to distract the guy at the counter while he swiped the empty soda bottles they stashed out back. Then he'd cash 'em in for the deposit, cool as could be."

Me, I'd pulled the deposit scam a few times myself at a store down the block from my house, so I kept mum.

"Switch is a good guy," Blake said, evidently putting aside the fact that old Switch would have had him iced if they weren't related. "Smart, too. He had guys working for him at Beaulieu siphoning off fuel, diverting food deliveries, hijacking everything from fountain pens to lumber. The army's got so much stuff, it's like it doesn't even notice when you take a bit here and there. And the Brits, Jesus, they'll buy anything. You ever go into the stores over here? Hardly anything on the shelves."

"Yeah, I hear there's a war on," I said, tired of listening to his complaints and rationalizing. I was still stuck on Alvin Blake bailing out over Nazi-occupied France. Colonel Harding had failed to mention that little tidbit.

CHAPTER TEN

"LOUSY DAY TO take a picture," Big Mike said the next morning as we hoofed it toward the gates of Buckingham Palace. The wind slapped at our trench coats as a light rain blew across Hyde Park, swirling tree branches and lifting green leaves toward a dull grey sky. The calendar had turned to June, but this wasn't like any June I'd ever seen back home in Boston. A damp chill rose from the ground and seeped into my bones as I turned up my collar and trudged on.

"Why are we doing this?" Blake asked, looking much improved after decent grub and a night's sleep in a real bed. "I've already seen the palace."

"Orders, kid," Big Mike said, a Leica camera hung around his neck. "We need a snapshot of you with Kaz and Billy out in the open, so Switch will know you're safe."

"What are you going to do, mail it to him?" Blake asked. None of us bothered to answer. I was glad he was free of the Morgan Gang, but his company was beginning to wear. Now that Blake knew he was safe and wouldn't be facing charges, he'd developed a smirk that I ached to wipe off his face. There was nothing as irritating as a petty thief who knew he'd beat the system.

"Okay, smile," Big Mike said as we stood in front of the ornate iron gates, the imposing royal palace looming behind us. Kaz and I stood on either side of Blake, grinning like tourists while he frowned, boredom etched on his brow.

"Smile!" Big Mike barked. Blake jumped, a grin splitting his lips before Big Mike could.

After a couple more shots for luck, we were done with sightseeing. We headed to Norfolk House in Saint James's Square, where Harding was based, along with General Eisenhower's Office of Special Investigations. As we navigated the narrow streets, Blake seemed nervous, glancing about as if expecting a salon car to come around the corner with a gangster aiming a tommy gun at him.

"You guys sure you can keep me safe?" he asked, keeping Big Mike between him and the curb.

"Safe as houses, as the English put it," Kaz said, a sly grin lighting up his face. We crossed King Street on our way into Saint James's Square, and smack in front of us was a bombed-out house. The rubble had been cleared long ago, but the scorched bricks were still there, stacked up neatly, smelling of smoky char. Blake didn't pick up on Kaz's little joke, which was probably best for his nerves.

Norfolk House was bustling, senior officers of every Allied nation and service scurrying through the halls, while enlisted men and women in a variety of uniforms carried stacks of papers and trays of coffee, dodging the flow of brass in the marble hallways. Big Mike went to drop the film off at the photographic unit as we took the stairs to the narrow warren of offices on the third floor.

"Have a seat," I said to Blake as I settled into a chair in our cramped office. It was a homey place if you had a thing for filing cabinets, maps, and the sight of a sooty brick wall through the single window.

"Can I go back to the hotel now?" Blake asked, leaning against my desk, disdaining the chair. "My arm hurts."

"Big Mike will take you to the infirmary when he gets back. You'll get your bandage changed, and then he'll show you where you're going to work."

"Work? I thought I was a witness or something. Don't I need protection?"

"You don't need to stay at the Dorchester to be protected," I said. "General Eisenhower comes by here regularly, and he's protected just fine."

"But you said I'd get shipped off to Naples," Blake said, pouting like a two-year-old. "When's that happening?"

"When I say so," Colonel Harding barked from the doorway. "Assuming you cooperate."

"Yes, sir," Blake said, smart enough to stand up straight and deliver the expected response.

"Boyle, Kazimierz, my office in five minutes. If Big Mike isn't back, get an MP to sit on him," Harding said, crooking his thumb in Blake's direction as he left.

"I don't like officers much," Blake said in a near whisper as soon as he was sure Harding was out of earshot. "Not counting you, Lieutenant," he told Kaz.

"I am delighted to be in your good graces," Kaz said as Big Mike squeezed into the crowded office.

"They'll have the photographs in an hour," he said. "Come on, kid, let's get your bandage changed." Blake followed, more docile now that he'd had a taste of Harding. The colonel often had that effect.

"What do you think Colonel Harding has in mind?" Kaz asked as he leafed through a stack of papers in his inbox.

"I don't know," I said. I had a pretty good idea, but I didn't want to say it out loud. That way, there was still a chance it wouldn't come true. I changed the subject. "It feels strange to be a private." Without my captain's bars, I felt naked and vulnerable, especially at Norfolk House, one of the bastions of SHAEF senior brass. I kind of agreed with Blake about officers, now that I wasn't one.

I knocked, and we entered Harding's office. Kaz and I sat and waited as Harding crushed out a smoldering Lucky Strike in an overflowing ashtray. He sighed, and with that single breath he betrayed the stress and worry that were constant companions to everyone at SHAEF involved in the invasion plans. Sleepless nights, heavy responsibilities, and unknown enemy intentions had left Harding ashen and pale, the only color in his face the greyish-blue bags under his eyes. He slapped a file closed with the flat of his hand.

"Desertions are on the rise," Harding said, leaning forward and rubbing his red-rimmed eyes. "The latest report came in today. We have enough deserters on the loose in England to form a full infantry division. And we've lost enough goods to organized gangs to supply a couple more."

"I did not know it was that many men," Kaz said.

"Too damn many," Harding growled. "A lot of them are British, but plenty of Americans, too. It's a dangerous combination, the Brits with their criminal connections and American access to vast stockpiles. That's what makes the Morgan Gang so dangerous."

"Colonel," I said, knowing what was coming, "let's cut to the chase, okay? You want us to head to France along with everyone else and find Sergeant Alvin Blake." It wasn't hard to figure out. I didn't relish the idea of storming the beaches, but guessed that Harding would at least wait until the first few waves had landed and secured the area. No reason to get us all shot up before we found Cousin Switch.

"Something like that," Harding said, his eyes avoiding mine.

"Do you have his general location?" Kaz asked. "It must be somewhere close to the invasion beaches." That made sense if we were going on a search-and-rescue mission, tagging along with the infantry as they spread out from the invasion bridgehead. "Unless he's already in a POW camp."

"He hasn't been captured, and I have his exact location," Harding said, opening a file and unfolding a single sheet of paper. "Along with several other downed fliers."

"Why do I sense this is nowhere near the invasion area?" I asked. Kaz and I were BIGOTs, meaning that we knew some of the D-Day secrets, including the location of one specific beach code-named Utah in Normandy. It didn't take a military genius to see that there'd be more than one along that stretch of coast. We'd stumbled upon that secret information during our last investigation, when General Eisenhower himself had brought us into the elite ranks of the BIGOT club.

"It's not," Harding admitted. "Blake and the other fliers are trapped in a château about a hundred and eighty miles southwest of Utah Beach."

"But there have to be landing areas closer to Blake?" I pushed, dreading the answer.

"Not close enough," Harding said. "They're about ninety miles from the nearest point on the coast."

"With a lot of guys named Hans and Ernst in between," I said.

"Along with their tanks and artillery," Kaz added. "Which will be heading to Normandy from all over France."

"Yes," said Harding, unfolding a road map of northern France and laying it out between us. "But you will be in place before that happens. Here." He pointed to the town of Dreux, west of Paris. "Blake and the others are hidden in the Château Vasseur, where we have an SOE team."

"Why?" Kaz asked. "I thought the Resistance and the Special Operations Executive had connections to take them south, over the Pyrenees and into Spain."

"The connections are blown," Harding said. "The Dreux circuit, code-named Noble, was originally taking escaped POWs and downed fliers from Minister, the SOE circuit based in Paris."

"Minister was compromised a month or so ago," Kaz said. "Or so I read in a recent intelligence summary."

"Yes," Harding said. "As was Carver, the circuit based in Orléans to the south. Noble has nowhere to send the fliers; they're trapped in the château. Carver was betrayed, and all the operatives killed or captured."

"SOE circuits are given code names based on professions," Kaz explained, knowing I didn't always keep up on my official reading.

"Yeah," I said, a gnawing fear growing in my gut. Diana. Harding kept talking, but I couldn't pay attention. Diana Seaton and I were an item. As head over heels in love as anyone could be, separated by duty and the threat of death too much of the time. She was with the SOE, Churchill's spy and sabotage outfit. Me, I hoped to come out of this war in one piece. Diana, having served in the British Expeditionary Force, survived Dunkirk by the skin of her teeth. She'd been with the First Aid Nursing Yeomanry, working as a switchboard operator at army headquarters before everything fell apart. She got out on a destroyer, only to have it sunk out from under her. Watching dozens of wounded men, many strapped on stretchers, slide into the cold Channel waters had left her with a serious dose of guilt, which she kept bottled up in the classic English manner. She joined SOE to do her bit, as the Brits liked to say, but I thought it was to see if she deserved to live after watching so many die.

"Boyle?" Harding said, his voice loud enough to tell me it wasn't the first time he'd called my name.

"Yes, sir," I said. "Sorry. Are we going to parachute in?" I hoped he hadn't already told us.

"Negative. There's no time to train you. A Lysander will fly you in." Lysanders were low-flying aircraft used for landing agents behind enemy lines. "There will be three of you on this mission."

"Big Mike?" Kaz asked.

"No. I need him here. We have a trained radio operator ready to go. He'll parachute in right before you land, along with the supplies you'll need."

"Does the Noble circuit expect us?" I asked. "Do they know about Switch?" I was trying to focus on the job and stop worrying about Diana, which was hard after hearing two SOE circuits had been blown in France. Blown. As if they'd been carried away on the wind, instead of killed or captured by the Gestapo. Each circuit had at least three SOE agents, plus any number of Resistance. Was Diana part of Carver or Minister? Was she in a Gestapo cell right now?

"No and no," Harding answered. He pushed the paper listing the airmen toward me. "This is the last communication we had from Noble. There was a scheduled Lysander pickup in the hills south of Dreux earlier this month. Two high-ranking members of the Resistance were brought to London. Noble coordinated it all, and one of the passengers brought this note."

I took the paper and smoothed it out on top of the map. It was crumpled and torn as if it had been hurriedly jammed into a pocket by someone about to take off in a slow-flying Lysander in the dark of night from deep inside occupied France.

"Adrien dead, L. Radio taken," I read. "No further contact possible. Names of fliers below. Danger of discovery great." I scanned the list and confirmed Sergeant Alvin Blake was among them. "It's signed 'Juliet Bonvie.'"

"Adrien is the code name of their radio operator," Harding said. "At least we know the Germans won't be using him to transmit false signals."

"What does the L mean?" I asked, studying the brief message. It looked hastily scrawled, probably because it was too dangerous to carry for any distance. I imagined Juliet Bonvie writing it out in the minute or two before the Lysander turned around and took on its passengers.

"Code for the suicide pill," Harding said. "Cyanide." I caught him staring at me, waiting for something. What? I looked at the agent's name again. Juliet. Of course it wasn't her real name, but it was familiar.

Not the name. The writing.

"This is Diana," I said, barely a whisper. "She's alive."

"Yes," Harding said, the faintest of smiles creasing his face.

"How soon do we leave?" Kaz said, nearly out of his seat and ready to go. He was fiercely loyal to Diana, their bond forged over the death of her sister Daphne. Daphne and Kaz had fallen in love during the Blitz, when every day could have been their last. Their joy was infectious, and I liked both of them immediately, that spring of 1942 when I first arrived here. Then Daphne was killed, and for a long time, Kaz didn't give a damn about carrying on. He and Diana had that in common—a carelessness about their own lives—which allowed them to take chances that frightened the hell out of me.

"This morning," Harding said. "You'll be taken to the Royal Air Force base at Tangmere, meet the third member of your team, and receive a final briefing from the SOE people. Then the following night, you head for France."

"Three of us," I said. "And we're landing blind, since there's no way to communicate with the Noble circuit."

"That way you're certain no one on the ground can betray your mission," Harding said, clearly working to find the bright side of this mission. "We have a landing area mapped out. Your other team member will parachute in, and then contact the Lysander with the all-clear."

"He's taking a big risk," I said.

"It's a secluded spot, a clear field in a small valley off the beaten path," Harding said. "We're dropping a number of equipment canisters, too, with weapons for the *Maquis* as well as for Noble. Food and medical supplies for the airmen." The *Maquis* were Resistance bands that had taken to the hills, some eager to fight, others more eager to flee the Nazi roundups for forced labor camps.

"And, I assume, a radio," Kaz said, leaning in to study the map.

"Yes," Harding answered. "Your other man is a trained wireless operator. He'll take over communications for Noble."

"Okay," I said, trying to focus on the practicalities. "We touch down in a deserted pasture. This guy is waiting for us, and there's equipment canisters scattered all around. We collect them and lug them how many miles to this château?" I was eager to see Diana—I needed to get used to calling her Juliet—but I wanted to be sure this little journey actually made sense. Outside of a London office, that was.

"No, you carry out the wireless and your weapons. Hide the canisters as best you can, and organize a party to recover them once you've made contact."

"Makes sense," I said, checking with Kaz, who nodded. "Then we grab Switch, call for another Lysander, and head home?" I wanted to add Diana to the passenger list, but I doubted that was in the cards.

"Basically," Harding said. "Once you know it's safe."

"Colonel," Kaz asked, "if it is safe for us to land, should it not be safe for us to depart as well?"

"We'll go over that on the way to Tangmere," Harding said, glancing at his watch. "Right now, Boyle, the general wants to see you."

I always enjoyed seeing Uncle Ike. For some strange reason, he'd taken a liking to me, even though I'd been in short pants at a family wedding the last time I saw him before the war. Out here, I think he liked having a relative around, someone he could relax with for an unguarded moment. He also didn't mind having a detective he could trust, which occasionally meant sharing a burden of truth with him.

But right now, I had my own burden—the certain knowledge that Colonel Harding was holding something back.

CHAPTER ELEVEN

I RAISED MY hand to knock on the door to the first floor conference room. As I did, it opened, and I nearly gave Deputy Supreme Commander Leigh-Mallory a rap on the nose.

"Steady on, Boyle," Leigh-Mallory said as I tried to recover. He clutched a pipe in one hand and a thick folder in the other. He studied me, his clear blue eyes a perfect match to his Royal Air Force uniform. "They've finally demoted you, eh?"

"It was bound to happen, sir," I said, stepping aside. He raised a feeble smile, not much interested in whatever story was behind the loss of my captain's bars. He had more on his mind.

"Ike's waiting for you. Be a good lad and cheer him up, will you?"

I shut the door behind me, entering a room hazy with tobacco smoke. Two wooden trestle tables were pushed together, surrounded by huge maps of France and Europe, mounted on boards and leaning against polished walnut walls. Uncle Ike stood at the window, gazing out at the road, smoking one of his ever-present Lucky Strikes.

"William," he said, turning to greet me. "It's good to see you. Come, have a seat."

"Thanks, Uncle Ike," I said as we sat down next to each other, the huge map of northern France looming over us. I only called him *uncle* when we were alone, and if it looked as if he wanted me to. This was one of those days. His face was drawn, the bags under his eyes grey with fatigue. He smelled of ashes and stale coffee. "How are you?"

"I'm fine, William. I hope your time in the stockade wasn't too terrible."

"No, not at all," I said, surprised Uncle Ike knew about it. "Colonel Harding has been going over the next step in this mission."

"I know," he said. "That's why I wanted to talk to you. I need you to know how important this is, William. One thing we can't afford in this war is to let our own people work against us. I don't want anything to get in the way of supplying our fighting men with every single damn thing they need. And these gangsters and deserters are doing exactly that."

"They're running a huge enterprise," I said. "I knew there was pilferage going on, but this Morgan Gang is operating on a massive scale."

"It's like dry rot, William," he said. "You think everything is fine, and then one day the roof caves in. We can't let that happen. Our boys have to trust us. They have to know we're doing everything we can to give them the best odds in the coming fight." He twisted his cigarette out and stood, walking to the window while the last wisp of smoke swirled and faded away. I gave him a minute. He was about to send thousands of young men into the unknown, invading Hitler's Atlantic Wall. Many wouldn't come back. I guessed Uncle Ike couldn't stand the thought of anyone sitting things out and getting rich while some kid died on a beach in France.

"Leigh-Mallory thinks the airborne assault may be a disaster," Uncle Ike said, his voice a hoarse whisper. He fired up another Lucky. "He wants to call it off. Says the paratroopers will sustain seventy-five percent casualties. Worse for the glider troops."

"That's horrible, General." It was time to be military. Now I understood why Leigh-Mallory told me to cheer him up.

"Yes. As will be the casualties if we don't have airborne troops in place to block German reinforcements. The French Resistance will do what it can, but it won't be enough without the airborne divisions."

"I get the idea it's getting too close to call that operation off," I ventured.

"The clock is ticking, William, for us all. I have to get down to Southwick House on the coast. Time to check in with the weatherman." I stood, and he gave me a wan smile as he placed his hand on my shoulder. "Godspeed, William. I'm entrusting this mission to you because it's that important. I know you can do it. Bring that fellow back safe and sound."

"I will, General. Don't worry, sir."

"William, at this point all I can do is worry. The entire enterprise is about to be placed in the hands of brave young men. Commanding officers will sit and worry while these boys do the fighting and dying. Now go finish up with Colonel Harding. I've taken enough of your time."

The busiest man in Europe had apologized for taking a few minutes of my time. I rubbed my eyes, which stung from the thick cigarette smoke, then squinted and tried to find Dreux on the map. There it was, west of Paris and due north of Chartres. Not a big city, but a number of roads converged there from the south and east. Roads German reinforcements might take on their way to Normandy, roads that would need to be blocked to ease the pressure on the bridgehead.

I had a good idea what might keep us from making this a quick round trip.

"KAZ AND SAM are waiting for you out front," Big Mike told me when I returned from Ike's office. "We're going to the Red Cross Club in Piccadilly Circus for some chow." He had Blake in tow, freshly bandaged, and we walked downstairs.

"You guys going to be bunking together?" I asked as we exited the front door, standing aside for a couple of admirals.

"Yeah, a coupla sergeants at SHAEF," Big Mike said. "Hiding in plain sight." Blake frowned, but stayed close to him.

We stood on the front steps as I scanned the curb for Kaz and Harding. Olive-drab staff cars were a dime a dozen in Saint James's Square, and it took me a few seconds to spot them. I waved and turned to say my farewell to Big Mike.

A second later, a shot echoed against the buildings. Granite flaked behind us as two more shots rang out. Big Mike dove on top of Blake. I knelt and searched for the source of the gunfire, trying to focus as people scattered and screamed all around me.

I spotted a truck at the far side of the square. The rear canvas flap came down as it pulled away, heading fast for a side street. I ran after it, drawing my pistol and pushing aside a couple of slow-moving colonels as I tried to keep the truck in sight. I heard honking and turned the corner in time to see my quarry disappear in a cloud of smoke.

Smoke grenades. The street filled with thick white clouds, traffic halted, and panicked pedestrians began running in my direction. I holstered my weapon and stood aside, letting the crowd pass. On the other side of the smoke screen they had probably already switched vehicles. Pursuit was useless, so I made my way back to Norfolk House.

Big Mike was holding Blake upright while Kaz stood guard, Webley at the ready.

"Is he hurt?" I asked.

"Only where I fell on him," Big Mike said

Blake's face was pale, his eyes wide with fear. "How'd they know I'd be here?" he asked. It was a good question.

"No idea," I said. "But be thankful they're not marksmen. Those shots were high." Still, Blake was rattled, and with good reason. We knew CID was compromised, which was why our small group had taken over. Yet word had leaked out, or the Morgans had somebody at SHAEF on the payroll.

"Change of plans," Harding said, coming out of the building. "I made a call. We have a safe place to hide Blake."

"Where?" I asked. Harding didn't answer. He whispered to Big Mike, who nodded his understanding. He said his goodbyes to Kaz and me, telling us we'd better come back in one piece, then hustled Blake around the corner.

"Let's get out of here. I'll drive," Harding said. He took the wheel of the big Plymouth staff car, and we maneuvered through London traffic, me up front and Kaz in the back. We both kept our pistols drawn until we were well clear of the city.

"Where did you send Blake?" I asked, holstering my weapon.

"To Archie Chapman," Harding said. "He'll keep him safe and well guarded."

"Are you sure he can be trusted?" Kaz asked.

"I know he can. He has a personal as well as a professional interest," Harding said. "The third member of your team is Topper Chapman."

"Good Lord," Kaz murmured. "What a coincidence."

I didn't believe in coincidences. Topper's old man was Archie Chapman. We'd sparred in London awhile back, when Topper was still nothing but a gangster helping Archie run his territory. But Topper had that British itch to do his bit, and he ended up being recruited by Kim Philby, who last I heard was running SOE down in Italy.

"Let me guess," I said. "Archie had a condition for playing that part in my court-martial."

"He did," Harding said. "It was Archie who alerted CID to Alvin Blake in the first place, hoping to do some damage to the gang that was moving in on him."

"Then he found out about Blake being shot down, and figured we'd go after him," I said, trying to see things from Archie's perspective. "But why Topper? I thought he went with Philby to the Med."

"Philby's back, running the XX Committee," Harding said. Double cross, the symbol of the counterintelligence game. "Topper came with him. He's an explosives expert and trained as a radio operator. Talents in demand for missions to occupied France."

"Damn, Archie doesn't miss an opportunity," I said. "He knows Topper is in for dangerous work, so why not benefit the family business at the same time?"

"His words almost exactly," Harding agreed. "He has a notion that Topper will command more respect among his criminal pals if he protects their territory at the same time he's killing Nazis. Everyone wins."

"A strange family," Kaz put in. "I am glad we never ran into Mother Chapman. She must be a nightmare."

"I wonder how Topper's doing," I said. "He's probably seen some fighting during the last few months." Not the kind where two bruisers held a guy by the arms while you pummeled him, either. Topper could have sat out the war. He had a phony medical certificate to prove it. For a gangster, he had guts.

We continued south on roads that were normally filled with convoys and military vehicles of every description. Today we had the roadway to ourselves.

"We spend tonight at Tangmere and fly out tomorrow night?" I asked Harding.

"That's right."

I did a quick calculation, counting on my fingers. "So D-Day is June fifth."

"Why do you say that?" Kaz asked, leaning into the front seat. "Did General Eisenhower tell you?"

"No," I said, watching Harding very carefully not saying anything. "Just think about what we know. We're BIGOTs, and no BIGOT is allowed in a combat area prior to D-Day."

"Right." Kaz nodded.

"We're going to have an easy trip in, or as easy as flying behind enemy lines can be," I said. "Which means the invasion won't have started quite yet. By the time we land in the early hours of the fifth of June, things will have started. Paratroop landings first, I'd guess, then amphibious landings at dawn."

"So we won't be violating the BIGOT policy," Kaz said. "The invasion will have begun. And that will also complicate our leaving, since the Germans will be rushing reinforcements to the front. Obvious, now that you say it."

"Your logic is sound. Some of the first troops are already aboard transports, stretched out along the coast all the way from Dartmouth to Portsmouth. They'll set sail tomorrow night and hit the beaches at first light," Harding said.

"That's why there's no one on the roads," I said, gesturing at the empty lane opposite.

"No one gets out of the restricted coastal area," Harding said. "And everyone who needs to be in it already is. Except for us. Needless to say, mum's the word, even if everyone else seems to have figured it out."

"What else can you tell us, Colonel?" Kaz asked.

"You're going in as Jedburghs," Harding said. "That's the code-name for three-man teams, a joint operation between SOE, the Office of Strategic Services, and the Free French. Boyle, you'll go in as a sergeant. Blake would naturally mistrust an officer, so you'll have the same rank as him: buck sergeant."

"Are there many Jedburgh teams?" Kaz asked.

"We're dropping them all over France to hook up with the Resistance and provide weapons and support. You could meet up with others or their Resistance groups."

"Why the cover story?" I asked.

"Our latest information is that at least one other member of Blake's B-26 crew is a member of the Morgan Gang. A goon, a real knuckle-buster. We don't want him to get suspicious. And your cover story is partially true, which will help. Topper Chapman is an excellent wireless radio and explosives expert. He'll work with the local Resistance and the Noble circuit. It's got to look like you are all there as a Jedburgh team, so you can keep Blake safe and wait until a rescue can be organized."

"By Lysander, I assume?" Kaz asked.

"Yes. We can take four passengers out in a pinch," Harding said. "Make sure Blake is in the first group. Once Noble is back in radio contact with London, plan to arrange an escape route for the rest across the Pyrenees to Spain. Or a Lysander pickup if the situation is stable."

"General Eisenhower thinks this is pretty important," I said.

"It is, rest assured," Harding said. "GIs are going to be flooding into France. Once we get off the beaches and capture a port, there'll be thousands more. Some are bound to think about deserting."

"There'd be plenty of places to hide in France, with bombed-out towns and refugees on the run," I said. "It would be easy to desert and live off the supply chain."

"Indeed," Kaz said. "Everyone will be armed to the teeth."

"Blake said he'd name names," Harding said. "Now that his cousin is safe, thanks to us, we need him to keep his word. Show him this as soon as you can." He tapped a file on the seat. Inside was the photograph of Kaz and me with Cousin Donald in front of Buckingham Palace.

"What if he keeps his mouth shut now that his cousin is safe?" I asked, folding the photo and stuffing it in my pocket.

"Convince him," Harding said, staring at the green fields beyond, as rain began to streak the glass.

That sounded easy. The hard part was going to be finding our way from some remote field to the château. And then what would we do? Knock on the front door and ask if there were any Allied airmen hiding in the attic?

I settled back into the seat as the miles slipped by. The close-cropped emerald fields of the South Downs gave way to fog-draped hills and the scent of sea salt as we neared the coast. I thought of Diana—code-named Juliet—across the Channel, and wondered what SOE would have her do once the invasion was launched. Would she even be at the château? Or would she be out blowing something up, doing her bit, seeking that moment of truth when she'd be forgiven for surviving Dunkirk?

Or would she be dead?

It was war, I told myself. Lots of people would soon be dead. I sent silent prayers skyward, more of the deals I offered the Almighty on a regular basis. *Spare her. I'll be a better man, I'll take any punishment, but spare Diana.*

More realistically, if we both have to die, let us live a little more. Love a little more. One more day, one more night.

It occurred to me that many men—German, English, French, American—had only one more night.

CHAPTER TWELVE

THE SNARL OF aircraft woke me up. Despite my prayerful good intentions, I'd fallen asleep. I hoped God wouldn't hold a quick nap against me. Harding said we were nearing Tangmere Royal Air Force base, and our destination was a cottage on the outskirts that served to keep SOE types isolated for security reasons.

He turned down the last lane before the main airbase entrance. The cottage was a long two-story house, whitewashed and plain. Nondescript except for the Royal Military Police guards with Thompson submachine guns at the gate. Big Mike produced the appropriate papers, and they waved us through, letting the gate close behind us with a firm finality.

"Welcome! Good to see you all again." Topper greeted us at the door, looking tan and fit in his battle dress, complete with lieutenant's pips. His hair was shorter, and sported far less pomade than the last time we'd met. His eyes remained dark pools of ruin. We shook hands like old pals and set aside the strange nature of this meeting.

"They have rooms for you both upstairs," Topper said. "Your gear and weapons are already there. Not a bad spot for a last supper, eh?" He gestured to a large sitting room with a fire crackling in the hearth, a dining room beyond already set.

"In England, that is," Kaz corrected him.

"Of course," Topper said. "Drinks?" He headed to a small bar, at home as if he were lord of the manor.

"I'll take mine neat," I said. "Like how this all worked out for you and Archie."

"Sit down, Boyle," Harding said, pouring himself a healthy dose of brandy. "That's not how I want this to go." He took a chair near the fire, while I slumped onto a comfortable couch. Kaz and Topper took chairs opposite, crossing their legs and holding crystal tumblers as if they were at a London club. Topper had manners and a pleasing smile. He wasn't half mad like his father, but he was just as ruthless. I had to keep staring at his dark eyes to remind myself of that.

"Listen, Billy, and Lieutenant Kazimierz, of course," Topper said, with a polite nod to Kaz. "I had nothing to do with this arrangement. I only learned about my father's part two days ago. I thought this was a normal assignment, if there is such a thing with SOE." He took a swig of his drink, which made it hard to study his eyes, where lies lived out their brief lives.

"You weren't in contact with your father before that?" I asked.

"No, and Colonel Harding can confirm that," Topper said. "I was at Wanborough House in Surrey, finishing up an explosives course. I went straight there from Italy after I got my orders."

"He's right," Harding said. "No reason for you three not to work together."

"Still," Topper said, raising his glass, "you have to hand it to the old man. Always looking for an angle, and often finding it."

"Angles I can drink to," I said, and did. It looked like we were stuck with each other.

"What happens next, now that we are confident we will not be going at each other's throats?" Kaz asked.

"You'll be briefed this evening by someone from SOE headquarters. I'm off to Southwick House in Portsmouth," Harding said. "I'm joining Ike and will monitor your mission from there."

We shook hands all around, Harding wise enough to forgo the usual platitudes. He knew the deal. We might see him again, we might not. Words did nothing to alter that basic reality.

"Well, boys, it's only us until Vera shows up," Topper said, settling in with another whiskey.

"Who's Vera?" I asked.

"Vera Atkins, of the SOE French Section," Topper said. "She's running this circus. Nice lady. A bit stiff-necked, but that gives one confidence, don't you think?"

"I'm not sure I have a lot of confidence in anything right now," I said, wandering over to the bow window. The sky was clearing, and the wind barely stirred the leafy branches. Good invasion weather. "Like you supposedly being a demolitions expert, and finishing an explosives course two days ago."

"Billy, I *taught* the course. I've been blowing things up since I first ran with a jelly gang back in '38."

"Jelly gang?" Kaz asked.

"Gelignite," Topper answered. "A blasting gelatin. It's moldable and safe to handle. Perfect for blowing safes. Or bridges. Lovely stuff."

"And the wireless?" I asked.

"Top of my class," Topper said with a grin. "I can transmit at a fair rate. I'm a bit slower at coding and decoding, but that's not what matters. It's how long you're on the air."

"Since the Germans can track your signal," Kaz said.

"Yes. Bloody Jerries have it down to a science," Topper said. "They tell me the average life expectancy of a wireless operator in France is six weeks. So let's be quick about this job, boys."

"Can we trust you?" I asked, still staring out the window. "With our lives?"

"You can trust me to do my job," Topper answered. "Can I trust you not to muck things up?" He sprang up and made for the drinks table, pouring himself another healthy dose.

I glanced at Kaz, who lifted one indifferent eyebrow and nodded. He was satisfied. I guess I had to be.

"Sure," I said, lifting my glass in Topper's direction. "Here's to a good six-week run."

"Confusion to our enemies," Kaz offered.

"Here's to them that wish us well. All the rest can go to hell," Topper responded, and we drained our glasses. "We'll have a grand time, wait and see."

I almost believed him. I willed myself to believe it, but was jolted out of that fantasy by the crunch of tires on gravel and doors slamming. Moments later a woman entered the room, wearing a dark-blue skirt and jacket and carrying a briefcase.

"Vera!" Topper exclaimed, with an overabundance of enthusiasm. He was acting as the life of the party, which perhaps wasn't a bad way to deal with things the night before D-Day.

"Lieutenant Chapman, how are you? Not overdoing the liquor, are you? Parachuting with a hangover would be dreadful, I think." One corner of her mouth went up, the briefest of smiles offered to Topper. She looked to be in her mid-thirties and had dark hair piled up and thin lips done in a slash of red lipstick. Her wary eyes studied Kaz and me in turn.

"Vera Atkins," Topper said, kicking off the introductions.

"Pleased to meet you, Baron Kazimierz," she said. Kaz did a little bow, ever the Continental aristocrat. "And you as well, Captain Boyle."

"I'm of indeterminate rank at the moment, ma'am," I said.

"Rank means little in this endeavor," she said. "I understand you are acquainted with Diana Seaton? I saw her off in this very room. She and her two teammates."

"You've had no further word?" I asked.

"No, not since Adrien was taken. Not counting that desperate note she sent, of course."

"Do you disapprove?" Kaz asked.

"It was a risk, but Diana has a level head about her. I'm sure she didn't write it until the last moment. But if the aircraft had been shot down, the Germans might have made something of it. Still, it worked, and gave us an opportunity to send in a new wireless operator and move those fliers along. You want one in particular, so our interests coincide." Vera unsnapped her briefcase, clearly eager to get on with business.

"How has Diana been?" I said. "Is there anything you can tell me? Is she safe?"

"Captain Boyle, no SOE operative in occupied France is safe. And neither will you be; have no illusions about that. It will be best for you to leave sentiment behind. Diana is in a dangerous spot, and we don't need romantic heroics from you making it any worse. I only accepted your participation in this mission since Diana knows both you and Baron Kazimierz by sight. She'll trust you immediately."

"Why do you need two of us?" I asked. I didn't like being lectured, and enjoyed pointing out a flaw in her plan.

"Because it's likely one of you will be captured or killed before making contact," she said. "And trust me, killed is preferable. The Germans will treat you as agents and interrogate you quite harshly. Before shooting you."

"But we'll be in uniform," I said, hoping it was simply a misunderstanding.

"Adolf's Commando Order, old boy," Topper said. "In or out of uniform, he wants us all shot. After a spot of torture, of course, courtesy of the Gestapo." Topper's forced bravado was beginning to wear thin, but it hardly mattered, given what Hitler had in mind for us.

"Okay, let's get to work," I said, going for the brandy decanter.

"I'd suggest coffee, gentlemen," Vera said. "A very large pot."

She began with the basics of the plan. Tomorrow night Kaz and I would take off in a Lysander. Topper was going in a Stirling four-engine bomber, converted for clandestine missions. He'd be dropped over the landing zone along with equipment canisters containing arms and supplies. We'd carry our own gear and the wireless for safekeeping. If the landing field was secure, Topper would set off flares in a prearranged pattern once he heard the

Lysander approach. If the area wasn't secure, well, then, goodbye, Topper.

"You'll land in the Forest of Dreux," Vera said, running her finger over a swath of green north of the town. "Don't worry, it's not all trees. It's a large tract of land with fields and meadows, mostly used as pasture."

"We won't come down on a herd of cows?" I asked.

"Not to worry, it's fairly deserted," she said. "The Germans have requisitioned nearly all livestock, so it's not much used these days. You'll have the same pilot who did the last pickup there, so he knows the spot. Nice, soft meadow grass, a good landing field."

She spread out photographs of the château. I glanced up as I heard sounds from outside; branches blew against the house as the wind increased. Fat raindrops began to splat against the windows as the sky darkened.

"What's our route to the château?" Kaz asked.

"Along this farmer's path," Vera said, pointing to a thin line on the map. "Then around the village itself—not through it, mind you—until you come out on the main road to the south. Then in a mile or so, take this turnoff for the château."

The pictures showed a three-story white stone structure with a slate-grey roof, spires at either end. The main building was long, with a gravel drive leading to the center. At either end, wings jutted out in opposite directions. To the rear of the property stood a parallel building, not as tall or fancy.

"That's the stables," Vera said. "It's where the fliers are hidden. Diana and her courier are in the main building with the count."

Diana was Juliet Bonvie, secretary to Count Alexandre Vasseur, an elderly gentleman who owned the château and a good deal of surrounding property. Her courier was Sonya Charlet, who worked as the count's estate manager. Sonya traveled frequently to collect rents and handle various business matters for Count Vasseur, which enabled her to keep in touch with the Resistance. Sonya was also English, but had grown up in Toulon, where her father managed a shipping business. Like Diana—Juliet, I reminded myself—she spoke French fluently.

Their local Resistance contact was Christine Latour, head librarian at the Dreux public library. She was the link to Commander Murat—another code name—who was the leader of the armed Resistance in that part of the Loire Valley, the *Maquis*, meaning the bush or the trees and thickets that hid the fighters from the Germans.

"If for some reason you can't get to the château, you'll need to approach Christine Latour at the library. Baron Kazimierz, with your language skills, that task falls to you," Vera said, spreading out pictures of each of the women for us to study. "I'd advise obtaining civilian clothes if it comes to that."

"Are there German troops in the area?" I asked.

"There's a large garrison in Chartres, about twenty miles south. There's a security detachment of about a hundred men in Dreux. But as you can see, Dreux is a main intersection. Troops are constantly moving through. If there's been Resistance activity, the Germans will be out in force."

"They'll be mad as hornets soon enough," Topper said. I could tell he'd never been stung by one.

"Those are all the major players, except for Major Gustav Zeller. He plays chess with the count," Vera said, tossing a picture of a German officer onto the pile. He had close-cropped hair, fleshy cheeks, and a bemused expression.

"Which side is this count on?" Kaz asked, his brow wrinkled as he studied the major.

"Count Vasseur believes that French honor must be upheld. He offered his help freely and understands the consequences if the network is found out. He's not active, given his age, but his real value to us is the cover he provides for Noble."

"Why does he play chess with a Nazi?" Topper asked. The rumble of distant thunder rolled against the walls.

"Zeller looked into the château as his headquarters," Vera said. "He found better accommodations, but struck up a friendship with the count, as both of them are chess enthusiasts."

"He'd have to play along, so as not to arouse the major's suspicions," Topper said.

"And he does have his son to consider," Vera said. "He was captured in 1940 and ultimately sent to a forced labor camp. Diana thinks the count is trying to cultivate Major Zeller in order to free him."

"How could an ordinary German major accomplish that?" I asked.

"Because he's with the *Abwehr*. German counterintelligence. Your nemesis."

With that cheery bit of news, Vera continued the briefing. The stables housed a few remaining horses and a dilapidated truck, not that there was any petrol for it. It was the cellar we were most interested in. It was an old root cellar which was accessed from stairs in the tackle room. Another door connected the root cellar to a secret chamber beneath the stables. The fliers were all hidden there, cramped but comfortable.

"Huguenots," Vera said. "French Protestants persecuted in the sixteenth century by the Catholic majority. After thousands were slaughtered in 1572, many fled or went into hiding. Châteaus like this one provided hiding places for them."

"Is Count Vasseur of Huguenot blood?" Kaz asked.

"He is," Vera said. "But it is a closely held secret. If the Germans discover that fact—especially one as smart as Zeller—they might suspect the building has its secrets."

Light flashed, blindingly white, and seconds later the crack of thunder rumbled like distant guns.

CHAPTER THIRTEEN

IT WAS DARK when the telephone rang. It was for Vera. She cupped her hand and spoke softly, then nodded and replaced the receiver. "The invasion. It's been postponed."

We stared out the window. The wind had come up fiercely, rain spattering against the bow window. I moved closer to the coal fire and thought about the thousands of men on transports out in the Channel, wallowing in this filthy weather, having to endure another day.

"We'll go over this again tomorrow," Vera said. Then she poured herself a drink and took a seat on the couch.

I sat next to her, leaning in to whisper, "How long has Diana been in Dreux? I worry about her."

"A month now," she said. "She's terribly smart and fit in very quickly. She's keen to do her job. Don't get in her way, Captain Boyle. I can understand the temptation, but you have your job, and she has hers."

"After the invasion, her job changes, doesn't it?"

Vera took a slow drink, savoring it and staring into the fire. "Yes. But we don't want to lose the cover story she and Sonya have created. Or endanger the count. The Resistance will become active, but I don't expect Diana to be leading the charge. Her job is to coordinate Noble and maintain contact with London. We'll want information on German troop movements, that sort of thing. We don't need her running about with a Sten gun shooting Nazis, if that's what you're worried about."

"I think I'd rather take my chances with the Sten," I said. "I don't know if I'd have the nerve to play her game."

"She's got nerve, all right," Vera said. "Let's hope she has equal parts luck."

We sat down to a dinner prepared by the British MPs who guarded the place. Afterward, I had no idea what we ate.

The next day we poured over maps, memorizing routes around Dreux. I studied the face of Major Zeller, wondering what kind of guy he was. He looked cheerful. But perhaps that was because he'd recently captured an SOE agent. Or won at chess.

I went through the gear that had been stockpiled in my room. A uniform with sergeant's stripes. Paratrooper jump boots. Thompson submachine gun, lots of ammo. Grenades, flashlight, trench knife, .45 automatic, first-aid kit, canteen, and K rations. I cleaned the Thompson, sharpened the knife, and then checked in with Kaz. He packed a book as I cleaned his Sten gun. We had everything we needed.

"We must not appear too friendly," Kaz said. "Topper and I should begrudge the burden of a criminal in our ranks. It will lend credence to your identity."

"I'll do my best to show my resentment of all officers," I said. "We need to make sure Diana doesn't spill the beans. There's no reason she should know either of us." *Juliet*, I reminded myself. I had to get used to that name. The less anyone knew about her identity, the better.

"It will require only a few seconds. A quick shake of the head, the right look," Kaz said. I hoped he was right.

The rest of the time was a blur. All I knew was that the rain finally stopped. After another nondescript meal during which no one said a word, Vera told us to get ready.

Oddly enough, I couldn't wait to leave. I wanted to get to Diana, sure, but that wasn't the reason. It was the waiting. I wanted to get going, to see if we'd land in once piece. To see what lay beyond.

Keen. That's how Vera had described Diana. The word fit her perfectly, and maybe it was because I'd been thinking of her so much, but I felt keen as well. Even though there were only a handful of us in this little cottage, I knew we were part of something greater, something that the history books might talk about someday.

It would be nice to live to read about it.

PART TWO

BELOW US, SHIPS filled the Channel. To the far horizon, wakes churned the inky water as vessels of every size departed English ports and made for the French coastline. Moonlight rippled across the waves, shimmering slivers of silver in the night. I glanced at the luminous dial on my watch. Forty minutes past midnight. It was the sixth of June.

Off to the west, over the Cotentin Peninsula, splashes of light arced high into the sky. Antiaircraft fire. Pinpricks of light burst brightly and then faded as C-47s loaded with thirty men were hit, burned, and crashed.

The tiny Lysander flew on, slipping by the devastation, nearly invisible in its matte black finish. The high canopy afforded a grand view all around, from stars glimpsed through the thin cloud cover to the vast fleet beneath us. We were cramped, our gear stuffed around us. Kaz had a tight grip on the priceless wireless cradled in his lap, nestled in a small, nondescript brown suitcase.

"Look ahead," he said, shaking my arm.

We were entering a new realm of darkness. No moonlight reflecting off waves, only inky shadows cast from the full moon. Landfall; the coast of France. It slipped under the plane, and soon we were traveling across the blacked-out enemy landscape.

"Where are we?" I asked Lieutenant Vaughn, our pilot, leaning forward and raising my voice over the engine's drone.

"We've crossed west of Deauville on the coast," he said. "Le Havre is on our port side. You can make out the mouth of the Seine, see?"

I did. The glassy sheen of water thrust itself into the landscape, undulating through the curves of the river. "How do you find your way?" There were no navigation instruments on the Lysander. These flights were done by compass and dead reckoning. Bad choice of words.

"I keep the river in sight, but not too close. See how the land rises up ahead? We stay with those heights for another half hour. The valley of the Seine to the left, the valley south of Caen to our right. Couldn't be simpler, mate."

"What happens in half an hour?" I began to make out the features below and saw what he meant. We were following the spine of a series of low, rolling hills, with flat plains on either side. It would have been impossible without the moonlight.

"We follow a main road east. Takes us over Dreux, then we touch down, and off you go. That's supposing your pal sets the flares."

I nudged Kaz and tapped on my watch. Five minutes before one. By now, Topper should be on the ground. Hopefully alive. If there had been any Germans near the drop zone, the sound of the four-engine Stirling and equipment canisters floating to the ground would definitely have tipped them off.

As the minutes wore on, a sense of isolation crept up on me. The invasion fleet was far to our rear, vanished from sight. The antiaircraft fire was nothing but a faint glow in the distant sky. Our plans and hopes seemed foolish now, nothing but fine ideas fed by a warm fire and brandy. Was I really going to find Diana down there? Hell, even finding Topper looked like a thousand-to-one shot.

The aircraft banked, and I picked out the roadway below. The *route de Paris*, Vaughn informed us. He recited the towns as we passed them, the names familiar from studying the map. Verneuil, Tillières, Nonancourt. Each was barely visible, no more than a clump of buildings at a crossroads, lit by the glow of silvery moonlight. He banked again, giving Dreux, a much larger town, a wide berth.

"The Forest of Dreux, dead ahead," he announced. Again, a poor choice of words, but I understood. The land rose into a long plateau, a swath of unbroken woods cloaking the ground. Here and there patches showed through the dense canopy. Fields and meadows, visible for a second, then gone. The plane slowed, descending in a wide circle. If the Germans were waiting, we'd be an easy target.

Vaughn flew another circuit, banking the Lysander now and then to better scan the ground below. I realized I had been holding my breath and finally gasped for air.

"There we go," he said, the relief in his voice palpable. He signaled downward, slashing his hand to the right. Five pinpricks of light, arrayed in an inverted L, marking the landing area. Kaz and I grinned at each other like kids. Topper was okay, and we'd found him.

Vaughn went in for the landing. That was when I realized those tiny lights weren't getting any bigger, and we were landing in the dark on an unknown field in the middle of the woods. Suddenly Germans didn't seem that big of a problem.

My stomach dropped as the Lysander descended, faster than seemed safe. Vaughn eased up on the throttle as the ground seemed to surge up and strike the undercarriage, hard, jolting my spine. We bounced, once, twice, before the aircraft settled down, and we were taxiing, the wind and the prop blast blowing the grass in every direction. Vaughn turned the plane, lining up on the flares.

"This is your stop, gents. Good luck," he said, sliding the canopy open. I went out first, stepping down a ladder permanently bolted to the side of the plane. Lysander pilots didn't like spending much time on the ground, and this made for a quick exit. Kaz handed me the wireless set, then our rucksacks and weapons.

A figure trotted out from the tree line. Vaughn aimed a pistol at him but held his fire when he saw it was Topper.

"Welcome to France," Topper said, a mad gleam in his eyes. We hustled the gear away from the plane as our pilot waved and pulled the canopy shut. He roared off down the field, rising and vanishing in the darkness. He'd been on the ground three minutes, tops.

"Everything go okay?" I asked Topper.

"I think so. We still have to collect the canisters." We were whispering, even though moments ago the Lysander's engine had been roaring away. There was a breeze rustling the leaves, the only other sound the thumping of my heart.

"Where?" Kaz asked, his back to us, Sten gun at the ready as he stared into the dark.

"First the flares," Topper said. He told Kaz to move our gear farther into the trees and stand guard. Then we ran the length of the landing field, scraping holes in the ground with bayonets and burying the still-burning flares. We paused at the far end of the meadow, moonlight breaking through as the thin clouds parted. Deep woods were at our back, the tree trunks thick, with gnarled roots spreading at the base. Beyond the field on one side, the land sloped downward, the pattern of cultivated fields and a distant church spire visible in the gloom.

We caught our breath and dashed off to rejoin Kaz. Now the only sound came from our boots brushing against the long grasses. As we drew closer, Kaz leaned out from the shadows, motioning with his hand for us to go low. We stopped a few yards short of cover. Topper stood with his back to mine, our weapons aimed at an unknown threat.

Silence.

Cold sweat dripped down the small of my back.

Slowly sounds from the woods overcame the silence. A rustling of leaves. A scurry in the underbrush, a small creature on the prowl.

A *boom* echoed in the distance. An explosion miles away. We duck-walked to Kaz, who held a finger to his lips as his gaze flitted about. He raised his hand in the direction of a worn path that skirted the edge of the field and vanished into the woods, then cupped his ear.

We strained to hear anything unusual. A soft wind whispered through the leaves. Kaz shrugged. "I thought I heard voices," he whispered. "What do you think that explosion was?"

"The Resistance," Topper said quietly. "Maybe a bridge. London would have alerted them by now. A coded message to attack."

"Of course," I said, trying not to betray my nervousness. It was eerie being out here, alone on a hilltop in enemy territory, not knowing who might be closing in or what was going to happen next. A lot of guys must be having that same feeling right now. "Should we get the canisters?"

Topper raised his hand to silence us. This time it wasn't the wind.

Footsteps thumped within the forest. A man's voice, indecipherable.

We crouched behind trees, weapons aimed at the sounds. More noise from the footpath—a group of men advancing toward the field. A figure emerged from the gloom, rifle in his hands, then faded back into cover.

"They must have seen the parachutes," Kaz whispered.

"Or heard the bloody Lysander," Topper countered in a low voice. "I'll take the radio; you two grab your gear. They might be circling around us, for all we know."

We began to crawl backward, dragging our equipment. If the Germans spotted us, we'd be dead in seconds. Even worse, captured. Behind us, the land sloped away, a ravine promising cover for our escape.

A quick, high-pitched laugh echoed from within the darkened lane, then nothing.

A nervous German? A Gestapo agent anticipating an interrogation?

More footsteps and thrashing about in the woods. Then they were running into the field, ten or more of them, some waving rifles. Topper went up on one knee, his Sten gun aimed dead center.

"*Où êtes-vous? Qui est là?*" It was French. I laid my hand on Topper's arm, signaling him not to fire.

"They're asking where we are, who we are," Kaz whispered.

"It could be the *Milice*," Topper answered, meaning the Vichy fascist militia. It was evident they hadn't spotted us yet, but any movement might attract a hail of bullets.

"*Vive la France! Vive de Gaulle!*" This was a girl's voice, and was followed by others shouting the same. "*Vive la libération!*"

"*Voici!*" Kaz shouted, standing up and announcing our presence. I was pretty sure it wasn't a clever trap, but I still kept my finger on the trigger.

Within seconds, we were engulfed by fifteen or so French partisans. A few grey-haired men, two young girls, some boys barely old enough to shave, and the rest sturdy working men, to judge by the rough hands and the smell of manure on their worn boots.

"*Blessent mon cœur d'une langueur monotone,*" one of the men said, kissing me on both cheeks. I glanced at Kaz, who was busy being embraced by one of the girls as an old man pumped his hand.

"Wound my heart with a monotonous languor," said another man, nodding as he spoke each word slowly and deliberately. "Yes?"

"Yes," I said, shaking his hand, hoping to forestall another Gallic smooch as I tried to puzzle out his meaning. "Do you speak English?" I wanted to ask if he was nuts, talking about monotony, but he was carrying a German rifle.

"A little," he said. "I am Cyril. *Bienvenue!*"

"Welcome, welcome," one of the boys said, grasping my hand.

"I speak English. I learn in school. Until the *Boche* tell us we must learn German." He was grinning ear to ear, thick, curly black hair hanging over his forehead, his dark eyes wide with excitement.

"What does he mean," I asked, "wounding his heart?"

"It is a poem from Radio *Londres*," he said. "My name is Jean. We came as soon as we heard!"

"Radio London, he means," Kaz said, extricating himself from several embraces.

"Yes, yes," Jean nearly shouted. "The invasion, the liberation, it is at hand!" *Liberation* was the same word in French, and everybody whooped and hollered when he said it. One of the grey hairs produced a bottle and passed it around. I was ready for the marching band to show up.

"Silencieux!" Kaz said, as loudly as he dared. The crowd looked disappointed, but they simmered down. *"Où sont les Allemands?"* Yeah, the Germans. Be nice to know if they were following this bunch.

"Yes, yes, many Germans in Dreux," Cyril said. "We fight them now, yes?"

"Un moment," Topper broke in, pulling Kaz and me away from the crowd. He had a firm grip on the wireless. "We don't know who the hell these people are. Don't mention any names. We ask questions, but we don't tell them a damn thing, right?"

"Agreed. Let's ask them to take us to the local Resistance leader," I said. "If that's Murat, we've got the right people."

"We can have them carry the canisters," Kaz said. "They are eager to help."

"If they stay sober long enough," I said, watching another bottle make the rounds. "How did they know we'd be here?"

"Cyril was quoting the French poet Paul Verlaine. 'Autumn Song,'" Kaz said. "It was probably one of those messages the BBC reads out every night."

"Right. Meaning the invasion is coming, or a call for a general uprising," Topper added. "This drop zone has been used before, so they guessed it would be tonight."

"I'd like to be sure about that," I said, studying the growing party that was going on a few yards away. "But there's no time for questions now. Let's get them to work."

Kaz took charge, and I took the bottle. It was cognac, mostly gone. I raised it to Topper and took a swig. Then he did the same, wincing after a healthy gulp. He trotted off, leading a group of chattering Frenchmen in search of canisters. Kaz led another group, the two young women at his side, of course.

Had these people guessed correctly about a drop tonight? Or had word somehow leaked out? *Impossible*, I decided, peering into the dark shadows around me. No one outside of a handful of security-minded types in England knew we were coming. And from the few firearms carried by the *Résistants*, they were in dire need of weapons. Their arsenal consisted of one German rifle, a shotgun, one pistol, and a couple of old bolt-action rifles that might have been surplus during the Franco-Prussian War. A hike up here was safer than attacking anything short of a sleeping sentry.

I considered another drink, but instead I stashed the bottle in the bushes and covered it with a branch. The bar was closed.

"No!" It was Topper, emerging from the trees, following a blur of white with feet.

"La soie, la soie!" Cyril shouted, grinning madly.

"We have to bury the parachutes, damn you!" Topper said, the rage in his voice buried beneath a whisper. "The *Boche*, don't you bloody well understand? They'll know there was a supply drop."

"But it is *la soie*, silk," Cyril said, as the others arrived, weighed down by the canisters. "The *Boche* will never know unless they take down my trousers!" He translated and the other *Résistants* laughed and clapped him on the back. Kaz joined us, his group carrying four canisters while the women held white silk parachutes neatly rolled up.

"I could not dissuade them," Kaz announced. "In their village, no one has seen new clothing in three years, including knickers. They promise the parachutes will disappear within hours, never to be seen by any German."

"They hope," Topper said. "Let's go before Jean and his pal fall down drunk." He gestured with his thumb in the direction of the two *Résistants*, staggering as they held an equipment canister between them, passing a wine bottle back and forth.

"*Allons! Prenez-nous à Commandant Murat,*" Kaz said, trying to get the group moving. At the mention of Murat, a cheer went up, followed by evident disagreement that quickly turned into bickering. I didn't understand much French, but I knew slurred words when I heard them.

"They don't know where Murat is, do they?" I said.

"They know of the famous commander," Kaz said with an exasperated sigh. "But they do not know where he is. At the moment."

"This moment or any other, I'd wager," Topper said.

"Where's their village? The place with no knickers?" I unfolded a map of the area around Dreux and shined my red-lensed flashlight on it.

"Coudray?" Kaz asked one of the women. She took a second to trace her finger across the map, then stabbed at a point off the main road to Dreux. It wasn't far.

"Tell them to take us to Coudray," I said. "We'll hide the canisters and then move on. No mention of our destination." Kaz and Topper nodded their understanding. These people were enthusiastic, but that might get them into trouble. The less they knew, the better. Better for us, that is. If they were captured and had no information to offer, their torture would only last longer.

Kaz's instructions were greeted by another round of cheers, probably because Coudray was a lot closer than wherever Murat was right now. We set off, leaving the moonlit field for the murk of the rutted lane leading to the valley below. Topper took point, and I had the rear, with Kaz and the precious wireless in the middle of the group. With the six canisters, each carried by two men, and the bundles of parachute silk, our pace wasn't the fastest. But at least the work quieted the assembly as we neared the village of Coudray, where I imagined the inhabitants asleep in their tattered and worn undies.

We halted on a hilltop, the small village below us. In the light of the full moon, I could see buildings along a narrow lane and a couple of farmhouses off in the distance. There were small, cultivated fields close to the village. A quiet country scene. I glanced at my watch. Farmers would be rising soon. Men would be dying on the beaches.

"Hide the canisters here," I said, pointing to the woods crowning the top of the hill. "Tell them Commander Murat will come for them, and they must wait for him."

Kaz explained, and was met with a barrage of objections. They must have weapons for their group, he translated. For all their work. They would leave the rest for Murat, but honor demanded they be armed. It was hard to disagree. Topper opened one canister and distributed Sten guns and ammo, explaining how they worked. Pretty basic stuff.

We hid the canisters, all but one, covering them with dead logs and branches, out of sight from the road. Then we had a round of hugs and double-cheek kisses from all, along with shouts of *Vive la France* and *Vive de Gaulle*, until the glow of lamplight appeared in the window of one house. We extricated ourselves, carrying the remaining canister between Topper and me. We worked our way around the village, not wanting to give our friends a clue as to our direction.

"I hope they stay busy at their sewing machines," Kaz said as we moved through the thick forest. "They were in no shape to engage in combat."

"I hope this Murat chap has a more disciplined crew," Topper said. "I don't mind a drink and a hoot myself, but not in a drop zone on D-Day, for God's sake."

We stumbled on through the woods, circling homes and staying clear of roads. The canister—full of K rations for the aircrew, gelignite, and extra ammo for us—grew heavier with each step, the narrow metal handle cutting into my palm. Stopping now and then for a compass reading and a glance at the map, we made it to the main road south of Dreux as the first hint of dawn lit the eastern horizon.

"We're here," Topper said, stabbing at the map. "A half mile up the road is the turnoff for the château. Or we could take this trail through the woods."

"Should we chance taking the road?" Kaz asked. "It seems quiet." He was right. I stepped out from the cover of the woods onto the roadway, Thompson at the ready. The road was empty and silent, the damp air heavy and still. It wasn't far, and we'd be able to hear an engine long before it got close. Plus we'd get there sooner. I grabbed my end of the canister and we set out at a trot, counting on a fast pace to keep us ahead of trouble.

Kaz took the lead, his carbine slung and the wireless held close to his chest. I kept one hand on my Tommy gun and the other wrapped around the canister's handle. Everything made noise—web gear bouncing against our bodies, canteens sloshing water, and especially the stomp of our boots on the road surface. After the silence of the woods, it sounded like a herd of elephants on the march.

We tromped on, building up a steady rhythm, boot heels striking pavement in parade-ground unison. I saw a bend in the road ahead and figured we were close to the half-mile mark. I told Kaz and Topper to hold up. We halted.

The stomp of boots didn't. It continued, a distant echo from beyond the bend in the road. It grew louder.

Topper moved first, grabbing the front of the canister and dragging me along. We scampered across a drainage ditch and slipped on the wet grass, hoisting ourselves and the heavy load into the spindly trees and grass a few yards in. Kaz followed, falling hard as he slid into the ditch. I reached out a hand to help pull him in and saw him wince.

We went flat behind the thickest of the trees and waited as the marching men came closer. This definitely was not a ragtag group of celebrating *Résistants*.

"You okay?" I whispered to Kaz. He nodded, but I knew he was hurting. Topper and I aimed our weapons toward the road as Kaz gripped the wireless. German soldiers came into sight. A column of twos, rifles slung, moving at a fair pace, their hobnail boots making a harsh metallic sound against the pavement. I counted forty-four of them as the last man passed by.

"Rifle platoon," Topper said. "Probably coming from Dreux."

"Early morning calisthenics, or an invasion alert?" I asked. "They didn't seem to be looking for anyone."

"The map shows a bridge a few miles in the other direction," Kaz said, giving a small gasp. "Perhaps they are reinforcements. If the local commander received word of the invasion, he would want to guard vulnerable targets."

"Are you hurt?" Topper asked.

"No, I had the wind knocked out of me when I fell, nothing else. Shall we go?"

"Yes, we shall," I said, helping Kaz up. "Slow and easy this time. If we'd kept running, we might have barreled right into those Krauts."

We made it to the turnoff without meeting up with any more of the German army. Now came the hard part. Diana, her SOE partner, and the hidden fliers were only a few hundred yards away. Well hidden and armed. All we had to do was sneak in, find their hiding place, and announce ourselves.

CHAPTER FIFTEEN

WE CIRCLED THE Château Vasseur, giving the three-story white building a wide berth. Tall windows were arrayed along each floor, providing a perfect view of the gardens and the gravel drive. An open lawn provided no cover close to the château. We darted through the trees, taking cover behind large ornamental shrubs along the driveway. By the time we worked our way around the count's digs and caught sight of the stables, the sky was a dark blue with blazes of orange at the horizon. Soft light glowed from a few windows in the château on the lower floor in the rear. The kitchen, maybe.

"I could knock at the rear door," Kaz said.

"We can't take a chance," I said. "If we approach the wrong servant, they could betray us. I bet the Germans pay well."

"It's a foolish Frenchman who sides with the Germans at this late date," Topper said. "But I agree. We should work around to the rear of the stables and keep watch. Sonya or Juliet might show up."

"Or not," I said. "Remember the stable and the château are connected by secret tunnels, which they probably use to go back and forth."

"What do you suggest?" Kaz asked. "Waiting and watching would be the safest course."

"Bloody hell," Topper said. "If we wanted safe, we'd be waking up to tea and crumpets in England right now. Let's visit the stables and knock about."

We worked our way to the back of the stables and unlatched

a door. We stashed the canister in an empty stall and began to look for the tackle room, which led to the hidden underground chamber. Kaz kept a tight grip on the wireless as we moved along, passing by three horses that were too old and thin for even the Germans to steal. Hoping we'd brought breakfast, they raised their long necks and nickered at us. Beyond the stalls was a truck even more broken down than the trio of nags. Engine parts littered the oil-stained floor. We stepped over the debris and opened a door that creaked and groaned on its hinges. Leather bridles and harnesses hung from the walls, covered in dust and cobwebs.

"Where are the stairs?" Kaz whispered. The walls were rough-hewn planks of wood. Farm tools took up any space that wasn't festooned with riding gear. I pressed against the wall, testing for any give or sign of a secret entrance.

"They have to be here," Topper said, checking the floorboards for a hidden hinge.

"No, they do not." The unfamiliar voice was followed by the sound of a hammer being pulled back. It was feminine. The voice, not the revolver. "Turn around slowly."

We did. A young girl with wavy black hair stood behind Kaz, one hand on his shoulder, the other pointing a Walther P38 automatic at his head. Her gaze darted between Topper and me.

I held my Thompson low, not wanting to spook her into shooting. "Who are you?" I asked, working to keep my voice calm.

"Never mind. Who are *you?*"

"Parachutists, *mademoiselle*," Topper said. "We were blown off course and are looking for a place to hide."

"We have no idea where we are," Kaz said, trying not to look at the German automatic a few inches from his eyes. "Can you tell us? Your English is very good."

"You are in a very small room, looking for stairs. Where do you think they will take you?"

She looked a good deal like the picture of Sonya Charlet that

Vera had shown us. But the quality hadn't been great, and there was something different about her. The hair? The pistol? I didn't dare say her name in case it wasn't her. If this young lady was a collaborator, that would be a death sentence for Sonya.

"To someplace safe," I answered, hoping it was both vague and true enough to satisfy her, whoever she was.

"You've dyed your hair," Topper said, narrowing his eyes as he studied her. Keeping his Thompson hanging loosely from one hand, he took a step forward. "Auburn, wasn't it?"

He was right. In the photograph she'd had longer reddish-brown hair.

"Who told you that?" She moved the pistol a few inches away from Kaz.

"Vera," Topper said. "You know Vera, don't you?"

"Yes. Now tell me my name."

"Sonya Charlet. From Toulon. Estate manager for Count Alexandre Vasseur," Kaz said rapidly. "Now please put that pistol down."

"We'd almost given up hope," Sonya said, lowering her weapon. "We can't be too careful, you understand. The Germans have been known to send out false agents in order to infiltrate our networks. I hope that's a wireless set you're clutching like your firstborn."

"And with as much love," Kaz said, a flash of pain flitting across his face.

"Come quickly," Sonya said, heading back to the horse stalls. "We boarded up that door a few weeks ago, in case any of the fliers who passed through here were captured and interrogated."

Topper and I retrieved the canister and followed. I ached to ask her about Diana—Juliet, I meant—but I couldn't reveal I knew her. I tipped my helmet low over my eyes, hoping to buy a second or two before she realized it was me. I'd have to signal her somehow and pray that it would work out.

Sonya entered one of the stalls, gently pushing the ancient

horse to one side and grabbing a shovel to move a pile of manure and straw. When she pushed hard against a wall board, a section of flooring loosened enough for her to raise it and reveal a steep set of wooden steps that disappeared into darkness.

We waited while she descended the stairs. A muffled conversation below was followed by the glow of candlelight and Sonya returning to beckon us forward. Kaz went first, protecting the wireless, with Topper and me behind him. I made sure to bring up the rear, head low, on the lookout for Juliet. Because that's who she was now. Her life depended on her identity, and my mission depended on mine. Lies were our most trusted ally.

"Thank God," an unmistakable voice declared. As Topper and I manhandled the heavy canister down the narrow stairway, I heard a sharp gasp and a stifled "Oh!"

"What is it, Juliet?" Sonya asked.

"Nothing. I stumbled, that's all," Juliet answered. I figured Kaz had been able to give her a sign.

At the bottom of the stairs, we found ourselves standing in a small chamber with two tunnels barely five feet high running off in opposite directions. It was damp and smelled of chalk. The walls were limestone, and water dripped from the arched ceiling.

"I'll close up," Juliet said, still hidden in one of the gloomy tunnels. "Excuse me, Lieutenant." This was addressed to Kaz, a signal that she'd understood the need for secrecy.

"Juliet Bonvie," she said to Topper as she passed him. She was dressed in a short leather jacket, a brown skirt, and her hair tucked under a wool cap. The butt of a pistol stuck out from her jacket pocket.

"Lieutenant Chapman," he responded. "This is Sergeant Boyle. We have food for your guests."

"They'll be pleased, gentlemen. I'll be right back." She shot me a quick glance, no more. I knew it had to be that way, but I found myself wishing for a brush of her hand against my own, or even a sly wink. But this wasn't a lovers' game, this was war, and her face was set for it.

The trap door shut above me, casting the chamber into an even dimmer light. I heard the sound of a shovel reapplying the manure camouflage.

"Through here," Sonya said, taking us into a tunnel lit only by a single guttering candle. We stooped sideways, the passageway not even wide enough for our shoulders. Finally the space widened, and we found ourselves in front of a stout wooden door reinforced with ironwork.

"Where's the latch?" Kaz asked.

"It only opens from the other side," Sonya said, giving the knocker two quick raps, waiting, and then one more. "The door is solid oak. It's been here for centuries."

Dull metallic sounds echoed from the other side, followed by the creaking of hinges as the massive door slowly opened. Sonya led us from the wet, cramped passage into a long room with a vaulted ceiling and a trestle table. Electric lights were strung along the ceiling, giving the white limestone a soft, bright glow at odds with the darkness outside. Coats hung on pegs driven into the stone, along with rifles and Sten guns.

We were swarmed by a gaggle of airmen, each of them peppering us with questions. "What's happening? Is it true? The invasion? When are we getting out of here?"

"Hold on, boys," I said, and remembered a noncom would defer to an officer, at least in his presence. "Lieutenant Chapman will explain everything. Give us a second."

Kaz wearily took a seat as Topper and I set down the canister and opened the latches. The K rations distracted them, and we passed them to the eager takers.

"Who's in charge here?" Topper asked. This was greeted with an exchange of glances among the men.

"Well, Juliet runs the show, her and Sonya here," one of the men said, extending his hand. "First Lieutenant Harry Babcock, Royal Canadian Air Force, senior officer." Babcock had thinning blond hair, crow's-feet at the edges of his eyes, and a jagged scar along his jawline that hadn't yet healed. He wore the blue tunic of the RCAF with a *Canada* shoulder patch. So did two sergeants, mixed in with Yanks in leather flight jackets and khaki coveralls.

"Second Lieutenant Pete Armstrong, US Air Force," said one of the Americans, clutching a tin of chopped ham and eggs. "We're sure glad to see you fellas." He was tall, with a muscular build and a delicate face that seemed at odds with his body: thin lips, sunken eyes, white skin, and gaunt cheekbones. But that could have been from the diet and confinement. None of these guys looked healthy.

The ground trembled. Explosive *crumps* echoed from above as dust and grit cascaded from the ceiling.

"Damn," Armstrong muttered. The room went silent. The fliers cast their eyes toward the ceiling as if they could see through the solid limestone.

"What?" I asked.

"That might have been one of ours," Armstrong said. "Dropping their bombload early." He looked away, turning the tin of food over in his hand.

"B-26 Marauders from the Ninth Air Force," Babcock explained, watching as Armstrong sat to talk with his men. "Those guys are from the 323rd Bomb Group. They were shot down not far from here, after hitting the marshaling yards in Dreux. Their pals keep coming back, but the Krauts strengthened their defenses with lots of heavy antiaircraft stuff. That sound you heard was a Marauder dropping bombs short of the target 'cause they were hit."

"We have to go," Juliet announced, entering the room via a door at the far end. She was armed with a German Schmeisser submachine gun and carried a bulging pack. Two Frenchmen were with her, armed with German rifles. They wore dark coats, wool caps, and determined expressions. These were not the cheerful *Résistants* who greeted us last night. These had to be the hard men of the *Maquis*, who lived in the hills and woods and fought the Nazis full-time.

Babcock and one of the other Canadians grabbed weapons, along with two of the Americans. Juliet was definitely in charge here, and our mission was taking a backseat right now.

"What's happening?" Topper asked.

"A railroad bridge is about to be blown up," she said, not giving me so much as a glance. "Join us if you wish, but don't get in the way."

"I have a supply of gelignite, and I know how to use it," Topper said.

"But you are also the wireless operator," Kaz said, a pained look still on his face. "I think I may have damaged the radio when I fell. Not to mention my ribs."

"Sort it out, then," Juliet said. "We need that radio. Besides, we have *explosif plastique*, and we know quite well how to use it. *Allons-y!*"

"I'll go with you," I said, grabbing my helmet and Thompson. She shrugged, a perfect Gallic gesture of indifference. I followed Juliet, Sonya, the two *Maquisards*, and the rest of our little international force out the way we'd come, except when we got to the stairs, we took the other tunnel. The way was lit only by a lantern held by one of the Frenchmen. The ground began to slant down, becoming increasingly wet and cramped as we moved on.

The Frenchman doused the lantern, and I saw daylight ahead, beyond a rusty iron gate that moved surprisingly quietly on its ancient hinges. The opening was less than four feet high, and we scuttled out through thick weeds and down a streambed until we came to a spot where a rutted dirt road crossed the water. I wanted to ask where we were going, but everyone was moving too fast to stop for questions.

On the far side of the ford sat the broken-down truck that had been in the stable. A man stepped out of the cab and held the door open for Juliet, who handed off her submachine gun to Babcock. She got in up front with Sonya, who also relinquished her weapon. The rest of us jumped in the back as the silent driver walked away with an unsteady, shuffling limp. We tied down the canvas flap, and the truck took off with a lurch through the woods.

"Okay, someone tell me what's going on," I said. I had a lot of questions, like how were we going to blow a bridge in broad daylight, how many tunnels did that château have, why were downed airmen going along on a raid, and was Juliet mad at me? I looked at the Frenchmen. They didn't look at me. "Babcock?"

"We're going for a ride," he said, pushing back his blond hair. "What did you say your name was, Sergeant?"

"Billy. Billy Boyle," I said.

"Ronnie Fawcett," said the RCAF sergeant next to Babcock, extending his hand. He was a small guy, with wiry brown hair and a trace of childhood freckles across his cheeks. We shook hands, and he nodded to the Yank next to him. "This is Earle McCabe."

"They call me Dogbite," McCabe said in a slow southern drawl. He rubbed the side of his cheek where scar tissue was puckered up in two semicircles highlighted by black stubble growing around the clear, shiny skin. He made Kaz's scar look like a shaving nick.

"I can see how that'd be a hard name to shake," I said.

"Lot less hard than the damn dog was," he said, laughing and slapping his thigh. He looked to the *Maquisards*, who gave no response.

"Don't mind those two," Fawcett said. "When Juliet brings them in for a job, there's little said, whether they speak any English or not."

"Let me guess: need to know."

"Right," Babcock said. "You have to assume if anyone's captured, they'd talk, sooner or later. Best not for anyone to know too much. No one except Juliet and Sonya know all the tunnels and exits out of that place, for example. Smart women, those two."

"How smart is it to be attacking a bridge in broad daylight and driving around in a truck? Won't the Germans stop us?"

"Billy, I got this here bite goin' into a henhouse in the dead of night, back when I had next to nothing to my name and less on my feet," Dogbite said. "Figured I'd snatch a few eggs and be on my way. Never saw that dog until he knocked me down and started chawin' on my face. You know why?"

"Why?"

"Because that's what a farmer's dog does, dammit. And because I was too hungry to wait for him to go off with his master in the mornin'. I coulda walked in there and took a damn chicken after the sun went up if I'da waited."

"I guess the Germans guard this bridge at night, then," I said. "What about the truck?"

"Hell, I don't know nothing about the truck," Dogbite said. "I'm just glad not to be walkin'."

"No airman likes to march," Babcock said with a grin, his fingers playing along the red and swollen line on his jaw.

"How'd you get that wound, Babcock?" The scar wasn't much compared to Dogbite's, or even Kaz's, but it was worthy of comment.

"Nicked by shrapnel when we were shot down," he said. "Down to the jawbone. Fawcett patched me up, and the Resistance got me to a doctor. Didn't find out until later he was a vet. Not that stitching up a cow or a Canadian is that different."

"Cow's gotta be tougher," I said. It looked like the vet had done the job well, but with as much cosmetic concern as he'd have for a bovine patient. "You know where we're headed?"

"This is part of the Forest of Dreux," Babcock explained. "The Germans don't often patrol here. We can drive to within a mile of the bridge, then use cover to make our approach. No one has petrol, but the *Maquis* stole a few jerricans to keep this heap running."

"Tell me about the target. Why is this bridge so important?" I asked.

"It's part of the rail line between Chartres and Dreux," Babcock said. "It's a small bridge, too hard to hit from the air. It crosses over a road, which makes it hard to see, not like spotting a river crossing."

"How many guards?"

"Combien de gardes?" Babcock asked the *Maquisards*. One of them raised four fingers.

"Only four guards? Should be easy," I said.

"If we're quick about it," Dogbite said. "Damn quick. We gotta be gone quicker than cake on a fat man's plate." He cackled, looking to the Frenchmen, who sat impassively, clutching their weapons. The truck rolled to a halt, and that ended the conversation.

We left the truck in a shaded grove and scrambled down a hill to the edge of a field of sunflowers, dazzlingly yellow and green in the bright morning sun. Sten gun in hand, Juliet motioned for all of us to go low. The plants were less than five feet high, and we had to run in a crouch to avoid being seen. We hustled through the field single file, cutting a swath through the young plants on our way to kill young men.

I was behind Babcock. The advance slowed until he and the others went prone and began to belly-crawl. I followed suit, slithering out of the field into a wet drainage ditch next to a hard-packed dirt road. Pushing off on my elbows and knees, I kept my head down as mud soaked my torso. The earthy, damp smell of fetid standing water and decaying vegetation filled my nostrils. Ten minutes of slogging got us to a spot where the road curved, and Juliet called a halt, whispering to Sonya who passed the order down the line.

"Billy, up front," Babcock said. I should have been excited, but I was too focused on keeping my hands from shaking. I couldn't see a thing except for mud and slime, and I had no idea how close we were to the Krauts. But it was nice to be wanted.

"I'm here," I whispered as I got close to Juliet. I almost whispered *Diana*, but held my tongue.

"Sergeant Boyle, take a quick look," she said, her head inclined toward the top of the ditch. I took off my helmet and inched my head up slowly until my eyes cleared the edge.

I saw the bridge. It wasn't much more than a cutout under a raised embankment. The railroad ran over it, and the road we were following went under it. A thick vaulted arch of red brickwork with several feet of soil on top supported the tracks. Two Germans stood guard facing us, and one sat on the bridge, his legs dangling. That meant one or two more on the other side.

"I see three," I whispered to Juliet.

"How far can you throw a grenade?" It was about a hundred feet.

"I should be able to make it on a bounce. It'd be easy if I stood up, but one of them is up on the bridge. He'd spot me in a second." I couldn't get any closer. The ditch curved with the road ahead, which would put us right in their line of sight.

I took a grenade from my web belt and waited for the signal. Whispers went down the line. Juliet gave me a nod when everyone was ready. I pulled the pin, keeping a tight grip on the safety lever. I arched my arm back and rose up enough to see the target. The tunnel under the railway seemed smaller, and at the same time the Germans seemed to be right on top of me. I threw, putting as much weight and momentum into it as I could. The German on the bridge lit a cigarette, his feet swinging back and forth. The grenade bounced in the road, and he dropped the cigarette, his mouth in a round *oh* of shock and surprise.

I ducked.

The grenade exploded, a harsh echo sounding from within the tunnel.

I stood and fired a short burst from my Thompson at the guard on top, his legs still hanging over the edge. I dropped him, and he slid off, hitting the road as everyone else fired, filling the bricked arch with hot lead and ricochets.

"Now!" Juliet screamed, and we ran for the bridge. Rifle shots came at us in quick succession. There were two or more Germans on the other side. I ran to the left side of the bridge and flattened myself, another grenade in hand. Dogbite grabbed a potato masher grenade off one of the dead guards and went flat on the opposite side. We exchanged glances as he unscrewed the bottom cap and held the detonator cord. I pulled the pin. He pulled the cord. We tossed our grenades into the tunnel, aiming for the far side where the Germans had taken cover.

Twin blasts sounded, and we moved in, the enclosed space thick with smoke. I fired a few quick bursts, and a scream rose from a form writhing on the ground. One of the *Maquis* silenced him with a rifle shot. Juliet dropped her pack, and the two Frenchmen began to work with the plastic explosive, setting it along an ornamental ridge that ran the length of the tunnel.

Juliet sent Dogbite and Sonya to watch the way we'd come, and Fawcett up top. Babcock and I stood guard on the far side as she checked the explosive charges. I walked a few paces out, scanning the terrain ahead. Thick-trunked trees lined the roadway, whitewashed for visibility at night in the blackout. I caught movement from the corner of my eye and saw Babcock take cover behind the nearest tree. A submachine burst came from ahead, aimed at the tunnel. Another shriek, and then another burst.

I ran full-tilt, hoping the Kraut bastard wouldn't expect anything so stupid. I had no idea who'd been hit, but this was going to stop now. I went left, firing a burst as I rounded the first tree.

No one there. I skidded past the next tree, emptying the magazine. I heard footsteps and dropped my Thompson, pulling my .38 Police Special from my holster. I zigged inside the trees this time, running straight up the road and finding my Kraut kneeling, ready to fire at where I would have been. One shot through the helmet took care of him. I looked around, waiting for the next threat, but there was no one.

Through the distant trees, I saw the faint outline of a large building, a grand château, maybe half a mile away. The muffled sound of engines rumbled across the fields, my ears still ringing from explosions and gunfire. Vehicles were streaming out of the château and headed in our direction.

"Come on!" Babcock yelled, waving his arms. I picked up my Thompson, ran back to the tunnel, reloading as I went. I was relieved to see Juliet still standing, but one of the Frenchmen was down and, judging by the amount of blood, dead.

"We have company," I said.

"Right, we'll set a two-minute fuse," Juliet said. "Sergeant Boyle, come with me. The rest of you get ready." The remaining *Maquis* busied himself with setting the timing detonator in the *explosif plastique* on both walls. Everyone stepped around our dead companion without a second glance.

Juliet took a block of plastic explosive and a detonator. I followed her outside to the road, keeping an eye on the steadily approaching vehicles. She worked the block into the roots of a tree, and jammed in the pencil detonator. She glanced at the Germans, then back to the tunnel. None of our people were in sight. She crushed the end of the detonator.

"Two minutes," she said, looking me straight in the eye for the first time. Then she leaned in and kissed me. It was a kiss that could have lingered forever on my lips. Enemies approaching, friends fleeing, and less than a hundred and twenty seconds to oblivion, nothing else mattered but the taste of her, the scent of her hair, the salt of her tears, her warm lips, and her body pressed close to mine.

We opened our eyes, and in a second we were running, jumping over the bodies of the dead, elbows pumping, heads thrust forward as we burst into the sunflower field, making for the Forest of Dreux.

The explosion was sudden and sharp, shock waves bending the stalks and sending us stumbling in the dirt. Debris rained down around us as we turned to watch the arched bridge collapse, steel rails twisted and tumbling to the roadway. Smoke and dust filled the air, covering our escape in case any Germans were left standing.

CHAPTER SIXTEEN

HALFWAY BACK TO the château, we dropped off the surviving *Maquisard*. He vanished into the greenery without a word. We rattled on in the ancient truck, Juliet at the wheel and Sonya at her side. The idea, Babcock had told me, was that it might give us a couple of seconds to get the jump on the Germans if we had the misfortune to run into a roadblock. A couple of smiling girls might distract the Krauts if they didn't stop to wonder how the girls had managed to get any petrol.

"Lucky for us, we haven't had that problem yet," Fawcett said, grinning as if this had been nothing more than a grand adventure. With his small stature and freckles, he looked more like a Boy Scout than a commando.

"You've done this before?" I asked as the truck negotiated some deep ruts.

"Couple of times," he answered. "Small stuff, cutting telegraph and phone wires, raiding for weapons, that sort of thing. Risky, but the boredom was driving me crazy."

"We're careful not to attract any attention to the château," Babcock said. "That's why the location is perfect. The forest lets us drive undetected for miles in almost any direction."

"I think it spooks the Krauts," Dogbite said. "They done sweeps through the woods, but always in broad daylight."

"Nah, they can't take those stories seriously," Fawcett said.

"What stories?" I asked. Before he could answer, the truck braked, and we readied our weapons.

"It's Vincent Labiche," Babcock announced, peering through the canvas flap. "Time for us to get out."

I caught a glance of the same fellow who had limped away earlier, hoisting himself up into the cab. This time, we followed the truck right to the driveway, clearing away tire tracks in the dusty lane with leafy branches. When Juliet was satisfied the coast was clear, she signaled him to proceed down the drive.

At the back of the stables, where the land sloped away to reveal the stone foundation, Juliet opened a weathered wooden door. Inside were empty barrels and dusty shelves—the root cellar Vera had told us about.

"Here," Sonya said, handing me her weapon as Juliet lit a candle. "I will clear away our tracks and return to the house." She took a deep breath, brushed off her clothes and shut the door, leaving us in the dark, crowded room. Juliet pressed on the far wall, and a section of shelving swung outward, leading to another tunnel. Or the same tunnel we'd entered before, it was impossible to tell. I ducked my head, following the feeble light as Juliet led the way, her hand cupped around the small flame. I felt dizzy, uncertain of where we were, the fear of being lost deep underground growing stronger with each step. By the time we came to a door that opened out into the larger and well-lit tunnel, my heart was hammering in my chest and sweat soaked my shirt.

"Next time, Sergeant Boyle, secure permission from your commanding officer before going off on your own," Topper said once we'd reached the main underground chamber. He stood with his chest puffed out, playing the role of the aggrieved officer. "You showed decent initiative, but follow the chain of command from now on, eh?"

"Yes, sir," I said to his back, rolling my eyes and playing the aggrieved noncom for Dogbite's benefit. "We blew up the bridge, by the way."

"That will buy a day or so," Juliet said, her brief but confused glance telling me she was unsure how to play this. "If the wireless is working, we can notify London. Until the Germans repair it, there should be a nice backup in the Chartres rail yards."

"Not yet, it isn't," Topper said. "Boyle, come take a look."

"Wait a minute," Juliet said, laying her hand on my arm. "What about my equipment canisters? We need those weapons and supplies. Our orders are to keep that rail line out of service."

"Lieutenant Kazimierz is hurt," Topper said. "Bruised ribs, maybe broken. He'd be useless in the field. I need to get that radio working. That leaves Boyle here. He could lead you to them, couldn't you, Boyle?"

"Sure, after some shut-eye. I'm exhausted."

"Right," Topper said. "Can you wait, Juliet? We haven't slept for thirty-six hours or more."

"We leave at dusk," Juliet said. "I'll have some food brought down, and you can eat, meet the others, and get a few hours of sleep."

That last part sounded good. As much as I wanted time alone with Juliet, I could feel my eyelids getting heavier by the moment. I watched her leave as I introduced Topper to Fawcett, Babcock, and Dogbite. Dead on my feet, I shuffled along with Topper down a limestone corridor reinforced with timbers. Electric lights were strung along the beams, giving the stone a soft yellow glow.

"How big is this place?" I asked after a couple of turns. We'd passed sleeping quarters cut from stone, set up with two or three cots in each. Not the Ritz, but better than a POW camp.

"No idea," Topper whispered. "It's a honeycomb with plenty of locked doors. I got lost looking for the loo."

"All the comforts of home," I said as we entered a large room with a workbench. Kaz looked up from the wireless parts spread out in front of him and shot a look at Topper. He gave Kaz the all-clear—no one within earshot.

"Are you all right, Billy?"

"Yeah. One of the Frenchmen didn't make it, but the trains won't run on time tonight. How's the radio?"

"We can't find anything wrong. Topper has replaced all the parts for which we have spares. Coils, adapters, fuses, valves, nothing works."

"What about the vacuum tubes?" I asked, pointing to a variety of tubes on the bench.

"Those are valves, at least in England," Topper said. "Whatever they call them in France or America, they're not the problem. We're about to take the whole thing apart and put it back together. Again."

"Good luck," I said, my voice low. "And keep riding me, Topper. That'll play well with Blake. Maybe we should throw a few punches at some point."

"Leave me out of it," Kaz said. "My ribs hurt enough already."

"Blame Billy for your fall," Topper said. "Then I'll step in, and we'll let the fireworks happen."

"Okay, after some chow and shut-eye," I said, and headed out, checking for the end of the tunnel. I came to an intersection and took a right. It was unlit, pitch black after a couple of steps in. I steadied my hands against the cool limestone and walked farther. The tunnel curved, and when I turned around, there was no light at all. I backtracked, feeling that sensation of being buried alive again. The main corridor branched out into a series of connected spaces. Sleeping quarters, weapons storage, even a washroom with a faucet attached to a pipe. Running spring water and an old galvanized metal bathtub. I'd been in worse hotels.

"Have a seat, Sergeant," Sonya called to me. "Welcome to our *salon*." I took a spot on the bench as she ladled hot turnip soup from a pot. There was warm bread and wine. I hadn't realized how hungry I was. Here in the larger room, I didn't feel the dread of the shadowy tunnels. I didn't normally get spooked that easily, but this setup reminded me of nights when I was a kid scampering up the dark stairs at the back of the house, certain a ghost was at my back.

"Do you cook down here?" I asked Sonya as I inhaled the steaming soup.

"No, the cook brought this through the tunnel, fresh from the kitchen," she said. "She's been with the count forever, so there's no need to worry." She must have read my mind.

Babcock and Fawcett were already digging into their food, and I nodded to the other men sitting around the wood table, the planks shiny with age and use.

"How soon we gettin' outta here?" The question came from one of my fellow Americans, a squat guy who needed a shave and a lesson in manners. "I can't take no more turnips."

"Billy Boyle," I said, extending my hand across the table. He took it and gave me the briefest of shakes, as if he wasn't used to friendly gestures.

"Roy Meyer," he said, crooking his thumb in the direction of the guy sitting next to him, leather flying jacket draped across his shoulders. "Me an' Switch is with Armstrong. We been here since our Marauder got hit awhile back."

"Alvin Blake," Switch said, standing to give me a solid handshake and a once-over. "Everyone calls me Switch." He had an easy smile and striking blue eyes that bored into mine. Switch had an air of easy authority about him, as if he were more used to giving orders than obeying them. He was freshly shaved and wore his brown hair short, unlike his pal Meyer, whose thick black hair curled around his face and blended in with the dark stubble.

"There's what, seven crewmen on a B-26?" I asked. "Any others make it?"

"Copilot and bombardier got it when a Focke-Wulf 190 came at us head-on," Switch said. "Rest of us bailed out, but Armstrong, Dogbite, Meyer, and me lost sight of the other guys on the way down. We got separated on the ground, and the Resistance brought me, the skipper, and Dogbite here. Meyer a few days later."

"That bastard Riley better be alive," Meyer put in. "He owes me fifty bucks. Say, Boyle, what are you, some kind of hero, goin' out with them others?"

"I like a walk in the country now and then," I said. "And I like putting distance between me and officers even better. Where's Armstrong?"

"Dunno," Meyer said with a shrug.

"Armstrong's a good pilot," Switch said. "But he's nothing special on the ground. He spends all his time moping around and reading. A lot like Brookie the Canuck, except *he* don't read." They both laughed, a harsh cawing that made the kid at the end of the table flinch.

"Paul Brookes," he said, giving me a weak wave, and then returning to an intense study of the wood grain. He was pale and thin, with long shallow cheeks and a droopy mouth that looked like it had forgotten what a smile was.

"So you don't like officers?" Meyer said, lighting up a cigarette with all the joy of a smoker long denied. "Thanks for the smokes, by the way, even though they're Chesterfields."

"Chapman ripped into me for going along on the raid without asking," I said, keeping my voice to a whisper. "He thinks I'm his goddamn servant."

"I don't like officers on principle," Switch said. "Asshole or prince, their job is basically to get us killed, that's how I got it figured."

"Dogbite doesn't seem to agree with you."

"That guy is certifiable," Meyer said. "One helluva gunner, I'll give him that. But he loves a fight, and it don't matter with who."

"Fawcett didn't seem to mind going along, either," I said. "What's his story?"

"Ask Brookie, why don't you?" Switch said, his lips forming into a sneer. "You and Fawcett are buddies, aren't you, Brookie?" He and Meyer rocked with laughter as Brookes rose and left the room, his eyes riveted to the floor and his hands stuffed into his blue RCAF tunic. His drawn, pale face was expressionless, as if he'd hidden all emotion away. I was about to ask what the hell they were talking about when Juliet burst into the room.

"The Germans searched the château this morning," she said. That got everyone's attention.

"Was anyone taken?" Sonya asked.

"No. It was only Zeller and a few men. He said there were reports of parachutists and that he was obliged to search. He was almost apologetic, according to the count," Juliet said.

"No one's seen Armstrong for a while," Switch said, shaking a cigarette loose from his pack.

"No more smoking," Juliet said.

"There are air vents," Sonya explained. "It wouldn't do for a German to smell cigarette smoke in an empty stable. Especially American cigarettes. And Switch is right. We need to look for Lieutenant Armstrong."

"How many places can he be?" I asked.

"He's been to the château," Juliet said. "There had to be someone down here who knew his way around. There are lots of secret panels and hiding places. Maybe he heard the Germans and hid himself."

"I'll help," Switch said, pocketing his smokes. Meyer said the same, which surprised me. These guys didn't impress me as the volunteering type.

"No," Juliet said. "I want everyone in this room in case we need to leave in a hurry. Sergeant Boyle, Sonya will show you to a place where you can sleep. One of us will get you when it's time to leave."

"What about Armstrong?" I asked.

"Sonya will look for him," she said. "I need to go to Dreux.

The count told Zeller I was there on business. I'll be back as soon as I can."

"Zeller, that's the *Abwehr* captain?" I said to Sonya as she led me to my room.

"Yes. Juliet knows he might check on her whereabouts, so if she gets stopped at a roadblock, it will be an alibi. Or close to one, at least."

"Do you think Zeller suspects anything?"

"No, he is naturally suspicious," she said, pulling aside a curtain and showing me a room with a rough cot and a wooden table with a single unlit candle. "Our finest accommodation. Sleep well, Sergeant." She smiled and dropped the curtain, leaving me in darkness.

I dropped my gear and found the cot. Unlaced my boots, pulled off my field jacket, and began to take off my shoulder holster. Then I thought about Zeller and his pals. They might be back, looking for those parachutists who blew up his bridge. The Police Special revolver dug into my ribs, but it was a comforting pain, and I left it there. I stretched out on the bed and felt exhaustion claiming me as its own. I'd awoken almost two days ago in England, and now I was falling asleep in occupied France, buried deep in the count's limestone caves. Strange.

More strangeness swirled through my mind. What was there about the Forest of Dreux that frightened the Germans? They'd conquered all of Europe; what was so scary about a patch of woods in France? Or was it a story people told because it made them feel safe?

And who was Switch's Morgan Gang partner? Meyer? Dogbite? Or maybe Armstrong, which would be clever, disguising their racket with apparent disdain.

Where had Armstrong gotten to? If he was stir-crazy, he could have come along on the raid. Maybe he'd had enough of fighting and hiding and headed for the hills. Or a comfy German POW camp.

Who were the mystery parachutists, and why had they landed here? Or were the Krauts seeing parachutes everywhere since the morning of June the sixth?

There was a faint frame of light from the corridor leaking around the edges of the curtain. It looked like daylight at the end of a long, dark tunnel, and I must have been dreaming, because I found myself with Diana—not as Juliet—walking into the sunshine, our feet bathed in soft green grass and summer flowers. I tried for a kiss, and she faded away, light turning to darkness, the sky as heavy and forbidding as the tons of rock I slept beneath.

CHAPTER SEVENTEEN

I'D FOUND HER. She'd disappeared into the murk, but now she was back. I could feel her hands, sense her smell, and hear her voice.

"Wake up, Billy!" Not a lover's summons, but a hissing, insistent whisper. "Wake up."

"Diana," I mumbled. She gave my shoulder a quick shake.

"No, it's Juliet." I could see her glance at people milling behind her. I'd almost spilled the beans. The curtain opened and closed, casting splashes of light on the cold stone. She struck a match and lit the candle as Sonya ushered the others away.

"Yeah, of course. Sorry, I was dreaming. Is it time to go?"

"We have a problem," she said. "We've found Lieutenant Armstrong. He's dead."

"Germans?" I asked, lacing up my boots and trying to clear the cobwebs from my brain.

"Not unless they've gotten into the tunnels," she said. "He's been murdered."

Trying to grasp the implications, I trailed Juliet and Sonya into one of the dark corridors I'd explored earlier. Had Germans gotten in? Or one of the household staff? Perhaps one of the fliers had a grudge against Armstrong, nurtured by tension, boredom, and close proximity. Juliet flicked on a torch and shined the light toward the ceiling, which grew lower and lower as we went.

Bent over, we came to a stout wooden door, no more than four feet high. Sonya fit a large lever lock key into the rusted lock and turned it with both hands. The door opened with a metallic *clang*, the rusty iron hinges creaking loudly. A dank, damp murk carried into the air. Juliet aimed the light ahead, and I ducked through the doorway, blinking to focus on the chamber.

"We're directly under the house now," she said. The room was round with a high arched ceiling. Huge slabs of granite rose up on all sides, with layers of chiseled limestone rock set in brickwork patterns between them. The stone floor was worn smooth, like the steps in an ancient cathedral.

"What is this place?" I asked, my voice unexpectedly hushed.

"The remains of an old Druid temple," Juliet said, as if that were not the least bit remarkable. She ducked again, taking us through an opening barely three feet high under a massive stone lintel. The next chamber was narrow, braced by a series of smooth boulders and roofed with giant aged beams. At the far end, Juliet's light settled on a crumpled figure.

"Has anyone touched the body?" I asked, taking in the sizable pool of blood soaking the stones around his head, creating a ghastly halo.

"No," Juliet said, handing me the light. "Sonya found him and came right to me."

"Did you tell Kaz and Topper?"

"No, Juliet thought it best to let them sleep," Sonya said, a note of irritation in her voice.

"The wireless still isn't working," Juliet added. "But they were falling asleep at the workbench, so I told them to rest."

"Don't you think your officers should be informed, Sergeant?" Sonya said. It was the first sense I'd gotten of any disagreement between the two women, but some friction was to be expected in any high-pressure situation, and here it had just gone to full boil.

"No," I said, not bothering to explain. I knelt next to the body. Armstrong was on his side, legs crumpled beneath him, one arm pinned under his torso, the other at his side. It looked like he'd been walking in our direction, but it wasn't always easy to tell. I didn't look at his head yet, knowing that was going to be distracting. He'd either been shot or bludgeoned, and neither method made for a pretty picture.

I started with his legs. Nothing unusual on his boots. I patted down his pants' pockets and found a single shilling. A good-luck piece? Or loose change from his last night on the town? I rubbed my finger over the image of King George. Only Armstrong knew.

I checked the pockets of his leather flying jacket and was rewarded with a pencil stub and lint. Nothing in his shirt pocket.

I moved the flashlight to his head and knew right away he'd been shot. His face had the misshapen look that came from a bullet careening through the skull, releasing pressure and churning tissue as it sought to expend its energy against the grey matter that made up the mind and memories of humans.

I found the bullet hole at the base of his head, right at the occipital bone, where the trajectory would take the slug through his cerebellum and brain stem, wiping out everything that mattered. It was quick; he never knew it was coming. Which told me something.

I flexed his neck and felt for the muscles in his face. He was beginning to stiffen up. I studied his hands; muscles were hardening in place at the wrists. The thumbs were dashed with red. Same at the base of his palms. Dried blood. Spend as much time with a coroner as I did back in Boston, and you couldn't help but pick up a few things.

I stood and shined the beam around the area. "Do you have many flashlights down here?" I asked. "Torches, I mean."

"No, that's the only one, not counting the ones you brought. We use candles or a lantern if we have to leave the lighted areas. Batteries are impossible to come by," Juliet said.

"What about keys? How did Armstrong get this far?"

"As I said, he knew the tunnels and where the extra key set was kept." Juliet knelt close by and stared at the body. "He didn't want to take any chances outside. He said he'd used up all his luck in the air. I gave him tunnel duty so he could lead people out if need be. He liked the idea that he might save lives if the worst happened."

I looked a few feet in the direction he would have come from, then back again. There was no candle wax. He definitely had his hands on his head. If he'd been carrying a candle, it would have dropped and left some trace. His killer was behind him, with some light of his own. Or hers, for that matter.

I got down on my hands and knees and swept the light along the edge of the floor, looking into the crevices where the stones met. I was about to give up when I spotted it. About a yard back, where a paving stone tilted toward the wall. It had rolled into that tiny crack, but glowed in the flashlight beam.

"Shell casing. Looks like he was shot with an automatic," I said. There was no way to tell if the killer didn't care about leaving a casing behind, or if it had been too hard to recover in the frantic moments after committing a murder. If this killer was the frantic type. "Rigor mortis is beginning to set in. It's already advanced in the smaller muscles. He could have been killed within the past eight hours, maybe longer. The stone floor is cold, so that might slow the process."

"So anytime today?" Sonya asked. I glanced at my watch. It was six o'clock. Evening, I was pretty sure. Above, the earth turned and the sun rose and set. Deep in the rock tunnels, time had a way of standing still, the solidity encasing us in a permanent present.

"Possible," I said. "More than a few hours ago—of that I'm certain." I shined the flashlight on the shell casing, then back at Sonya. "You had a Walther pistol last night."

"Yes, so?"

"This is a nine-millimeter Parabellum round," I said. "Used in Lugers and Walthers." I shined the light on the head of the casing, showing them the *9mm* mark.

"We have both in the weapons room, taken from dead Nazis," Juliet said. "I carry a Walther myself at times."

"Who has access?"

"Everyone. There's a war on, Sergeant," Sonya said. "What happens now?"

"We bury our dead. And count your pistols." I took Armstrong's dog tag and followed the ladies back, wondering what the hell he had been up to.

There were seven pistols in their weapons room that fit the bill. Two Lugers and five Walthers. All were clean, the sweet, pungent odor of gun oil clinging to each of them. Any of them could have been the murder weapon, or it could have been a pistol hidden away after lifting it from a dead Kraut officer. It was useless to speculate. Juliet was more productive, coming up with a large white sheet and Dogbite, who'd volunteered to help carry the body.

I kept Dogbite in front of me and watched his reactions in the tunnels as best I could. He kept one hand on the wall, steadying himself, hesitant in his steps. He might have been a good actor, but I got the strong impression he was disoriented and unfamiliar with the path we were taking.

"Goddamn," he muttered when we came to the body. "What'd he do to deserve that?"

"Good question. Got any ideas?" The beams from Juliet's and my flashlights waved like searchlights as we shook out the sheet and laid it next to Armstrong's body. I caught a glimpse of Dogbite's face, his scars lit like craters on a half moon.

"Hell, no, that boy wouldn't hurt a fly. 'Cept for all the Krauts we killed, but you know what I mean." He grimaced, shook his head, and looked away. I did know what he meant. Some guys reacted to war that way. They became subdued when not engaged in the act of killing, almost numb, as they retreated deep into their souls.

"Help me roll him," I said to Juliet, handing my flashlight to Dogbite.

"No, I'll do it," he said, straightening Armstrong's arms and legs. "It's only right. He was my skipper." The arms took some work; they were starting to stiffen. He pulled the body onto its side by the shoulders, cradling Armstrong's head in his palm, and rolled him onto the sheet. The head came to rest as Dogbite withdrew his hand, now sticky with blood. He then tucked the sheet under the body on both sides, leaving it swaddled in the white sheet, with enough fabric at either end to carry.

"You look like you know what you're doing," I said.

"Back home, you were rich if your family could afford a coffin. I buried kin in shrouds plenty of times. Old and young. Where we takin' him?"

"Into the woods," Juliet said, setting her hand on Dogbite's arm. "It will have to be an unmarked grave for now."

"Don't matter much. Dust goes to dust, and the spirit goes to God, so they say. Come on, Billy, lend a hand," he said. "How'd you come to find the lieutenant anyway?"

"We searched everywhere," Juliet said, lighting our way. "I've no idea what he was doing here."

"How about you, Dogbite? What do you think he was up to?" I asked, grunting as we clumsily carried the body.

"He kept to himself, you know? It was the same back in England. When he got leave, he'd go to a museum or a fancy church. Spent a lot of time reading. Most guys, even officers, wanted booze and broads, but not Armstrong. Had a girlfriend back home, and he wasn't the type to stray. Knew his own mind, I have to give him that."

"Good pilot?" I asked.

"Damn good," Dogbite said as we stopped in the Druid temple, setting Armstrong down to take a breather. "Brought us down with our hydraulics all shot up once, and that ain't easy. Can't say him and me woulda been pals back home, but he was a good skipper, and that's what counts over here. Wish I knew why anyone'd want him dead."

"Same here," I said. "I don't like the idea of being knocked off by the same bastard. Let me know if you get any ideas." We resumed our journey through the tunnels, carrying Armstrong into the salon and laying him out on the table.

I stepped back as Meyer and Switch came in, their faces drawn and serious. They stood with Dogbite, silently gazing at the corpse of their skipper, none of them betraying what they really felt about him or each other. It was the perfect imitation of respect for a fallen comrade, a solid front that I knew for the lie it was. But did that make any of them a killer?

As I left to find Kaz and Topper, I passed Babcock, Fawcett, and Brookes shepherded in by Sonya, who carried a shovel and a pickax. Everyone was shaking their head, wondering how this happened, whispering about what a fine fellow Armstrong was. Someone was a steely calm liar.

Kaz and Topper were already awake when I got to their chamber, Sonya having delivered the news moments ago.

"Is Sergeant Blake involved?" Kaz asked, his voice low.

"I have no idea," I said. "Unless Armstrong was part of the Morgan Gang, and from what his crewmen said, he wasn't the type."

"Or he was damn clever," Topper said. "Until today."

"Or the real Morgan member was sending a message," Kaz offered.

"Keep your eyes and ears open. See what you can pick up from these guys; there's probably going to be a lot of gossip and conjecture after we bury him," I said.

"We're ready," Juliet said, appearing in the doorway.

"You guys go ahead. I need to speak with Juliet for a second."

Kaz and Topper left, and Juliet glanced into the corridor before pulling the curtain. "What in God's name is going on, Billy?" she whispered.

"Diana—"

"No. I am Juliet Bonvie. Please don't think of Diana Seaton, not until we're out of here. Juliet is who I must believe I am if I want to live. And I do, Billy, very much."

"Okay, Juliet it is. That's how I'll think of you." I gave her hand a quick squeeze and gave her the lowdown. "We need to get Sergeant Blake out as soon as possible. He's a top honcho in a big black market operation, and he's willing to testify against his partners. He took exception to how they mistreated his cousin. Someone in his crew is part of the gang, but we don't know who."

"Do you think Lieutenant Armstrong was involved?"

"Haven't a clue. All I know is that they're a violent bunch, and Switch is no exception. He's not turning on them out of the goodness of his heart. Matter of fact, he doesn't yet know his cousin is safe. The gang nabbed him when Switch was about to tell all as an insurance policy. He clammed up, we rescued the kid, and here we are."

"So you're not a Jedburgh?"

"Topper is the real deal. Kaz and me are here to deliver your radio and supplies, keep Blake safe, and get him out as soon as possible."

"Thank God," Juliet said, the tension draining from her face. "I doubt many Jedburghs will survive. I suppose your sergeant's rank is part of the show?"

"Yeah, I'm a crooked officer who was busted down and given one last chance."

"Fits you well, Billy." She smiled and winked. No kiss, but we had a funeral to attend, so I understood. Although I smarted a bit over her relief that I wasn't a real Jed. Sure, it was dangerous, but did she think I couldn't handle it?

I followed her to the salon where everyone was gathered, staring at the white shroud with the deep-red stain.

CHAPTER EIGHTEEN

WE FILED THROUGH the labyrinth of tunnels, emerging into the dusky light via the root cellar. Dogbite had the shroud by the legs, with Meyer and Switch fumbling at the shoulders, the dead weight causing them to stumble in the narrow passages. Outside, they set down their load, Meyer giving out a loud grunt.

"Quiet," Babcock whispered.

"Officer or not, you ain't my skipper," Meyer snarled. "And a Canuck to boot."

"Shut up," I said, wanting to get this over with before a fight broke out. Switch gave Meyer a nod, and they picked up the body, following Juliet and Sonya, who bore the ax and shovel like a couple of gravediggers. We crouched as branches pulled at our sleeves and snapped at our faces, closing green ranks behind us like sentinels.

"Here," Juliet said, as we emerged into a glade. The fading light cast a silvery glow on the birch trees, their delicate leaves dancing in the breeze. She and Sonya laid the tools on the ground, offering them to the men. I took up the ax and began to cut into the soil, snagging roots and rocks as I went. Brookes grabbed the shovel and followed me as I broke ground, digging out the earth as I loosened it.

"Anyone want to take over?" Brookes asked ten minutes into our labors. He was sweating in the cool evening air, his thin frame not made for grave digging. No one answered him. Not the most popular guy in this hotel. Babcock stepped up to spell me on the pickax, but Brookes was left to his shovel.

As I stepped away from the widening hole, I saw Vincent shuffling forward, carrying an ornately carved wooden chair with ruby-red upholstery. A bit fancy for the woods, probably a Louis something-or-other. He set it down, carefully checking to be sure the legs were steady. Behind Vincent, an elderly woman came into view, clutching a shawl and stomping through the bushes in scuffed but sturdy shoes. On her arm was an even older man, a black cape on his shoulders and holding a cane with a silver handle. His goatee matched the handle, but the rest of his face was hidden by a fedora pulled low across his forehead. Vincent helped settle him into the chair, then stood at his side, flanked by the grey-haired woman.

"The count," Juliet whispered. "And that is Madame Agard, the cook." No one else paid them any mind, as if the viewing of clandestine interments was standard procedure. Quite possible, I thought as I began to walk toward the count, ready to shake hands or kiss cheeks as the situation demanded.

"No," Juliet whispered, pulling me back. "Do not speak to him yet. I will introduce you later."

She returned her gaze to the grave as Kaz raised an eyebrow and gave a barely perceptible shrug. This wasn't the time for questions, but I had a few.

Brookes stopped, leaning on his shovel and breathing hard. I took it from him, clapped him on the shoulder, and told him to take five. He grinned weakly, obviously not used to friendly gestures. Fawcett took over for Babcock with the pick, and we quickly enlarged the hole, getting a couple of feet down.

"Keep digging," Sonya said. "There are animals in these woods. Wild boar, badger, fox. Bury him deep."

Fawcett took a deep breath and swung the pickax in huge arcs, breaking up clods of soil and moving back as I followed, digging out and deepening the grave. I worked at the sides, driving the spade into the earth and prying up stones Fawcett's pick had missed. One of them didn't come out easily. I pressed down on the handle and tried to force it, only to be thrown backward when it finally popped out and rolled between my legs.

It was no rock. It was a skull.

"What the bloody hell?" Topper exclaimed, squatting over the hole for a closer look. I scrambled out of the now twice-dug grave, wiping away the dirt clinging to the skull as best I could and handing it to Kaz, who examined it in the lingering light.

"Is this a graveyard?" I asked Juliet. "Have other escapees been buried here?"

"We've buried no one here," she said, glancing at the count.

"That stands to reason," Kaz said. "This unfortunate person has been buried quite some time. Perhaps in a past war, but not this one. Look at the coloring—almost dark brown."

"Puis-je, monsieur?" Vincent had left his post with the count and appeared at Kaz's side, his palm outstretched. Blue flecks of paint decorated his fingers and the sleeve of his jacket.

"Mais oui," Kaz answered, placing the skull gently in Vincent's hand. It was missing its jaw, but I'd had enough of digging and had no desire to go bone collecting. Besides, we had a whole body to deal with. After more excavation without discovering any other skeletal remains, Sonya approved of the depth.

Dogbite and Switch laid Armstrong in the ground. Meyer joined them, the rest of us lined up on the other side of the grave. The count remained in his chair, stroking the dome of the cracked brown skull with his wrinkled hand. Madame Agard was wide-eyed, while Vincent's face was a blank.

"Does anyone wish to say a few words?" Sonya asked, looking at Armstrong's crewmen. Silence draped itself over the grave. Meyer grimaced, seeming more likely to spit into the grave than say anything over it. Switch shook his head slowly, glancing at Dogbite.

"Aw, shit, I was with him the longest," Dogbite said. "Might as well say my respects out loud. I was proud to fly with him. He was a good pilot, always brought us home, and only a few fellas got killed or hurt real bad. Lotta pilots done worse. The skipper wasn't a guy who made friends easy. Didn't drink much, kept to himself. Didn't visit whores, stayed faithful to his girlfriend. You mighta thought him boring, which he was, 'cept that lively don't mean a thing stacked up against good flyin'. Me an' Riley came over from the States with the lieutenant, and since then the three of us been through hell and half of Georgia together. Now Lieutenant Armstrong, he's in the ground, and I don't know where Riley's got himself to. Hope he's alive, 'cause sad to say, I think he's the only other person who'd care. But I give a damn, and when I find the bastard who shot my skipper, I'll kill him, skin him, and leave his carcass for the badgers to gnaw on. That's a goddamn promise."

Dogbite strafed the group with his eyes, not stopping until he took in the count and his entourage. Then he began to shovel and didn't stop until the ground was smooth and even, leaving only the darkened soil to betray the burial site. We stood in silence, gazing at the turned earth, and I was curious who else was wondering when their turn might come, and if any better words could be spoken over their grave. After a minute, by unspoken consent, we turned to go.

The count was gone, his chair empty, no trace of the skull left behind.

The last time I'd looked, while Dogbite was still shoveling, the count and his acolytes were still there. Now the three of them had vanished into the gloaming.

I shivered. No one spoke, nervous glances darting to the freshly dug grave and to the edge of the darkening wood. Watching for the ghost from another time, another war, who might rise from the violated tomb as his skull was marched off like a macabre souvenir?

Or had Dogbite's bloody promise of revenge spooked someone in the burial party? The ancient skull, the silent count, the glade of silver birches, the murder of Armstrong, the image of wild animals digging up the body, all these thoughts flashed and swirled through my mind, making some sort of strange sense before they slipped away under the scrutiny of what logic I could muster.

"You want to explain any of this?" I whispered to Juliet as we filed back to the house, the setting sun a blood-red line at our backs.

"Beware the White Giant. He lives within the Forest of Dreux, deep underground, and guards an abandoned Druid treasure chamber. He's eight feet tall and swathed in luminous white linen."

"I don't need riddles or fairy tales, I need answers," I said. "What gives with the count?"

"Count Vasseur came to pay his respects," Sonya said sharply as she opened the door to the root cellar. The others entered, Babcock carrying a candle, the flickering light disappearing down the corridor as Juliet lit another, Kaz and Topper dark shadows behind her.

"That clearing may well have been a burial site in centuries past, who knows? But Count Vasseur appreciates the value of a good ghost story. He'll have Vincent clean the skull and put it on display. The servants will be frightened, and the story of the Druid priest's skull will spread to the village. Many people will not admit to believing that the old spirits still inhabit the forest, but neither will they take a chance. And those who do believe won't come within miles. It's a ruse, one the count enjoys perpetuating, and one which works to our benefit," Sonya said.

"Fawcett mentioned something about the Germans not wanting to enter the forest," I said.

"We've heard the legend of the White Giant has some of them spooked," Juliet said. "Or perhaps they simply believe the locals are too frightened to hide anything in the deep woods."

"Either way, it's a useful tool. You've seen the remains of the temple. There certainly was a Druidic presence here at some point in the distant past," Sonya said.

"A Druid temple? Beneath the château? This I must see," Kaz said, his voice rising with excitement.

"Please fix the damn radio first," Sonya said, her irritation a match for Kaz's enthusiasm.

"We're getting close," Topper said. "It may be a problem with the power cord from the transmitter to the power supply. I didn't want to tackle it before getting some rest; I was seeing double."

"We'll bring you coffee," Juliet said as we wended our way through the tunnels. "Some of the real stuff you brought, mixed with chicory. And bread."

"Any cheese? I'm starving," Topper said as we entered the salon.

"There is no cheese other than what you brought. Fix the radio, and move these men on," Sonya said, her voice a great and tired sigh. "We've had very little to eat. Without ration tickets, there is not enough to go around for all these men. Can't you see we are slowly starving?"

"We will get to work," Kaz said, motioning for Topper to follow while holding his ribs, the pain evident.

"And I need to figure out where everyone was when Armstrong was killed," I said, watching the two of them leave. "I'll have to talk to the count as well."

"No!" Juliet said, grabbing me by the arm. "We don't have time for that now. You need to get the canisters to the *Maquis*. We've been waiting weeks for those weapons. We have our duty, and so do you."

"What about Armstrong?" I asked. "Doesn't anyone have a duty to him?" Switch watched us with those clear blue eyes as the rest of the men milled around the table. Juliet still had hold of my arm and steered me out of the room.

"Billy, you're not here to investigate a murder," she whispered.

"Your job was to deliver a wireless and weapons, then get your man out of here. We have the radio, for what it's worth, and now you need to get the weapons to the *Maquis*. That's what we're here for. This isn't a murder inquiry back in England, where the life of one man matters above all. This is the real war, the liberation of France, and a lot of people have died waiting for this day. Lieutenant Armstrong was a nice man, and I liked him. But finding his killer will have to wait while you do what you came for."

"Do you think the killer will only strike once?" I asked, wrenching my arm free. I knew she was right, but I didn't like the idea of leaving a murderer loose.

"I don't know, Billy. I don't like it, but we don't have a choice. This is the invasion. We've been waiting years for this, and we need to get those weapons into action."

"Okay," I said, raising my hands in surrender. "Let's get going, then." Not that it would be safe running around the French countryside after curfew, but at least it would put distance between Juliet and the killer, whoever he or she was.

"I'm not going," she said. "I have to be here to decode incoming messages, assuming they ever get the radio to work."

"But I don't want to leave you alone," I said, knowing it was the wrong thing to say as soon as I said it.

"Thank you, Billy, for the vote of confidence. But I've managed to survive the Nazis so far without you, so one more night shouldn't be a problem, killer or no killer."

She stormed off, leaving me in the dark.

CHAPTER NINETEEN

"CHRISTINE WILL GET you to Coudray by automobile,"
Sonya explained as we waited inside the stables. "Close anyway."

Christine Latour was the municipal librarian in Dreux, and
she often traveled between the library and Rouvres, a town with
an old folk's home and a hospital. She had a pass to be on the road
until curfew, which was only an hour away.

"And she'll bring me to Commander Murat?" I asked.

"Yes, and then you bring him to the weapons. I hope the *Résistants* from Coudray have not taken any. They are amateurs, and
you should not have armed them as you did."

"It was the only choice," I said. "Otherwise they would have
taken all of them after we left. This way, we secured their promise
to leave the rest for Murat. They seemed to respect his name."

"Murat is feared among the French as well as the Germans.
There are many factions to the Resistance, and it takes a leader
of great strength to pull them together. It is not easy, especially
with all the fence-sitters rushing to arms now that the tide is about
to turn."

"The Coudray group, for instance?"

"Some of them, yes," Sonya said. "Several men ran off to
join the *Maquis* early on, after the Germans swept up the most
able bodied to be sent to the Reich for slave labor. Two of the
women have helped us as couriers. I suppose that's how they
knew about the landing field."

"We couldn't have gotten far without them," I said. "But they
didn't seem focused on security."

"I only hope they will wait for orders," she said. A sputtering, wheezing engine interrupted her as an ancient Peugeot propelled itself down the drive, smoke billowing from the rear. "Don't worry, it's not on fire. It's a gasogene engine, powered by wood gas."

"That's one way around fuel rationing," I said. A large firebox was built onto the back of the vehicle, with pipes leading to the engine up front, where the gases apparently made the thing go. The light-blue Peugeot slid to a stop, grey smoke wreathing it as the engine continued to rattle. With the headlights directly behind the slanted grille and taped over to allow only a sliver of light to escape, it had the look of a smoking metal dragon.

I glanced toward the château, where a shadowy figure stood at a window, silhouetted by the glow of candlelight.

The driver stepped out of the car. She was dressed in a raincoat cinched tightly around a thin waist. Her hair was dark red, strands spilling out from under a man's wool cap. Her eyes, bright and alert, were the best feature on a face that otherwise was unremarkable. Sonya introduced us, and Christine got right down to business.

"Weapons?" she asked. I wondered if she didn't speak much English or was in a hurry to beat the curfew. Or if she was short on firewood.

"Five canisters," I said. "Sten guns, pistols, grenades, explosives."

"The wireless?" This she directed to Sonya, who shrugged.

"They say they can fix it. They also said that before they went to sleep."

"*Merde!* Sergeant Boyle, we must have more weapons. We have many who want to fight, men and women."

"Our wireless operator thinks he's found the problem, but they had to get some sleep," I said, giving Sonya a look. "They're working now."

"Good," Christine said. "There will be more Germans soon. The Coudray group ambushed a German convoy, not long after your people blew up the train crossing. Major Zeller is setting up roadblocks everywhere. He is determined to catch the terrorists responsible."

"How can you be sure?" I asked.

"Because he told me so in the library today. Come, get in." She opened the rear door, moved boxes of books and a good-sized ax, and then pulled on the seatback cushion. It revealed a space about a foot wide running the length of the seat. "Most of the trunk is used for the wood. But there was enough room for this hiding place. It may be a little warm, but do not worry."

I looked at the size of the space she wanted me to get into. I handed Sonya my helmet and Thompson, then took off my web harness with the extra clips and grenades. I still wasn't sure I'd fit.

"You're certain this is safe?" I said as I looked again to the château. The window was dark, the curtains drawn. I eased myself into the hiding place.

"If you wished for safety, you should have stayed in *l'Angleterre*, Sergeant," Christine said with a hint of a smile as she slammed the cushion in place. "Do not move. Do not speak. I will say when it is safe." Once again, I was in total darkness.

The automobile lurched off, pressing my body against the metal wall separating me from the firebox. I settled in, trying not to think about being locked in a crawlspace next to a hot fire, driven around by a woman who'd come from a friendly chat with Major Zeller, and that I'd left a lot of firepower behind. At least I still had my .45 automatic on my belt and the .38 Police Special revolver in my shoulder holster, both of which were digging into different parts of me.

The ride was slow and bumpy, and I guessed Christine was taking a route through the Forest of Dreux. The luminous dial on my wristwatch told me we had forty minutes until curfew, when anyone found outside would be shot on sight. A wood-burning rattletrap was sure to attract attention, so I prayed that Rouvres wasn't too far away.

As we bounced along the bumps and ruts, I thought about how little we'd accomplished so far. A bum radio, a handful of supplies, and no opportunity to get Switch Blake alone to let him know his cousin was safe and sound. One dead body and no time to interrogate suspects. No chance to be alone with the woman everyone knew as Juliet, either.

One final rough patch, and we were on a smooth road, picking up speed.

Then Christine hit the brakes.

Voices. German voices. Christine answered, her voice light and airy as if she didn't have a care in the world. I could make out her rapid-fire French, followed by slower-paced German. Then a male voice, asking questions, his tone stern and harsh. Christine responded, her voice cheerful as my heart beat faster and faster. I wanted to get a hand on my automatic, but I was afraid to move, certain that they'd hear the rustling of my clothes. I waited.

Finally another voice, this one pleasant, calling her by name, if I heard right.

Then a cheery *"Auf Wiedersehen,"* and we were off. I'd been worried about her chat with Zeller, but she got us through the roadblock, so who was I to complain?

A few minutes later we stopped again. Christine cut the engine and pried me out, her finger to her lips. *"L'hôpital,"* she whispered, giving a nod in the direction of the structure behind us. We were wedged in between two ambulances, both with the same gasogene setup. It was close to nine o'clock, and lights winked out in all three stories of the brick building. *"Silence,"* and then she darted off into the shadows, slinking along a line of cypress trees. I drew my pistol and followed.

We were soon into the woods, Christine clambering over the rocks and branches with ease as we made our way up a slope. She'd been this way before. Clouds blew across the night sky, shimmering bursts of blue moonlight shining through and creating strange, dark shadows, then fading away, like waves receding on a beach. We crested a ridge, the rolling countryside spread out before us, lit only by the intermittent moon.

"There, Coudray," Christine said, leaning against a tree and catching her breath. "Can you see the church?"

"Yes," I said, spotting the squat tower in the distance, past the folds of rolling fields. On the far side the forested knoll rose up, looking down on the village shrouded in inky blackness. "If that's northwest, then that's the hill where we hid the canisters."

"It is," Christine said, gazing along my outstretched arm. "We wait now. For the *Maquis*."

"For Murat?" I asked.

"We shall see. Be patient, Sergeant."

"While we wait, tell me what Major Zeller was up to in the library today," I said, pulling up a piece of ground and stretching out my legs.

"Why, borrowing a book, of course," she said, smiling as she sat next to me. "What else does one do in *la bibliothèque*?"

"Brushing up on his French literature, was he?"

"No, he knows very little French, and it sounds horrible. But he does like to read, and we have some English titles and quite a few books in German."

"I'd have thought German books wouldn't be too popular in a French library," I said. "Especially since this is the second war with them this century."

"Oh, I see. You are suspicious, yes? Because I have books for the Germans. You think I am a *collaboratrice*? A double agent, perhaps?"

"I was a police officer before the war," I said. "I can't help being suspicious. Of everyone."

"As am I, Sergeant. Now about the books—when the Germans came, I searched everywhere for anything written in German. I hoped to do something, do you understand? I thought that if we had books in their language, some of the Germans would come to the library."

"And chat with the friendly librarian, who also happens to be a spy?"

"*Exactement!* But I was not a spy when I started. I was afraid to approach anyone for fear they would turn me in. People thought Marshal Pétain, with his silly regime in Vichy, had saved the honor of France. But really they wanted to ignore what happened, to wish it all away and pretend to be normal. If you spoke against the Germans, you reminded them of what cowards they were."

"How did you come to be involved with the Resistance? And with Juliet and Sonya?"

"I knew Sonya from Toulon. I saw her in town one day, and I could see I'd frightened her. Her father was English, you know. He had a shipping business in Toulon, and she grew up there. Of course, Sonya wasn't her name at the time."

"She thought you blew her cover," I said.

"What?" She furrowed her brow, unsure of what I'd meant. "Oh, yes, her cover story. *Bien sûr.* When she told me I must forget about Toulon, I knew I could confide in her. I told her of my plan, and what I'd learned. Most of it was about military units in the area, who the senior officers were, where the headquarters were located."

"So your plan worked?"

"Yes, but I was surprised that most of the information came from the enlisted men. Young boys who were lonely. I found a box of adventure novels at a bookseller's. Many by Karl May, who wrote cowboy stories. The Germans love those, isn't that strange?"

"This feels like cowboys and Indians," I said, gazing at the fields and forest surrounding us. "I wonder who the Germans think they are."

"They are savages, not at all noble. But I do listen to them. The young boys who are lonely, who miss their girlfriends and mothers, the ones too shy to speak to a French girl, the ones who want some kindness that reminds them of home. And they tell me their troubles. No leave because of invasion warnings. Sharing tight quarters with reinforcements. Transfers to the coast. Their officers, especially the harsh ones."

"What about Zeller?" An owl hooted in the distance, its call answered seconds later, echoing against the distant hills.

"He fancies himself a cultured man. Not a member of the Nazi party, he's reminded me more than once. Reads Thomas Mann, Rilke, Kafka, that sort of thing." Christine squinted in the gloom, her gaze traveling across the open and empty fields.

"Have you learned anything from him?"

"That he is dangerous. He worries that he looks bad to his superiors. After all, the nearby networks were all destroyed. But he's captured no one from this area. He said this morning he believes Dreux must have its own nest of spies. A desperate man is to be feared."

Something rustled in the trees behind us, and I drew my pistol, not certain if it were a man or the breeze. I waited, catching Christine's eye.

"The wind," she whispered. "If it were the Germans, you would hear their heavy boots. If it were the *Maquis*, you would hear nothing."

"Not the White Giant?" I asked.

"Oh, you know of the giant who haunts the Forest of Dreux? If it were he, you would see an unearthly white glow. My grandfather told me the giant will guide you underground, to the treasure house of the ancient Druids, where mounds of gold and precious stones are kept. He will tell you that you have all the time in the world to take what you wish. Which is true, because if you enter, he shuts the iron doors behind you, and you are entombed until the end of time."

The leaves *whooshed* in the wind. I couldn't help looking over my shoulder, feeling foolish that her story had given me a tingly feeling like someone was right behind me.

There was. I rolled, hand on my pistol.

"No, no, Sergeant," Christine said, one hand covering her mouth in an unexpectedly girlish gesture as she laughed. "It is not the White Giant."

"Il faut se hâter," said the man with the Sten gun. He wasn't a giant, but he was a big guy, and he wasn't laughing. Christine took in the look on his face and stood, firing volleys of French at him too fast for me to understand a word. He'd said something about hurrying, or being in hurry, but that was all I got out of it.

Other figures stepped out from the forest. Christine had been right; they'd been yards away, and I hadn't heard a thing. There were a dozen of them, drifting into a wide semicircle around us, watching the fields and the woods at our backs, while the big guy and Christine yammered at each other. Something was wrong. The group was silent and wary, clutching a variety of weapons, and ready to use them.

"We have little time," Christine finally said. "We must get to the canisters quickly. Come."

She broke into a trot, pulling me along as the men ran through the fields, grouped protectively on either side of us, the big guy close by. We ran through calf-high plants that smelled of onion as we crushed them.

"What's happened?" I managed to say between breaths.

"One of the *Résistants* from the village has been captured," Christine answered. "Cyril. He was with the group that met you."

"Yes, I remember him," I said. We slowed as we crossed a stream that divided the fields and made our way through the brush.

"He will talk," she said. "He will tell them where the canisters are."

"How can you be sure?" I asked before breaking into a run.

"Everyone talks," she said as she led the men up the next hill. "It is only a question of when."

I stopped asking questions.

The Resistance group from Coudray had used the weapons we gave them to attack a convoy. Cyril must have been captured during that attack, or another I didn't know about. I felt responsible, since we gave him and his pals the guns, but he was an eager volunteer. Maybe too eager, which was pretty much the story with a lot of guys fighting and dying today on the Normandy beaches. I tried not to think about what was ahead for Cyril. Torture until he talked, followed by a Gestapo cell or a bullet. Either way, he was a dead man.

We ran a race against time, a race pitting our lungs and legs against Cyril's stamina and willingness to suffer. There was no way to know if the race had already been won by the Germans, or if Cyril was neck and neck with death. The Germans would want to know about his group first. Names and locations. They might not ask about their weapons right away, but they'd get around to it. Sten guns meant supply drops, and the Krauts would want to know when and where. There was a chance our landing site would be compromised as well.

Christine signaled a halt. We'd reached a line of oaks that bordered one of the farmhouses at the edge of Coudray. A road led up the hill to where the canisters were hidden. To our left, the road forked, one lane going off into the woods and the other curving around the farmhouse on its way to the village. She held a whispered conference with the big guy, and in seconds one of the other men slipped off into the darkness.

"He is going to look," she said. "What is the word? To go ahead and see?"

"Scout?" I suggested.

"Yes, he will scout. We cannot use the road in case the Germans have an *embuscade*, yes? Maurice is very quiet, a good hunter. He will see."

"Was that Murat's idea? Is that him, the big man?" I said, pointing to who I guessed the commander was.

"Yes, it was Murat's idea," she said, the wisp of a smile playing across her face as she watched the farmhouse. I might be slow at times, but I wasn't stupid.

"You are Murat," I whispered.

"Oui," she said. "And if I die, there will be another."

"You're not the first?" She shook her head and held up three fingers. It made sense. Murat would never die. It gave people a hero.

We settled in for the wait, listening for any movement or the distant approach of trucks. Wind blew the clouds to the east, leaving the moon bright as a searchlight. Another owl hooted, and then one of the *Maquis* hooted back, a signal that all was clear from the look on Christine's face.

Four of the men crossed the road and disappeared into the trees. We stayed in the woods on our side and worked our way up the hill, weapons at the ready, taking no chances. We found Maurice at the top of the hill, crouched at the side of the road, studying the downward slope.

He stood and shouldered his rifle. *"Personne."*

"Zéro," I said, remembering that *personne* meant no one. I'd picked up a few French phrases from the Canucks I'd rousted back in Boston, mostly French Canadians who'd had too much to drink on Saturday night, or gotten caught with stolen loot. Between that and what I'd learned in Algiers, I could make out a few words here and there, especially if they were about the black market, booze, or a good alibi. *Personne* was usually who could vouch for a proffered alibi.

"It seems we have beat the Germans, or that Cyril has held out," Christine said.

"Let's hope they don't think he has any information. He's just a kid, after all. Come on," I said, heading into the woods near a fallen pine I recognized. I tried to find the exact spot where we'd hidden them, at the base of a lichen-covered rock, covered in branches. Having lost my bearings, I headed back to the fallen pine and almost stumbled over the canisters. They were all there, unopened. Cyril and his people had kept their promise, leaving the bulk of the weapons for Murat.

We got the canisters out to the road, where Christine gave the men their marching orders. They snapped to, taking up the canisters and heading down the other side of the hill, leaving us alone.

"We have a hiding place, an old cellar, not far," she explained. "Thank you for leading us here. The arms will be well used against the *Boche*, believe me."

"I do. What next?"

"We walk back to *l'hôpital*," she said. "I hide you there for the night. They are used to seeing me stay after curfew, so it is not dangerous. Not so much anyway."

With that cheery qualification, we took the road back, staying in the shadows cast by the silvery moon. The landscape was silent, the only sound coming from our heels hitting the road.

Until we heard the engine. Grinding gears and tires on gravel, coming from the forest lane near the farmhouse. We bolted for the oaks, taking cover at a spot that gave us a clear view of the fork in the road.

"Looks like we beat them to it," I said. "Too bad we didn't think to set up an ambush of our own."

"It was too important to get the guns away," Christine said. "If we lost men, they could not carry them." Simple arithmetic. I began to see why she was Murat.

One truck emerged from the woods, followed by a second, beams seeping through the black tape covering their headlights. The first continued on to the village while the second braked in front of the house. The canvas flap was thrown back, and half a dozen men jumped out, rushing for the farmhouse door.

"Milice," Christine hissed. Their blue tunics and large floppy berets marked them as members of the French fascist militia, the *Milice française*.

Rifle butts pounded on the front door as the *miliciens* swarmed the house, covering the back. Soon they were inside, and shouts and screams echoed in the night. Shots boomed from inside the house, flashes of muzzle fire illuminating the progress of the search, until a final blast lit an upstairs window for a split second, leaving darkness and silence within the riven home.

Christine gasped so loudly I was afraid the killers must have heard. I rested my hand on her shoulder, and she grasped it tightly. Moments passed, and then the silence was broken by the smashing of glass, the *thuds* of furniture being overturned, the desecration of a family's patrimony. Laughter rippled through the house, the forced jocularity of those who needed to convince themselves that all was well, their actions right and just, even as they stepped in the blood of the slain.

Men stumbled out the front door. Bottles were handed around, brandy or calvados from the kitchen cupboards. Flames ate at the curtains lit in an attempt to further punish the dead before the *miliciens* climbed into their truck and motored off.

Without a word, Christine bolted to the farmhouse, her coat flapping as she ran. I followed, racing up the stone steps and through the open door. She was pulling at the curtains in the sitting room, stomping out the fire. I went through to the kitchen. The farmer was on his back, mouth open, his body wreathed in blood from two shots to the chest. On the stairs I found a boy, fifteen or so, the back of his head blown away. In the bedroom, a woman was huddled in the corner as if she'd run out of places to hide. She'd been shot in the neck, her hands still clutched around her throat in a futile attempt to staunch the blood as it pumped out of her dying body.

"There's a girl as well," Christine said. "She'd hidden in the closet."

"Dead," I said, not bothering to make it a question.

"Yes."

"Why?"

"It is simple. Cyril is from this village. God only knows what they are on their way to do now. Come, we must see."

"Wait, Christine," I said as I followed her out of the charnel house. "What can we do? We have nothing but our pistols."

"Nothing but bear witness. For now. Go back if you wish, but I must see."

I looked back at the house. A sign was posted at the door, a requirement of the German occupiers. Names and ages of the residents within. Clara had been eighteen, Jérôme fourteen. There was nothing else I could do. I followed her, taking the road I'd traveled not so long ago with the *Résistants* of Coudray, joyfully celebrating their new weapons and white silk.

We left the road and circled around the village, finding a vantage point along the stone wall surrounding the churchyard cemetery. The two *Milice* trucks were parked in front of the church, the militiamen patrolling the main street with its white-washed houses and dark slate roofs. The houses crowded the roadway, close enough for the men to tap the darkened windows with their rifles and taunt the inhabitants as they passed.

"What's going on?" I asked. The leisurely approach was at odds with the attack on the farmhouse. The growl of approaching engines gave the answer. Reinforcements.

"Mon Dieu," Christine whispered. From the other side of the village a column came into view, led by an open staff car. Head-lamps were on full beam in defiance of the blackout. The harsh lights reflected off the stone church and the white walls of the houses and shops, creating an arena of garish whiteness, as fright-ening as it was unexpected. *"Le SS."*

A German officer stood in the staff car, barking out orders in French and German. The *Milice* scattered to the perimeter, form-ing a cordon around the village. One of them was about twenty yards from us, but his gaze was fixed in the opposite direction, seeking those who might try to escape.

Troops in dappled camouflage smocks and hobnail boots descended from the trucks, smashed their way into houses, and dragged out the inhabitants. Shots rang out from behind the buildings, picking off those who tried to escape.

"They are from the Twelfth SS Panzer Division," Christine said. "See the emblem on the trucks?" I did—a skeleton key set against the runic letter S. "Hitler Youth, the *Hitlerjugend* division. Fanatic Nazis."

"They're going to kill everyone," I said, not able to believe what I was witnessing. Christine didn't need to answer. I wanted to bury my head in my hands and pretend such things didn't really happen. But I couldn't, not with Christine locking her eyes on the scene in front of us, taking it all in.

As the women and children were dragged into the church, screams slashed the air. Mothers and wives reached for their men and boys, who stood with their hands held high in front of the houses where they had gone to sleep that night, counting the days until liberation. One mother broke free, running to her young son. Her arms and her nightdress enfolded him in a final gesture of protection. The SS troopers looked about the same age as the boy, but stared at the scene with indifference, their faces masks of darkness and reflected light.

The officer leapt from his vehicle and shouted at his men to hurry. *"Macht schnell, macht schnell."* The woman and her son were hustled into the church, joining about thirty others who had been herded inside. As the heavy door was slammed shut, silence draped itself over the tableau, broken only by a truck parking in front of the church steps. The village men, a couple of dozen by my count, were pushed back against the walls of the buildings across the street.

The officer waved his arm, a languid, almost graceful motion.

Gunfire ripped the night. Submachine guns, rifles, pistols, all let loose into the gathered Frenchmen. Their bodies twitched, tumbled, and fell back against the white walls now spattered with crimson. It was over in seconds, and when the shooting stopped, cries of anguish rose up from within the church, even more terrible than the volley of fire that still seemed to echo off the stones.

The truck pulled away from the church, revealing two of the *Hitlerjugend* upending jerricans of gas at the wooden door. Other troopers surrounded the church as the officer stepped through the pile of corpses, delivering pistol shots to any that moved. There was no further need for orders; everything was going according to plan. The gas cans had been hidden from view, so the men wouldn't guess what was planned for their women and children. They'd awaited their fate quietly, accepting it as best they could.

Whump.

An orange explosion ignited at the church door, sending a cloud of black smoke swirling into the night sky. Flames licked at the stout wooden door and lit the inside of the church as the fuel that had flowed under the door torched the interior. SS troopers shot out the stained glass windows and tossed grenades through the narrow shattered openings, the explosions drowning out the pleas for mercy and the terrified screams of the burned and dying.

Hands clawed at the windows, only to be beaten back by shots and more grenades. A woman threw a small child out one window. She screamed at the nearest soldier, cursing him while flames licked at her back. Two troopers shot at her, and she vanished into the inferno. The small form lay still and smoking between the two SS men, who kept firing at the windows until the interior was fully engulfed, the centuries-old wooden pews burning like kindling in a stove.

Christine wept, tears dropping like raindrops. She'd bitten her lip to keep from crying out—or in despair, perhaps—and a trickle of blood ran down her chin.

We crouched behind the wall, unable to move or think about what to do next. Running away seemed cowardly, remaining foolish. We knew what had happened, we knew who'd done it. We'd borne witness. And it all seemed so useless. I gripped my pistol, aching to take vengeance, knowing that I'd be nothing but another corpse in seconds.

I laid my hand on Christine's shoulder. She shook it off.

The *Milice* came in from the perimeter, their job done. No more laughing, no bottles in sight.

The SS mounted their trucks and halftracks quickly and efficiently. Dispassionately. Like the job they'd come to do. The column roared out of town, scattering the *miliciens* who milled about near their trucks as if they were playing *boules* in a village square.

By unspoken accord, we slumped down, resting against the cold stone wall, waiting for the complicit French to leave the murdered French. The fire sparked and crackled behind us, casting an orange glow against the leafy branches above us. I was empty, my mind numb but my body craving revenge, action, the feel of a man's throat in my grip.

The *Milice* trucks finally drove away, leaving the village to the dead.

"Let's go," I said, my voice still a whisper. I helped Christine to stand, and turned to look one last time at the fiery church.

A ghost walked toward us. A child, wisps of smoke curling from her clothes. The girl who was thrown from the window.

"Mon enfant!" Christine cried, and vaulted over the wall. She ran to the child, who burst into tears. I tore at her garments, certain she must have been badly burned.

She wasn't. The thick woman's coat she wore had taken the brunt of the flames. She gripped Christine and wailed, sobbing and choking on her words. We scurried out of the graveyard, away from the church, hurrying down the road and away from Coudray, the village and the memory of it.

We carried the child for miles, but the memory only burned deeper into my brain with each step.

CHAPTER TWENTY

HER MOTHER HAD told her to lie still when she hit the ground. And that she'd be right behind her. Instead, she'd distracted the soldiers with her curses, taking bullets as her child lay unnoticed on the ground.

Her name was Emeline. She was five years old.

She wanted her *maman*.

I slept in a toolshed outside the hospital. Christine brought Emeline in with her and spun a story about finding her lost in the woods. The nurses accepted it, but by morning, a jittery doctor began to ask questions about where Emeline had come from. The story of the massacre had spread, whether by other survivors, bragging *Hitlerjugend*, or drunken *Milice*, it was impossible to say. But my money was on the militia. A guy with a guilty conscience couldn't stop flapping his gums to justify himself. Either way, we had to get her out before the doctor lost his nerve and reported her.

So that was how Emeline came to return with us to the château. I was hidden behind the backseat again. Emeline was wrapped in a blanket in the back, and I listened to her snuffling tears as we drove slowly through the forest.

I UNFOLDED MYSELF from the backseat as Juliet was holding Emeline, who seemed half asleep or too afraid to let anyone know she was awake. "Who is this?" Juliet whispered.

"Have you heard about Coudray?" I asked.

"Yes. I thought as much. What are we going to do with her?" Juliet said.

"I must leave," Christine said. "I am already late for the library, and I don't wish for any questions. Care for her, please. I am sure Count Vasseur will take her in."

"But what if the count doesn't agree?" Juliet asked.

"He must. He has many hiding places, doesn't he?" Christine leaned in to whisper to Emeline, stroking her hair and murmuring gently in French. I couldn't make out a word, but I got the gist. *Be a good girl, be brave. I'll be back soon.* Emeline nodded, her face burrowed against Juliet's breast.

"Did you see Murat?" Juliet asked.

"Yes, Murat was there, and the weapons were delivered," I said, not wanting to lie to Juliet or reveal the secret of Murat. "After we left the *Maquis*, we witnessed the SS attack on the village, with the assistance of the *Milice*."

"We must find the Germans who did this," Christine said, adding wood to her firebox. "They were with the Twelfth SS Panzer Division. I want the officer who ordered this massacre, and as many of his men as we can kill."

"What about the *Milice*?" I asked.

"We know exactly where they are. They set up their headquarters in Dreux at the synagogue on rue Vernouillet, since the Jews had no further need of it, according to Pierre Rivet, their leader. He shall not be making bad jokes much longer. *Au revoir.*"

With that declaration, Christine drove off for another day at the library.

"We'll talk to the count, Billy. He'll want a firsthand report," Juliet said as she carried Emeline down the basement steps.

"What about the radio? Please tell me it's fixed."

"Yes, finally, late last night. I was in the midst of coding a message when you arrived."

"Good news," I said. But the news I really wanted to hear was that Count Vasseur would willingly take in little Emeline and hide her from those who wished to leave no witness to their crimes.

It suddenly occurred to me that Christine and I were witnesses, too, and that the *Milice* in particular would want to eliminate anyone who could testify as to their complicity. Unless the Germans threw the invasion back into the Channel, sooner or later they'd be retreating to the Reich, tails between their legs. But the homegrown French fascists would have nowhere to go. There'd be hell to pay for their collaboration, and wholesale murder meant the hangman for sure. Unless they blamed it all on the *Hitlerjugend*, and there was no one alive to claim otherwise.

We surfaced in a pantry off the kitchen, the narrow door disguised behind shelves of canned goods. Her eyes squeezed shut, Emeline whimpered in Juliet's arms. Madame Agard greeted us, her apron dusty with flour, and her eyes wide at the sight of the child. She swooped up the girl and sat her at the wooden table, in the chair closest to the warm stove. In seconds, a bowl of milk appeared along with a hunk of crusty bread. Madame Agard took Emeline's small hands in hers and wiped away soot and dirt with a wet cloth. She cleaned Emeline's face, pressing the cloth to her eyes. Emeline rewarded her with the slightest of smiles as she scrubbed.

"Maman?" Emeline whispered, finally opening her eyes. Madame Agard spoke softly, telling her lies as she dipped the stale bread into the milk and fed her pieces, coaxing her to eat. I fell into a chair myself, fatigue overtaking me. I wanted nothing more than to lay my head on my arm and fall asleep in this warm kitchen and forget what I'd seen.

"It's not exactly coffee, but it's warm," Juliet said, handing me a cup of something steaming and dark brown. Or maybe yellow, it was hard to tell. "Toasted barley mixed with chicory. I've gotten used to it, God help me."

Madame Agard moved to the counter to cut a slice of bread for me, and Emeline reacted with a quivering lip and arms outstretched. Juliet took over with my bread, and the cook went back to Emeline, whispering kindnesses as she fed her.

"Dunk it in your drink," Juliet said. "It's quite stale. Bread rations are pitiful, and flour hard to come by. Madame Agard experiments with potato, rice, and maize, whatever she can use to substitute."

It helped to soak it in the coffee, which was how I preferred to think of this concoction. The grey bread was improved, if only in color and texture. Whatever the ingredients, the food and drink helped wake me up. As we got up to find the count, Juliet gave Emeline a hug, crumbs of milk-soaked bread sticking to her shoulder. Then Emeline put out her arms in my direction, the smell of smoke still clinging to her hair, and I hugged her.

From the moment it had happened, I'd wanted to get back at the men who had committed this atrocity, but now I wanted it in the deepest, darkest part of my heart. Poor Emeline would smell that smoky scent for the rest of her life, always at the edge of memory, the sight of flames and fire more terrifying than they had any right to be as the years passed. I couldn't do much about that, but revenge, *that* was within my grasp.

I followed Juliet, intent on more short-term needs. Get the count to care for Emeline, then send a radio message out, and finally get Switch Blake alone to show him the picture and convince him Cousin Donald was safe and sound.

We walked along a wide corridor, the faded wallpaper peeling off the walls, the ceiling cracked and water-damaged. Empty rooms on either side, except for a toppled chair or a three-legged table on its back.

"This wing is not used," Juliet said. "It's safer to go this way. There are hidden entrances to the tunnels in these rooms; we can leave and return without any of the staff taking notice."

"They don't know what's going on here?"

"None other than Vincent and Madame Agard know exactly what we do. I'm sure some have their suspicions, but it is best if they're not aware. They are all loyal to the count, loyal enough to look the other way when necessary."

At the end of the corridor we came to the foyer at the main entrance. Here it was gleaming marble and polished brass, a sharp contrast to the decay we'd walked through. Juliet beckoned me along and led me through the foyer and into a grand hall with a giant fireplace I could have stood in.

Portraits were hung along one wall, the nearest looking like a younger version of Count Vasseur. As we walked, the clothes became more old-fashioned, until we were back in the time of Napoleon, the men in high-necked military uniforms, the women in gauzy dresses and high hairdos. The frames were thick with dust, the carpet on the floor threadbare. The windows were grimy, letting in barely enough light to see by. Two doors on the opposite wall were ajar, and I stopped to listen for footsteps.

"Is it safe? Won't we run into one of the servants?" I asked.

"No," Juliet said. "They're too afraid."

"Of what? The White Ghost?"

"No, of him," she answered, pointing to the largest portrait in the room, hung over the massive fireplace.

A dark-haired man stood in front of a curtain of scarlet brocade decorated with fleurs-de-lis, his gleaming armor breastplate a bright silver, his red plumed helmet at his side. His royal-blue doublet was embroidered in gold, and his right hand rested on the hilt of a shining sword. His eyes were narrow, glancing sideways as if aware of a nearby danger. They were startlingly blue, and they seemed to follow me as I moved.

"Everyone says the eyes move," Juliet whispered. "It frightens the servants." I could see why. The effect was spooky.

"The first Count Vasseur," a frail voice said from a stairway to our left, an ornate, wide, curved staircase, where I imagined at one time the ladies of the château made their entrance to fancy balls and dinners in the great hall. But today, only a stooped, elderly man leaned on the balcony to watch us. "Frédérick-Charles Maronneau, a true visionary. Come," he beckoned, and opened a set of double doors.

We followed him into the library. Tall windows let in the morning light, dust motes floating over shelves of leather-bound volumes. Count Vasseur sat behind an oaken desk and gestured for us to sit in two armchairs facing each other. Behind him a series of intricately carved wood panels, showing woodland scenes and animals of the forest, filled the wall. A chess set sat on a small table near the window. Between the two windows, a solitary painting was hung, obviously special given its placement. The face of a young woman, surrounded by a veil of vivid royal blue, her eyes cast downward in a melancholy gaze, dominated the room. It was small, but powerful. I thought of the mother in the church, a Madonna for our own terrible times.

"You are Sergeant Boyle," the count said as I forced my eyes away from the painting. His English was precise, each word clipped and exact, with only the slightest lilt of a French accent. "Forgive me for not greeting you previously. Welcome to the Château Vasseur. I was most saddened by the death of Lieutenant Armstrong. He and I spent many pleasant hours in this room."

"It was a murder, sir. *Le meurtre.*"

"Yes, murder. But by whom? Do you have any idea?"

"No, sir, but I will do my best to uncover who did it. I was a police detective before the war, so it won't be my first investigation."

"Whatever I can do, please call upon me. Or Vincent; he has my complete trust."

"Something terrible has happened, Count Vasseur," Juliet said, wringing her hands.

"Ah, Coudray, is it? All the servants are talking about it. You understand, Sergeant Boyle, the maids and gardeners live in Dreux for the most part. They bring news and gossip every day. Today it is the killings at Coudray. Is it as terrible as they say?"

"I saw it with my own eyes. Even more terrible, I'd guess. Everyone, men, women, children. Shot or burned alive in the church."

"*Mon Dieu*," he said, his head bowed.

"Not quite everyone," Juliet said. "A small child escaped. The sergeant and Christine Latour brought her here."

"Here? What does Mademoiselle Latour wish us to do?"

"Hide her. Care for her," Juliet said. "It was the SS and the *Milice*. The *Boche* will probably be on their way to Normandy soon, but the *Milice* remain. They will want to silence any witness."

"I think of my son every day and hope he survives the labor camps by acts of kindness from those in a position to help. So I cannot fail to help this child who is so in need of kindness. Where is she?"

"In the kitchen with Madame Agard," Juliet said.

"Then she is in good hands for now. What of the wireless?"

"It has been repaired. I am coding a message now," Juliet said.

"There is much to ask for. Has London contacted you?"

"We have not gone on air yet," Juliet said. "Major Zeller undoubtedly has his *OKW Funkabwehr* units operating around the clock. We cannot afford to transmit for long."

The count nodded his agreement. The *OKW Funkabwehr* was the German Radio Security Service, dedicated to pinpointing transmissions in occupied nations. It was very good at what it did. "Yes, he seems fixated on tracking down a band of terrorists in Dreux," he said.

"Do you think he has any suspicions?" I asked.

"Of us, no, not at all," Count Vasseur said. "He even apologized the other day for the loss of electricity. He gave me an hour's warning."

"The Germans routinely cut power, district by district," Juliet explained, "while listening for wireless transmissions. That way, when a transmission is cut off, they know the general area to search. Which is why we often go into the woods and operate with batteries."

A knock sounded at the door. Vincent stuck his head in and announced, *"Les Allemands arrivent."*

"Germans," Juliet said, rushing to the window. A staff car and a truck rolled down the gravel drive and came to a stop outside the front door. "Zeller."

"He may conduct a search," the count said. "As he did the other day. Come, hide quickly."

Vincent pressed a section of wood paneling behind the count's desk. There was a faint click, and the panel shifted back. He then slid it sideways, gesturing for me to step inside. It was a small chamber with a bench. As Juliet and I entered, the count instructed Vincent to hurry to the kitchen and warn Madame Agard to hide the child.

"I'll show you how it works," Juliet said, stepping in with me as soon as Vincent limped off. Grabbing a handle, she slid the panel back in place, pressing it forward until it clicked. The darkness was total. Then I heard another sound, like a latch being loosened, and pinpoints of light appeared through the panel. "These holes are part of the carving. They're barely noticeable, but we can see and hear."

She was right. By putting my eye to one of the holes, I had a decent view of the room, especially the count's desk and chess table. We heard boots clomping up the steps, and Juliet put her finger to her lips. Not to worry—with a truck full of Nazis prowling the place, I wasn't about to get chatty.

"Major, to what do I owe the pleasure of another visit?" Count Vasseur asked. I remembered Christine telling me Zeller knew English, but not French.

"Have you heard of that dreadful business at Coudray?" Zeller said, exasperation drawing a sigh out of his throat as he tossed his cap on a chair and sat opposite the count. His voice had a discernable British accent, as if he'd gone to school there or learned from an Englishman. "Those SS bastards!"

"Rumors are flying," the count said. "The entire village?"

"Yes. Fifty or so poor souls. Apparently the Resistance attacked a column of the Twelfth SS Panzer. The Twenty-Sixth *Panzergrenadier* Regiment, to be exact. One of the attackers was captured and had been foolish enough to keep his identity card."

"I take it he was from Coudray," the count said.

"Yes. *Sturmbannführer* Erich Krause took it upon himself to conduct the reprisal. He had lost men in the attack and was quite angry. Terrible, what he did."

"And the *Milice* helped, I hear," Vasseur said. "It is hard to understand."

"It all could have been avoided, count. There was an attack on a rail bridge that caused a backup in Chartres. The Twenty-Sixth Regiment was off-loaded from the train and was making its way by road when they were attacked. If the Resistance had not made those two attacks, the good people of Coudray would be going about their business as we speak. Now they are in the ground, and Krause has accomplished nothing but stirring up a hornet's nest. More attacks, more reprisals, mark my words."

Zeller's voice rose, and I saw him stand and pace the room. He was tall, with thick black hair and beefy jowls. Duty in occupied France agreed with him. He rested one hand on the hilt of the dagger at his belt, drumming the other on his leather holster as if he were itching for a fight.

"I do not disagree, Major," the count said. "But as you know, young people feel the need to take action. They are swept up in the propaganda from London. They think little of the consequences."

"Yes, I know," Zeller said wearily, flopping back down in his chair. "You understand, I must go through this charade of searching the château and grounds again. I apologize, but if I do not do it, you will have the SS everywhere."

"Major, the building and grounds are at your disposal. I appreciate that the *Abwehr* conducts itself with a dignity the SS and the Gestapo lack."

"If there must be war, it should be fought between gentlemen, I say. Whenever we capture a British agent, I counsel them to cooperate. Because if they do not cooperate with us, we are forced to hand them over to the Gestapo. What they lack in finesse, they make up in efficient brutality."

"Major, if I may ask . . . have you had any news of my son? Frédéric?"

"Yes, Count Vasseur, I have had some success. Frédéric has been transferred from a coal mine outside Essen to a farm in Augsburg. Much better working conditions, believe me."

"But when can he be released? He has been a prisoner since 1940." The old man's voice trembled, and I'd bet he wasn't playacting now.

"Count Vasseur," Zeller said, leaning forward, his arms on the desk, "you must understand the currency with which we deal. Information. The work camps for prisoners are run by the army. The *Abwehr* cannot issue orders concerning military prisoners. I must have more than vague rumors and bits and pieces of gossip. Give me something which shows your loyalty to the Reich, and the army will release him to your custody. Otherwise, I can do nothing."

"Major, no one tells an old man like me anything useful. If they did, I would tell you, for the sake of my son." I began to worry that the count would be tempted, but if he hadn't betrayed the whole operation yet, there was no reason to think he'd start now.

"Find out who gave the weapons to that foolish boy from

Coudray. That would be quite important. Or the identity of Commander Murat, who has eluded me for far too long. Now, forgive me, I must attend to the search. I hope not to inconvenience you greatly."

"I will ask the servants what they know after you leave," the count said. "Perhaps a game of chess tomorrow?"

"I look forward to it," Zeller said as he donned his cap. He clicked his heels and left.

"Quickly," Count Vasseur said, after listening to Zeller's footsteps as he descended the staircase. Juliet opened the panel and secured the covering for the spyholes.

"What about Emeline?" Juliet said as we unfolded ourselves from the tight compartment.

"We must trust Vincent and Madame Agard to have hidden her," the count said, leading us to one of the tall built-in bookcases. He reached behind a row of books and pulled at something. The entire bookcase swung out like one massive door, as smoothly and quietly as if the hinges had just been oiled. Juliet pulled me along, lighting a candle that sat on a shelf above a winding staircase behind the shelves.

"What kind of place is this?" I asked, marveling at the design of this and all the secret chambers within the château.

"When there is time, young man, I will tell you how my ancestor, Frédérick-Charles Maronneau, came to construct the Château Vasseur. But now, you must get to the others and warn them of the search. Hurry!" With that, he closed the bookshelf, leaving us in darkness except for the flickering candle.

"Quietly," Juliet said, her voice hushed. "The stone walls echo." I followed her down the circular staircase, coming to a door which opened into a narrow tunnel barely five feet high. Stooped low, I followed Juliet in the glow of the candlelight. The walls were damp and chalky, soft and crumbly to the touch. I tried not to think about cave-ins.

Soon we were in front of a thick wooden door, the same one we'd gone through when Kaz, Topper, and I first entered the tunnels. It seemed like weeks ago, not a couple of days. Juliet rapped on the door, and it was quickly opened by Sonya.

"I must get back," Juliet said. "Major Zeller may ask where I am. I'll return as soon as I can and finish coding the message." With that, she shut the door behind her, and I was greeted with expectant gazes from around the long table. The electric lights were out, the room illuminated only by a few candles.

Everyone was there. Babcock, Fawcett, and Brookes, the Canadian contingent. Dogbite, Meyer, and Blake, the Yanks. Kaz and Topper as well. All with their packs and gear, ready to bolt if the Krauts found a tunnel entrance.

"Standard procedure, Sergeant," Sonya said, her voice hushed. "The candles are in case the power goes out or is cut by the Germans. Be as quiet as possible. Sound can carry through the vents."

"What happened in Coudray?" Kaz asked in a whisper. "We heard rumors of a massacre."

"It was," I said in a hushed voice, taking a seat on the bench next to Blake. I went through it all: bringing Murat's men to the weapons, the *Milice*, the SS in the village, the burning of the church, the mother throwing her child from the window, and spiriting Emeline back to the château.

"Bastards," Babcock muttered. "I'd like to drop a bombload on the lot of them."

"It's hard to believe anyone could do that," Brookes added. "Burn all those people in a church."

"What the hell do you think you were doing, Brookie, bombing all those German cities?" Meyer said, his voice low but sneering. "You burned plenty of people, little babies and their mothers, just like those Krauts did, except they looked 'em in the eye while they did it."

"Shut up," Brookes said, turning his face away from Meyer.

"War is terrible," Kaz said, leaning across the table and placing a hand on Brookes's arm. "And we must do terrible things to defeat the enemy. But what the fascists did in Coudray was not about fighting the enemy. It was revenge, terror, call it what you like."

Brookes nodded, slowly, then pulled back into himself, eyes lowered like a beaten dog's. Fawcett looked the other way, disgust plain on his face. There was bad blood between them. Even Lieutenant Babcock couldn't be bothered to offer a word of support. Whatever Brookes had done, it haunted them all.

"Do you know the unit?" Topper whispered, getting back to the atrocity at hand.

"Yeah, the local *Milice*, headquartered in Dreux. They assisted the Twenty-Sixth *Panzergrenadier* Regiment of the Twelfth SS Panzer Division. A *Hitlerjugend* outfit, *Sturmbannführer* Erich Krause commanding."

"We first heard of them when they were stationed outside Rouen," Sonya said. "Cold-blooded Nazis in spite of their age. Or because of it, perhaps. They've been brought up to believe Hitler is a god."

"We must do something," Kaz said. As a Pole, no crime the Germans committed in France would come as a surprise to him. He'd want revenge, not only for the people of Coudray, but for his own fellow Poles. For his family.

"Whoa, whoa, hold on there," Meyer said. "We already got *beaucoup* Krauts sniffin' around. Don't go causing no more trouble, not when we're about to get outta here."

"If I can follow the double negatives, I think you mean to say you'd rather hide in a hole in the ground than fight," Kaz said, staring down the table at Meyer.

"You want a double dose of negative? I got 'em right here," Meyer said, standing and brandishing his meaty fists.

"So you are not afraid to fight. Good for you; this is encouraging," Kaz said, waving a hand as if swatting away a fly.

"Please, gentlemen, keep it down," Sonya said, her finger to her lips. Switch put his hand on Meyer's shoulder, urging him to sit. Meyer shook him off and stalked out of the room.

"Brookie, take a candle and give him a hand, will ya? He's liable to get lost in there," Switch said.

"Sure," Brookes said, eager as a puppy. Shielding a candle with his hand, he shuffled off in the direction Meyer had taken.

"This is not good," Sonya whispered. "We should stay together."

"Aw, how many times have we done this?" Switch said. "The Germans are only going through the motions, you know that. Zeller likes the old count, doesn't he?"

"He does respect him, it seems, but that will only go so far. If there is any hint of Resistance activity, Zeller will tear down the château to find what he's looking for," Sonya said. "And put a bullet in our heads while he's at it, so please remain quiet."

"Meyer's jumpy," Dogbite said. "Don't pay him no mind. He don't take to bein' cooped up like this."

"Sort of like being in the slammer," I said, sliding in next to Switch. "You got to live by someone else's schedule."

"Hell, that's the army," Dogbite said. "But at least they give us three squares and good boots. Never had it so good growin' up. You been inside, Billy?"

"Reform school when I was a kid, no big deal. And the stockade, not too long ago."

"How'd you get out?" Switch asked. The three of us huddled together, our voices low, while the others whispered among themselves. I could see Kaz chatting with Babcock and Fawcett, drawing their attention while I laid down my crooked GI patter. It seemed Kaz and Babcock were comparing scars.

"Had to come along on this operation. I got busted down to private and sentenced to a couple years' hard labor, on account of a few gallons of gasoline the army lost track of. Then these guys came for a visit, looking for volunteers, offering a full pardon and my stripes back. First time I ever volunteered for anything." I figured two years would impress these guys more than the three-month sentence I'd actually been assigned.

"How many gallons?" Switch asked, his eyes narrowing as he studied me.

"One hundred. Along with the truck they'd been loaded in," I said. "Not that they ever found the stuff. It was all circumstantial evidence, but that didn't matter to the army. So here I am."

"Two years?" Switch said. "I might take that over what you've been through."

"Yeah," Dogbite said. "Two years, and you walk out alive. Who knows what's going to happen now?"

"Hey, I'm here in the same spot you guys are. Wasn't so bad. Besides, I figure once we're clear of this place, who knows what else France has to offer?"

"You going to desert?" Dogbite said, his eyes wide.

"I never said that, and don't repeat what I didn't say, all right? All I know is I don't want to end up dead or behind barbed wire, German or American."

"That's a wise choice," Switch said, nodding. "I wish you luck, friend." His eyes were steady, revealing nothing. Dogbite glanced between us, catching the undercurrent, but looking perplexed. Or maybe it was the dim light. Either way, I needed to get Switch Blake alone and show him the photograph.

"I hear the radio's fixed," I said in the general direction of Kaz and Topper, not wanting to appear too eager with Switch. "About time."

"Watch your tone, Sergeant," Kaz said, playing along. "Otherwise I'll put you on report. I had half a mind to do so for your role in damaging the wireless."

"He tripped!" I said, keeping my voice muted but pointing an angry finger at Kaz.

"Show proper respect, Sergeant. Or else you'll end up back in the stockade, remember that."

"Okay, Lieutenant, sorry," I said, winking at Switch. "Glad to hear about the radio. Have you contacted London?"

"No, we're waiting for Juliet to finish coding the message. Takes some time to get right. As soon as the Germans leave and she finishes, we'll string up the antenna," Topper said.

"Does that mean we'll get out of here?" Fawcett asked.

"Sooner or later," Kaz answered. "They might smuggle you through Spain if we can make contact with another network. Or send in Lysanders, but that would take time. We only have a few nights with sufficient moonlight left until next month."

"So when we gettin' outta here?" Meyers said, returning with a shearling-lined flight jacket over his arm.

"Don't know yet," Fawcett said. "That's a good idea—I'm going to grab my flight jacket as well. It'll come in handy if we need to spend the night outdoors."

"I doubt it will come to that," Sonya said. "But hurry, and bring Brookes back with you."

"Where'd Brookie get to?" Meyer said, shoving me as he took back his place on the bench.

"He went after you," Babcock said. "You didn't see him?"

"Naw," Meyer grunted, folding his jacket on the table and using it for a pillow. With all the twists, turns, and hidden chambers, it was easy to picture how they could have missed each other.

Fawcett returned with his heavy jacket, giving a shrug when asked if he'd seen his crewmate. It was obvious he didn't care one way or the other.

Ten minutes passed. Twenty. Now it was getting hard to see why Brookes wasn't back.

"Could he be lost?" Topper asked.

"He's not one to explore on his own," Sonya said.

"And he's always on his own," Switch said. He, Meyer, and Dogbite all snickered before looking to Fawcett.

"Why?" I asked. "What's the deal with him?"

"That's our concern," Babcock said. "You Yanks mind your own business."

"Sorry," I said. "Didn't mean to offend the Royal Canadian Air Force." I rolled my eyes in the direction of Meyer and Switch to show I could snicker with the worst of them.

"Maybe you'd like to look for him, Sergeant?" Kaz said in his most imperial tone.

"No, I will go," Sonya said. "I know the tunnels better than any of you. No one leave; is that clear?" We all agreed. She took a flashlight from the shelf, flicked it on, and removed a small automatic pistol from her jacket pocket.

I followed her to the wide archway leading to the tunnel, which went off in both directions. To my right were our rooms and the armory. Sonya had gone left, in the direction of the other sleeping chambers, where Meyer had headed. I watched the beam of light dance against the stonework as she proceeded along the curving walls, the faint echo of footsteps fading as the light disappeared.

I waited under the arch, listening for the pounding on heavy wooden doors and harsh commands which would signal Zeller's discovery of one of the secret entrances. Or for the hushed tones of Sonya and Brookes, whispering as she led him back to the main room. For five minutes or so, the tunnels were silent.

Then came the steady pad of feet, light shining straight ahead as she made her way back. She brushed past me, stopping to stare at Fawcett, who'd appeared with his jacket slung over his shoulder. Something was not right.

"He's dead."

CHAPTER TWENTY-ONE

"EVERYBODY OUT!" SONYA said, her hushed voice raspy and raw. With a pistol in one hand and flashlight in the other, she herded us into the tunnel and through the cellar.

"What about Juliet and the others?" I whispered as she secured the door. Shaking her head, Sonya put her finger to her lips. Dogbite signaled for us to follow him, single file, into the woods.

Babcock and Fawcett gathered twigs and leaves, scattering them around the door to hide the evidence of our footsteps. They brought up the rear as everyone in the group ran low, making for a stand of pine trees on a small rise about a hundred yards out.

"What happened?" Babcock said as he hunkered down next to Sonya.

She raised her hand, the palm sticky with blood. "I think he was stabbed," she said. "I found him near the entrance to the Druid temple. I have no idea what he was doing there."

"Meyer, you sure you didn't see him?" Babcock said.

"I didn't. Never went that far." Meyer crawled to the base of a nearby tree, keeping watch on our left flank.

"Fawcett?" Babcock hissed. "What about you?"

"No idea, Lieutenant. Really. Never laid eyes on him after he left." It was the *really* that bothered me. Why did Fawcett feel the need to say that? Was the problem between him and Brookes so serious he needed to convince his own lieutenant he wasn't lying?

"Later," Sonya said. "We need to listen for the Germans. If they got into the tunnels, we shall know soon enough." She was right.

Brookes wasn't going anywhere, and if a Kraut had killed him, they'd be spilling out of the stables and château anytime now.

But if it wasn't a German, we had a whole different problem.

The suspect pool was pretty small, most of it gathered around in the pine grove. Plus anyone in the château who knew about the tunnels: Vincent, Count Vasseur, Madame Agard, and Juliet. It was hard to imagine Brookes being a threat to anyone. He was meek, afraid of his own shadow, and eager to please. Maybe the taunting today had pushed him over the edge. Could he have attacked someone he ran into out of fright or rage or frustration?

Speculation was useless. I let my gaze linger on Fawcett and Meyer. No visible bloodstains. It would be revealing to see where Brookes had been stabbed. If there had been a lot of blood spray, they'd be off the hook.

Kaz caught my look and shook his head. He hadn't spotted any blood, either. We turned toward the château, and I knew he was wondering the same thing I was. What would the Germans do if they'd found the tunnels? Shoot everyone? Torture them? The thought of Juliet at their mercy was too much to bear. She'd endured capture before, and it had cost her. And me.

But it didn't feel right. There'd been no shouts, no alarm raised, no boot heels tramping through the stables. I had no sense of how much time had passed since Brookes went off to look for Meyer. Half an hour? Forty-five minutes, maybe. So why weren't the Germans ripping the place apart? Questions buzzed through my mind as we waited, watching and listening.

Almost an hour later, an engine coughed to life, then another. Sonya pointed to the right, where the trees thinned out enough to afford a view of the drive curving away toward the main road. A staff car appeared first, followed by two trucks with their canvas tops rolled up. Each carried a dozen soldiers. Their search was over.

Ours was about to begin.

■ ■ ■

I WANTED TO hug her, kiss her, call her Diana, but all I did was nod as Juliet opened the root cellar door. It was enough for now to know she was safe.

We filed inside, Sonya bringing up the rear, her pistol still in her hand as she herded us through the entrance. Did she think the killer was about to bolt? Or had she been the one to knife Brookes? The SOE trained all their agents, male and female, in lethal killing. She and Juliet were probably more deadly with a blade than any of us, excluding Topper, who'd never left the room.

"Did you see?" Sonya asked her.

"Yes, on my way back to you. My God, what happened?" Juliet said, her eyes searching out mine. All I could do was shrug.

"Meyer left the room, and Brookes went to find him. Meyer came back, then Fawcett left as well. We never saw Brookes again," Sonya said as we took our places in the salon, not quite as crowded as it had been a few days ago. The electric lights were on, casting harsh shadows on the floor.

"You left the room as well," I said. "That's how you found him."

"Of course," she said. "You don't think I killed him?"

"Just getting our facts straight." I smiled. "Four people left the room. One was found dead."

"It could have been any four of them," Babcock said. He sounded relieved, as if that took the pressure off his crewman Fawcett. "Or someone from the château. Doors work both ways."

"Who's gonna be next?" Dogbite asked, taking a seat at the big table. "Why stop at two?"

"We need to understand why Armstrong and Brookes were killed," I said. "That will tell us if we have to worry about the killer striking again."

"All I know is, I'm going to be watching my back," Switch said. "Like now, when I put my pack away."

"I'll go with you," Meyer said, grabbing his own gear and jacket. If Switch was nervous about Meyer following him into the tunnels, he didn't show it. But any crook worth his salt had a decent poker face.

"We must attend to the radio. Communicating with London is our priority at the moment," Juliet said. "Lieutenant Babcock, I am sorry about Brookes. We will try to sort out what happened. But right now I need to finish coding my message."

"I'll get the radio ready," Topper said. "I need to string the aerial outdoors; there's sixty feet of it."

"Sonya, help him set up the wireless in the attic. Show him where the aerial can be strung between the rafters. Lieutenant Kazimierz, will you and Sergeant Boyle see what you can learn from the body? We'll organize a burial after dark. The rest of you, stay here. There will be questions." Orders issued, Juliet strode out of the room.

"Who does she think she is anyway?" Switch muttered. "It could have been her, sneaking in from the château."

"In which case, best keep your comments to yourself," I said, working at not sounding defensive. "You could be next on her list." I grinned to show it was a joke. No one laughed.

"No dame ever got the drop on me," Switch said. "No man, either, come to think of it." We played the hard-stare game for a few seconds, and then I broke off before following Kaz into the tunnels.

"How's your rib?" I asked.

"It only hurts when I laugh. Fortunately, there is not much to laugh about. Are you getting any friendlier with Switch and his companions?"

"Not friendlier," I said. "I'm cultivating the brotherly bond of crooks. Not much luck so far. Have you picked up anything about them?"

"According to Sonya, Blake seems intelligent, but content to remain quiet. Meyer is not well liked, and the last to offer assistance in any regard. Dogbite is colorful and amusing as well as restless. He has accompanied them on missions and killed Germans with a knife on several occasions."

"So either Meyer or Dogbite would fit the bill as Switch's partner in crime. Or neither," I said as we approached the dark tunnel that held the entrance to the Druid temple.

The beam from Kaz's flashlight played over the still form ahead. It looked like a pile of rags in the dank shadows, seeming to meld with the stones on which it lay. The dead never ceased to surprise me, no matter how many bodies I'd seen. Life animated us, made us whole. Death swept all that away, leaving a twisted imitation of the living, instantly recognizable as no more than cooling dead flesh.

Kaz shined the light on Brookes's face. There was nothing it could tell us.

"The hands," I said, kneeling a foot or so away from Brookes. I hesitated to use his nickname Brookie. Everyone who used it treated it as a curse, as if they spat when they said it. Most guys got a nickname in their unit, but this hadn't been a shared camaraderie. *Brookie* was a diminutive, a verbal lessening of the man. I needed to find out what had brought that on.

But first things first. I held up his right hand, looking for signs of a fight, scratches, anything that might hint at what happened here. Nothing. I took the other, the beam of light showing only dirty fingernails and soft, young skin. No cuts, nothing to show he'd had a chance to fight back or ward off a knife thrust. He was on his left side, so I rolled him onto his back and opened his jacket. A bloodstain darkened the right side of his shirt above the belt. I unbuckled his belt and loosened his trousers.

"Perfect kidney stab," I said, pointing to the entry wound between the rib cage and pelvis.

"Is that fatal?" Kaz asked. "I mean, so quickly?"

"Yeah, if you know what you're doing. The kidneys are small, but a lot of blood goes through them. Hit one right, twist the knife a bit, and it's lights out. He bled to death internally. There's not much blood on him."

"It sounds like our killer had some specialized training," Kaz said. "Or was very lucky."

"Luck had nothing to do with it," I said, rolling Brookes's body back as we'd found it. "Shine the light around the body."

Working the edges, Dad called it when we worked a homicide. Looking for any trace the killer might have left. He always said the best chance for a hands-on killer to leave a clue was at the last moment of contact, when the deed had been done. Before that, the murderer was likely on high alert, conscious of every move, waiting for the moment to strike. Then, with the victim dead or dying, the killer might let down his guard if he was overconfident or relieved. Who knew what a guy who'd just knifed a kid and twisted the blade felt? Or a woman?

"There," I said, as Kaz passed the beam along Brookes's leg. Blood. Not from the wound, but from the blade. "The killer cleaned the knife on his pants leg. See the line of blood?"

"He was not in a great hurry, then," Kaz said, kneeling to study the stain.

"Don't say 'he.' Two of the suspects are female."

"You can't mean Diana," Kaz said, then lowered his voice. "Juliet, I should say."

"We have to treat her as we would anyone else, for appearance's sake. And remember, it could have been someone from the château, male or female."

"Yes, of course. Very well, what's next?"

"Keep working the light around him," I said, kneeling closer to the corpse.

"There certainly is not much blood," Kaz said.

"No, not with this wound. I wouldn't expect to find our killer walking around decorated with bloodstains. Unless he or she got careless. Look!" Three tiny droplets of blood on the stones, a few inches from the wound.

"From the knife, after it was withdrawn," Kaz said.

"Probably," I muttered, trying to recreate the scene in my mind. They must have been walking together. Not standing still, since Brookes would have seen it coming. Walking along, talking. About what? Where were they going? Into the temple? Who had a key to that door? Suddenly the killer pulled a knife. Easier if they were right-handed. Dropped back a pace, reached their arm around Brookes's back, and stabbed into that soft midsection. Twisted the blade and lowered the body to the ground. Pulled out their knife, and as they moved to wipe the blade on their victim's trousers, they leave a trail of red drops.

"He—I mean the killer—might have a drop or two on their shoes," Kaz said.

"If the killer is stupid and we're lucky, yes," I said. "There's another possibility. It's easy enough to slice yourself, especially if you grabbed ahold of your victim and pulled the blade out hard. There's a chance our murderer has a cut."

"Or that this person has clean shoes by now and no cut," Kaz said. "Basically we know nothing."

"We might not know much," I said, walking over to the temple door and giving it a try. Locked up tight. "But I think I have an idea."

"What?" Kaz asked. I didn't answer yet. I wanted to give my own common sense time to talk me out of it.

CHAPTER TWENTY-TWO

"I HAVE TO check your shoes," I said, opening the curtain to Juliet's underground room. It was about ten by ten feet, adorned with an electric light, a cot and chair, and one wood-plank table covered in loose sheets and pads of paper. A candle in a sconce was the only decoration on the limestone walls.

"Oh, please, Billy, I am quite busy," Juliet said, as she wrote out a long column of letters.

"Please," Kaz said in his most soothing tone. "We must ask. It wouldn't do for the others to wonder why we gave you special treatment."

"Of course. But be quick about it." She swiveled in her seat, lifting her feet to show a pair of worn and scuffed leather lace-ups, not a speck of dried blood to be seen.

"That's it, thanks," I said, giving her a smile. "Sorry to bother you."

"Oh, it's not that. I shouldn't have been short with you, but this is all so frightening," she said, turning back to the jumble of letters. "It's hard enough to do the job we came to do, but a killer among us is too much to bear." Her voice caught, and I saw her hand tremble before she laid it flat on the table. She didn't meet my eye.

"We'll find whoever did it. Meanwhile, I have an idea to help out the count. I'll tell you about it when you're done."

"I could use some good news. I'll be finished in about an hour." With that, she sighed and returned to her coding.

Sonya was keeping everyone else corralled in the salon. With a fair amount of griping, we got everyone to show us their boots. Dusty and dirty, but bloodless. Sonya had white socks folded down over the tops of her shoes, clean and neat. I pulled her aside, out of earshot of the others.

"Is there somewhere we can put the body for a while? Someplace cool, perhaps?"

"Why? We can bury him tonight as we did Lieutenant Armstrong," she said.

"I have something else in mind," I said. "I'll tell you and Juliet about it later. But for now, what's the coldest part of these tunnels?"

"There's an unused ice pit off the root cellar. They used to store ice during the winter and it lasted all year, I understand. It's empty now, but I know it's cold and damp. We stored weapons in it for a while."

"Perfect," I said. "Can we get some sheets to wrap the body?"

"Of course," she said. Kaz and I followed her as she gathered up a couple of sheets and a length of twine. We rolled Brookes in the sheets, and bound him up as best we could. It wasn't so much a gesture of respect as a matter of convenience. It's easier to carry a corpse if the arms and legs aren't flopping around. Brookes was going on one last mission before he was laid to rest.

"What are you up to, Billy?" Kaz grunted, as we lumbered through the tunnels with our awkward load, Sonya leading the way.

"Maybe getting Zeller off our backs," I said, leaving out the tricky part. Which described most of my idea admirably.

Sonya took us into the root cellar and opened a hatch that led to a brick-lined chamber. We carried the body down four steps and immediately felt the chill. The room was perfect. As we set the body on matted straw, Kaz shook his head slowly.

"There are many ways to die in this war," he said. "This one seems particularly senseless."

"It makes sense to someone. That's what we need to understand," I said.

"When these poor boys come to us they are frightened, often in shock from what they've endured in the air," Sonya said. "We give them shelter and hope, and the fear fades away. But Sergeant Brookes was always afraid, always worried. None of the other men, even his own crew, gave him a kind word."

"Do you know why?" I asked.

"No. They would not speak of it, and he hardly spoke at all. When I did ask him directly, he simply stared at the floor. For a long time."

"Poor lad," Kaz said.

"He carried guilt. Over what, or whom, I have no idea," Sonya said. We stood for a few moments, paying what respects we could. Then we left him in the ice pit. Sonya went off to see if Topper was done rigging the aerial, and we returned to the salon.

"What next?" Kaz asked as we neared the entrance. We had a while until Juliet was done coding and I could reveal my scheme, such as it was.

"Let's talk to Fawcett and find out if he had a beef with Brookes. Then Babcock."

"Lieutenant Babcock was his commanding officer," Kaz said. "Perhaps he knows more than he was willing to say when his sergeant was alive."

"I had that sense, too," I said. "But he might have been protecting Fawcett. And remember, Fawcett was one of the people out of the room. Let's tackle him first."

"Very well. I shall play the imperious officer and order you to assist me," he said. "This may also give us a good cover for speaking to Blake alone, since we'd be interviewing each man separately."

"Yeah, after we talk to the Canadians. Right now, this killer is our biggest problem."

"Second only to the Germans," Kaz said.

"But as far as we know, they're not the ones wandering through the tunnels killing our guys, so let's focus on that. Come on."

We entered the salon, where Babcock and Fawcett sat silently at one end of the table, while Switch, Meyer, and Dogbite played cards at the other.

"We will be conducting interviews with each of you," Kaz said. "To determine what light you might be able to shed on the killing of Brookes."

"You mean put the screws on until you get a confession," Meyer said. "Tell me why I should listen to a Polack in a Brit uniform anyway." He didn't look up from his cards.

"That is not quite what I had in mind. As for your question, suffice it to say the Polack officer, who outranks you, will communicate with London over the Brit radio for a Brit aircraft to get you out of here. Here being the safe house provided by SOE, a decidedly British organization. Or would you rather wait for the war to roll over the château? Assuming the Germans don't discover you first and have you shot?"

"What the hell do you mean, have me shot? I ain't been with the Resistance." Meyer was interested enough in the answer to his question to look up at Kaz.

"Don't matter. Enough of us been runnin' around killing Krauts," Dogbite said, grinning as Meyer lost some of his bluster. "Ya gotta figure by now, some Jerry spotted one of those blue RCAF uniforms, or me in my flight suit and leather jacket. Hitler don't appreciate commandos so much, and I bet the Gestapo'll be happy to gun us all down."

Kaz took some joy in filling Meyer in on the *Führer*'s infamous Commando Order. It only made me more nervous, since it applied directly to us, whether we were shooting up the local garrison or not.

"Okay, okay," Meyer finally said. "You made your point. I'll fit you in my busy schedule whenever you want to chat."

"We'll begin with the victim's fellow crewmen. Sergeant Fawcett, you first," Kaz said, gesturing for Fawcett to follow him. "Sergeant Boyle, come along."

"Can we get some chow first? I'm starving," I said, giving it the right amount of disobedient petulance.

"*Now*, Sergeant. We have a lot of work ahead of us." Kaz herded Fawcett out ahead of him. I shrugged in the general direction of Meyer as if to say, *What can you do with a stuck-up officer?* He grinned, the first sign of anything mutual between us besides disdain. He shuffled the cards, murmuring something about that runty Polack bastard. I was tempted to warn him about underestimating Kaz, but I didn't want to be his pal that badly.

"Sit down, Sergeant Fawcett," Kaz said, as we entered the room where he and Topper had repaired the radio. The workbench was covered with tools and spare parts. Kaz and Fawcett took the two chairs facing the bench; I grabbed a crate and sat across from them, the junior partner in this interrogation.

"It's Flight Sergeant, actually," Fawcett said, resting one arm on the bench. "Not that I care much about rank. Ronnie will do fine, if this is a friendly talk." His face might have looked youthful with those freckles, but his voice was firm as he stated his full rank.

"We're all on the same side, Ronnie," Kaz said, crossing his legs and shaking out a crease that had never been there. "Obviously, it makes sense for us to speak with you first, since the victim was a fellow crewman, and you were in the tunnels at the same time he was."

"I was only gone a few minutes. I stopped in the latrine, had a piss, then went to my room and grabbed my jacket. Never saw Brookes."

"Do you have a knife?" I asked.

"Sure. Take a look," Fawcett said, handing Kaz a black metal pocket knife. "Standard issue for aircrew. I keep it sharp, but I didn't use it on Brookes." Kaz opened the blade. It was four inches or so, and I could tell by the sheen that Fawcett took good care of it. Which could mean he was handy with it or that he had a lot of time on his hands. Kaz handed it to me, and I inspected the opening that held the blade. No telltale blood or gore stuck inside.

"If I killed Brookes with that knife, when did I have time to clean it?" Fawcett said. "Not to mention the blood I would have gotten on myself."

"Had to ask," I said, glancing at his fingernails as I handed the knife back to him. They were clean.

"Did you see anyone else?" Kaz asked.

"Not a soul. But the latrine is down a lateral tunnel, so I could have missed someone while I was in there."

"How well do you know your way through the tunnels?" I asked.

"I got lost a few times when I first got here, but I'm okay if I don't wander far. They keep the doors that lead to the château locked, so sooner or later you wind up back where you started."

"What about Armstrong? He had the run of the place, didn't he?" Kaz asked. It was a good question. Perhaps there was a connection between him and Brookes.

"Yeah, he did. Juliet wanted someone who knew where all the keys and secret passages were, in case something happened while she and Sonya were out with the Resistance. She made him promise to keep it all to himself."

"And did he?" Kaz asked.

"Far as I know," Fawcett said. "It was right after we found out we were stuck here. Juliet told us the next network on the escape route had been rolled up, and it might be awhile before we got out. She stressed that we had to stay underground and not attract attention, and asked for one volunteer to learn the ins and outs of the place. Armstrong spoke decent high-school French, and was interested in the tunnels and the Druid temple, so he was the logical choice."

"How did he get along with Brookes?" Kaz asked.

"As well as anyone," Fawcett said, his mouth set in a grim line.

"Why don't you tell us the story?" I said. "The truth about

Brookes. Why did Meyers and Blake ride him so hard? What did you have against him?"

"I despised the man. Not that he was much of a man."

"Tell us," Kaz said, settling back in his chair. Fawcett sighed, closed his eyes, then opened them, seeing the past he'd rather not remember.

"We were flying out of RAF Topcliffe when Brookes joined us. We were getting the Mark III Halifax after our old ship had been shot up during a raid on Essen. We had two killed, one of them the mid-upper turret gunner. Brookes got that job. I was the rear gunner." He stopped, and rubbed his eyes as if simply beginning the story had fatigued him.

"It must have been hard for Brookes and the other fellow to become part of the crew," Kaz said. "Were you all together a long time?"

"I came over from Canada with Babcock and Colin Carter, our copilot. We picked up the rest of the boys over here and had good luck until Essen. We ran into heavy winds, heavier than expected. Our squadron arrived over the target fifteen minutes late. By then, every antiaircraft battery in the Ruhr valley was filling the sky with flak. Three aircraft went down, and ours was shredded. Three men wounded, two dead. We were flying so high to avoid the night fighters it was forty degrees below zero inside the aircraft. Their blood froze instantly, everywhere in the fuselage."

"Were you hurt?" I asked, mainly to give him a breather.

"Not a scratch," he said, a slight shiver of memory trembling through his body. "Anyway, that's not the story you wanted to hear, sorry. So Brookes and another lad, Johnny Miller, join us. Miller is the wireless operator. We have a few milk runs to Brest and Cherbourg, and the new boys do fine. No sign of trouble from them or the new aircraft." He picked up a small screwdriver and began to tap it against the wooden workbench.

"And then?" Kaz asked.

"Then Hamburg, Nuremberg, Leipzig. All deep into Germany. We watched the cities burn, watched our planes explode and crash, and waited for our turn at the flames. Then Berlin. And again Berlin. We were all on edge, dreading each mission, but we kept on as best we could."

"Except for Brookes?" Kaz prompted.

"He was shaky, no doubt. I was worried about him, about whether or not he could do his job. He was either jumpy or clammed up, a lot like you saw here. And his job wasn't just to defend the ship, it was to help me in case we had to bail out."

"How?" I asked, remembering the stories I'd heard about tail gunners and their survival rates.

"It's too damn cramped to wear a parachute in the rear turret. It's the mid-upper turret gunner's job to help the rear gunner out of the turret, lend a hand with his 'chute, and let the pilot know they're both clear to jump."

"I'm guessing that didn't happen," I said.

"March thirtieth, it was," Fawcett said, either not hearing or ignoring my question. "A big raid on Nuremberg. Nearly eight hundred bombers, they told us in the briefing. Then they pulled the sheet off the big map showing our route. It was a goddamned straight line. They sent us into the teeth of the enemy defenses without any evasive maneuver."

"That is not normally the case?" Kaz asked.

"Hell, no! You fly a zigzag route to confuse their defenses. Keep them guessing about what the target is. But a straight line? Might as well call ahead and let them know we're coming."

Fawcett leaned back in the chair and rubbed his hand over his eyes, blinking away tears, or perhaps visions of that mission. He sat upright, then rested his elbows on his knees and held his face in his hands. The room was silent. The smell of limestone chalk filled my nostrils. The electric light threw harsh shadows across

Fawcett, shreds of the nighttime darkness over Germany still clinging to his skin.

He blew out a long sigh. "It was a bright moonlit night. No cloud cover. The slaughter began as soon as we crossed the German border. If the flak wasn't pounding us, it was the night fighters. I started to watch bombers go down, thirty before we even got to Nuremberg. I could make out a trail of glowing fires marking our route. We dropped our bombload and got turned around as quickly as we could. It was a mess. No formation to speak of, everyone scattered across the sky. But we were in one piece, and I thought we had a chance to make it home."

"Was this your last mission?" I asked.

"Yes. Somewhere over Belgium, a night fighter hit us from below. Miller, the new wireless operator, was killed. Babcock told us the plane was fine, and to hang on and watch for the fighter to hit us again. On the second pass, the intercom was knocked out and the fuselage began filling with smoke. I could see one engine on fire, and figured it was time to bail out. Normally the pilot would give the order, but there was no way to hear him, or anything, really. The sound of the engines drowns out everything, you know. So I rotated the turret to get out, and I see Brookes, standing over the escape hatch. He looked at me for a second, then jumped.

"The smoke got heavier, then we were hit again. The tracers made a horrible, metallic, shredding sound I'll never forget. Flames sprouted from the electrical circuits, and the sudden brightness blinded me, so I felt around for my parachute, stumbling and falling as Babcock took evasive action. Finally I got the thing on and crawled to the hatch. The midsection of the fuselage was burning, there was no way to get up front and let Babcock know I was about to jump."

"Why would you need to tell him?" Kaz asked. "What else was there to do?"

"It was Brookes's job to help me with my parachute and notify the pilot we were ready to jump. I knew he didn't do it when I saw his face in that split second. He was saving himself, and no one else. By the time I got the 'chute on, I couldn't get through the flames to go forward."

"And Babcock kept flying, thinking you needed more time," I said, realizing the enormity of what Brookes had done.

"Yes. Right after my 'chute opened, I saw the night fighter hit them again. The rest of the crew was killed, except for Babcock. He jumped right before the plane exploded. I watched the burning pieces fall to the ground. If Brookes had done his duty, three good men would be alive today. He almost got me killed, and he is responsible for those three deaths. Was, I should say."

"Do you think that's why he was murdered?" I asked. It was hard to stay focused on the interrogation after hearing that story, but I had a job to do.

"No idea," he said.

"Did you see him in the tunnel?" I asked.

"I told you I didn't."

"Did you kill him?" Kaz asked, getting to the point.

"No. I'll tell you I shed no tears over the man, but I had no hand in it. Think about it; we've been here for weeks, and the three of us traveled together before that. If I wanted to kill him, I'd have done it while we were hiding out in the hills."

"How did you find him, and Babcock?" I asked.

"Once I was on the ground, I went in the direction the plane was headed. I spotted Babcock gathering up his parachute, and told him what had happened. We set off due west, looking to make contact with the Resistance. Hoping we were actually in France or Belgium, not Germany. We hid out during the day and walked for two nights before we dared approach a farmhouse. Luckily, the farmer wasn't a collaborator. He put us in touch with the Resistance, who took us to a safe house in Sissonne. A couple of days later, they brought Brookes in. I laid into him, starting with a punch to his jaw. Babcock pulled me off and calmed me down, promising he'd see to a court-martial when we got back to England."

"That satisfied you?" Kaz asked.

"It did. The thought of telling the world what that little worm did kept me going. The last thing I wanted was for him to die before being brought to justice. Anyway, the Resistance moved us on, through a series of isolated farms and hideouts in the woods. We ended up here, and you know the rest. Traffic jam on the escape route to Spain."

"What about Meyer? He seemed to have a grudge against Brookes," I said.

"Grudge? No. He's a mean one, a real bully. If he can push a guy around, he will, for the fun of it. I have the feeling it wouldn't have bothered him to knife Brookes, but I can't see him caring enough to do it."

There wasn't much more to get out of Fawcett. Kaz and I agreed we believed his story about wanting Brookes alive to be court-martialed. I could see him getting violent with Brookes in a fit of rage, but not following him into the tunnel and calmly driving a blade into his kidney. We brought in Meyers next.

"Sure, I couldn't stand the little weasel," Meyer snapped as soon as we got seated. "But I never laid a hand on him. Ask anyone."

"Why couldn't you stand him?" I asked.

"Fawcett told us what happened, how Brookie left him in the lurch. Bet he was surprised to find Fawcett alive and kickin'!" Meyer snickered.

"Why did you leave the salon?" Kaz said.

"You know why. To get my jacket."

"Is it not standard procedure to have everything ready in case of a search? So you can get away with whatever you need?" Kaz asked. A good question.

"We done it so many times and nothing ever happened," Meyer said. "This was taking longer, and I got to thinking it could be the real thing. So I wanted that flight jacket. It's warm, just the thing for spending a night out in the woods, which I did after we was shot down."

"How'd you get along with Armstrong? Ever have any problems?" I asked.

"Nah. We had a good crew, everyone did their jobs. Armstrong was a damn good pilot. Always calm up there, even when the flak was hot and heavy. That's what you want in your skipper. You want to trust that he won't lose it when things get tough."

"How about on the ground?" I said.

"We went our separate ways. He was a quiet guy, kind of an egghead. You might have noticed I ain't. I like the booze and the broads, Armstrong liked books and museums, that kinda stuff."

"Do you have any idea who would want him dead?" Kaz asked.

"Nah. No reason for anyone here to do him in. Brookie, I can understand. But Armstrong, you got me."

"I have no other questions," Kaz said, rising from his seat. "Sergeant Boyle, you may ask any questions that come to mind. When done, bring in Dogbite, then Blake. I shall take a brief respite."

"What's that mean, he's gotta take a leak?" Meyer said, leering, after waiting for Kaz to be out of earshot. I laughed.

"If I'd known I'd be saddled with that twerp, I'd never have volunteered," I muttered.

"What choice did you have?"

"I could have done a two-year stretch in the stockade. The army and me had a misunderstanding about peaches."

"What's to misunderstand?" Meyer said.

"Oh, where sixty-four cases of 'em got to," I said. "Plus some gasoline went missing. I was cooling my heels in the stockade at Cheltenham when this Brit comes through looking for volunteers. Charges dismissed, rank reinstated—all I had to do was sign up for a vacation in France. Guess he wanted a bodyguard."

"Two years is tough, but then you're out. And out of the army. This ain't no picnic you signed up for."

"Listen," I said, leaning forward and whispering, "I don't know about you, but I've never seen so many supplies, guns, fuel, you name it, as I did in England. I figure it's going to be the same here in France once the Krauts are on the run. I wouldn't mind staying put for the duration, you know what I mean?"

"Ah, a businessman," Meyer said. "Looking to strike it rich."

"Hey, how rich were you getting flying around in that Marauder?"

"I do okay," he said. "Almost a hundred bucks a month. I send most of it home, otherwise I'd blow it all."

"On booze and broads, right?"

"What else is there? We done here?"

"Sure," I said. "Say, you ever thought about going into business yourself?"

"I'd steal sixty-four cases of peaches right now if I could. See you later, Boyle."

"NOTHING," I SAID to Kaz as I left to bring in Dogbite. "He played innocent, even when I offered him a business proposition. He liked the *brief respite*, by the way."

"I thought it would provide for a comical observation," Kaz said. "Did it help for you to mock me?"

"Not much, but it was fun," I said, and went off to fetch Dogbite.

"What the hell do you want to talk to me about?" Dogbite said as I led him into the room. "It had to be Fawcett or Meyer."

"Hey, I'm not accusing you of anything," I said. "The lieutenant has a few questions, that's all." Dogbite sat and shrugged, waiting for Kaz to speak.

"Let's start with Armstrong," Kaz said. "Did you get along with him?"

"Sure. He was easygoing. Not a barrel of laughs, but a decent pilot. Quiet and calm. We didn't have a lot in common, on the ground anyway."

"And in the air?" Kaz prompted.

"We both kept our bird flying. I'm a damn good gunner, if I do say so. And Armstrong kept his head when things got hot. We did our jobs best we could."

"No one seems to have been close to him," I said. "That true for Blake as well?"

"Yeah, pretty much. The only guy Armstrong was friendly with was Brookie. I think he felt sorry for him, you know? They both liked museums and all that stuff. I remember them talking about the ones they visited in London, and hoping they'd see that one in Paris everyone talks about."

"The Louvre," Kaz said.

"Yeah, that one. Poor bastards."

"Do you think either of your fellow crewmen capable of killing?" Kaz asked.

"Jesus, that's what we do all day long. Drop bombs and shoot things up."

"It's not the same," I said.

"You don't think so? You ever been in the nose gunner position in a Marauder? That's where Meyer sat. All alone up front with that big .50 machine gun. We fly high, we fly low, and when we're low, he loves to strafe anything in sight. Hopefully it's Krauts most of the time."

"What about you?" Kaz asked.

"I'm in the top turret with my twin fifties. Can't hit ground targets from up there, unless we're in a dive. I've shot down a few

Kraut fighters, but it ain't the same as machine-gunning a convoy of trucks. Know what I mean? I'm fighting metal up there, goddamn Me-109s. But Meyer's hunting people. Krauts, but people all the same. Big difference."

"You don't like him?" Kaz asked.

"Didn't say that."

"Do you think he killed Armstrong or Brookes?" I asked.

"No reason for him to kill Armstrong. That old horse just won't run."

"What about Brookes? Will that horse run?" Kaz said.

"Meyer can be nasty, that's for sure. Worse when he's drunk, but we ain't had enough liquor here to get mean over. Killing Brookes? Naw, that horse ain't even got outta the stable."

CHAPTER TWENTY-THREE

WE DECIDED DOGBITE was exonerating Meyer with his homespun logic. Which was almost as interesting as learning Armstrong was the only person to befriend Brookes. They were both quiet guys, more bookish than the average Joe. One was steady and calm, the other shaky and frightened. Now they were both dead. Was that all they had in common?

Juliet stopped in as Kaz and I were scratching our heads over that very question.

"I'm done with the coding," she said. "I'm taking it to Topper, and he'll transmit. I hope he's fast; it's a long message."

"Are the Germans always listening?" I asked.

"Yes, their *Funkabwehr* section is quite good. If a mobile radio van is in the area, it could mean trouble. Or if they cut the power, as they've done before."

"I hope you were not too wordy," Kaz said.

"Words could be the death of us," she said. "When we're done, I'm eager to hear this idea of yours, Billy."

"As am I," Kaz said. "We will be ready after we interrogate Blake. Do you have any suggestions about him?"

"He doesn't give much away, that one. Always watching and listening, letting others do the talking. He's been no trouble. No great help, either. Good luck." Juliet left, cheerily waving her sheets of paper covered in deathly code.

I brought in Switch. He didn't complain, didn't ask why we wanted to talk with him. He studied us, trying to get a read on the situation, as Juliet had described.

"First, tell us if you have any ideas or suspicions about the deaths of Armstrong and Brookes," I said. I knew that once we sprang our surprise about cousin Donald, it'd be hard to get him to focus, so I wanted to pump him for information first.

"First? What else do you want to talk about?" Juliet was right on target. Switch was a sharp customer.

"Something to our mutual benefit," I said. "But answer the question, okay?"

"Meyer said you had a business proposition. I didn't know it included the Boy Scout." He hitched a thumb in Kaz's direction. If he only knew.

"All we want is the inside dope. Who had it in for those two?" I said, leaning forward and trying for the earnest look. "Did Meyer have a beef with your pilot? Did he ride Brookes too hard, and he fought back? You must have some idea."

"Look, I don't know anyone short of the Germans who'd want Armstrong out of the picture. He was a steady pilot, ran a tight ship, got the most out of everyone in his crew. I wish I knew who did it—I'd take care of them myself."

"Perhaps Brookes in fact killed Armstrong, and you did just what you suggested," Kaz said.

Blake laughed. "Brookes wouldn't have had the balls to do it, and for that matter, why kill the only guy here who'd give him the time of day?"

"They were friendly?" I prompted.

"Yeah. Armstrong took pity on him. Or maybe it was just to have someone to talk to about art. They were both crazy about art."

"What kind of art?" Kaz asked.

"Paintings. You know, *art*." I made a mental note to ask the count about this. He'd mentioned spending time in his library chatting with Armstrong. "The stuff they hang in museums. I never paid much attention to what they were jabbering about."

That was the first false note in anything he said. Switch was the kind of guy who paid attention to everything.

"Do you have any ideas, anything that could help us?" Kaz asked.

"No, I'm stumped. Can't believe Fawcett killed Brookes—he was chomping at the bit to get him back to England for a court-martial. I'm outta air speed and ideas. What about you fellows?"

"We're really here to talk about something else," I said, giving Kaz a glance. He nodded. That got Switch's attention.

"What?" he said, alert to the shift in tone.

"It's about your cousin Donald," I said. His eyes widened.

"I told them they had nothing to worry about," Switch said between gritted teeth. "How'd they get you here? Both of you?" He looked back and forth, shifting back far enough to widen the gap between us.

"It's not what you're thinking," I said, reaching into my pocket for the folded photograph. Switch tensed, expecting something more lethal. "We're not from the Morgan Gang. As a matter of fact, we sprung your cousin. They were ready to shoot him."

I unfolded the photo and laid it out on the table in front of him.

"We were with Donald in London a few days ago, as you can see," Kaz said. "He is quite safe."

"Where'd they have him?" Switch said, studying the photo, his voice suddenly soft.

"Bromwich," I said. "Place next to the Spitfire factory. The noise covers up a lot."

"Who was there?" Blake was quizzing me, making sure I was on the up and up.

"Willie and Nick, and a third mook whose name I didn't catch before I put three slugs in his chest. He was the one about to execute Donald."

"Yeah, I know those guys. So who sent you?"

"We were loaned out to CID by our boss, Colonel Harding.

Agent Hatch thought it best if this operation was handled outside CID," I said.

"Hatch is smart," Switch said. "Not his fault CID leaks like a sieve. So what's the deal?"

"Same deal as before, except this one includes your cousin. You testify, CID rolls up the Morgan Gang, you two have a family reunion, and everyone's happy. You both get a transfer somewhere safe and far from England."

"Well, well. The three of you came all this way for me? I'm impressed with my own importance," Switch said.

"Actually, Topper is a real Jedburgh. We used him as cover," Kaz said. "We know that at least one of your aircrew is also a Morgan, but not which one."

"Meyer. He's been watching me ever since Donnie came looking for help. I had no idea he was involved until he asked me to get him out of a jam. Meyer might have been the one who set up the grab, but that's only a guess. In any case, he was just doing what he was told."

"Are you still willing to testify?" I asked.

"Damn right I am. I'm no angel, but I draw the line at using family against a guy. Donnie's like my kid brother. I owe his old man a lot for taking care of me, so I won't let this stand. As long as I see Donnie alive back in England, you can count on me. You sure he's safe?"

"That's his bodyguard and new best friend," I said, tapping the image of Big Mike.

"He'll do. What's next?"

"We check on the status of the wireless. Part of the message is to bring in a Lysander to take you out," I said.

"Obviously, Meyer can suspect nothing," Kaz said.

"Speaking of Meyer," Blake said, rubbing his chin as he leaned in. "There is something, now that we're pals and all. He's been acting funny lately. I can't put my finger on it, but I can't help feeling he's hiding something from me. We've been together a long time, and done a lot of things. I can tell."

"He must know about your initial deal with Hatch," I said. "Could it be because he's suspicious of you?"

"No. When they took Donnie, Meyer was the one who delivered the message. It was straightforward. I knew he had no more choice than I did. I didn't like it, but we still flew and worked together. I wish I could tell you more, but it's just a gut feeling."

"Do you think it had anything to do with Brookes?"

"He wasn't acting any different toward Brookes. He always gave him a hard time. He enjoyed seeing people squirm. If Brookes put up a fight, Meyer would beat him senseless, sure. But that knifing ain't his style."

"Okay, thanks," I said. "We'll let you know about the Lysander."

"I can't believe you two came all this way for me," Switch said, shaking his head.

"Listen, I'm not the gung-ho type, but this Morgan business is way out of hand," I said. "It's beginning to interfere with the war effort, which is another way of saying that guys on the front line aren't getting everything they need. Odds are its only going to get worse here in France."

"They're counting on it." Switch smiled. "It'll be like the Wild West, plenty of loot for the taking." He had the gleam of greed in his eyes, even though he'd promised to betray his gang.

"Who are the Morgans anyway? I mean, the head honchos," I asked.

"England and Donnie, Boyle. Then I spill. So keep me alive and get me home. If this turns out to be a double-cross, I'll clam up for good. And I'll find a way to make you pay, believe me."

"Simmer down, Switch. We pulled little Donnie's fat out of the fire, so save your breath. The only double-cross is the one you pulled on your own side, stealing from GIs."

"Don't snap your cap, Boyle. You wore blue before Uncle Sam's khaki, didn't you? I bet you lifted plenty back then. Boston, I'd guess by your accent. I heard half the coppers up there are on the take, and the other half are too stupid to figure the angles. Which were you?"

By this point we were both on our feet, chest to chest. My right hand was a fist, and it was headed toward his jaw until Kaz stepped between us and took a glancing blow to the shoulder for his trouble.

"Enough!" Kaz commanded, and then sat, wincing and cradling his ribs.

"Sorry," I said, not looking at either of them so Switch might think it was directed at him. I had a job to do, and personal likes or dislikes had little to do with it. So far, I wasn't a big fan of the Blake family, but that didn't mean I needed to deck the guy. At least, not until we got back to England.

"Tend to your pal, and let me know when we're getting the hell out of here," Switch muttered, turning on his heel. I couldn't wait to get back on English soil.

"Is it bad?" I asked Kaz, who sat stiffly in the chair, clutching his side.

"Bad enough that I wish I had let you strike him, but not terribly bad. Please, Billy, now that we've completed this part of the mission, I would like to bring Sergeant Blake back in one piece. And myself, for that matter."

"You're right. I'm not thinking straight. Too little sleep and too much running around the countryside. I think I'll grab a catnap."

"Not now," Juliet said, pulling the curtain aside. "We're done with the transmission. Come along and tell us about your grand idea."

I was beginning to think I'd oversold it.

CHAPTER TWENTY-FOUR

WE WENT THROUGH the tunnels and surfaced again in the kitchen through Madame Agard's pantry. Emeline was sitting at the table, doing her best to help shell peas. She smiled at the sight of me, or maybe because we came in from the pantry as if by magic. Juliet pressed a finger to her lips, and Emeline nodded in silent agreement. Of course she could keep a secret.

"Don't go up yet; that silly girl is with the count. She's hysterical again," Madame Agard said. "She insisted on seeing Count Vasseur, and Sonya had no choice but to bring her to him."

"One of the maids, Yvonne," Juliet explained as Kaz and Topper joined us in the kitchen. "A young girl, she takes all the ghost stories far too seriously."

"It's the painting this time," Madame Agard said, shaking her head in disapproval. "She came in here and frightened Justine."

"Who is Justine?" I asked.

"Why, you've met Justine, my grandniece, haven't you?" She gave Emeline a reassuring squeeze on the shoulder and spoke soothing words in French to her. "We're getting identity papers fixed for her, aren't we, dear Justine?" Emeline giggled at the sound of her new name. I hoped she'd be good at this game.

"*Enchanté*, Justine," Kaz said, who took a seat next to her and started shelling peas. "Madame Agard, what is it about this painting that frightened the maid?"

"It's the big one in the great hall. The first count, the man who built the château. She claims he looks at her, that the eyes move. Superstitious girl!" Madame Agard cleaned the table with a cloth, furiously rubbing at stains and crumbs with great indignation.

"Frédérick-Charles Maronneau," Juliet said. "There is a story about that painting, to be sure. But it's an old ghost story, according to the count. I didn't think anyone took it seriously."

"Do tell, if we must wait," Kaz said, and popped a pea into his mouth. The newly christened Justine did the same and laughed. We all did. Madame Agard cut slices from a large, crusty loaf of bread and passed the plate around. I'd lost track of time and was low on sleep, but I knew I was hungry as soon as I bit off a mouthful.

"The first Count Vasseur had his portrait painted after he had built the château. The painting is said to have been done by Jean Clouet, a sixteenth-century painter. There is no proof, unfortunately, other than the story that has been handed down by the family," Juliet said. "One of Vincent's jobs is to establish the provenance."

"Even without provenance, it is a handsome painting," Kaz said. "Does the old count haunt the château?"

"Not exactly," Juliet said. "The story is that he haunts the painting."

"That's a twist on the old haunted house tale," Topper said. "Never heard of a haunted painting."

"It all started with Margaux Vasseur, the third countess," Juliet said. "In those days, somewhere in the middle of the seventeenth century, meals were served in the great hall, under the eye of Frédérick-Charles. The count sat at the head of the table, with the portrait to his back. Margaux, seated opposite, hated looking at it."

"I don't blame her," Madame Agard said, spreading butter on Justine's bread. "He has such a dreadful look on his face. The eyes do follow you, I'll say that much."

"So Margaux complained?" Topper asked.

"Every day, so the story goes. Finally her husband couldn't stand it any longer and had the portrait carted up to a room on the top floor. It was covered with a cloth, and Margaux became much easier to live with. One day her sister came to visit and wanted to see the evil portrait she'd heard so much about in the letters Margaux had written her."

"She refused?" Kaz asked, splitting another pea pod with his fingernail.

"No, not at all," Juliet said. "She'd vanquished Frédérick-Charles and won out over her husband's wishes. She proudly took her sister upstairs and yanked off the cloth with a flourish. But the fabric caught on the edge of the frame. It toppled, sending Margaux reeling. She struck the window as the painting fell on her. A jagged piece of glass tore her throat, and she bled to death pinned under the deadly eyes of Frédérick-Charles himself."

"Mon Dieu," Madame Agard muttered. "I shiver every time I hear that story. That room has been locked for four hundred years. The bloodstain is still bright upon the floor, they say."

"You've never tried to unlock it?" Topper asked.

"Eh, I am not sure which room it is," Madame Agard admitted with a shrug. "There are many small rooms up there. Who has time to look?"

"An excellent story," Kaz said, giving little Justine the last pea pod. "I take it no one has actually looked for those bloodstains?"

"Not in this century. Why ruin a good story?" Juliet said with a grin. "But I do know for a fact that one of the upstairs rooms has a window that is not original. Vincent did have that confirmed by a fellow who knows the history of architecture from that era."

"What is Vincent's job, exactly?" I asked.

"The poor man," Madame Agard said with a heavy sigh. "He had a wonderful business in Dreux before the war. A small gallery, with a frame shop as well. Painters from all around, even from Paris, came to have their canvases framed by Vincent. He was a happy young man, even though the gossips would not leave him alone."

"What were they gossiping about?" Kaz said.

"Oh, there was some talk of stolen artwork being sold in his gallery," Madame Agard said. "The police obviously didn't take it seriously, and neither did I. We were all pleased to have such a cultured shop in our town."

"Vincent was a promising artist himself, and showed his work along with other local painters," Juliet said. "But then he was called up in 1940 to serve in an artillery unit. He was wounded in both legs, as is evident by his gait. While he was recovering in hospital, the Germans shelled Dreux as they were encircling Paris. His shop, along with many other buildings, was totally destroyed. His parents were killed."

"The Germans left him alone, only because he was too crippled to be of use to them," Madame Agard said. "One day he came here, walking with two canes, and asked the count if he had any work for him. Who would have thought he'd still be here?"

"What does he do?" Kaz asked.

"He cares for the count's art collection, restoring and reframing canvases," Juliet said. "Many of them were in sad shape. He is also working on a history of the château and the count's family."

"He has a place to sleep, food, and a few francs for the work he can do," Madame Agard said. "Little enough, compared to what he once had." She was interrupted by echoing voices, a high-pitched tirade with the occasional counterpoint of soothing words, all concluded by the slamming of doors and an expressive sigh of defeat as Sonya entered the kitchen.

"Yvonne has quit," Sonya informed us. "She is terrified of the haunted portrait."

"She has always avoided the great hall," Madame Agard said. "What brought this on now?"

"She claims the eyes follow her, that this time she saw them move," Sonya said, a sad laugh escaping her lips. "I am sure her mother will bring her back as soon as she calms down. There is no work to be had in Dreux, none that can be done standing up, at least. Come—the count can see you now."

Madame Agard cackled as we filed out, heading for the count's library. I studied the portrait of the first count as we went through the great hall, imagining Margaux dying under the steely gaze of the bloodline's founder. His eyes *were* expressive, but I didn't see as much as a wink.

"Please, sit," Count Vasseur said as we entered the library. Vincent rose from his seat to offer it to Juliet. While chairs were being gathered, I took the time to study the painting of the Madonna in blue. Her eyes were cast downward, but expressive nonetheless.

"Beautiful, isn't she?" Count Vasseur said, then took me by the arm and guided me to a seat. "I understand you have a plan to propose?"

"Yes," I said, aware of all eyes upon me as the count settled into his chair. "It may keep Zeller off our backs and help you as well."

"This has nothing to do with the murders, then?" he asked.

"Not the murders here, no. But it does involve our latest victim. We know that Zeller is desperate to find out who is helping downed fliers in this area, and that he's pressuring you for useful information in exchange for freeing your son."

"That is true, but I only give him small bits of gossip, or perhaps some minor detail. Nothing vital enough to get my son released."

"We pass on things to Zeller when we can," Juliet said. "A few small weapons caches, or a warning of an attack, just too late to be of any real use."

"He's not suspicious?" Kaz asked.

"No, I think not," Count Vasseur said. "Early on I told him where to find a large number of rifles. Old relics from the last war. We decided that it was too soon for the local *Maquis* to use them, and that when the invasion drew near, we would receive adequate supplies. Major Zeller was impressed. It was a worthwhile gambit. But I fail to understand what you are driving at."

"My idea is to hide Brookes's body at the *Milice* headquarters in Dreux, the old synagogue on rue Vernouillet. You tell Zeller that Pierre Rivet, the *Milice* leader, is working both sides, hedging his bets in case of an Allied victory."

"That's crazy," Topper said. "Even supposing we could get Brookes there, what proof would a corpse provide?"

"It doesn't matter. The count tells Zeller he's heard what Rivet is up to, and that he's got a Canadian flier hidden there right now. Zeller arrives to find a dead Canadian, but he has no idea how or why he was killed. All he knows is that the count was right. And how could Count Vasseur have arranged such a thing? It would be impossible," I said, beginning to believe it myself.

"At the very least it would distract Zeller," Kaz said. "And it would be revenge for Coudray. Ironic justice if the Nazis put a bullet in Rivet's skull. After a decent torture session, of course."

"It may be what Zeller has been demanding," Juliet said. "Something significant for the release of your son."

"And at the same time, driving a wedge between our own French fascists and the Nazis," Count Vasseur said. "It is an inspired concept, Sergeant Boyle. If you can hide a dead man in the *Milice* headquarters, it may have the effect you describe. But how can that be done?"

"I imagine it's easy to walk in," Topper said. "A little harder to do so with a corpse, and damned difficult not to end up a corpse oneself."

"We need a vehicle and a diversion," I said. "Then we find a back door and a place to stash the body. In the basement, perhaps."

"We can arrange the diversion and the automobile," Juliet said, looking to Sonya. "Along with someone who knows the layout of the synagogue." Sonya nodded and left the room.

"This must happen quickly," Count Vasseur said. "Where is the body?"

"In the ice pit," Juliet answered. "If Christine agrees with the plan, we can leave before curfew."

"I will call Zeller immediately upon your return," said the count. "I leave the arrangements to you. Is there anything else I can do to help?"

"I need to sleep if there's time. Thank you, Count Vasseur. I hope this works," I said.

"Please do not take any terrible risk," he said. "We will deal with the *Milice* in due course, I promise you."

"Count Vasseur," Kaz said as the others left, "we were entertained by stories of the haunted painting of your ancestor as we waited. I understand one of the maids has quit because it frightened her?"

"Ah, Yvonne," the count said, turning to Vincent and speaking in French. They both chuckled. "I am certain she will be back, somewhat embarrassed. It is my own fault, of course. I pretend to take these stories seriously—the White Giant in the Forest of Dreux, and the tragedy of Margaux Vasseur. Her story is true enough, but she must have been unbalanced, the poor thing."

"The painting did really fall on her?" Kaz said.

"Yes, in a storage room upstairs. She fell against a window and slit her throat, according to the story handed down the generations. I find it useful to let the villagers think the château and grounds are haunted. The *Boche* know of the Giant as well. I think when they search the Forest, they do so quickly!"

"I have a weakness for such stories, count. May I see the room where it happened?" Kaz gave him his best smile, the grin on one side running up against scar tissue that stopped it cold.

"Some other time, perhaps, Baron Kazimierz. When we have dealt with the present-day deaths. Vincent will take you to the tunnel now. *Bonne chance.*"

"*Crois-tu aux fantômes?*" Kaz asked Vincent as we trooped through the great hall. Vincent halted, gazing up at the grand portrait of Frédérick-Charles Maronneau. He smiled, perhaps the first sign of joy I'd seen on his face, and answered Kaz, then shuffled on in his painful gait. After going through the kitchen and seeing us into the now-familiar tunnel, Vincent waved and shut the hidden cupboard door behind us.

"You asked if he believed in ghosts, didn't you? What did he say?"

"He said yes, if you bring them back to life."

CHAPTER TWENTY-FIVE

I HAD ANOTHER reason for stashing Brookes's body with the *Milice*. It was one of the things Dad taught me about murder investigations. When they're going nowhere, shake things up. Do something, even if it doesn't make sense. Then watch how people react. Well, right now people were reacting like I was nuts, which wasn't exactly a news flash.

"You out of your mind, Boyle?" Switch asked as soon as I walked into the salon. They were eating supper, slurping up thin soup and dipping crusty bread. I glanced at my watch. Six o'clock. I tried to remember how much sleep I'd gotten last night, but the mental cobwebs were too damn thick. Living underground was disorienting even with enough rest.

"Here," Sonya said, ladling soup and pushing a plate of bread my way. "You'll need your strength."

"And a whole lotta luck," Meyer said, stuffing a crust into his mouth.

"Shouldn't you be sorting out who killed Brookes and Armstrong?" Babcock said, absentmindedly rubbing the scar on his jaw. "I mean, pulling one over on the *Milice* is a fine idea, but we have our own problems right here."

"I'm working on an angle," I said. "But in the meantime, why not draw the heat away from us?"

"I'm all for that," Fawcett said. "Let me know if I can help. As long as *help* doesn't mean a suicide attack."

"What about you, Dogbite?" I asked. "Up for another jaunt?"

"Depends on who else is goin'," he said, his gaze lingering on everyone at the table. "Or stayin'. I don't cotton to a murderin' bastard in the dark any more than the next fella."

"You talking about anyone special, Dogbite?" Meyer said, dropping his spoon into the bowl. Soup splashed onto the table.

"Nope. Why'd you think I was?"

"Can it, guys," I said, frustrated, hungry, and tired. "Let me eat in peace."

"What about the radio?" Meyer asked, picking up his spoon as if nothing had happened.

"We got our message through," Topper said. "We have a set schedule for communications from London. We'll have a response at midnight, so I have to stay here."

"Lieutenant, I can tell you're still in pain," I said, turning to Kaz and still playing the obedient noncom. "It'd probably be good for you to rest."

"I am fine, merely a hint of discomfort now and then, but thank you for your concern, Sergeant," Kaz said, sitting upright and twisting his torso to demonstrate. He winced, and tried to hide it.

"Yeah, every time you breathe," I said. "Sir."

"I would gladly go," Sonya said. "But I must bicycle to Épernon. We have a letter drop there that must be checked. A hiding place for messages from any network trying to contact us."

"Have you heard from anyone?" Kaz asked.

"No, but we must try. It is twenty kilometers, so I should leave now. I will return in the morning."

"Be careful, Sonya," Juliet said, entering the room. "It could be a trap."

"We must try," she said. "I plan on arriving early and watching from a distance. *Au revoir.*"

We all wished her *bonne chance*, and I hoped the same for us. If another network did establish contact, it would help to move their guests down the line. Minus Switch, of course.

"I telephoned Christine," Juliet said. "She'll be here shortly. She's bringing someone who knows the synagogue."

"Don't you worry about the Germans listening in?" Topper asked, mopping up his soup with a piece of bread.

"We have code words. I asked her to come for dinner and to bring her friend who knits. I told her we had fresh fish, which means we have to plan a quick operation."

"And the friend who knits?" I asked.

"A hidden Jew, a member of the congregation. She knits." That got a laugh, not that a Jew in occupied France was all that funny. "She and her husband attended services regularly for years, so she knows the entire layout."

"What of her husband?" Kaz asked.

"Gone, like all the others," Juliet said, taking soup for herself. "Rounded up and sent to the transit camp at Drancy. Then never heard from again. Madame Morency—her new name—was working at the time, doing alterations in a clothing shop. In exchange for food, since Vichy had declared it illegal to employ Jews. The owner hid her until contact could be made with the Resistance. They obtained *vrais faux papiers d'identité* for her."

"True false papers?" Kaz said.

"Yes, better than the *faux faux papiers d'identité* from London," Juliet said. "False false papers are created in England and could miss something vital. Then true false papers, created by the Resistance using copies of the real thing. Finally, there are the false true papers, which can only be obtained directly from a contact in the *préfecture*. Real papers, issued for a false identity. See?"

"No," I said, draining my soup. "Which is why I need to sleep until Christine gets here."

"WAKE UP, BILLY. Wake up!" I heard Kaz's voice and felt someone nudging me in the shoulder.

"No, I just went to sleep," I said as I pulled the wool blanket over my head.

"Two hours ago. Christine has arrived with Madame Morency. They are dining with the count now."

"Okay, give me a minute," I said, managing to sit up and lace my boots. I felt groggy from sleep—or the lack of it. I couldn't tell. "There's something I need you to do while I'm gone."

"Of course. And I could go with you, Billy. You may need reliable help."

"I know. But the route we take into the headquarters could be tricky, and we can't afford your injury holding us back. But there is something important you can do. Talk to the count and get the low-down on this château and all these tunnels. The real story, not a fairy tale about ghosts and giants."

"Certainly. Perhaps he will show me the room where poor Margaux met her end. Do you think he is keeping something from us?"

"I don't see any reason to mistrust him, but the more I think about it, the less reason I see for anyone here to kill Armstrong or Brookes. I can't see a motive, or even the hint of one, beyond a sudden, violent argument."

"Which we have no evidence of. Brookes was disliked, but not argumentative. Armstrong was, by all accounts, a quiet man."

"Right. So that leaves someone from the château. We've seen a lot of tunnels and hidden chambers, but maybe not all of them. See what you can find out. And be careful. If there's a secret, it's one worth killing for. Twice."

Madame Agard led us through the kitchen to the dining room, where the count sat with Juliet, Christine, and Christine's companion. They were sipping coffee, and it smelled like the real deal.

"This is Madame Morency," Juliet said. "She has agreed to help us."

"Thank you, ma'am," I said, taking the seat next to hers.

Grey-haired and thin, she wore a plain blue dress and jacket, the perfect outfit for dining with the local count. Her dark eyes went wide as she took in the sight of Kaz and me in our uniforms.

"*La libération?*" she asked, smiling as if to say she understood that was still to come.

"*La petite libération,*" I answered. "Madame Morency, can you describe the layout of the synagogue? It will be a great help."

"*Je ne parle pas anglais,*" Madame Morency said as she withdrew a folded sheet of paper from her jacket pocket.

"She has no English," Christine said, "but she is as good with a pencil as she is with a needle and thread."

She was. She'd sketched out a front view of her old synagogue. A three-story brick structure with small turrets at the corners, easy to spot from the street. The third floor was an attic shaped by a peaked slate roof, with rounded windows at each end.

Below the drawing was a layout of the two floors. Translating, Juliet explained that the attic was one large room. The basement was divided into storage areas, mostly old furniture and the usual junk that collected dust and cobwebs in any basement.

"Is there a back entrance? Any way up into the attic from the outside?" I asked. Madame Morency answered Juliet's queries as she marked a spot on the side of the building.

"Yes, there is a rear door," Juliet said. "It was always kept locked. The rabbi's office was off the entrance, and she guesses the office will still be in use. There is no way to get up to the attic except through a stairway next to that office."

"What's that mark?" Kaz asked. Madame Agard poured us coffee. Mixed with chicory, from the taste of it. Still, it gave me a jolt.

"*Le charbon,*" Madame Morency said. Count Vasseur stood and poured a brandy for her, which she accepted with a nod.

"The coal chute," the count explained, looking over her shoulder as she drew another building next to the synagogue. "In the alley."

Madame Morency spoke with the count, then raised her glass in a toast and downed the rest of the brandy.

"She says her husband was responsible for repairs to the synagogue. The lock for the coal chute had gone missing, and it was his job to replace it. Fortunately for us, he was a busy man and never got around to it," the count explained.

"Don't you think the *Milice* would have replaced it?" I asked.

"I put that question to her. She asked who would be fool enough to sneak into the *Milice* headquarters?" Count Vasseur laughed, and Madame Morency joined in. The lady had a point.

I told her *merci* and gave Kaz a nod toward the count. He got the message, patting my arm as he passed me to accept a brandy. Tough assignment. Juliet and Christine brought me into the kitchen, where Madame Agard had a long wool coat and a slouch hat for me.

"You will have to sit in the backseat, since the compartment will be taken up by our silent passenger," Christine said. "It is not a long drive into Dreux, and there were no checkpoints on the way in."

"Why the back?" I asked, trying on the coat. It was short in the sleeves and smelled of mothballs. I wouldn't pass muster as a civilian for long, but it would do as long as we weren't stopped.

"Because I shall be in the front with Christine," Juliet said. "It is too dangerous for anyone else to go, and you will need help with the body. Be glad I'm letting you come along at all."

"But it's my idea," I said, following as she opened the cupboard door.

"And it's my network, and Christine is our Resistance contact. It may be your macabre scheme, but we are your best bet for getting you there."

"And back, I hope."

"One thing at a time, Billy," Christine said with a smile. "I like your plan. We get the Germans at the throat of the *Milice*, then we go after the SS. Delightful."

Not exactly how I thought about it, but the notion did have a certain charm. With help from Babcock and Fawcett, we carried Brookes's body out of the ice pit and around to Christine's gasogene automobile, stashed out of sight in the stable. Fortunately, rigor mortis had passed, and his slight frame was easy to maneuver into the compartment.

"Well, I can't say he was a good man, but I'm sorry he had to die like that," Fawcett said. "This might be the most useful thing the pitiful bastard ever did." With that, he turned on his heel and left.

"Don't judge him too harshly," Babcock said. "It's a terrible feeling when someone you rely on lets you down. Hard for some to deal with. Good luck, all of you."

"No one seems to spare any feelings for this young man," Christine said as she started the car.

"It's a long story," I said, climbing into the back. "What's the plan?"

"We drive to the library, which is now closed. We wait until dark, after the curfew. At eleven o'clock, the *Maquis* will attack the rail line. That is when we will approach the headquarters."

"How far is it?"

"Perhaps a quarter of a mile," Juliet said. "The library is on the rue des Marchebeaux, north of the rue de Vernouillet where the synagogue is. The rail line crosses that road about five hundred meters south, where it branches off to the south and west."

"An excellent spot for sabotage," Christine said, flexing her hands on the steering wheel until her knuckles went white. "When the charges go off on both lines, the *Milice* will certainly come to investigate. Usually the *Maquis* scatter, but tonight they will remain and fight."

"For ten minutes," Juliet said. "Then they disappear into the woods on the other side of the rail line. The *Milice* will probably return to their headquarters as soon as the threat is gone."

"And the Germans?" I asked, slouching in the backseat as we left the long driveway behind and motored down a quiet country lane.

"The security garrison is based at the *préfecture*, on the far side of the river which runs through Dreux. We have an ambush set up which will delay them, but only briefly. The *Maquis* have orders to stall the *Boche*, but not to engage in battle. The biggest problem we will have is dealing with any *Milice* who might remain in the headquarters," Christine said.

If we had to deal with even a single one, it would be a disaster. We had to get in and out without anyone being aware of our entry. Otherwise, the presence of a corpse could be chalked up to another fight with the *Maquis* and a downed flier who'd thrown in with them. We were each armed with a pistol, but that was only in case things went south. Our best bet was to rely on luck, the *Maquis*, and the *Milice* doing exactly what we expected them to do.

Luck, at least, was with us on the road into Dreux. A convoy of trucks passed by in the other lane. The German soldiers looked bored, leaning on their rifles as the canvas flapped around them. It was a fine evening for a drive, but they didn't look like they were enjoying it. I had a brief glimpse of sullen grey faces under the shadows of their helmets.

"They take to the roads as night falls. To avoid your fighter planes," Christine said, pointing to a black-and-white signpost at an intersection: *zur Normandie Front*

"Were those SS troopers?" I asked, craning my neck to watch the trucks vanish around a curve, hopefully to be dispatched by the Resistance or Allied aircraft before they got into the fight.

"No, that was a *Luftwaffe* unit; you can tell by the blue uniforms. The Germans are running out of aircraft, so they turn their ground crews into infantry," Juliet said. "Not very good infantry, either."

"We've learned where the SS *Hitlerjugend* are bivouacked," Christine said. "They will not escape unscathed."

"Unscathed sounds good to me right now," I said, turning up my collar as we entered Dreux proper, weaving through narrow streets with shuttered brick and stone buildings set only a few feet back from the road. A German soldier on a motorcycle roared by, but no one else was to be seen. It was almost curfew—time for the French to be at home, curtains drawn, with no lights showing. I felt exposed even as I huddled in the backseat, hat pulled down low over my eyes, a dead man at my back.

"Here is the library," Christine said. It was two stories of white granite and tall windows. Twin columns flanked the front door, with *Bibliothèque Publique* inscribed above. She took a side street that led to the rear of the building and parked the car out of sight.

"Come, we will wait inside," she said, looking around to be sure we hadn't been spotted. Behind us, buildings stood silent, their doors and windows barred against the night. The last rays of sunlight caught the rooftops, leaving the illusion of brightness before fading into dusk and darkness, our most trusted allies.

Christine turned the key. The lock released with a metal *clunk* that sounded like thunder in the quiet evening air. The heavy door swung open, and we slipped in, entering a wood-paneled hallway leading to a work area behind a counter. The tall windows let in the fading light.

"This is where I hear a lot of gossip and occasionally some useful information," Christine said. "See, there is the section of German-language materials." One bookcase to the right of the counter was filled with books in German. Comfortable chairs and a low table were conveniently located close to the checkout counter.

"We will have to set the record straight once the Germans are on the run," Juliet said. "People with little else to do have criticized Christine for her kindness to the Occupation. Little do they know."

"It is nothing," Christine said, waving her hand to dismiss such silliness. As Murat, she faced many more lethal dangers than wagging tongues. "We have a few hours to wait. You should rest."

I was too keyed up to think about rest. I walked around the main reading room, running my fingers across the spines of books and wondering if the Nazis had gotten around to burning books in France the way they had in Berlin. It was a crazy world they wanted to build, one where ideas and words were so dangerous they had to be incinerated.

I wandered back into the German area and plopped down into one of the comfy chairs. Had Zeller himself rested in this seat? What was it like for a Kraut like him, enjoying years of easy duty with the Occupation, while his pals suffered and died in hordes on the Eastern front? Knowing that it was only a matter of time before the Allies rolled through France and sent him hightailing it back to the Fatherland and the approaching Russians? Not a pleasant thought, I imagined.

For him. Me, I enjoyed the idea of helping him on his way. I tried to relax, watching the shadows lengthen and darken. I closed my eyes.

"Billy," Juliet said, shaking my shoulder. "It's time." It was fully dark as we walked into Christine's office. The curtains were drawn, and Juliet shut the door as Christine aimed a small flashlight at a map of the town.

"Our route," she said, tracing a line from the library to rue Vernouillet. We had to begin on the street to our front, but most of the path took us down side streets and alleys. "We stay in the shadows. If anyone sees us, most will look the other way."

"And those who don't?" I asked.

"No one dares venture out. If they have a telephone, they will call the police. Depending on who answers, they may or may not act. In any case, who would think to look among the *Milice*?"

"Only a crazy man. How soon?"

"We should begin now. The explosives will be set off at eleven o'clock," Christine said. I checked my watch. Quarter to eleven. Time to deliver a body.

I ditched the coat and hat in the car. A disguise wasn't going to help if the Germans spotted me carrying a corpse after curfew. There was a damp chill in the air, but I figured I'd be sweating bullets in no time. Then I wished I hadn't put it quite like that.

I pulled Brookes from the hidden compartment, glad he was still wrapped in a sheet so I wouldn't have to look him in the face as I gave him a tour of Dreux's back streets before dumping him down a coal chute. I hoisted him over my shoulders in a fireman's carry and followed Christine, Juliet bringing up the rear. We ran across the street, our heels sounding a drumbeat against the cobblestones. Then we ducked into an alleyway, waiting to see if anyone took notice. The dark quiet was complete except for the sound of my own breathing.

Christine scurried through the alley, coming out in a street barely wide enough for a single vehicle. It was a long way to the next street, no exits in sight. On one side was a bare wall, the back of a two-story structure. Along the other ran a series of barred windows leading to a corner where the street emptied into a wider thoroughfare. Juliet took out her revolver, gesturing for us to proceed. Christine went ahead, a Walther P38 automatic held at her side—the same type of weapon used to kill Lieutenant Armstrong. But I had no energy to think about that, what with the second victim bouncing against my shoulders and feeling heavier by the minute.

It was difficult to run with Brookes's dead weight. I had to slow down to a fast walk, and watched Christine approach the corner ahead. She flattened against the wall and checked to the left, then the right. She signaled, her head still at the brickwork edge of the building. I thought it was to come forward, but I made out too late that she was making a stay-back motion. I stopped a few feet from her, Juliet right behind me. We froze.

I heard footsteps.

Christine held her Walther ready. Juliet cocked her revolver. I thought I might throw Brookes at whoever was coming. *Milice*, the local cops, or a Kraut security patrol—it made little difference. Armed ladies and an American GI carrying a dead Canadian would rouse the suspicion of even the most anti-Nazi *gendarme*.

The footsteps halted. The brim of a wool cap appeared, followed by a face in shadows. Christine put her pistol on his cheekbone.

"Qui êtes-vous?" she whispered, asking who he was.

"Personne, mademoiselle. Vous?" He was no one. So were we.

"Allez!" Christine commanded, satisfied that this was not the *Milice*. Two men darted by, each carrying a sack slung over their shoulders, not giving my burden a second glance.

"Black market or burglars," Christine said with a shrug. "I doubt they will raise an alarm."

We crossed a small bridge, then darted and weaved through the streets until Christine called a halt. We took refuge on the steps of a shop entrance. She pointed down the street, and I saw the old synagogue, the small turrets at the corners a clear landmark. I squatted and leaned against the shop window, glad of the rest. Juliet glanced at her watch and nodded. Christine smiled.

An explosion ripped the night, followed by another, a crack followed by an intense booming sound like thunder. Lesser sounds punctuated the air as debris scattered from the blast, wood and rock from the railbed falling like hailstones. A red glow lingered in the distance, then faded as at least a dozen armed *Milice* poured from the building, some pulling on shirts and the others racing to the site of the attack.

Another five or six waited out front, weapons at the ready, flashlight beams searching the shadows cast by the waning moon. Christine held up her hand.

We waited.

Gunfire erupted. Bursts from submachine guns and the crack of rifles blossomed and grew as the ambush was sprung and the *Milice* returned fire. A man exited the headquarters, adjusted his beret, and signaled for the others to follow him to the battle. Was that Pierre Rivet, the leader of the *Milice*? And what had he been doing inside? Telephoning the Germans?

"Now," Christine whispered, waving her gun hand forward. We skittered along the sidewalk, seeking shelter in doorways and an alley we shared with a growling dog at work on an overturned garbage can. We hustled out before he got distracted from dinner and began barking, hurrying straight across to the side street that abutted the headquarters. At the end of the building was the coal chute. It had a heavy iron door two feet wide with a handle that ran the width of it. I could see where the lock would go, but thankfully Madame Morency was right. Who would enter the lair of the dreaded *Milice* for a few pieces of coal?

Juliet gripped the handle and pulled the door forward. Stiff on its hinges, it creaked and groaned. I set Brookes down and motioned that I'd go first. There were no objections. I felt around inside, expecting to find the chute to slide down, like we had at our place back in Boston. My hand clutched air. The rattle of gunfire increased, and I was conscious of the ten minutes ticking by. I stuck my head into the pitch-black basement, getting my shoulders through so I could chance a quick look with the flashlight. I flicked on the beam and shielded it as best I could.

The basement was a jumble of junk. I switched off the light, trying to accustom my eyes to the complete darkness. I turned it on again. The junk wasn't junk. There was an upright piano, a tables and chairs, upholstered couches, armoires, china, candlesticks, small statues, stacks of paintings, all crammed into every square inch of the cellar. Below me was an ornate writing desk next to a fancy side table with a set of cut-crystal glasses on a silver tray. One step, and I'd send everything crashing.

"No room," I whispered after I wriggled out. Shots still rang out, but they were random. "The place is filled with loot. Expensive loot."

"*Bâtards!*" Christine muttered. "From the houses of Jews and *Résistants*, no doubt. Now what?"

"We walk in the front door, of course," Juliet said, standing up straight. "I'll bet Rivet took everyone with him. Safety in numbers. Come, as if we own the place."

There was nothing to do but follow. I hoisted Brookes over one shoulder and prayed that no dutiful fascist had taken the time to lock the door. Hands stuffed in her pockets, Juliet sauntered out from the side street, took the few steps up to the entrance, and grabbed the handle.

It turned. Juliet shut the door quietly behind us, and the latch gave off a metallic *snap* drowned out by a renewed volley of gunfire and the sound of grenades. The dimly lit foyer gave way to an open space, likely where the congregation had peaceably worshipped for decades. Now it was a warren of desks and tables, the raised platform up front an armory. I knew that was where the rabbi read the Torah—I remembered that much from going to my pal Abe Tascher's bar mitzvah. It held a Bren gun that had been in the midst of being cleaned. The *Milice* were mainly armed with weapons captured at supply drops, adding insult to lethal injury. Abe was flying B-24s out of Italy, last I heard, and I hoped he was hitting the goddamn Krauts hard.

A tap on the arm shook me out of my thoughts. Juliet pointed to an open door at the far end of the room. We headed that way as I gingerly maneuvered Brookes through the aisles, trying not to knock anything over.

"Let's look for a door to the attic," I whispered as we came to a halt. "That's a logical hiding place." Christine nodded and held the door fully open, one hand on the latch and the other gripping her Walther. I crossed the threshold into a small chamber where coats and uniform jackets were hung. It opened onto a wide hallway that ran to the back of the building. I saw the rear entrance, and the open door to what must have been the office Madame Morency described. Light spilled out into the hall.

Someone spoke.

"Allô, allô," followed by the repeated clicking of a telephone receiver. They'd left someone behind, and with our luck tonight, he was calling for reinforcements.

Juliet pointed to the door opposite his, then pointed up. The way to the attic. There wasn't much of an option, unless you counted on running back through the streets with a dead body as a swell notion. I set Brookes down as quietly as I could, letting the shots and the noise of the telephone mask the inevitable thump. I drew my pistol and strode into the office.

He wore the dark tunic of the *Milice*, their trademark oversized beret flopped down over one ear. That's where I hit him. One hard swing from the butt of my pistol, and he was down for the count, if not the decade. I put the phone back on the cradle.

"Upstairs. Hurry," Juliet said, giving my handiwork a quick glance. "Is he dead?"

"No. Don't think so, at least," I said, picking up Brookes for what I hoped was the last time.

Christine glanced in, then took the lead going up the attic stairs. Gutsy, since someone could be waiting. She got to the landing and waved us up. The coast was clear. Blankets were hung across the two round windows, and a single bulb glowed at the end of a cord. Four cots and a couple of chairs were arranged under one window, the rest of the attic taken up by boxes and the usual attic debris. No loot.

"Look here, wine bottles and tins of food," Juliet said. "They must sleep here on night duty."

"Or this is a hiding place for Allied airmen," Christine said. "What do you think?"

"Perfect. But we have to hide the body. As if one of the *Milice* killed him in an argument and had to leave in a hurry once the shooting started." I was beginning to think this plan had a chance. I carried Brookes over to the far end of the attic and unwrapped the sheets that covered him.

He looked so young. I couldn't think about his cowardly act thousands of feet in the air, his bomber shot up and on fire. He was only a kid; that was all I could see. I hoped Fawcett would see that someday as well. I stacked boxes around Brookes and draped one of the sheets over him as if it were a hasty attempt at hiding a body.

"That is good," Christine said. "I am sorry, young man." She went quiet for a moment, then motioned with her pistol. "Come. We have to deal with the *milicien* downstairs. We cannot leave him."

"We have to leave now," I said as we clattered down the stairs. "What does it matter?"

"Because it will be obvious," she said. "The guard is knocked out, and a mysterious body is discovered upstairs? Not even the *Boche* are so stupid."

"But if the guard deserts, and a body is found, he is of course the culprit," Juliet said. It made sense.

"What do we do with him?" I said.

"Take him with us. I know how to deal with him. But you carry him, Billy." Christine smiled until the gunshots stopped.

"Let's go," I said, grabbing the unconscious man. The sturdy, well-built unconscious man. "Take his coat and weapon." Juliet took his jacket and a Sten gun that was draped over the chair. Christine rifled through the desk drawers and found a small cashbox. It was unlocked, and she grabbed a fistful of francs. Her grin returned.

We went out the back. I had to stop and balance my load, doing the fireman's carry again. This guy had fifty pounds on Brookes, and I felt every one. We crossed a street moments before two truckloads of Germans flew by, reinforcements who'd be too late. The good news was, no one was going to dare look out their windows with Krauts on the streets and the sound of gunfire still ringing in their ears.

"Stop here," Christine said, as we came to the bridge we'd crossed on the way in. "Our thief is about to meet with an accident." She eyed the steps leading down to the river. "It flows into the Eure River. With any luck, he'll drift miles away. If not, it will seem that he ran into terrorists who robbed and killed him."

"You want to execute him?" I said, his breathing body still across my shoulders.

"Yes. I do. For what they did in Coudray, if nothing else. This is what we do with the *Milice*. They are worse than the Germans. They are traitors who prey on their own kind. Now no more talk, into the water with him. Pretend you killed him when you struck him, if that makes you feel better."

Juliet nodded toward the river. I knew they were right. But they weren't the ones doing it.

I took the stone steps to the water's edge and shrugged the heavy load off my shoulders. Blood matted his hair. His mouth gaped open. I was glad he wasn't young. I put him face down in the cold water and shoved him off into the rippling tributary, an easier death than he had meted out to others.

CHAPTER TWENTY-SIX

"AUSWEIS!"

I could hear the demand for identity papers from behind the backseat where I occupied Brookes's former spot. It was morning, and we were on our way back to the château. The roadblock wasn't surprising, not after last night's shootout in town. I could make out some Krauts chattering to one another, keyed up, excited and frightened, not knowing if the *Maquis* might strike again. I preferred bored Germans to jumpy ones. Christine and Juliet answered in lilting and jaunty tones, not a care in the world, just two French girls out on an errand.

A hand thumped on the rooftop. I clutched my pistol, but it was only the signal to move on. Christine stepped on it, and I don't think I breathed until I heard the crunch of the gravel drive under the tires and felt the automobile brake to a halt at the rear of the château. I unfolded myself from the hiding place and followed Juliet and Christine into the kitchen. The first thing I saw was Meyer, a basket of baguettes in his hands. He was wearing an old brown sweater over his wool shirt, frayed at the cuffs and dirty.

"What are you doing here?" Juliet asked, her gaze darting about, looking for Madame Agard.

"I came for breakfast," he said. "You and Sonya weren't around, so I wanted to see what we had to eat. Madame Agard just took these out of the oven."

"Of course," Juliet said. "Sorry. It's been a long night. I didn't realize you were so familiar with the tunnels."

"Oh, I keep my eyes open, ma'am." Meyer winked. He was one of those guys who sounded the most insulting when they were being polite.

"Where'd this come from?" I asked, fingering the worn fabric of his sweater.

"The count. He gave us some old clothes a while ago. Armstrong had this one, but I figured it was up for grabs. You got a problem with that?"

"No, merely curious," I said. "Did Armstrong have any other stuff?" It would be normal procedure to check a victim's effects, but I hadn't thought of these guys as having anything but the clothes on their backs.

"Nah, only this sweater and an extra pair of socks, courtesy of the count. I gotta go. The guys are hungry," Meyer said. "Open the door, will ya?"

I went ahead of him into the cupboard, pressing the panel that released the secret door. As he passed, a smattering of blue on one elbow caught my eye. Where had I seen that before?

I shut the door. Then Madame Agard burst into the kitchen, one hand held over her heart as if it might burst. "Sonya has been arrested," she said. *"Dieu nous aide."*

Never mind us. God help Sonya.

"I must go," Christine said. "There are people to warn."

"Be careful," Juliet said, hugging her. "Take no chances yourself."

"To live is to take chances," she said. "When I telephone, I will tell you the book you wanted is still not available. If all is well, tell me you will wait for it."

She rushed out as we hurried to the count's library. Kaz and Topper were already there, worried looks on their faces.

"What happened?" Juliet asked, glancing out the window as if the Gestapo were coming up the drive.

"I received a message this morning from a friend at the

gendarmerie in Épernon. Sonya was apprehended at a known meeting place for Resistance contacts," Count Vasseur said, his voice weary.

"We have forty-eight hours at best," Juliet said.

"What do you mean?" Kaz asked.

"No one is expected to withstand Gestapo torture," the count answered. "We expect no more than forty-eight hours. Two days is enough time for everyone else in the network to disappear. After that, the captured agent may tell all they know."

"If they haven't already," Juliet said. "No one can predict how long they will hold out." She knew more than most.

"What will you do, Count Vasseur?" I asked. The rest of us could scatter and wait for the war to come our way, but not this elderly gentleman.

"What I can, young man. What I can. Today I will send Madame Agard away with little Justine. I have already sent the other staff home, giving them the long weekend. But now tell me, were you successful?"

"Yes, the body is hidden in the attic. You can tell Zeller that Rivet is using the *Milice* headquarters to hide escaping Allied airmen," I said. "Any sense in asking him to help get Sonya out?"

"Sadly, no," Count Vasseur said. "That would only draw attention to the château. Until our guests depart, we cannot afford to take such a risk."

"We need to inform London," Juliet said from her post by the window. The Madonna in blue hung over her shoulder. They both looked sorrowful. "Did the midnight sked come in?"

"Sked?" Kaz asked.

"Scheduled transmission," Topper said. "Yes. It's waiting for you to decode. If you want to transmit a message now, I'll take the radio a mile or so into the woods. No sense letting the Jerries track our signal here."

"Good idea," Juliet said, facing us. She took a deep breath, then focused on what had to be done. If she was thinking of what Sonya might be enduring at this very moment, those thoughts had to be put away. "Topper, get one of the men to go with you, and tell the others to gather in the salon. And to take it seriously this time. I'll code a brief message while you get the radio packed up. Billy, Kaz, keep a lookout up on the top floor. It will give us a few moments' head start if the Germans come. Count Vasseur, make the call to Zeller. We should proceed as planned. There's always the chance she was picked up in a routine roundup."

When being picked up as a hostage or for slave labor transport to Germany was the good news, the bad news was very, very bad.

"It may not be the Gestapo," Count Vasseur said, reaching for the telephone. "If it was the *Abwehr*, it could be worse. For us, that is."

"What do you mean?" I asked.

"The Gestapo gets what it wants by torture for the most part," Juliet said, locking eyes with the count. "They call their cells 'kitchens,' to give you some idea of what happens there. But the *Abwehr* uses skillful interrogation. They promise life and protection if you betray your network. Money, for those who care to earn it that way. All backed up by the fact that they will turn you over to the Gestapo if you fail to cooperate."

"They are skillful, indeed," Count Vasseur said. "Now excuse me. I must act as a Judas myself."

"I'm going to check on Switch," I said to Kaz as we left the room. "How are things here?"

"Everything was fine until this news," Kaz said as we descended the steps into the grand hall. "Meyer has been testy, or I should say testier than usual."

"Do you think he suspects anything?" I stopped in the center of the empty room, looking up at the portrait of the first count. The eyes *were* odd, at that.

"I can't see how he would," Kaz said. "I don't believe Switch would say anything. He begged me for news once he had me alone. All I could suggest was to hope for good news in that sked."

Ever the lover of jargon, Kaz had picked up a new word.

"Well, remember, the walls have ears." I stopped in my tracks. That reminded me of something. What was it?

"Don't be long, Billy. I'll be on the top floor, first door on the right."

"Sure. Say, Kaz, did you mention to Switch that I'd been a cop before the war?"

"No, I didn't. I am still keeping up the fiction that you are a disgraced scoundrel, and no friend of mine. Hurry up, please."

"Okay," I said as Kaz took the main staircase two at a time. I looked back at the painted count. What had Vincent said? Something about bringing ghosts back to life. I moved on, more concerned at the moment that we all might be ghosts by nightfall.

I found everyone in the salon, Meyer distributing the baguettes, Dogbite pouring water from a jug.

"Bread and water, that's what we're down to," Meyer said. "And look at this bread! It's grey and soft. When we gettin' outta here anyway?"

"Madame Agard makes it with potatoes," Dogbite said. "And rye. The lady does the best she can, but I have to say, it'd make better moonshine than bread." That got a laugh and shut Meyer up.

"Once we get the message decoded, we'll know more," I said. "For now, everyone stay put. Hopefully we'll be on the move soon." Maybe one step ahead of the Krauts, but I thought it better to leave that part out. I glanced at Switch, who gave me the slightest of nods and looked away. Meyer kept his eyes on Switch as he ripped a piece off his baguette. Then he looked at me, the wheels turning.

"You get lost coming back here, Meyer?" I said to distract him. "You left the kitchen awhile ago."

"Not that long," he said. "You know how it is down there. One wrong turn, and it gets confusing fast."

"Yeah, and dangerous, too. You heard about Sonya?" I said.

"Bad luck," Fawcett said. "She was a good woman."

"She's not dead yet," Babcock said. "Maybe it's a false alarm. You know, like a mission being scrubbed at the last minute. Happens all the time." It did, and so did the desire for normalcy, the wish for my friends and comrades not to die horrible deaths, the belief that it couldn't happen to them. Or to me.

"Did one of you boys volunteer to go out with Topper?" I asked.

"Yeah, me," Meyer said, gulping water as he stood up. He grabbed a half baguette and headed into the corridor. "This is his breakfast. I ain't stealing rations, boys." He winked at Switch, snickering at the inside joke. I was surprised he'd offered to go; this was the first time he'd done anything constructive. Maybe he wanted some fresh air. I didn't really care as long as he watched Topper's back.

I followed him to the radio room, where Juliet was hunched over sheets of paper. Topper snapped the suitcase closed, ready to go. Juliet finished a line of letters and checked her handiwork as Meyer grabbed a Sten gun and a couple of magazines.

"This tells them Sonya has been arrested, and we will disperse within forty-eight hours," she said, handing Topper the paper. "I asked for instructions by six o'clock, before our regular sked. Hurry, will you?"

"We'll be quick, ma'am," Meyer replied. "Quicker than a preacher to the Sunday ham, as Dogbite might put it."

"And at least a mile away," Topper said. "We can't transmit from the same place twice, especially not now. We'll be back in a couple of hours."

"I'm sorry," I said, as soon as they'd left. "I know you and Sonya were friends. Are friends."

"In a way, yes," she said. "Sonya and Juliet are friendly, but who are they? Figments of the imagination, the dreams of SOE officers smoking cigarettes and drinking tea, complaining about the long hours. So proud of their creations, these false identities. False people."

"You're not false," I said, worried as I watched her hand tremble.

"I'm not in a Gestapo cell. Where if one desires life, the falseness must be cast aside. Or stay true to the falseness, even facing torture and death. What monstrous choices, Billy."

"I don't know what I'd do. I'd like to think I couldn't live with myself if I betrayed my friends, but who can say for sure?" I said.

"Precisely. And now all our lives are at risk. The Noble network is a failure. What good are we if we can't help these men?"

"Look, we have some time. After we get the message back tonight, we'll scatter if we have to. You still have a radio and Topper. Not to mention Kaz and me, as long as we can stay."

"You're right. It's simply that I was beginning to think we'd make it through. A dangerous notion for an agent. You give me hope."

I reached for her hand. It no longer trembled. Her palm was warm and soft.

"I have to decode this," she said, pulling her hand back and holding it before her face, as if to ward off the feelings assaulting her.

"What kind of code is it?" I asked, strictly business.

"A poem code," she said, spreading out clean sheets of paper on the table. "SOE used to use well-known poems, but that gave the Germans an edge. If they recognized a snippet, they'd have the whole poem. So Leo Marks, our codes officer, started writing original poems. Most of them were funny or incredibly risqué, mainly to make them easier to remember. Each message indicates which of the words in the poem are to be used to encrypt the message, identifying them by number. So if the message starts with '10,' that means the tenth word will be used. If that word starts with E, then every E stands for A. And so on. Very clever. Almost foolproof."

"Is the poem he wrote for you funny or filthy?" I said, trying to lighten the mood. "Should I be jealous?"

"It's rather special," she said, and recited it in a low, whispered voice, like a prayer.

> *The life that I have*
> *Is all that I have*
> *And the life that I have*
> *Is yours.*
> *The love that I have*
> *Of the life that I have*
> *Is yours and yours and yours.*
> *A sleep I shall have*
> *A rest I shall have*
> *Yet death will be but a pause.*
> *For the peace of my years*
> *In the long green grass*
> *Will be yours and yours and yours.*

"My God," was all I could utter.

"Leo wrote it for his girlfriend. She died in a plane crash. I think of you, Billy, whenever I recite it to myself. It's an odd comfort, to think about dying and leaving the gift of memory behind. Sometimes I envision you standing over my grave, the long green grass blowing in the wind. You smile, thinking of something we've shared. And then I smile. Strange how war makes one think of death as a rest, isn't it? Now leave, please, before I can't go on."

A tear made a tiny drop on the blank paper. The fibers soaked it up and it vanished, like a false identity long forgotten.

I jogged across the back lawn, knowing that the staff had been sent home. It felt odd to be aboveground, exposed, however briefly, under the morning light. I stopped in to see Count Vasseur, tossing off a wave to the painting of the old count in the grand hall on my way. Vasseur was alone with Vincent.

"How did the call go?" I asked as Vincent stepped behind his employer, his hands folded respectfully.

"Very well, Sergeant. Major Zeller said he would investigate immediately. He was quite upset by the severing of the rail lines last night, and wondered if perhaps Rivet and his men were in league with the Resistance! Laughable, but it will keep him busy for some time and cause the *Milice* a good deal of trouble."

"He won't reveal the information came from you, will he?"

"No, certainly not. He has been discreet in the past, and I expect he will continue. He is not unintelligent."

"Is he a Nazi? A fanatic?" I asked, strolling over to the Madonna for a closer look.

"No," the count said, walking from his desk to stand by me. "He has a degree in art history from the University of Heidelberg. Not that the Nazis don't fashion themselves as art lovers. But he says he joined the *Abwehr* because it is home to many who do not worship Herr Hitler."

"That's what I've heard as well. I've also heard that the Germans are looting art from all over France. How have you managed to hold onto yours?"

"By having an unremarkable collection, except for this one," Count Vasseur said. "*Blue Madonna*, by Carlo Dolci. Italian, seventeenth century. Beautiful, isn't she?"

"Yes. I don't know much about art, but I can tell this is something special." Mary's face, serene and humble at the same time, was surrounded by a veil of lush royal blue, almost luminous against her pale skin and downcast eyes.

"Vincent was doing repairs to the frame when the Germans

came calling. He had temporarily hung one of his own paintings in its place. A landscape he'd done recently, nothing the Germans would even bother with. They mainly appropriate property from Jewish homes, or from political opponents, but they also make offers to buy whatever they want. At ridiculously low prices, but which only a fool would refuse, with armed men at the ready."

"They didn't take anything?"

"Other than an inventory of my paintings, no. Vincent hid the Madonna, and since they have not returned, I trust they found nothing of interest. The portraits of French noblemen apparently hold little interest for the master race." The count smiled at his little joke and led me to the staircase. "Vincent will show you to where the baron is on watch. We are making arrangements for Madame Agard and Justine, so please excuse us."

"Where?" I asked.

"It is better that you do not know in case of the worst," he said with a shrug, as if to apologize for bringing up such an unpleasant topic.

He was right, of course. I might rat everyone out in minutes. I wasn't dumb enough to think it would be easy to play the hero, not all alone in a Gestapo "kitchen." As I mounted the steps to Kaz's top-floor lookout post, I thought about what I might try. Profess ignorance of anything vital? No, they'd never believe it, and they'd be pulling fingernails in two shakes. Lie. I was a good liar. I could give them the location of a phony arms cache or parachute drop. A lie would buy time, but for what?

Nothing. Torture, betrayal, a bullet in the head. Those were the likely outcomes, and salvation would not be in the cards.

"Anything happening, Kaz?" He was seated by a tall open window, the warm spring breeze wafting in.

"No. I can hear trucks on the main road, but nothing out of the ordinary. Is Topper sending the news to London?"

"Yeah. Meyer volunteered to go with him. Tell me, did you learn anything about the history of the château?"

"Only that the first count, Frédérick-Charles Maronneau, was a Huguenot from Toulon. They were French Protestants, you know."

"The Huguenots," I said, trying to act as if I did know.

"Yes. There were religious wars and persecutions over the centuries. The Catholic majority persecuted them horribly. Frédérick-Charles converted to Catholicism and was given this land and his title by the king as recompense for his actions. He was a rich textile merchant, and the count alluded to a sizable bribe as well."

"He built this place himself?"

"There was already a *petit château*, as the count called it. But Frédérick-Charles enlarged it and added the tunnels, discovering the Druid temple along the way. That's as much as he would say. I suspect the tunnels were used to hide Huguenots fleeing persecution."

"So his conversion was a cover?"

"That would be my guess, but the count was not very forthcoming. Is the history of the family relevant to our situation?"

"It might be," I said. "I'd like to know how many people know about it, for starters. But that can wait. First we have the Krauts to worry about, and whatever orders London sent us. Juliet is decoding last night's message now."

"It must be hard on her," Kaz said, pulling aside the curtain as it blew in. "First their wireless operator died, then Sonya is picked up."

"Adrien, wasn't it? The wireless operator?" I stood back from the window, not wanting to be spotted. If the Germans were watching the château, they'd have no reason to think we'd heard about Sonya yet.

"Yes. He took his cyanide capsule, as Major Harding told us."

"I wonder where he was," I said. "He obviously had his wireless with him."

"Perhaps putting some distance between the château and his signal. As Topper is doing."

"Topper and Meyer are heading off into the woods. I wonder if Adrien was doing the same, and how the Germans caught him."

"Perhaps he was taking the wireless to the Resistance," Kaz said, tapping his chin. "But why would he do that? Far easier for the *Maquis* to bring a message to him and transmit from nearby. No, it must have been somewhere close."

"I never thought to ask," I said, running the possibilities through my mind. "Until now. I'll be right back."

I darted downstairs into the kitchen. Glancing out the window, I spotted Vincent helping Madame Agard and Justine into a horse cart. He climbed in after them and snapped the reins. The ancient nag moved slowly, carrying the old woman and child to some safe place, if there was such a thing in occupied France. I went through the cupboard door, lighting one of the candles kept on the ledge.

The tunnels had become more familiar, but I still felt a sense of chaos and fear, deep underground with only a flickering candle for light. I felt my way, one hand on the cold limestone wall, stepping carefully to avoid a fall on the uneven floor. One wrong turn, one sudden gust, and I'd be a prisoner of the darkness, alone and disoriented. Two men had been murdered down here, the damp walls and clammy air making the narrow chambers a perfect crypt.

But now I was sensing a third murder, one committed in the open air.

I made my way through the Druid temple, wondering how many people in the area knew about it. Was it common knowledge, or simply a legend, like the White Giant?

I made it into the main tunnel connecting the salon and the living quarters. I left the candle and made my way through the dimly lit corridor, finding Juliet still at work decoding the sked. "Do you know where Topper was headed?"

"What? Into the forest, of course, Billy."

"No, I mean exactly where?"

"Other than a mile or so out, I have no idea. Why?"

I wasn't sure I could put all my suspicions into words yet. "What about Adrien? Was he in the forest when they grabbed him?"

"No. We decided it was too dangerous to keep using the wireless here. If the Germans got close to tracking the signal, it would be instantly obvious that the château was involved."

"Because there's no one else around."

"Exactly. So Christine made arrangements for him to be housed in an apartment in the town center. The owners had fled south in 1940 and were never heard from again. We thought there would be safety in numbers."

"But he never made it?"

"Right. He was taken outside the apartment building. How did you know?"

"Because things are finally starting to make sense. I think Adrien's death is related to the murders here."

"What's going on, Billy? Why is all this happening?"

"I'm not entirely sure yet, but I'm beginning to see a pattern. I thought Topper might be in danger, but I guess I may be wrong about that. I'll still feel better if I look for him and Meyer."

"All right, but be careful. I'll finish the decoding, and we can talk when you get back. Do you want anyone to go with you?"

"Right now, I don't know who else to trust. You be careful, too." I leaned over and kissed her cheek. The salty tang of tears lingered on my lips as I went to search for Topper.

CHAPTER TWENTY-SEVEN

I HAD NO idea in what direction they'd gone, so I went straight up the nearest hill, figuring Topper would want some height for his aerial. Then the next hill, and the next, until I stood in a clearing, hands on my knees, gasping for breath. Thoughts kept zipping through my mind, daring me to make any sense out of them.

Switch saying he knew I was a cop before the war. The upstairs room that Count Vasseur didn't want to show Kaz. The spooky eyes in the painting of the first count. The ghost stories. Blue paint. Vincent and his art gallery. The survival of the Noble network while all others in contact with it were betrayed. With all the worry about what Sonya might be able to stand up to, I should have thought about the implications. Had no one talked? Maybe knowledge was so compartmentalized that only a few people would know who and where Noble was.

And finally, Adrien.

Adrien, the biggest mystery of all. He'd solved all the problems of betrayal and identity. One little pill, and no more falseness, no more fear, no gruesome tortures, no guilt. Simple. In an instant, he was out of the equation. Which was perhaps the plan. Or more precisely, his wireless was gone. Noble was isolated, cut off from all contact.

Until we showed up, and two men were murdered. I thought about what my dad always said about coincidence. It was the word people used when they couldn't see who was pulling the strings.

A branch snapped. Footsteps crackled on dried leaves. I drew my pistol and eased behind a tree, waiting as the sounds grew closer. I heard the exhale of breath, a groan of exhaustion. I stepped from behind the tree and leveled the pistol at the figure emerging from the brush.

"Bloody hell, Billy, put that down and help me," Topper said, staggering forward. Blood matted his hair and streamed down his neck. His hands were empty. I grabbed his arm and draped it around my shoulder.

"What happened?" I said, knowing the answer.

"Meyer, that bastard. He bashed me good while I was setting up the wireless. What the hell was he up to? Why take the radio?"

"You hadn't sent the message yet, had you?"

"No. I suppose he couldn't wait. Do you think he's off to do a deal with Zeller and trade the wireless? But for what?"

"The radio may be smashed and tossed in a ravine by now," I said. "He doesn't want the radio. That's the point."

"Make sense, Billy. Or stop talking. My head hurts."

I stopped talking and saved my breath for the hills. I wasn't entirely sure I could make proper sense of it anyway.

By the time we got into the tunnels, Topper was woozy. He slumped against me, and I held him up as we entered the salon. Everyone but Juliet was there. Kaz and Dogbite took Topper from me and sat him down as Babcock went off for a medical kit.

"What happened? Where's Meyer?" Switch asked. "Did you run into Krauts?"

"No. This is Meyer's work. He took the wireless, too. Lit off to parts unknown," I said.

"Meyer? He can be a bum, but why'd he clobber Topper and take the radio?" Dogbite said.

"Beats me," I said, keeping my theories to myself. "Does he know how to operate those things?"

"He could work the radio on the aircraft, but that's a different story from sending Morse code on one of those sets," Switch said. "Besides, who the hell would he radio even if he could?"

"If any of you have any ideas, now would be the time," Kaz said, using a damp towel to clean the blood from around Topper's wound. Silence and shrugs all around.

"Aren't you on watch?" I asked Kaz.

"There's been another development," he said. "Sonya has returned."

"Yeah, how d'ya like that?" Fawcett said. "Meyer takes off, and the Gestapo lets Sonya walk. I say we get the hell out of here. Either she sang to the Krauts, or Meyer will."

"Pipe down, Fawcett," Babcock said, returning with the kit and handing Kaz bandages. "It could have been a mistake. Even the Germans can mess up paperwork."

"The count does have a friend on the police force," Kaz said. "Perhaps he saw to her release." He glanced at me and raised an eyebrow. I didn't believe it, either, but the last thing we needed right now was panic.

"I'm sure Meyer just lost his head after being cooped up in here for so long," I said. "I need to tell Juliet. Where is she?"

"In the count's library, with Sonya," Kaz said. "I'll join you as soon as I get Topper settled. She finished the decoding, but Sonya's arrival took us all by surprise."

Funny, I wasn't all that shocked.

It was a classic cop move, releasing a suspect in the hopes that his pals would think he'd given them up. Usually used as a threat, but sometimes you had to follow through. Like when you wanted to flush out the bad guys from their hiding places. It worked, too, because the gang would make it their first order of business to come after the stool pigeon. Criminals expected their confederates to do their time and shut up if they were caught. Like SOE expected agents to take the pill or put up with torture for forty-eight hours.

No one was expected to walk out scot-free. But Sonya had.

I made for the kitchen, noting Sonya's bicycle leaning against the wall by the door. Had the yellow license plate given her away? Every bicycle was required to be registered and the owner's identity kept on file. But no—if they were looking for her, they wouldn't have let her go so quickly. It had to be a case of the wrong place at the wrong time. Her identity papers were good, even if they were *faux faux* documents created by the SOE. What had she felt as she pedaled home? Relief, or did the fear of being followed gnaw at her?

In the library, relief was not the dominant theme.

Count Vasseur sat at his desk, worry creasing his brow. Sonya sat opposite him, the contents of her purse emptied onto the floor. By the look of her clothes, she'd been searched. Juliet stood over her, a Walther in one hand and a slip of paper in the other.

"What's going on?" I said.

"They don't believe me," Sonya said, tears streaking her face, her eyes searching for sympathy.

"It is difficult to comprehend how you could be picked up by the Germans at a letter drop site and then released only hours later," Count Vasseur said.

"And with this in your possession," Juliet said, waving a document in Sonya's face. "An *Ausweis*, good until curfew tonight. Signed by an *Abwehr* officer. Did you forget to destroy it?"

"No! They gave me that when I was released. They actually apologized and drove me out of town. I know it sounds strange, but it is what happened. Please believe me."

"We can't risk believing you," Juliet said, looking to the count, who raised his eyebrows in my direction, inviting my opinion.

"Were they waiting for you at the drop?" I said.

"Yes. Even though I watched from a distance, I didn't spot them until it was too late. There's a low brick wall in the park at Épernon. I sat on it and checked a loose brick for a message hidden beneath it. There was nothing, and they were on me in seconds. Frenchmen in plain clothes, and then the *Abwehr*."

"Not the Gestapo," I said. "You're sure?"

"Of course," she said.

"You didn't take your suicide pill," Juliet said, as if that was damning.

"It was in my jacket pocket, but they were on me too fast. I tried to get to it, but they wrenched my arms behind my back. It must have fallen out, since they searched me and found nothing."

"You were extraordinarily lucky, my dear," Count Vasseur said. "One might say unbelievably so."

"I have no idea why they released me, none at all," Sonya held out her hands, palms up. "They had me in a cell for a few hours, but no one even spoke to me."

"If she talked, where are the Germans?" I asked, glancing out the window, half expecting to see Zeller and his men swarming the grounds. "Why would they wait?"

"A good question," Juliet said. "What did they ask you to do, Sonya? Tell us now. I have no wish to make this unpleasant." By the time she finished her sentence, the Walther was pointed at Sonya's head.

"I have another question," I said. "How did you get your bicycle?"

"What? The officer who drove me out of town had it in the boot of his car. Why?"

"Never mind. I don't think we have to worry about Sonya. She didn't betray us," I said.

"How can you be so sure?" Juliet said, the barrel of the pistol still pointed at Sonya's temple.

"Because right now, the château is the safest place in France. But not for long."

"Explain yourself, Sergeant!" Count Vasseur said, as Juliet let the pistol drop a few inches, her stare wavering between me and Sonya.

"To begin with, I believe that Adrien's death was connected to our recent murders. He wasn't known as part of the staff here, right?"

"Right," Juliet said, the pistol finally relaxed at her side. "He had multiple identities so no one could trace him back to us."

"Which is why he had to die. He may have taken the suicide pill, or it was forced on him. The real target was the wireless. It was important to isolate the château. I think the person behind all this was also responsible for the betrayal of the other networks."

"You're making no sense, Billy," Juliet said. "Let's get back to Sonya. If she didn't betray us, why did the Germans let her go?"

"Because her arrest and absence would direct suspicion to the château and everyone in it. Adrien was different. He had no apparent ties to the place, but he might have revealed what he knew under interrogation. So he was silenced, along with his wireless."

"And what of Sonya's bicycle?" Count Vasseur said. "Why do you consider it important?"

"How valuable are bicycles in occupied France?" I said. The count shrugged.

"They are the sole means of transport for many people," Juliet said, her voice telling me she knew where I was going with this. "And none are being produced. The factories are all engaged in war work."

"There's no more rubber for tires, either," Sonya said, jumping in.

"And yet your bicycle is returned to you. None of the French collaborators or a German guard swiped it to make a bundle of francs. Or if they did, they returned it toots sweet. Who could make that happen?"

"Not I," Sonya said, her hand to her breast. In the distance, the sound of automobile engines rolled closer.

Juliet darted to the window and pulled the curtain aside. "It's

Zeller," she said. "With a truckload of men." She glared at Sonya, who looked at me with wide, terrified eyes. "If the Germans weren't about to swarm the château, I'd shoot you here."

At that second, Kaz appeared from the tunnel entrance built into the bookcase, his mouth gaping in surprise at the scene.

"No time to explain," I said, grabbing Sonya by the hand and leading her to Kaz. "Watch her. Zeller's back, probably to make another search. Make sure no one wanders off this time, okay?"

"Absolutely," Kaz said, regaining his composure in an instant and taking Sonya by the arm. I grabbed the debris from her handbag, stuffed it all in, and handed it to her. She gave me a weak, confused smile, then disappeared into the secret passage.

"*Probably* another search?" Juliet said as tires crunched on gravel. "I hope you're right. The alternative is that Sonya betrayed us."

"Or he's coming to thank the count for revealing the treachery of the *Milice*," I said.

"With a full squad?" Count Vasseur said. "Well, we shall see. Perhaps you two should also take to the tunnels?"

"No, let's listen in," I said, preferring to stay aboveground. Juliet and I entered the small listening chamber behind the count's desk and waited for the sound of boot heels. They weren't long in coming.

"Count Vasseur, my friend!" Major Zeller's voice boomed out as he flung open the door to the library, letting it slam against the wall.

"Major, you are in excellent spirits. I trust my information was helpful?" The count rose from his seat, gesturing to a chair. Zeller ignored him.

"Oh, most helpful, my dear count. I learned that Frenchmen are not to be relied upon, not at all. Certain Frenchmen, that is." Zeller stopped to admire *Blue Madonna*, much as I'd done earlier.

Just as he'd done then, Count Vasseur guided his guest to a seat and joined him in the matching chair in front of his desk. "Will your men be searching the château? Again?"

"My apologies, but with the revelation of Rivet's betrayal, searches are being undertaken everywhere for other Allied airmen. Even here. No one must be above reproach, don't you agree?"

"It is understandable, Major." The count's voice was wary, and I didn't blame him. Zeller was playing with him, like a cat with a still-breathing mouse.

"Good! My men are searching the grounds. Purely a formality, do not worry. I myself will search the interior of the château."

"I am glad to accompany you, Major Zeller."

"No, it is best you stay here. The staff?"

"Vincent took the cook shopping in the horse cart. The others have the day off."

"Very well. I hope to be done soon," Zeller said, rising from his seat and standing over Count Vasseur. "Do not leave the library. My men have orders to shoot anyone interfering with their search. They are on edge, since there was a terrorist attack in town last night. As I am sure you are aware."

"Yes, I did hear of that."

"Stay put, Count Vasseur," Zeller said, his hand resting on the knife in the black scabbard on his belt. "That goes for all the residents of the château, including the lovely Juliet."

"And what of Sonya?" I had to hand it to the count. Even in the face of these unsubtle threats, he played along with Zeller and brought up Sonya.

"Did I forget to tell you? She was picked up by my men. An unfortunate error, and I had her released. See? I am not the terrible Hun, am I, count? I can save lives as well as take them. Both are within my power."

"I am glad you saved her from harm, Major. But what of my son? Can you show mercy on his behalf as well?"

"Ah, your son. You must hope that informing on Rivet would

help his case. I am not certain it has, count. It may have made things more difficult, as a matter of fact."

"Why? Wasn't that the kind of information you wanted?"

"Yes, but I was surprised to find the only Allied airman to be a corpse. Did you know of that?"

"No, only that Rivet was passing them onto the Resistance. In hopes of mercy, should the Allies get this far. Or perhaps for money. Who can say with such a man? Still, why should that affect the release of my son?"

"There is some good news," Zeller said, ignoring the question. "You son is in France. He is closer. So act with great constraint, Count Vasseur, if you wish your line to continue."

"I will do my best, Major. Your kindness will not be forgotten."

Zeller ignored him, standing in front of *Blue Madonna*, straightening the frame. "We have spent many hours in this room playing chess, discussing art and history, have we not?" He tapped his foot.

"Yes, we have, it is true."

"But do not forget, count, that I also know how to twist the knife." He pulled on the dagger and resheathed it in one fluid motion, the metallic *click* a deadly reminder of his power.

CHAPTER TWENTY-EIGHT

THE COUNT SIGNALED us to come out after Zeller had completed his search of the top two floors. In the empty château, it was easy enough to hear him slamming doors and stomping around on the ground floor. I edged close to the window, stealing a glance at the Germans outside. They stood around the truck, smoking and talking. Their search had been perfunctory. Zeller's was thorough. It was a half hour before he joined them, shouting at his men to *macht schnell*.

"The damned *Boche*," Count Vasseur muttered under his breath. "What was the point of that melodrama?"

"I'll explain once Kaz is here. But there's other news. Meyer has taken off. He attacked Topper and stole the wireless."

"My God," the count whispered. "What is happening?"

"Was Topper able to send the message first?" Juliet said, getting to the heart of the matter.

"No. Unless we find the radio, we're out of contact again."

"I have news as well," Juliet said. "I finished decoding the sked. We need to contact the Resistance; I called Christine earlier and told her to come as soon as she could. We have a target to hit tonight. And tomorrow a Lysander will come in to pick up three people." We both knew who those three would be.

"That is a start, at least," the count said. The telephone on his desk rang, startling us all. He answered, listened, and hung up. "Madame Agard and the child are safe. Vincent is on his way back."

"What should we do with Sonya?" Juliet asked.

"She's done nothing wrong," I said.

"Yes, if she had betrayed us, the Germans would have found the tunnels, *n'est-ce pas?*"

"I agree. Zeller would have had all of us in custody," Juliet said. "Whatever happened in Épernon, Sonya did not reveal our secrets."

"Christine will arrive shortly," the count said, his face more relaxed now that dealing with a traitor was off the table. "I suggest we reconvene in the kitchen and partake of whatever food the good Madame has left us. Should we bring in the airmen? Surely they need to be appraised of the situation."

"No, let's leave them in the salon for now," I said. If what I suspected was true, we already had too many people in on the secret. Not that I knew exactly what the secret was, but I was damned certain there was one.

I took the aboveground route to the salon. As I neared the stables, the distant drone of aircraft grew closer, until the air was filled with the snarl of engines. I instinctively ducked as four Hawker Typhoons flew in from the north, low and fast, flashing across the sky toward Dreux. The white invasion stripes on their wings glistened brightly, as if they'd been painted on that morning. I followed them as best I could until they disappeared below the wooded horizon, and listened as the steady hammering of their cannons marked an attack somewhere on the main road. I watched as they climbed above the trees in a graceful ascending arc, leaving behind a dirty smudge of smoke and agony for the Germans who would not be making the trip *zur Normandie Front.*

"Looks like we'll be moving on soon, boys," I said as I entered the salon, trying for as much cheer as I could muster. "The Krauts are gone, so relax."

"Relax? Like hell! When are we getting out of here?" Switch asked. Sonya gave me a big smile, probably thankful for not having her brains blown out.

"Soon enough. How you feeling, Topper?" He had color back in his face and a bandage wrapped around his head.

"Good enough. I'd like to go search for that bastard Meyer right now." Anger was a great healer.

"We need to make plans with the count first. Sonya, you, too."

"You sure about that, Boyle?" Babcock said, eyeing Sonya with suspicion.

"Yeah. Listen, guys, be patient. We'll be out of here soon, one way or the other." I studied the faces of the four remaining men. In the past few days, two of their buddies had died and one had legged it. They had to be thinking the odds were against them.

"You don't think we should take our chances out there?" Fawcett said.

"Yeah, joinin' up with the *Maquis* sounds damn good," Dogbite said. "Better than sittin' here like a buncha rabbits waitin' for the polecat to pay a visit."

"If it comes to that, I'll be the first to say so. Hang on, and don't do anything stupid."

"Wish you'd said that before I went out with Meyer," Topper said, carefully adjusting his black beret over the bandage. That got a laugh, and some of the tension went out of the air.

When Kaz, Topper, Sonya, and I got to the kitchen, Christine was already there, her gasogene car parked out back. She stared daggers at Sonya, who flushed red and cast her eyes to the floor.

"It is a mistake to include her," Christine said. "No one released by the Germans should be trusted. No one."

"I'd agree with you normally," I said. "But not in this case. Zeller did let Sonya go, but not for the reason you think." I pulled up a chair to the kitchen table. Plates of bread, cold beets, and potatoes were set out along with a bowl of cherries. I resisted the desire to eat and watched the faces around me. Kaz poured me a glass of wine. Topper exhaled as he sat, the blow to his head likely still giving him pain. Sonya's gaze darted from person to person, looking for acceptance and trust. Juliet sat next to the count, her network shattered, besieged by the occupiers and strange motives not yet entirely clear. Finally, Count Vasseur. Keeper of secrets.

"We have much to decide, Sergeant Boyle. Perhaps you should let your officers speak," the count said.

"I have a headache," Topper said. "Go ahead, Sergeant." Kaz nibbled a piece of bread and gestured with a theatrical wave of his hand for me to take the floor.

"Your ancestor, Frédérick-Charles Maronneau, was a Huguenot. He converted to Catholicism and received this château and the title you carry today, correct?"

"This is absurd, Sergeant! What does my family history have to do with our troubles today?"

"Billy, what is the point of this?" Juliet said, giving me a look that said I must be off my rocker.

"It has a lot to do with them, count. Please bear with me. He expanded the original château, didn't he?"

"Yes, a common practice."

"What was his reason for digging out the tunnels and all the secret passages and chambers?"

"To help other Huguenots. Since you insist on these questions, let me explain as quickly as possible so we can proceed with what needs to be done in this day and age."

He did. Long story short, Frédérick-Charles converted in order to build a place of refuge for Huguenots on the run. There were religious wars in the sixteenth century between the Catholic majority and the Protestant Huguenots. Frédérick-Charles foresaw a desperate future for his people, and he was right on the money. Over twenty-five thousand Huguenots were killed in Paris during the Saint Bartholomew's Day Massacre, which really was a three-month affair. There were periods of peace and treaties, but in the next century it started up again. Protestant worship was prohibited and property seized, and emigration was not allowed. Many Huguenots fled the country illegally, some of them hiding at the Château Vasseur, given sanctuary by the descendants of the first count. At one point, French soldiers were billeted at the château, using it as a base to hunt down Huguenots in the area.

The Vasseur secret was never discovered. Those who hid here eventually fled abroad, many to England just as the modern-day fugitives hoped to do. The story was passed down from father to son, in readiness for a time when the tunnels would be needed again, God forbid.

"The legends of the giant in the forest and the haunted painting, these were used to distract the locals, keep them from looking too closely?" I asked.

"Well, the stories are true enough," the count said. "When the buried temple was found, the legend of the White Giant was already well known. And poor Margaux truly was thrown against the glass window and bled to death. I did my best to keep them alive for the purpose you describe."

"Your son Frédéric, he knows the family secret?" I said.

"Of course," the count said, his face clouding over with worry. "Of course he does."

"Billy, will you get to the point?" Juliet said, mirroring the impatience I could feel all around the table.

"Count Vasseur," I asked, "is there anyone at this table you do not trust?"

"No. I believe Sonya. She could not have done us harm. And the rest of you are beyond reproach."

"So tell us. Tell us the secret. Tell us what is hidden."

"I cannot, Sergeant." He rested his head in his hands. "I must not."

The door opened, and Vincent stepped in, obviously perplexed by the scene and Sonya's presence. *"Que se passe-t-il?"* he asked, taking a seat and helping himself to the wine.

"He wants to know what's happening, Billy," Juliet said. "As do we all."

"Count Vasseur, should we ask Vincent? He knows, doesn't he?" Murmurs and whispers spread across the table as the count translated for Vincent. "The blue paint on his clothes told me that much. Kaz, how do you say *forger* in French?" I asked.

"Faussaire," he said, and Vincent's eyes widened. He knew who we were talking about.

"Enough!" Count Vasseur said, slamming his palm on the table. "Yes, the artwork on the walls, they are all copies. That is what I hired Vincent for. *Blue Madonna*, the portrait of Frédérick-Charles, all the other important paintings, he has painted those over the past four years. The real artwork is hidden in the tunnels. No one else must know of this!"

"Why didn't you tell us?" Juliet said.

"It is a matter of family honor. No Vasseur is to reveal the secret of the hidden chambers, except to trusted retainers such as Vincent and those in need of sanctuary. Frédérick-Charles implored all descendants to keep the purpose of Château Vasseur intact, in case of need in future generations. As it is needed today to help the cause of a free France."

"But we know, and the escaped airmen know," Sonya said, secure enough now to speak up.

"Of course; that was necessary. But no more than what you needed to know. And not the existence of the hidden paintings. Until now."

"And if Frédéric has not talked, you could not bring yourself to, either. Because that's what these murders have been all about," I said.

"Yes, I believe so now, after the visit today from Zeller," the count said, draining his glass of wine. "Do you think he is dead, my Frédéric?"

"All I can say for sure is that he has revealed nothing to Zeller. And it would be in the major's interest to keep him alive. I think he's probably been close by for some time now."

"But the Germans were already here, and inventoried the collection," Christine said. "They did the same at the library—we have a few minor pieces from local artists—and the officer said he'd been to the château."

"It's not *the* Germans," I said. "It's *a* German. Major Zeller is out to steal the paintings for himself."

"How can you say that?" Topper asked. "Not that I think he's necessarily a nice chap, but what do you base it on?"

"Juliet and I heard the major speaking with Count Vasseur earlier. I had the bright idea to use Brookes's corpse to throw suspicion on the *Milice*."

"And it worked," Christine put in. "Rivet and several others were taken away by the *Boche* earlier today."

"But Zeller was oddly menacing today," Juliet said. "What was that bit about twisting the knife?"

"Right. Just like the knife that stabbed Brookes in the kidney was twisted."

"What? You mean Zeller killed Brookes?" Sonya said, her face screwed up in disbelief.

"Yes. Think about it. We were wracking our brains to figure out who among us could have killed Brookes and Armstrong. Who did we leave out as suspects?"

"The *Boche*! The damned *Boche*!" Count Vasseur slammed his fist on the table. "Of course. *Mon Dieu*, imagine his surprise when he found the body!"

"Right. He knew we'd planted Brookes's body there because he killed him. Somewhere along the line, Zeller learned of the tunnels and the real artwork stored there. He sensed which way the wind was blowing and decided he could use an insurance policy. Unfortunately for Armstrong and Brookes, they bumped into him while he was searching," I said. "Since he's not a rabid Nazi, he doesn't feel the need to steal artwork for the Reich. But for himself, that's another matter."

"The searches, they were all cover for his own explorations," the count said. "But why didn't he simply force my hand? Use my son or torture me?"

"He couldn't afford to draw attention to the château. That's why he had Sonya released when he heard she was picked up. That's also why he didn't close down Noble with the other networks, or bring you in to be interrogated. I figure he covered up whatever information would have implicated you in order to keep everything secure until he could grab the artwork."

"That's why Adrien was taken," Juliet said. "To silence the wireless."

"Yes, and I'm afraid that's why he had to die. Perhaps he took the pill as reported. Or Zeller forced him to. He couldn't risk Adrien revealing anything about Noble under interrogation."

"But we got a new radio—" Juliet stopped, realizing the implications. "Oh my God. Meyer?"

"He has to be in on it. Switch told us Meyer got separated from them after they bailed out. Meyer showed up here a few days later. I figure he was picked up by the Germans, and when Zeller interrogated him, he found a likely confederate. Without going into details, we know Meyer is a thief and a brutal crook back in England. No reason for him to act otherwise here."

"With his background, it would not be far-fetched to think of him offering his services to Zeller, perhaps as an informer, never dreaming he'd be invited to join another criminal endeavor," Kaz said. "It does make sense for Zeller to have a partner, particularly one who would not inform on him to the German authorities.

But I have to wonder, with all due respect to your collection, count, is it worth so much risk?"

It was the same question that had been bothering me. Maybe the Vasseur art collection was worth a bundle, but that wasn't the sense I got. I was no connoisseur, but I hadn't recognized any big names or seen anything other than *Blue Madonna* that took my breath away.

"There is something else," Count Vasseur finally said. "Perhaps it would be better to show you."

CHAPTER TWENTY-NINE

"WHAT MADE YOU suspect Meyer?" Juliet asked as we followed Count Vasseur into the tunnels through the kitchen cupboard entrance. "I thought he'd gone mad from being cooped up so long. I know I've had that feeling a few times."

"It was when Switch taunted me about being a cop before the war. I didn't realize it then, since I was dog tired, but it came to me later that the only time I'd mentioned being a cop was in the count's library. Then it clicked after Meyer appeared in the château kitchen. He knew the tunnels better than I'd thought, and had been eavesdropping on our conversation in the library. It's the only way Switch would know." I shined my flashlight ahead, lighting the damp stones for the old count.

"But how did Meyer and Zeller stay in touch? They didn't meet during the searches, did they?"

"No, there was a simpler method," I said.

"Oh God, of course! If he knew the tunnels, he could enter the library whenever the count wasn't there and simply use the telephone," Juliet said.

"Right. I imagine there was some sort of code word for Meyer to give, and he'd be put right through," I said.

"Even easier, a direct line to Zeller would be my guess," Kaz said from behind us. "With calls placed in the middle of the night to ensure Zeller would be there to answer, and Meyer would be sure of access to the instrument."

"Be the way I'd do it," Topper chipped in.

"Okay, so tell me this, since you have a nodding acquaintance with the wrong side of the law. How would you set the whole thing up?" I asked.

We entered the Druid temple, our lights playing over the high arched ceiling.

"It makes sense that Zeller needed an inside man,"Topper said. "But my money says the main purpose for Meyer is to guard the paintings once they've snatched them. Zeller probably has the connections to sell them, not to mention access to phony identity papers from the *Abwehr*. But he can't cart around a bunch of valuable canvases. He must have a secluded spot set up for Meyer to guard them. They're a good team, as far as it goes."

"Sounds like a setup for a double-cross," Kaz said. "Meyer could hide the paintings from Zeller and wait for the Allied line to roll over Dreux."

"Maybe. But I doubt a lowlife like Meyer would know where to sell them, other than a cheap pawn shop,"Topper said. "I'd lay odds on Zeller taking him out once he has his new papers and a way to get into Switzerland or Spain."

"No honor among thieves?" Juliet said.

"Not in this situation, other than in the short term. There's nothing else to bind them together, and they are enemies, even if that means little to Zeller and even less to Meyer."

I had to agree with Topper. In his world of London gangs, there were relationships to be maintained, business connections and personal ties to be nurtured. Within that circle, there did exist a certain honor among villains. But outside of it, death was always on the table.

Count Vasseur led our party into the tunnel system on the far side of the temple. Flashlights flicked off as we navigated by the electric lights. I recognized the spot where Armstrong had been found dead. Farther into the tunnel, grey stone lintels ran overhead, supported on either end by rough-hewn oak columns. Following the count, Vincent by his side, we came to a dead end.

Empty barrels were stacked to one side, the wood brittle with age, the bands rusted through. A chair, minus one leg, sat on top of the pile. It looked like a long-forgotten rubbish dump.

"What you are about to see is something known only to myself, my son, and Vincent. I trust you will keep this secret to yourselves." The count nodded to Vincent, who inserted two fingers in what looked like an irregular surface between two cut stones. The group went silent as he grimaced, working his fingers deeper into the crevice. A dull metallic *clang* rang out, and the stone wall moved inward, revealing thin gaps from floor to ceiling along the lines of cut limestone. Vincent put his shoulder against the wall and pushed.

The stones gave way, the solid surface moving farther back with a harsh, grating sound, revealing the intact wall on each side to be about ten inches thick, while the movable section was closer to two inches of chiseled limestone. With one hand he pushed it to the left, and the opening moved, ancient iron wheels gliding with surprising ease.

"The most secret of all the secret chambers," Count Vasseur said, gesturing for us to enter. Vincent turned on his flashlight, electricity never having made it this far. As I stepped over the threshold, I had a momentary feeling of terror as I recalled a story that had scared the hell out of me as a kid. "The Cask of Amontillado," about a guy who was tricked into entering a basement niche and walled up inside. *Thanks a lot, Edgar Allan Poe.*

It was roomier than I'd imagined. From the inside, I saw the door was a massive wooden frame, with the limestone pieces bolted to it. Wooden planks covered the floor of the chamber, about twenty feet long and ten wide. A wooden rack ran along one side, white sheets draped over it. At a nod from the count, Vincent pulled at the first sheet. Frédérick-Charles himself, out of his ornate frame, stared back at me.

"The original," Count Vasseur whispered, as if in awe of his ancestor. "Vincent finished the copy only the other day. It takes some time for the paint to set and harden."

"The maid," Kaz said, leaning forward to study the portrait. "She noticed something different about the eyes."

"Yes, and of course she attributed it to the painting being haunted, which served our purpose perfectly. And here is *Blue Madonna*, the true copy."

Vincent uncovered the painting, set on an easel. In the dim light, it was hard to tell the difference. Might have even been hard in broad daylight. I liked both of them just fine.

The count gave us a tour of the rest of his collection, which included a few nice landscapes and a bunch of stern counts down through the ages. That left half the rack still covered.

"This is the secret, I take it," Juliet said, standing in front of the dusty shrouds. This time the count did the honors.

"These are from the Rothschild collection," he said, revealing half a dozen canvases leaning against one another. He flipped through them as if browsing at a discount art gallery. Portraits that were lit by a light that seemed to spring off the canvas, even in the harsh beams of our flashlights.

The next section was from the collections of other French Jews who sought to keep their artwork out of the hands of the Nazis. More portraits, landscapes, mythological scenes, Madonnas, peasants, seascapes, the whole repertoire of European painting. It was dazzling.

"There are works by Degas, Monet, Picasso, and Cézanne, to name a few. Now you know," Count Vasseur said as Vincent covered the exposed artwork. "It is not only for myself that I have kept this secret. It is for those who have placed their trust in me, as others in centuries past have trusted the safety of Château Vasseur."

"Vincent is quite adept at forgery," I said as we left the chamber. The count pulled the stone door shut behind us. After the mechanism locked in place, it was impossible to tell one stone from the other.

"Yes. There was some trouble before the war, but we must not blame him for youthful indiscretions, now that his talents have been put to great use against the *Boche*. The plan was, if they ever came for my collection, I would resist slightly, then sadly let them take everything, while the originals were safely stored here."

"But Zeller knows there's more," Juliet said as we trooped back to the kitchen.

"Yes, I'm sure," I said. "He's gone to a lot of effort. He must have picked up information about the château being used as a hiding place for Jewish-owned art. How did the owners make contact with you?"

"A few art dealers, a museum director, and in one case a family friend," the count said. "I imagine any one of them might have talked, if enough pressure were applied. Many families had the same idea, to send their artwork to remote châteaus in the country. I know much of the Rothschild artwork was hidden in this manner, but discovered very quickly. The Nazis went after art with a vengeance as soon as France had fallen. Many pieces were sold to raise cash for the German treasury, especially anything they designated modern degenerate art. The rest were sent to Berlin. We were lucky to be overlooked—until Zeller, that is."

"We need a plan to deal with him," Juliet said. "Meyer knows a Lysander is coming in tomorrow night. Thank God he doesn't know where, but it might lead Zeller to think the château will be empty. That's when he could make his move and force you to give him the artwork."

"Perhaps," Count Vasseur said as he climbed the steps to his library. "But first you need to work out the attack on the viaduct tonight. I will leave you to it, and think about what can be done about Zeller."

"A bullet would do nicely," Topper suggested.

"That would most certainly bring reprisals," Christine said. "You can rarely predict what the Nazis will do, but they always respond to assassinations with lethal repercussions. Attacks on bridges and railways, less so. There has to be another way. These paintings are priceless, but so are lives."

"We will speak in the morning," the count said. "Now I must think and rest." Vincent followed him upstairs while the rest of us made for the kitchen.

"Do you think there's a chance Frédéric is still alive?" Juliet asked as we sat down again around the table. "The count's heart will break if he's dead."

"I think there's an even chance," I said. "If he was alive when Zeller tumbled to the hidden artwork, it would be in his interests to keep Frédéric alive—and the count on the hook. Maybe we could work out a deal if he's still alive and kicking."

"Get Zeller to bring the kid here, then snatch him. We tell Zeller the hidden art was shipped off long ago and to help himself to the paintings on the walls, and then get the count and his boy to the Resistance." Topper was good at working the angles, but this plan had a flaw.

"If he doesn't believe us, he's got all the time he needs to tear the place apart," I said. "Maybe we could find out who his boss is." Now I was grasping at straws. All that would do is draw more attention to the château, or deliver us to an even bigger villain.

"Let's plan our mission for tonight," Juliet said. "If we're alive tomorrow, we'll deal with Zeller. It will be our last chance before you two leave with Switch."

"The two of you are leaving with one man?" Sonya said, clearly expecting we'd stay, and three of the airmen would fly out in the Lysander.

"It's a long story," I said.

"What story is not?" Kaz said, helping Christine unfold a large map of the area. That about summed it up.

CHAPTER THIRTY

"HERE IS OUR target, the Chérisy railroad viaduct," Juliet said, her finger tapping the map like a machine gun. "It crosses the Eure River east of Dreux. All trains from Paris have to cross it on their way to Normandy."

"Why haven't they hit it from the air?" I said.

"It is too close to the town," Christine said. "Chérisy is a small place, tightly packed against the east bank of the Eure. The rail line runs just north of there, where it crosses the river."

"Heavy bombers flying at twenty thousand feet would obliterate the town," Juliet said. "We know fighter-bombers have tried low-level attacks, but there are antiaircraft emplacements along the riverbank, and they've downed several aircraft. It's up to us."

"Looks like work for a jelly man," Topper said.

"Gelignite," Kaz said. "Topper has a lot of experience with plastic explosives."

"But this isn't a bank safe," I said. "What do you know about blowing bridges, Topper?"

"Mainly that it's something you want the RAF to do. I can set charges to wreck a rail line or a building, but bridges are quite another matter. I don't suppose you have a picture of what we're up against?"

"We do," Sonya said, producing a faded sepia print postcard. "It's from the turn of the century, when the viaduct was new, but it still looks the same." She laid it in front of Topper. Three stone arches over the Eure River, about a hundred feet high at a guess. The bases, which sat in the water, were massive granite blocks.

"Well, no problem at all," Topper said, slapping his hand on the table. "As long as we can find an extra hundred pounds of gelignite, drilling equipment, and a few hours' peace and quiet to work at it."

"Why do you need all that?" Juliet asked.

"Because you don't bring down a massive stone bridge with what I brought along. We gave the *Maquis* fifty pounds of gelignite, and I have twenty pounds with me. You don't need much to send a stretch of rail to kingdom come, but demolishing heavy stonework like this? Near to impossible."

"Come on, Topper," I said. "A jelly man like you? You must know some tricks."

"The only trick is to plant the stuff inside the bridge, so the blast doesn't dissipate in the open air. On or under, you waste half or more of your power."

"You wish to contain the explosion, right?" Kaz said. "So the structure absorbs all the energy of the blast." Topper nodded. It made sense to me.

"But we couldn't drill, even if we had equipment," Christine said. "The *Boche* have antiaircraft batteries on both sides of the river. There are twenty-millimeter antiaircraft guns along each bank as well as those big eighty-eight-millimeter flak guns, one on each side."

"Patrols?" Kaz said, cleaning his glasses for a better look at the postcard.

"No. The Germans often patrol with dogs along the rail tracks, but not that we've seen at the viaduct," Christine said.

"No wonder they don't patrol. If the bridge is surrounded by antiaircraft emplacements, why bother?" I leaned back in my chair, trying to see any way we could do this.

"London said if we don't knock out the bridge tonight, they'll send heavy bombers tomorrow," Juliet said. "Which will kill hundreds of civilians."

"A terrible choice," Kaz said, half to himself, as he studied the postcard. "If the Germans get more reinforcements through to Normandy, hundreds or thousands might die there."

"We could place charges beneath the rails," Sonya said. "Wait for a munitions train, and then set them off."

"We can't wait for the right kind of train to come along," I said. "If it gets to be daylight, some Kraut is bound to notice the detonating cord, at least."

"What are these round holes?" Kaz asked. He tapped on two dark circles high up on the span, one over each of the main supports.

"I don't know," Christine said. "When we scouted the bridge a few weeks ago, we wondered about those. Drainage? One of the men who worked in construction before the war said it might be to reduce vibrations from the heavy trains, to limit damage to the masonry over time. There's a central partition, so they don't go all the way through."

"Then we don't have to drill," I said. "Place the charges in there."

"It might work," Topper said, stroking his chin as he peered at the postcard. "But as with a drill hole, it would have to be covered so the explosion is tamped down. Otherwise the force will simply be blown out the opening."

"I'd say the cavity is perhaps four feet wide," Christine offered. "What could we use?"

"Sandbags, at least three feet deep," Topper said. "Or a lot of large rocks. Neither of which can be easily carried all the way there."

"Show me where the gun emplacements are," I said to Christine. She placed check marks along the road paralleling the river. Two by the road north of the viaduct, two on the far side, high up on a hill. A fifth was about a hundred yards from the bridge, positioned for defense across the river as well as antiaircraft fire.

If that gun crew spotted us while we were on the span, we'd be shot to shreds. She made two circles for the eighty-eights. One on the outskirts of the village, about a half mile from the viaduct, the other on a hill beyond the twenty-millimeter emplacements.

"The riverbank on both sides is overgrown with trees and shrubs," Christine said. "We should be able to work our way to the base of the viaduct easily."

"But then what?" Topper said. "That twenty-millimeter will chew us up if they spot us climbing onto the bridge."

"What's the terrain like between the village and the viaduct?" I asked.

"The land slopes down toward the river," Juliet said. "The road is built up, with a drainage ditch on one side. The rest is pasture up to the village. I've bicycled there many times. The gun crews take little notice. They're not military police or security troops."

"This emplacement," I said, tapping my finger on the gun with a field of fire across the viaduct. "It's dug in?"

"Yes," Juliet said, quickly understanding what I was getting at. "Sandbags!"

"The other antiaircraft guns are far enough away that they may not notice if we do it quietly," Christine said. "There are seven men at each gun."

"Tricky," I said. "We'd have to get them all at once without making a sound. That's a lot of knife work."

"We have two silenced pistols," Christine said.

There was immediate quiet around the table. This meant we had a real chance to succeed. Which meant that we had set ourselves on a collision course with seven men who we hoped we'd surprise in the night with a silent bullet or a knife across the throat. That was the optimistic outlook. If any number of things went wrong, capture, maiming, torture and death were in our likely futures.

"Well, then," Kaz said, with all the enthusiasm any of us could muster.

"They are assassination pistols created by SOE," Christine explained. "Totally silent, but they are bolt-operated. And after six or eight shots, the sound suppression will become less effective. We have used both already, so we only have several more shots. They are very practical for taking out a single person, but they are not made for an assault."

"Okay, so if we get close, two of the seven go down before they know what hit them. Work the bolt, drop two more," I said.

"Which leaves three men, if they have their wits about them, to open fire," Topper said.

"It can work if we get close," Kaz said. "After the second shot, three of us go in with knives. The shooters will provide backup in case one gets away."

"We need a diversion," Juliet said. "One that won't cause an overwhelming response, but sufficient to focus their attention for a moment."

"A fire," Sonya suggested. "Perhaps a shed or a barn at the edge of the village. The gunners look that way as we approach from the river bank via the drainage ditch."

"Good," Kaz said. "They'll lose their night vision if they stare at the flames. And a small fire may be construed as an accident. Hopefully it will not draw any Germans to investigate."

We counted on it. This wasn't going to be a large-scale attack. Juliet and Sonya would stick with Topper, providing protection and acting as lookouts. Kaz and Christine would each have one of the silenced pistols. Maurice—the *Maquisard* who'd rendez-voused with Christine and me the night of the massacre at Coudray—would bring half a dozen men and the fifty pounds of explosives. Three of us would finish off the gun crew after Kaz and Christine hit their targets. As Topper planted the charges, we'd carry sandbags from the gun emplacement to the bridge. It sounded simple, the way things do when you break them down and check off each step in a warm, well-lit kitchen. Out in the dark, with death a trigger pull away, it would be a different matter indeed.

Christine left to make a coded telephone call to a contact who'd alert Maurice to the mission. *Six people are coming to the party tonight. Bring potatoes.* They'd come in through the woods after dark, and then we'd hoof it to Chérisy, about two hours to the east. Longer if we ran into German patrols.

Juliet and Sonya opened what K rations were left. Meat and vegetable stew for all. No one was in the mood for jokes about a last supper, so we went quietly about our business. Kaz left to bring up the remaining airmen for a meal in the kitchen, and I went to see the count. I found him in the library, seated before *Blue Madonna*.

"You have a plan, Sergeant?"

"Yes, we do, and it's a good one," I said, talking myself into it. "What about you, sir?"

"I think it may be time to give Zeller what he wants, if he does the same for me. The life of my son for some paint on canvas. A worthwhile trade, I believe."

"If you can trust him, and if you feel it's the right thing to do."

"I only trust a man like Zeller to act in his own self-interest. Which makes him predictable, I think. I can turn that against him."

"He's a murderer, count."

"There have been so many deaths. Executions are hardly to be remarked upon, they are so common these days." His hand brushed the air as if waving off such a naïve idea. "What is more important? Bringing Zeller to justice or my son's life?"

"I'd prefer both," I said, looking closely at the downward gaze of the Madonna. It was as if she were staring into Count Vasseur's heart. I wondered what she found there. "But if you're certain about this, we should clear out your guests tomorrow. Will you give us that much time?"

"Of course. You have a way about you, Sergeant Boyle. I think you may be something more than a noncommissioned officer."

"Things are not always as they seem, sir."

"No, indeed they are not," he said, smiling, his head tilted up at the Madonna. I asked him to join us downstairs for the meal, but he shook his head, his eyes riveted on the painting. Saying farewell, perhaps?

Switch intercepted me as I made my way back to the kitchen, glancing over his shoulder to be certain we were alone. "What's happening, Boyle? When are you getting me out of here?"

"We have a job to do tonight," I said. "We're leaving tomorrow night. Keep it under your hat, okay?" I didn't want any trouble about Switch taking the express while the other three contemplated a long, dangerous hike to the Spanish border.

"What the hell happens if you get yourself killed out there?" Switch hissed the question between clenched teeth, his eyes darting down the hallway.

"Well, I guess the War Department will send my folks a telegram," I said. I brushed past him, slipping outside for a breath of fresh air. The longer I spent here, the less I cared about Switch and his cousin. England seemed a lifetime ago, and the concern over a gang, no matter how well-organized, didn't hold up against massacres, betrayals, and suicide missions. Worries over pilfered supplies seemed quaint as the sun began to near the horizon, cloaking the surrounding forest in a shadowy grey.

CHAPTER THIRTY-ONE

MAURICE AND HIS six men filtered in from the woods in twos and threes, their backpacks bulging with one-pound blocks of gelignite. We shared what food we had and set out on our journey at midnight. Count Vasseur saw us off, offering a salute as we passed. Switch was nowhere to be seen, having turned even surlier as the evening progressed.

Babcock and Fawcett were reluctant to stay behind, either out of a desire to help or a fear of being abandoned, it was hard to tell. The reality was, I wanted them to keep an eye on Switch. I told them he was looking nervous, and to make sure he didn't do anything stupid. Having a job to do seemed to make them feel better, so I put them in charge of cleaning out all evidence of their stay if none of us returned by noon. I didn't dwell on the implications for them—or me—if that came to pass.

Dogbite couldn't be talked out of coming with us. When I gave him a sense of what we were up against, he took his knife from its sheath and told me to check the blade. It drew blood from my finger and a wide grin from Dogbite.

"Butchered my first pig when I was ten," he said. "Well, he wasn't rightly *my* pig until I laid hands on him, then I owned that porker. Ain't never been afraid of blood, and let me tell you, when they say bleedin' like a stuck pig, there's a reason."

To tell the truth, I felt better having him along.

"Your ribs hurt much?" I asked Kaz as we made our way through the woods.

"They are much better, thank you. Sonya wrapped me in a

tight bandage before we left. Don't worry, I can manage with the pistol."

"It looks clumsy," I said. The thick silenced barrel was over a foot long, anchored by a magazine that doubled as the handle. Called the Welrod, it was good only at close range.

"It wasn't made for looks," Kaz said. "But the bolt works smoothly. We should have no trouble getting off two or three shots."

Maurice gave us a stern glance, which meant "keep quiet" in any language. We threaded our way through a grove of thick-trunked trees, the soft, rotting leaves cushioning our steps. Maurice signaled for a halt, his raised hand easy enough to see in the filtered moonlight. Engines revved in the distance and we all instinctively ducked, taking what cover we could. The vehicles drew closer on the narrow forest road. I could make out horizontal splashes of yellow from the taped headlights as they slowly made their way toward us.

I gripped my Thompson tightly, aiming it toward the road. Was it a patrol looking for us, or simply more reinforcements heading for Normandy? Maurice signaled for us to stay in place, and shook his head at my raised weapon. It wasn't time for a fight, and the three canvas-topped trucks rolled past us. Whiffs of cigarette smoke and a sharp laugh flowed from the rear of the last truck.

"Did you see?" Christine whispered, as she crawled back from the edge of the road. "The key insignia? *Hitlerjugend.*"

"The same regiment?" I asked, watching Maurice's reaction. Hate smoldered in his dark eyes as he caught the word.

"Impossible to know," Christine said. "But Chérisy lies in that direction." Maurice whispered to her, and she nodded before he set off at a trot down the road. They'd agreed to something, and it probably didn't have much to do with the viaduct. Revenge for Coudray was fine with me, but we had a job to do before we risked our lives a second time tonight.

We stayed on the road, Maurice taking point and two of his

men bringing up the rear. It made for faster going, but was more dangerous. If the Germans set up a roadblock, it would be too easy to stumble into it. Soon we took to the woods again, crossing fields knee high in weeds. With so many men taken by the Germans for forced labor, wide swaths of farmland were going to seed. We closed in on a small village, a few farmhouses enclosed by brick walls in various stages of decay, a few cultivated fields showing what little the women, children, and old men left behind could manage.

We ran low along a wall, flanked by a grove of apple trees. At the corner, vague shadows moved across the road as clouds obscured the moon. A row of low buildings sat across the road, the structures blending together in the darkness. A break in the clouds cast a shaft of moonlight directly across from us. A dull reflection gleamed on a helmet. Two helmets.

"*Boche,*" Maurice whispered. One of the two Krauts lit a cigarette, cupping the match in his hand for the other to light up as they leaned against the rear of a *Kübelwagen,* Germany's answer to the jeep.

There was no debate about what to do.

I tapped Dogbite on the arm and he nodded, knife already in hand. Crouching low, we edged into the grove of trees, which gave us cover as we approached the front of the vehicle. I glanced at Kaz, who had taken my place at the end of the wall, silenced pistol at the ready.

We had the *Kübelwagen* between us and the Krauts. I signaled to Dogbite that I'd take the one on the left. He gave me a thumbs-up, and we took to the street, crouched low. I willed my feet to be as light as possible, floating on my toes over the pavement. I took a couple of deep breaths and looked at Dogbite. He wore a what-are-you-waiting-for expression, his face as calm as a still lake.

I lifted three fingers and counted down. When I made a fist, we moved.

I looked everywhere but directly at the German ahead. An instructor once told me never to stare at the back of a sentry's head when you're sneaking up on him. It awakens part of our ancient brain, he said, the part that senses hidden dangers in the night. Keep him in your field of vision, but don't lock onto him with your eyes.

My gut twitched. Sweat broke out on the small of my back. I was aware of the rustle of my clothing, the scent of cigarette smoke, the slightly sour smell that seemed to permeate their wool uniforms. Everything went in slow motion, the crisp night air vibrating with images: the vehicle, the man ahead, the village, all vivid and surreal at the same time.

One more step.

As I put my foot down, I grabbed his chin with my left hand, lifting his jaw to prevent him calling out before I stabbed the side of his throat, severing the carotid artery, the jugular vein, and the jumble of nerves I'd forgotten the name of. I pulled the blade side to side and caught the Kraut's rifle with one hand while I let his body settle against me, a soft gurgle marking the last gasp of air escaping his trachea. He was unconscious in seconds, dead by the time I laid him on the ground.

I heard a sharp *clunk*. Dogbite grabbed at his Kraut's helmet, which had fallen and clipped the *Kübelwagen's* fender. He held onto it, letting his quarry drop to the ground slowly by the strap of his rifle still slung over his shoulder. We froze, waiting for a response to the sound, but no one appeared. Murmurs drifted out from the nearest house, a squat red-brick-and-timber affair, with shutters closed tight against the night. The faintest line of soft light showed between the shutters. Dogbite nodded toward the house.

"Officers," he whispered as we lifted the bodies, careful to avoid the glistening spray of arterial blood. Maurice and two men appeared, helping us to dump the corpses in the back of the *Kübelwagen.* I pointed to the house, and he nodded, sending the two men around the back in case the Germans made a break for it.

Christine approached the vehicle, checking the uniforms of the two Germans. They were the dappled camouflage of the *Waffen* SS, but I hadn't looked too closely at the collar tabs, thick with their blood.

"Hitlerjugend," she mouthed, tapping on the right front fender. It was the runic S and key insignia. She raised her Welrod and gave me a questioning look. Maurice drew his own knife, his face full of fury and certain intent.

I raised a finger. One shot. We'd need the others for the viaduct.

"I open the door. You shoot once. Then Maurice and I go in and finish the job," I whispered. Christine translated while I told Dogbite to stay near the door in case one of them got out. I was confident there'd only be two Krauts inside. The *Kübelwagen* wasn't that big, and it stood to reason the officers would leave the enlisted men outside to stand guard. So two of them. Probably drinking brandy and looking at a map, trying to figure out where they were.

I went to the door, the voices from inside clearer now, definitely German. If the residents were still inside, they were probably off in a bedroom waiting out their visitors.

Or dead.

We were in position. My hand on the door, Maurice to the left, Christine facing the entry, pistol at the ready. I pressed down on the latch, letting the door open. Straight ahead was a stairway, and on the right, a sitting room bathed in soft lamplight.

"Ja, was?" The voice was sharp, irritated.

Christine walked in, smiling. She lifted her arm, and all I heard was a slight click before the German closest to her let out a gasp and fell against a table. She backed up, working the bolt as Maurice and I rushed in.

There were three of them, damn it. One down, one for each of us. A map was half off the table, the dying German pulling it down with him as he grasped at air, sliding to the ground, wondering what had happened. His pals were open mouthed, in shock at the appearance of Christine as well as the silent death of their comrade.

But not for long. They both reached for their pistols, unsnapping holsters at the same second. I raced at one, lunging with my knife, aiming my forearm at his throat and thrusting the blade at his chest. He backed up against the wall, one hand on my arm and the other on the butt of his pistol. His breath was rank with brandy and fear, his pale skin hot and flushed. I slammed into him, pinning his gun hand between us and shoving my arm against his throat. I couldn't pull back to use the knife for fear he'd get his pistol free. I put my shoulder down and hit hard, the two of us sliding to the floor as I heard a strangled cry from Maurice's man, who stared dumbly at the hilt of a knife buried in his chest. Blood dribbled from his lips as he looked at Maurice's snarl, the last thing he ever saw.

"Halten Sie, bitte," my guy pleaded, letting go of his pistol, his hand open wide. *"Bitte!"*

Christine stepped forward, taking his Walther pistol. "Outside," she said.

Kaz stepped into the room as the two *Maquis* from around the back came through the kitchen, trailed by an old man in his nightclothes, his grey hair disheveled but his eyes fierce. He spat on the dead German as Maurice withdrew his knife and cleaned it on the camouflage tunic.

"Aufstehen!" Kaz said, kicking the live German. He pushed himself up. Confusion flitted across his features as he took in the obvious *Maquis* but also our British and American uniforms.

"Amerikaner? Engländer?" He sounded hopeful. His light brown hair fell across his face and he brushed it back, the inadvertent

gesture making him look young, like a high school kid. But after all, these soldiers were drawn from Hitler Youth.

"A *Leutnant*," Kaz said, pointing at the three silver pips on the German's collar tab. "These other gentlemen were majors. Or *Sturmbannführer*, in the ridiculous parlance of the SS."

"What's *his* ridiculous rank?" I asked, stepping closer and staring into those frightened brown eyes.

"Untersturmführer," Kaz said.

"Please ask the *Untersturmführer* where they were going," I said. Kaz put the question to him, but all he got was frosty silence.

"Chérisy," Christine said, after huddling with the old man. "They were lost and didn't know where they were. Monsieur Dablin told them Croisilles. But this is Charpont." She smiled and patted his shoulder. "They ate all his bread and cheese and drank his brandy. He is pleased you killed them."

"Chérisy?" I said, standing nose to nose with the Nazi bastard. He shrugged, looking as haughty as he could manage. "I wonder if he knows where Coudray is."

At the sound of the name, he stiffened.

"He knows," Christine said. "Take him outside." She spoke to Maurice, who snapped his fingers. Two men roughly pulled off the camouflage tunic and shoved the German outside. I knew what was coming next, but after what I'd witnessed at Coudray, all I could think about was that Monsieur Dablin had enough blood to clean off his parlor floor, and wasn't it nice that we weren't adding to it.

"Look," I said to Kaz, pointing to the map as they dragged the SS officer outside. "There are circles to the southeast of Dreux. This one, outside of Maintenon, may have been where they were bivouacked." From that spot, a line drawn by grease pencil meandered north, ending outside of Chérisy. By the railroad tracks.

"They are boarding a train there," Kaz said. "Perhaps to avoid the chance of a bombing raid at the rail yard in Dreux."

"Tonight?" I said.

"I would think so. Otherwise they would be waiting in the open. The trucks we saw must be part of the troop movement. This could mean trouble."

"Yes, for the *Boche*," Christine said. "We had word they were hidden in the woods around Maintenon, but it was difficult ground for the attack, yes? Now they come to us, and we will blow them up with the bridge."

"If they are too close to the viaduct, it will be impossible," Kaz said. "They would cut us to pieces."

"I do not think they will be close. The ground near the river is too overgrown, very difficult for loading. But east of Chérisy a small road branches off into the fields, where the ground is level along the rails. It makes sense the train would stop there, don't you think? Here, the bad fortune of these *Boche* becomes our good fortune." She tossed the SS tunic to Kaz. "Not the best fit, but it will do. We can get very close. We shall drive up and wait for them to salute. Now let us leave." That took a few rounds of *vive la France* with the monsieur, but as we disengaged, I began to think about it. It could work.

An argument was in progress outside. The Kraut was on his knees, guns leveled by the *Maquis*, two of whom were in a serious disagreement. The *Leutnant* looked at me, a glimmer of hope in his eyes, perhaps looking for mercy from the man he'd surrendered to. No dice.

"What's the delay?" I asked Juliet.

"Those two both had relatives in Coudray," she said as the argument grew louder. "They each want to kill him."

"We don't have time for this," Kaz said, stepping between the two men. *"Je suis de la Pologne."*

They looked at each other and nodded. Kaz was from Poland, a place of a thousand Coudrays. The SS man gasped. Kaz raised his pistol.

"*Für meine Familie,*" he said. The German shook his head and mouthed, *Nein, nein,* as if all his crimes might be forgotten in that single split second before the grim Polish officer standing over him squeezed the trigger. The only sound was that of a bullet hitting bone as a rosebud of blood blossomed between his eyes before he slumped to the pavement.

"Are you all right, Billy?" Juliet asked as we grouped around the German vehicle, loading it with corpses. I didn't know if she was talking about the fight or the execution.

"I'm fine," I said, and I was. Could I have been so cold-blooded two years ago when I first left the States? Would I have thought only a callous murderer could be capable of killing a prisoner? Probably. But that kid hadn't been to Coudray.

"There was no other choice," she said, and I realized she might need to convince herself as well as me.

I took her by the hand. "No, there wasn't. If he ever got loose, they'd come back and burn this village to the ground. And he had to pay for Coudray."

She nodded, squeezed my hand, and got back to business.

The uproar had brought people out of their houses, eager to view the dead Germans and congratulate Monsieur Dablin on his good luck. Men appeared with bottles of wine and buckets of water. The former were passed around and the latter used to wash away the blood in the street, in case more Germans came looking for their pals.

We got out of there before the party engulfed us. Maurice drove ahead with the knapsacks of gelignite next to him and the five Nazi supermen a bloody heap in the backseat. By the time we caught up with him, he'd dragged them off into the woods. The vehicle would give us an edge, getting us close without risking a fire that might attract unwanted attention.

The *Kübelwagen* wasn't built for a dozen passengers, but we crammed in, hanging off the sides along with two men balancing on the front fenders. Maurice stopped and killed the engine several times, listening for the sound of other vehicles. Nothing came to us but the muted sounds of distant bombing, searchlights, and the glow of fires giving the night sky a vivid electric hue.

We came to the outskirts of L'étang, the last village before Chérisy. Maurice pulled to the side of the road under the overhanging branches and switched off the engine. Motorized vehicles were moving through the village, coming in from the west and turning north at the crossroads ahead.

"We have to go around," Christine said. Around was through a field, this one cultivated with cabbage plants. We took down a section of stone wall and followed on foot as the vehicle made its way through the soft soil, finally reaching a farmer's lane which ran by a dilapidated barn and emptied out onto the main road. Maurice turned off the engine and coasted up next to the barn, signaling two of his men to scout ahead. The sound of engines receded, and it seemed the tail of the convoy had finally passed through the village.

Minutes passed. Quiet filled the air, the silence intense after the passage of so many vehicles. Then footsteps. Not the hurried steps of our men returning, but the slow, methodical slap of leather on pavement. I glanced around the corner of the barn and saw two silhouettes headed our way. One wore the familiar German helmet, the other the oversized beret of the *Milice*.

I motioned for Maurice to look, and crawled back to the others.

"One Kraut, one *Milice*," I said, keeping my voice low.

"A *collabo*, most likely," Christine said, using the derisive term for a collaborator. "Someone in that village got to a telephone. Why else would they be guarding the crossroads?"

"How many?" Kaz said.

"I only saw two, but if Maurice's scouts haven't shown themselves, there may be more."

"I'd guess two on each cross street, plus a machine gun aimed along the road we would have driven in on," Topper said.

"What's the chance it's a normal patrol?" Sonya said, giving a little shrug as if to apologize for such a simple notion.

"Let us ask one of the gentlemen walking toward us," Kaz whispered. "The Frenchman, I think."

"*Oui,*" Christine said. "We will have no trouble getting the truth from him."

"We can't keep using the Welrods," I said, glancing over to Maurice, who put a finger to his lips.

"If we need more than two shots each at the gun emplacement, we are already in trouble," Kaz said. "And if we don't get there, it won't matter."

"He's right," Dogbite said, his knife drawn. "Ain't got time to do a lot of thinkin' on this one."

"Okay," I said. "Take two men. One to catch the Kraut before he hits the ground. The other to grab the Frenchie while you put that knife to his throat. Go."

Kaz tapped two of the *Maquis* and scooted around the barn, aiming to get behind them. I leaned over Maurice and watched the two sentries strolling the quiet street. Suddenly the German dropped to his knees and lurched forward. A figure rushed from the darkness and caught him, dragging the body into the barn. Dogbite and his partner grabbed the *milicien*, knife blade pressed to his lips. He got the message.

"*Vite!*" Christine commanded as they brought him in. She was right to tell us to hurry. We didn't have much time.

Kaz did the questioning. It made sense; the guy might expect mercy from an English soldier. From the *Résistants* he'd hunted, tortured, and killed, a quick death was the best offer he'd receive.

At first, all he did was shake his head. Dogbite placed the blade against his throat, and the shaking turned to trembling, but he still didn't talk. Kaz whispered soothingly, and I could imagine all the lies he was telling the man. Dogbite moved the knife to his belly, and he began to weep. Then below the belt buckle, pressing against the buttons. He talked. Fast.

There was a German armored car hidden near the crossroads. They'd been on patrol and sent here after a report of an expected Resistance attack on Chérisy, and to watch for a stolen German vehicle. A *collabo's* work for sure.

"We should leave the vehicle," I said.

"No, it will only tell them we passed this way," Christine said.

"So will the bodies," Juliet said, nodding to our prisoner, who had returned to a vigorous trembling.

"Perhaps not," Kaz said. He spoke to the *Maquis* who'd helped with the German's body. The Frenchman smiled, grabbing the rifle the *milicien* had been carrying, and snatching the beret from his head. From inside the barn we heard a hard splintering sound, followed by softer, spongy blows.

Kaz patted the man down, removing his identity papers from his jacket. Speaking quickly, he handed them to Maurice, then motioned for him to go, pointing across the open fields. The *milicien* jumped up, eyes wide in disbelief. Maurice gave him a hard stare, and he was off, clearing the stone wall like a jack-rabbit.

"I told him the Germans would find his beret next to the body of their friend, whose head is now smashed in with his *milicien* rifle. Nicely disguising the bullet hole I put there," Kaz explained. "And that if he were stupid enough to warn the Germans, we would find him and cut him most grievously—if they did not shoot him out of hand. Also that this was his chance to be a hero of the Resistance, that his name would be known by all as an agent of the *Maquis* who had saved the day."

"Better than gettin' your balls handed to you," Dogbite said, flashing his blade. For some reason, everyone understood that perfectly.

We rolled the *Kübelwagen* out onto the road and pushed it away from the crossroads, starting it up only when we came to a turn that led the long way around to the Chérisy viaduct. We'd run into the Germans twice, and our luck had held. Better than theirs anyway.

CHAPTER THIRTY-TWO

DOGBITE CRAWLED LIKE a guy who'd raided a few hen-houses in his time. Elbows and knees, butt down, face caked with mud, careful with each branch and twig in his path. I was right behind him, crawling through the brush at the edge of the river, trying to be half as quiet. Maurice, being a big guy and not what you'd call light on his feet, was wading through the water below. His plan was to climb up the riverbank at the base of the viaduct, over a thirty-foot jumble of roots and rocks, which would put him about thirty yards from the gun.

Dogbite turned to face me, palm down. I followed his lead, slithering into a drainage ditch. It wasn't deep, and we could see across the road to the field where the twenty-millimeter antiaircraft gun was set up. Of course, that meant they could see us as well.

A gentle wind rustled the trees behind us, covering the sounds we made advancing on the gun and the viaduct. There was Maurice, making his climb from the base of the bridge; Topper and three men in the brush behind us, knapsacks of explosives and lengths of rope at the ready; Kaz and Christine, outfitted in SS tunics and Kraut helmets, ready to start the *Kübelwagen* at exactly two o'clock and drive to the emplacement, headlights with the pencil-thin slits aimed away from our line of approach; then Sonya and Juliet, in position to sprint across the viaduct and watch for trouble from the other side. One man to guard the road from Chérisy, in case of a surprise visit from the nearby eighty-eight-millimeter gun crew. Two more behind me, holding our weapons. If we needed more than knives, we were lost.

I glanced at my watch: ten minutes to go. We crawled a few more yards and halted, the sandbagged emplacement about twenty-five yards straight ahead. Moonlight glinted off the long twenty-millimeter gun barrel as the gunner in his bucket seat swiveled back and forth, idly searching the starlit sky. He depressed the barrel and aimed it right along the bridge, and we both instinctively ducked. Seconds later it pointed skyward again, the routine of a bored crew playing out as we closed in around them.

A scrabble of rocks fell to the water to my left. Maurice? I watched the emplacement but saw no reaction, just the lazy movements of the gun above the sandbags. The sandbags we desperately needed.

One minute before two. I'd expected to catch a glimpse of Maurice by now, but he was either well hidden or not in place yet. I scanned the field ahead, watching for signs of an unexpected patrol. It was quiet. Tobacco smoke drifted in the breeze, along with murmurs and a quick, cutting laugh. Peaceful, in an odd sort of way.

The Germans heard the engine as we did. Two of them moved to the side, leaning on the waist-high sandbags to see who was coming. Curious, not alarmed, since it was probably normal for an officer to make the rounds. The smoker flicked his cigarette in the air, the glowing tip arcing toward me before hitting the ground. In the dark, two thin slits of light approached the Germans, demanding attention. It was what we counted on.

We rose, crouching, ready to sprint, knives unsheathed. The vehicle drew closer. I made myself count to three, not wanting to jump the gun. *That's funny*, I thought, then tapped Dogbite and launched myself, head down, watching the ground ahead, careful not to trip or give any warning. I ran over the still-smoldering cigarette, my stride lengthening, and saw a figure in the *Kübel-wagen* stand, arm extended. Two figures within the emplacement dropped as I timed my leap, jumping over the sandbags and stab-bing the first German I blundered into, my knife going between his ribs as he looked me in the eye before the blade sliced into his heart and stopped everything. Pushing him aside, I scrambled around the gun, grabbing at the gunner's helmet, trying to pull him off his seat before he could squeeze off a shot and alert every Kraut within a mile.

Too late, I saw it was a waste of time. The bullet hole in his helmet marked him as dead already. Dogbite grabbed a Kraut who had one leg over the sandbags, slit his throat, and pulled him back in. Six down, or maybe all seven, if Dogbite had gotten two. Where was Maurice?

Instinctively I put my arm up as I sensed movement from the side. A shovel hit me and bounced against the gun barrel, and I felt a boot in my gut. I reeled backward as a German vaulted the sandbags, running in the direction of the next emplacement. I bolted after him, barely able to get a lungful of air as I recovered from the kick he'd given me. An officer, judging by his fancy black boots, which didn't do much for his running style. I was on him as he gasped out a cry, taking him to the ground and falling on top of him, crushing the *Achtung* or whatever he'd been trying to scream right out of him. He punched at me, trying to throw me off, terror in his eyes as he realized his mistake and went to grab my knife hand instead.

Too late.

With all the force I could muster, I plunged the knife into his chest, once, twice, then a third time. He gasped, one hand still in the air, his fingers fluttering like an injured bird trying to fly away. It hit the ground, and he was dead. I rolled off, pulling the blade from his chest, and noticed something about him.

He looked like me.

Same build, same color hair, even the same color eyes. A mouth and chin I easily recognized.

"You got him, Billy!" Kaz whispered, kneeling at my side. "We did it!"

"Yeah. Help me hide the body, okay?" We rolled him down the riverbank. I didn't say anything about his looks. I thought maybe I was seeing things. I didn't know which would be worse, killing my double or imagining my face on a man I stabbed to death.

We ran back to the gun where the sandbags were already being removed and hustled out to the viaduct. Maurice was in the *Kübelwagen*, one leg up on the rear seat.

"He is sorry," Christine said, as Maurice grimaced and nodded. "He slipped on the rocks. His leg may be broken."

"We'll get him somewhere safe when we're done," I said, figuring the Resistance had a friendly doctor or two in the area. I joined the group pulling sandbags and running them to the bridge. The burlap sacks were heavy and clumsy, and the best I could manage was one balanced on each shoulder. I dumped my first load near the rope tied off on the railing, where Topper had climbed to the first chamber, about five feet below. Knapsacks were being lowered by another rope and pulled in by a *Maquis* assisting Topper in the tight chamber.

"How's it going?" I asked, keeping my voice as low as possible.

"I'll need twenty minutes or so," Topper said, sticking his head out. "I wish we had more cordex. I had no idea how long this damn bridge was." He went back to work, and I ran for another load of sandbags. Cordex—we Yanks called it detcord—was faster than a fuse; when you set it off, the entire length exploded at once. Topper was running the detcord through blocks of gelignite. When he was done, he'd run it as far as he could along the bridge and connect a blasting cap, which would ignite the whole damn thing.

Being far enough away was pretty important.

I loaded Kaz up with two sandbags and hoisted another pair myself. Back when I'd first met Kaz, in the spring of '42, he probably couldn't have lifted one of these, much less run with two. War changed people. I bet both of us would scare the hell out of our former selves. I knew I wouldn't want to have met this new me in a darkened Boston alleyway.

When I got back for another load, the man we'd left to guard the Chérisy road was driving off with Maurice.

"I told them to wait down the road," Christine said, running back from the railroad tracks. "We can't leave Maurice alone in case something happens."

"Good idea. Anything happening in that direction?" I pointed downriver, where we thought the *Hitlerjugend* might be boarding a train.

"I felt the tracks vibrate, then stop. It means the train may have halted a mile or so away."

"Jesus, they could be on us any time," I said.

"Perhaps we should ready the twenty-millimeter gun?" Kaz said.

"It's not enough," I said. "We might stop the engine, but we can't take on a whole trainload of SS. Let's get the job done and hope the timing works out."

Christine eyed the twenty-millimeter and the stacks of ammo, and I knew she wanted to exact more revenge for Coudray. I did, too, but from a safe distance.

At the bridge, I dumped the sandbags and let myself down the rope to check on progress. Topper was bent over in the small circular chamber, a spool of detcord in his hand, a stack of sandbags about a foot high in front of him. "Done," he said, handing me the detcord as he crawled out. "Let's get the rest of the sandbags down. The more the better."

I climbed back up as the *Maquis* began handing the bags over the rail, fire brigade style. I handed the detcord to Topper, who began running it along the iron railing that ran waist high the length of the viaduct. I ran in the other direction to tell Juliet and Sonya we were almost done.

"Anything?" I whispered when I found them at a curve in the tracks.

"No," Sonya said, resting her Sten gun on the rock she'd hidden behind. "We can hear the Germans on the hill when the wind is right, but they're not close."

I told them about Christine feeling the rails.

"That's not good," Juliet said. "The Germans are known to patrol vulnerable stretches of rail when a troop train is due to pass through."

"Perhaps they think this area well guarded," Sonya said.

"I hope. Listen, I'll come get you when we're done with the sandbags. We'll have to hurry. We have more bridge than detonating cord, it seems."

I ran back. Topper wanted even more sandbags. We relayed another thirty, pretty much the last of them, and he thought we might have a chance.

"Damn thing is too well made," he said, lowering himself down the rope to pack in the last of the bags himself.

"Vibrations," Christine said, her hand resting on the rail. "We don't have much time."

"Pull me up," Topper said, grasping my hand. "I'll get the cord set. Toss the rope over."

I made for Juliet and Sonya, stopping in my tracks at the sound of gunfire. From the direction of the Chérisy road came a volley of rifle fire and repeated bursts of machine guns. German patrols. Had they found Maurice? I raced ahead slouching low as I advanced, Thompson at the ready.

Sonya spotted me. She was hidden behind a rock, pointing down the track. A German patrol, four or five men that I could see, advancing at quickstep in response to the shooting across the bridge.

Things were going to get noisy. And deadly.

We couldn't pull back across the bridge; they'd be on us before

Topper was ready. Shots picked up again across the river, and I began to worry we'd be trapped on this side if the Germans won that fight. Juliet and I were hidden behind the curve of the track, Sonya in the rocks ahead. The Germans entered a narrow cut, their boots echoing on the thick wooden ties. Even in the dark, they were bunched together. Easy targets.

Juliet whispered, "Now?" Sonya looked to me. I nodded, taking out a grenade from my jacket. I pulled the pin, let the safety go, and waited two seconds, then threw it into their midst.

An explosion, screams, and then I stood on the tracks, emptying the Thompson into whoever was left standing. One Kraut was still in business with his submachine gun, and I scrambled to the other side of the tracks as I reloaded. Sonya and Juliet each kept up with bursts from their Stens, forcing him to stay under cover. I crawled forward, looking to get an angle on him. Then I saw the grenade. The German potato masher with its wooden handle, sailing end over end. I yelled a warning, and then dove behind a rock, firing as the Kraut made his run for it, only to get a burst of .45 rounds in his back.

The grenade bounced about ten yards out. I huddled behind the rock as it exploded, the sound deafening in the narrow railway cut.

There were no screams. Only the silence that settled in after a fight, overlaid with the scent of blood, gunpowder, and violence. I checked the Germans to be sure they were dead. It needed to be done, but it gave me a few seconds to prepare.

I turned and saw Juliet standing over the body of Sonya.

"She's dead," Juliet said, her voice ready to break. I felt nothing but relief, relief that Juliet—my Diana—was alive. The fact that another person was dead would sink in later, I knew, and I'd be ashamed. But now, I only cared about life. Her life.

"Yes, but we have to go. Now." I tried to take her by the arm.

"No, Billy. We can't leave Sonya."

"There's no time to worry about the dead."

"It's the living I worry about," she said. "The Germans will try to trace the identities of anyone they find. We don't carry our papers, but she's well known in the area."

Of course. I hadn't thought of that. I knelt, picking up Sonya's shattered body, blood oozing from a terrible wound on her back. She'd tried to outrun the grenade, or hadn't seen it in time. Either way, it didn't matter. Sonya was gone, as was whoever she had once been.

Her body was slippery, the blood coating my hands and making it hard to keep a grasp on her dead weight as I stumbled along the railroad tracks.

"Here," Kaz said, gesturing with his hand for us to hurry. He was at the end of the bridge, near the base where Maurice had broken his leg. Topper was busy connecting blasting caps to the end of the detcord.

"Oh, no," Christine said as I approached, Sonya cradled in my arms. Her face crumpled. Then she recovered, calling for two *Maquis*, who took the body and headed downstream, leaving me exhausted and with bloodstained hands. "Maurice is dead. They fought off the patrol, but at least one got away. We must hurry."

"Done here," Topper said, wrapping waterproof tape around the blasting cap connections. We followed him down the riverbank as he unspooled the last of the detcord, stopping not twenty feet away. "That's it. I connect the detonator to the caps, and Bob's your uncle."

"We're awfully close," I said.

"That's all the wire I have. I'd head back if I were you," Topper said with a fierce grin. "This place will soon be crawling with Germans, followed by flying debris, I hope."

"I, for one, would hate to miss the spectacle," Kaz said. "But perhaps we could move back for a better view."

"We should wait for the train," Christine said, and issued a sharp order to her remaining men, who disappeared into the brush. "They will cover our escape. But we must try for the train."

"Those *Hitlerjugend* bastards?" Topper said. She nodded. So did Kaz. So did I.

We waited.

Topper had run the detcord under the iron railing. It was pulled taut, looped around the stanchions every yard or so. All the Germans had to do was look in the right place, but they were focused on the railbed, not thinking about the round chambers on the side of the stonework. Two patrols swept up and down the viaduct, flashlight beams on the tracks, looking for dynamite under the steel rails. Shouts and commands echoed from the bridge, the lights fading as the Krauts walked back to where the train had halted. Maybe they thought they'd fought off the *Maquis* before charges could be set, or that it had been an ambush gone wrong.

"Look, it's the SS," Kaz whispered. He was right. Under the bright moon, their dappled camouflage tunics stood out clearly. These patrols were from the *Hitlerjugend*, not the *Luftwaffe* flak crews or security troops. Who might have wondered where all the sandbags had gone.

"They must have halted the train when they heard the shooting and taken over the search," Topper said, connecting the ends of the wire to the detonator.

"And now they will pay," Christine whispered. No one moved back, but we did take cover behind the boulders and driftwood at the edge of the riverbank. The granite stonework shone in the moonlight like a giant beast straddling the river.

A sound. The scuff of a boot on stone. The snap of a small twig.

A heavier sound—the hissing chug of a locomotive.

From where we were, we couldn't see the train, but the mechanical sounds of the steam engine and the cars jolting forward told us it was getting closer. Topper grasped the detonator handle.

Shadows moved in front of us. Two, three men, making their way down the riverbank. The last of the patrol, perhaps. One of them turned to look at the bridge and the approaching train, which was picking up speed. He said something in a weary voice, which I imagined to be along the lines of, *Let's get the hell out of here.*

Then one of them knelt. He picked up the detcord and tugged at it. Topper grabbed hold of the wire, making sure the connections didn't come loose. Still no train on the bridge.

Now the three Germans were crouched low, rifles aimed forward, the lead man holding the detcord, letting it trail through his hand, trying not to give any warning of their approach, never thinking the demolition team would be so close.

I saw the flash of a knife. One of the Germans was about to slice the detcord.

A puff of steam close to the bridge, and in a second the train was in view, louder and faster.

Kaz and Christine stood, aiming their Welrod pistols at the three men. They fired.

The train pulled onto the bridge, the locomotive nearly to where the explosives were set.

One man dropped, the only noise the clatter of his rifle on stone. More shots, these audible now, soft *pop-pops* that felled another German.

Topper twisted the plunger.

The explosion was a blast of jolting sound echoing along the river: a core of flames blindingly bright for a split second, followed by black smoke belching from the hole as bits of stone and showers of burning debris spread out in front of us.

The last German standing looked dully at what was left of his hand, which had been blown apart by the detcord he'd been holding. Dogbite let him have a burst from his Thompson, ending the German's misery before it even registered.

The viaduct stood. The train started to cross the bridge, sparks flying as the engineer applied the air brake. But there was too much momentum, and as the locomotive continued on, the train seemed to pick up speed as if the engineer was racing to get over before the structure collapsed. As the dust settled, I could see the blast site more clearly. Everything looked intact.

The locomotive reached the center of the bridge, which held. Then, slowly, pieces of stone began to fall from the arch. The locomotive continued forward, the following cars wobbling as their steel wheels clacked over the rails. Finally, a large chunk of granite tumbled from under the railbed and fell into the river. A flatcar with two tanks slipped from the track, twisting and snapping its coupler, beginning a slow slide off the bridge. The wheels on the far side of the car almost caught and held onto the edge until the next car, and the next, smashed into it, starting a chain reaction that left the flatcar and four passenger cars shattered in the riverbed below. Bodies spilled out onto the rocks and were swept away in the water.

The tail end of the train ground to a halt, sparks flying as the emergency brakes were pulled. One more car tumbled over and burst into flames.

It was time to go.

Christine stood, her fists clenched as she shouted, "Coudray!" but the Germans could not hear her above the screams and cries of their injured and dying.

CHAPTER THIRTY-THREE

IT WAS A long hike back, and dawn was beginning to light the horizon as we returned to the château. The remaining *Maquis* had already vanished into the forest when we stumbled into the kitchen, exhausted, dirty, and hungry.

Sonya, Maurice, and three of the *Maquis* were dead. If this mission was ever written up, the report would say casualties were light, and the operation a qualified success. The bridge would be repaired, but we'd struck a deadly blow.

Still, five deaths weighed heavily.

We made ersatz coffee and scrounged for whatever food we could find. The kitchen was warm and the food welcome, but a night of killing had left us empty and in need of nourishment not to be found in the count's larder.

Juliet fetched Switch, Babcock, and Fawcett and brought them up to date.

"I'm sorry about Sonya," Fawcett said. "She was a brave woman."

"When are we getting out of here?" Switch asked. Topper stood, his fists ready, and Switch saw the wisdom in adding his reluctant condolences. Topper still looked ready to pummel him, and I wondered if he even remembered that getting Switch back in one piece would be good for the family business. All that seemed so far in the distant past.

"Tonight," I said. "Kaz and I are taking Switch out tonight. Then we'll set something up for you two."

"You're leaving us in the lurch?" Babcock said. "Fawcett and I have been here longer than Switch. And what about Juliet? She's all alone now."

"Orders," I said.

"And I'll be here," Topper said. "Perhaps we'll all join the *Maquis* and wait for the cavalry."

"That might be a good idea," Count Vasseur said, entering the kitchen. "I have made a deal with Major Zeller. He will be here at nine o'clock with your former colleague Meyer."

"What the hell are you talking about?" Switch demanded. He spoke for us all.

"I telephoned Zeller last night," the count said. "I told him I knew what he was after, and he could have all the paintings if he returned two things—my son and the wireless."

"What did he say?" Juliet asked.

"That he was not certain he could meet my terms. I then told him I was ready to burn down the château and everything in it if he did not. He accepted my offer. Evidently your Sergeant Meyer has new identity papers and is working directly with Zeller as an *Abwehr* agent. All for the purpose of stealing the artwork, of course."

"But what if he shows up with an armed guard?" I said.

"He will not," Count Vasseur said, shaking his head emphatically. "Why would he throw away a chance at what he has wanted all along? With the Allies closing in, this is his moment. All he has to do is give me my son. I thought to ask for the wireless because it would have been foolish for Meyer to destroy it. Better for him to give it as a gift to his new employer."

"How can you let him get away with his crimes, Count Vasseur?" Juliet said, her eyes glistening. "Adrien, then the two men here? Sonya, too, for that matter."

"I know it is a difficult choice. I am devastated to hear that Sonya has been killed, but that is the way of war. If I could bring back the men Zeller has murdered, I would. But that is in the past.

Now I can keep Frédéric alive, and you can have your wireless. It is not a good solution, but it is a solution."

"What about the people who entrusted you with their paintings?" Babcock said.

"They are paintings, not lives. Besides, the owners may all have perished by now," Count Vasseur said. "I think Christine should leave. There is no reason for Zeller to see her here."

"I vote for leaving now myself," Babcock said. "I'll take my chances with the *Maquis*. If you do get the wireless, make contact with us after all this is over. If any of you are still alive."

"I'm with you," Fawcett said. "I don't like the sound of this. Reminds me of Dieppe." Dieppe was a disastrous raid on the French coast back in '42, where Canadian forces landed and were chewed up, half of them not making it back.

"What about you, Dogbite?" I asked.

"I might not be much sharper than a butter knife, but I can tell a whole lotta things might go bad right around nine o'clock, so I'll head for the hills with these boys. Feel more at home in the woods anyway."

"We will leave now," Christine said. "I can take you men to a safe place in the forest with the *Maquis*." With that, she embraced the count. "I hope to find Frédéric safe at home with you when I return."

We all shook hands, wishing Dogbite, Fawcett, and Babcock luck. Topper made arrangements to rendezvous with them in the forest the following day, wireless or not. He was the real Jedburgh, and he still had a job to do. Switch went to pack his gear, planning to watch from the edge of the woods to make sure he had an escape route in case things went south.

"I ain't being trapped like a rat underground," he said.

"Just don't go too far," I said.

"Don't worry, Billy. You're my meal ticket. You stay in one piece and get me back to England. Donnie and me are counting on it."

"Are you sure we could not toss him out somewhere over the English Channel?" Kaz said, watching Switch leave.

"You boys deliver him safe and sound, or my old man will have my hide," Topper said.

"Archie must be so proud," I said, and sipped the chicory coffee, making believe it was the real thing. All I wanted to do was lie down and sleep for hours, but something told me I'd need to keep my wits about me for a while longer.

IT WAS CLOSE to nine. Topper was stationed at the end of the long driveway. If Zeller had troops with him, he'd fire warning shots, and we'd all scatter. Count Vasseur said he had a small supply of petrol and was ready to start a fire in the great hall if Zeller betrayed him. I believed the old guy, and I began to think maybe Zeller did, too.

Juliet and the count stood by the front entrance, Vincent at attention behind them. Kaz and I were inside, watching. Switch was who the hell knew where. I tried to square the fact that we were doing a deal with a Kraut officer the morning after we'd blown up a bunch of his pals on a train. But then I thought back to some of the deals we'd done with crooks at the Boston PD, and it felt a little more natural.

Five minutes past nine. I heard the crunch of tires on gravel. No warning shots. The sedan came into view, a big black Citroën Traction Avant. Zeller was planning on traveling in style. And hiding the rolled-up canvases in the spacious trunk.

The automobile came to a halt. Meyer stepped out, looking like a different man in his pressed pants, shined shoes, slicked-back hair, white shirt, and leather jacket. He opened the rear passenger door. Zeller slipped out, followed by a thin figure in tattered clothes who needed help to stand upright.

"Frédéric!" Count Vasseur gasped.

Zeller withdrew the wireless case from the backseat and a Walther pistol from his holster. He and Meyer stood in front of the count. "Tell me why I should not shoot you now," Zeller said.

"Because you want the paintings, and I am ready to give them to you. All of them. That is my solemn promise as a Vasseur," the count said. "How do you propose we proceed?"

"You are correct, count. I will get what I want, and so will you. Your son. And no one will ever suspect what you've been up to. Now for the arrangements: Meyer will remain inside with the wireless and your son. He will execute him at the first sign of trouble from any of you. My headquarters knows where I am, and should anything happen, you will be under immediate suspicion."

"Of course," Count Vasseur said. "Vincent will assist. Since you are aware of my other guests, I can tell you they all have fled. Except for two, who are waiting for the wireless."

"They will help us. No firearms," Zeller said, his own gun pointed straight at Juliet.

"Major," I said from the doorway, hands held high, "perhaps we should all put away our weapons. It will go faster that way." Kaz stood next to me, his hand resting on his holstered Webley.

"You must be Sergeant Boyle. And the baron, I see. No others?"

"Gone, as the count told you," Juliet said. "Let's get Frédéric inside. Is he hurt?"

"A mild sedative," Zeller said. "To make him more manageable. Pistols will remain holstered. But Meyer will keep his trained on the boy."

We agreed. Juliet would stay with them. Meyer took the count's son into the great hall and laid him on a couch before sitting down, the wireless between his legs and a revolver cocked and aimed at Frédéric.

"How do you like your new boss?" I asked.

"He pays better," Meyer said. "Better than the Morgans, even. Now get to work."

"Yes, come, Count Vasseur," Zeller said, clapping his hands eagerly. "I cannot wait to see your hiding place. You've been most clever."

"As have you," the count said, gracing Zeller with a small bow. "I assume you have known about the paintings for a while?"

"Since I came to Dreux from Paris," he said. "We picked up an art dealer who foolishly returned from Tours, where he had a number of hiding places. He confirmed you had taken a shipment on behalf of Jewish friends. It did not take much persuasion."

"Ah, yes, there is always someone who will talk, isn't there? Come." The count led us down the now-familiar steps, through the Druid temple, and into the long tunnel that led to the hidden chamber.

"Ah, the lair of the White Giant," Zeller said. "A convenient fairy tale to mask your activities from the locals. Such weak minds they have."

"I agree," Count Vasseur said. "The old stories have their hold over us." He led us into a darkened section, and Vincent flicked on his flashlight. Zeller produced one as well. We passed under the granite lintels and came to the dead end with the old empty barrels.

"Here?" Zeller said. "I could never find a thing in this tunnel. It's sealed off."

"You underestimate the ingenuity of the Vasseurs, Major," the count said. "Vincent, *s'il vous plaît.*"

Vincent reached into the crevice and began the process of opening the stone door. He pushed against it, the scent of grease and oil rising as he smoothly rolled it aside. Zeller shined his flashlight inside.

"Ach, du lieber Gott im Himmel," Zeller whispered as his beam played across the canvases. Then he regained his composure, and ordered us in ahead of him. "Not that I don't trust you gentlemen,

but please stack those barrels in front of the door. To ensure it doesn't close by accident, of course."

Kaz and I complied as Zeller spent a few seconds inspecting the paintings. He looked at the stretchers, nodding sagely as he ran his fingers against the grain of the wood.

"So your paintings in the château are fakes?" he asked, studying *Blue Madonna*. "This wood is obviously centuries old."

"Vincent is quite talented," Count Vasseur said, nodding. "He has fooled experts."

"Yes, yes. I am quite impressed. Now hurry and remove these canvases from the stretchers." Zeller produced pliers from his pocket and handed them to Vincent. To save time, he also pulled his knife from its sheath to begin cutting the larger canvases. "You two, help him!"

Soon we had about a quarter of the canvases done and rolled up. Zeller ordered us to take them to the car and to tell Meyer all was well. For now.

We did as we were told and returned to find Zeller and the count arguing over *Blue Madonna*. Oddly enough, it was about whether or not to take it out of the frame.

"Please, Major, it is such a small painting. You can hide it easily. I would hate to see the canvas damaged." Count Vasseur held it at arm's length, studying it one last time.

"Very well," he said. "I must agree with you. It is too lovely to risk. We can wrap it in one of these coverings. For the moment, enjoy it while you can."

Vincent loaded us up with rolled canvases while the count stood in quiet contemplation of the small masterpiece. With his back to Zeller, he gave us a quick wink and nodded toward the door. We hustled out, and as we crossed the threshold, the count dropped *Blue Madonna*.

Zeller sputtered in anger as the count backed up, waving his hands apologetically. Vincent vaulted forward, hitting Zeller with his shoulder and sending him reeling against the stone wall as Count Vasseur ran out, Vincent on his heels, moving as fast as his injured legs allowed. Turning on a dime, Vincent reached into the groove at the base of the entryway, where the hidden door moved on the metal track. A quick metallic *snap*, and an iron door shuddered down, slamming into the stone inches from his hand.

The pounding and the shouts began immediately, muffled by the heavy iron door and surrounding stone. Count Vasseur smiled and clapped Vincent on the back.

"But the paintings," I said, wondering what exactly we'd gained.

"As I said, Vincent has fooled experts," the count said.

"All that artwork?" Kaz said, hardly believing what we were hearing.

"Oh, yes. He has been very busy these past years," the count said, patting a beaming Vincent on the shoulder. "Now bring those paintings along, and we will speak with the treacherous Meyer. It is vital that he leave unharmed."

"What about Zeller?" I asked.

"It appears he should have paid better attention to the fairy tale," Count Vasseur said. "Remember the White Giant, who promises you all the time in the world with the treasure you seek?" He and Vincent were all smiles as we made our way back to the grand hall. All I could think of was the sound of that door slamming shut.

"Where's the major? What's taking so long?" Meyer demanded as soon as the four of us walked into the room.

"The major has decided these paintings should be yours along with the others in the automobile," Count Vasseur said, nodding to our armfuls of canvas. "He is otherwise detained and quite sincerely regrets he cannot join you."

"What's the idea, Boyle?" Meyer said, deciding to level his pistol at me.

"You're getting a free pass, Meyer," I said. "You and Zeller had a plan, right? A place for you to hide out with your new identity papers and to squirrel away the paintings? You were smart, thinking long-term like that. Now you just have to do it on your own. Once the war passes by, find a fence and live like a king."

"Why?" Meyer said. "Why let me go?"

"You did not imprison and torture my son," Count Vasseur said. "Zeller became my sworn enemy once he did that. And you are nothing but a loose end, you and that automobile. It is best for all if you drive away and disappear. You have the paintings. Make the most of them."

"Zeller's dead?" Meyer said, lowering his pistol, seeing little percentage in gunning any of us down.

"No. I promised him the paintings, and now he has his fair share. *Blue Madonna*, in fact."

"He liked that one," Meyer said, apparently deciding not to pursue the question any further. "Okay. Take those out to the car."

We dumped the artwork into the trunk and watched Meyer drive off. I didn't know if I should shoot or wave goodbye.

"What just happened?" Topper asked as he jogged down the drive to join us.

"I think that old fellow outfoxed us all," I said. "Let's see what other surprises he has in store."

We found them in an upstairs bedroom. Juliet was washing Frédéric's face as Vincent disposed of his filthy clothes and got him between clean sheets. The wireless sat on a table, the case open. Topper began to check it out.

"It works," Juliet said, once Topper gave a thumbs-up. "We'll send an emergency sked in a few minutes."

"Papa," Frédéric managed, his eyes opening and a smile gracing his face before he drifted back to sleep.

The count beamed. *"Mon fils,"* he said. Tears streaked his cheeks.

"Count Vasseur, I'm sorry to interrupt, but what are we going to do with Zeller?"

"Nothing, Sergeant. Look at this." The count pulled back the sheets. Bruises, some fresh, some old, discolored Frédéric's torso. His arms were covered in burns, as if cigarettes had been ground out against his flesh.

"You are not going to open the door?" Kaz said. I think he sounded hopeful.

"It does not open, unlike the stone door. It is a last-ditch defense. That chamber was the most secret of all the hiding places the first count constructed."

"But what good is the iron door if it locks you in?"

"Oh, there was an exit. A disguised trapdoor that led outside, meant to be used only if the hidden room was found by the King's dragoons. But it was sealed shut by a cave-in years ago. There is no way out. Major Zeller has what he wanted. The paintings for the rest of his life." Count Vasseur looked at us all, perhaps expecting an objection concerning Zeller's entombment. None were made. Besides, Zeller had his pistol. His suffering need not last.

"But what about his staff knowing he came here?" Juliet said, wringing out a washcloth into a bowl.

"I told you before I have a friend at the *gendarmerie* in Épernon," the count said. "The same man who contacted me when Sonya was taken, a fellow Huguenot. I asked him to contact the German military police in Dreux and file a complaint about the unauthorized seizure of artwork from my château. The Germans do not officially steal from French citizens; they make purchases for a pittance and provide receipts. And those purchases are for the Nazi treasury and party officials, not for mere *Abwehr* majors."

"So Zeller's men will be too busy answering questions to bother searching for him," Kaz said approvingly.

"Yes, especially if the Gestapo gets involved. As they certainly will if they pick up Meyer and find Zeller gave identity papers to an American. It all ends with Frédéric safe, for now at least."

"The Germans may take a renewed interest in your artwork," Kaz said. "It seems Zeller kept them at bay, perhaps through mislaid paperwork, for his own purposes."

"Perhaps they will," Count Vasseur said, a sly smile playing on his lips. "I believe we have kept enough secrets from you all." He spoke to Vincent, who crooked his finger for us to follow.

Vincent led us upstairs to the infamous room where Margaux went through the window and bled out. He moved a pile of furniture and reached up into the molding that ran beneath the ceiling. Then he grasped a sconce and pulled. The wall came forward, revealing a painting draped in a sheet. He removed it, and I saw *Blue Madonna* for the first time.

She was beautiful.

CHAPTER THIRTY-FOUR

KAZ AND I packed up what little gear we had as Topper and Juliet worked on the message to London: the bridge had been damaged, Sonya was dead, and three of us would be at the Lysander landing zone tonight. Simple, as long as SOE didn't ask too many questions.

Switch was getting anxious. He'd been cool and calm, even as the body count rose around him, but now with only hours to go, he was fidgety.

"I'll be okay," he said, pacing in the narrow confines of the salon. "I always got keyed up before a mission. I hated waiting for take-off, wondering what could go wrong."

"It'll be fine," I said, hoping he'd settle down for the long hike to the landing area. "Good weather, hardly a cloud in the sky. We'll have a *Maquis* escort all the way." Christine was sending men to clear out all the weapons and supplies from the tunnels. If Meyer got picked up and blabbed, we didn't want any evidence left to implicate Juliet and the count.

"Yeah, that's what they said about the milk run when we got shot down. It'll be fine. And here I am, the last man standing."

"You are the last man here because you're being flown to England tonight," Kaz said. "Unless you'd prefer to take your chances with Dogbite and stay with the *Maquis*?"

"You know what I mean," Switch said, slamming his meager pack onto the table. "Sorry, it's only a case of nervous in the service. Don't worry, I won't screw things up. And I'll hold up my end of the deal once I see Donnie, and we get our transfers and promotions squared away."

"We never mentioned promotions," I said. "But if you don't cause trouble, I'll put in a word for you." Why not, if it calmed him down and made things easier all around tonight.

"Okay. Tell me, you ain't really a sergeant, are you?"

"No. I'm a captain."

"You'd be surprised how many captains I got on my payroll, Billy. They come pretty cheap."

"So do a lot of things in this war. Now shut up."

We left Switch in the kitchen and took up lookout positions, watching the driveway from the upstairs windows. It was quiet. Quiet as a tomb.

An hour later, Juliet and Topper came in. The sked had been coded and sent. London confirmed a response in three hours. We were all dead on our feet, but Kaz volunteered to stay awake and stand watch. Topper would grab a couple hours' sleep and then hike a mile into the woods to receive the sked.

Juliet took me by the hand. Kaz smiled as she led me away.

There was already hot water in the bathtub. We stripped off our dirty clothes, and I felt strangely embarrassed. Maybe it was the dirt, or the rusty dried blood on my sleeves and shirt. Or the fact that I was leaving Juliet behind. No, Diana. I could call her Diana now.

"I'm sorry, Diana," I said. "Sorry I have to leave."

"Me, too, Billy," she said, settling into the steamy water. Her toes wriggled at my side. "It's been strange, hasn't it? We haven't had a moment together, not as who we really are."

"Juliet and Sergeant Boyle were a pretty good team," I said, relaxing a bit as the water soothed my muscles.

"I am so tired of them," Diana said, sliding her head underwater and coming up with her light brown hair plastered over her forehead. "Aren't you?"

"Yes, Diana, I am. Thoroughly." I doused my head as well, emerging as a new man, baptized Billy, an officer and a gentleman. Being a gentleman, I'll leave it at that.

We fell asleep in a jumble of white sheets, a warm breeze wafting in through the windows. When I awoke, I didn't think about Germans, betrayals, or secret tunnels for a full thirty seconds. Until I noticed Diana was gone.

I dressed and grabbed my weapons, heading for the kitchen. Topper was back, and Diana was already at work decoding the sked. I must have slept for hours.

"Oh my God," she said, finishing a line of letters, looking up at me with worried eyes. The news must have been bad.

"What's wrong?" I asked as she ran her finger along the words, double-checking her work. "Is the pickup canceled?"

"No, it's on. But you and Kaz are not going back. I am."

"With me, right?" Switch said. "Right?" Nobody answered.

"I'll wake Kaz," Topper said, grabbing Switch by the collar. "You, come with me."

When we were alone, Diana explained. The Noble network was being shut down. With Sonya's death and the front lines inching closer, moving escapees and downed airmen was too dangerous. Two Jedburghs would come in tonight with supplies to join Topper. Diana—Juliet Bonvie—was to return to England for reassignment. Kaz and I were to be at the landing site and receive orders via the Jedburghs.

"I never expected this," she said. "I don't want it. I'd rather stay here with you."

"They're right, you know," I said. "The fighting could get close very soon. You won't be able to move freely, especially now that both Adrien and Sonya are gone. Topper's assignment is to work directly with the *Maquis*, not the SOE. You'd be all alone."

"As will you and Kaz. What do they want you to do? You can't pass for a Frenchman. You can't pass for anything but a Boston policeman, as far as I can tell." She gave me a smile, and I grinned like an idiot, happy that she was going home and out of danger. It was easier than leaving her in occupied France. I might feel differently once I found out what my new orders were all about, but for now, all I could do was hug her.

WE'D BID *adieux* to Count Vasseur and Frédéric, who looked somewhat better once the sedative had worn off. He still was in bad shape, but with rest and care, he'd pull through. Madame Agard and Justine had returned, and with Vincent's help, they might all make it.

Christine's men cleared out the tunnels and carted everything off. Four of them escorted us to the landing zone, where we waited in the meadow, five fires ready to be set as the prearranged signal.

Diana and I walked the length of the grassy field, the fading moon giving just enough light for the Lysander to navigate by. Stars twinkled in the heavens, and searchlights lit the distant horizon, hunting for bombers as they unleashed thunderous salvos, bright orange explosions flashing against the scattered clouds. The eerie, strange beauty of our times.

"Remember the poem, Billy?" Diana asked as she leaned her head against my shoulder. "The love that I have/of the life that I have/is yours and yours and yours."

"I'll never forget it," I said, as the snarl of an aircraft engine drifted in from the north. We held each other close as we watched the skies, Diana's damp cheek nestled against mine. The fires were lit, and soon the black Lysander landed and rolled to a stop. The two Jedburghs clambered out and unloaded the supplies, handing Kaz and me each a musette bag. They hustled Switch inside, and Diana and I barely had time for an embrace before the pilot yelled for her to get a move on.

She squeezed my hand and let go, her head bent low as she

climbed the ladder and pulled the canopy shut. She couldn't look at me through the window. I couldn't have looked back, either, if she had been the one left behind in the face of unknown dangers. I tasted the salt from her tears as the Lysander roared off, the blast from its propeller flattening the long green grass at my feet.

> *Yet death will be but a pause*
> *For the peace of my years*
> *In the long green grass*
> *Will be yours and yours and yours.*

AUTHOR'S NOTE

THE US ARMY Criminal Investigation Division estimated that in 1944–1945, forty percent of all crimes within their jurisdiction were related to the theft of army materials. The vast tonnage of supplies, ranging from medicines and foodstuffs to petroleum products, that flowed into Great Britain prior to D-Day presented a tantalizing opportunity for military and civilian personnel alike. In Great Britain, the Billy Hill Gang took full advantage of the black market, stealing and selling food and fuel while engaging in the lucrative side business of forged identity documents. The fictional Morgan Gang also had its real-life counterparts in the Lane Gang and the Sailor Gang, comprised of deserters active in Italy during the same time period.

After D-Day, the situation in France was even worse, as Colonel Harding predicted it would be. For example, the 716th Railway Operating Battalion nicknamed itself "The Millionaires' Battalion" for its role in stealing supplies headed for the front lines and selling them to French gangsters.

Fifty thousand Americans deserted during World War Two, as did over one hundred thousand British troops. Some desertions were for short periods of time, or as a result of the stress of combat, with men ultimately returning to service. Others were more calculated, the lure of easy money too great to ignore. After the liberation of Paris, that city became a magnet for deserters, who were well armed, combat trained, and not afraid to use their weapons.

To give a sense of the kind of money that could be made, the going black market rate for a single can of coffee in 1944 was ten dollars. That equals $135 in 2014 dollars. A crate holding fifty cartons of cigarettes went for $1,000, which is $13,500 in today's dollars. Tempting to many, especially given the voluminous amounts available in supply depots all across England.

The massacre conducted by the SS in the village of Coudray, while fictional, happened all too often during the war. The most notorious of these was conducted by the Second SS Panzer Division at Oradour-sur-Glane, where 642 men, women, and children were murdered in retaliation for nearby partisan activity. The burned-out village was never rebuilt, and today stands as a memorial and museum.

The Special Operations Executive used many female agents in occupied France. Women had greater freedom of movement, given that men were often conscripted for war labor in Germany. Violet Szabo was one such brave woman. The poem "The Life That I Have," by SOE code master Leo Marks, was actually Szabo's poem code. She was captured on her second mission, just after D-Day, and ultimately executed at Ravensbrück concentration camp in February 1945, at the age of twenty-three. Thirty-eight other female agents were sent into France. Fourteen were executed. Their stories are all riveting.

The Jedburgh Teams (named after a town in Scotland) comprised about three hundred men and contributed greatly to Allied successes following D-Day, their impact on the battlefield out of all proportion to their numbers. The Jedburghs and other commandos faced execution if captured on the basis of Hitler's infamous Commando Order. Approximately eighty captured Allied personnel were murdered as a result of that directive.

Château Vasseur was imagined as a result of reading the *London Literary Gazette and Journal* of 1827, which contained an account of the Castle of Robardière in the Forest of Dreux outside Paris. It was built upon the ruins of an ancient Druid temple and rumored to contain underground vaults and chambers that had yet to be explored. It was overseen by the White Giant, an apparition who guarded the "vault secured with iron doors, which open once a year during the celebration of midnight mass. Any one may enter and enrich himself as much as he pleases; but the mass once finished, the iron doors close immediately and woe betide him who is enclosed in the cavern!"

The story of poor Margaux and the haunted painting is taken from *Tales of the Dead*, a superb collection of French ghost stories published in 1813.

The centerpiece of Count Vasseur's personal art collection was *Blue Madonna*, painted by Carlo Dolci, a major Florentine painter of the seventeenth century. It safely resides in the Ringling Museum of Art in Sarasota, Florida. Acquired by John Ringling in 1927, this luminous work avoided the widespread looting of artwork carried out by the Nazis during the Second World War.

ACKNOWLEDGMENTS

I AM INDEBTED to the entire creative team at Soho Press. I hesitate to name names out of fear of missing any one of that terrific crew; but I must mention that Diana Seaton's *faux* identity of Juliet Bonvie is a nod to Juliet Grames, associate publisher and the best advocate an author could ask for.

My wife, Debbie Mandel, continues to play an important role as first reader and first editor, lending her keen eye and supportive shoulder to this endeavor specifically, and all else in general.

The description of the destruction of the bridge at Chérisy owes much to a society of experts I frequently call upon: a WWII listserv whose members provide an extraordinary level of detail whenever I come up with a question for them. I had no idea of the complexities involved in blowing up a stone bridge, and the group helped me to portray it authentically, avoiding the error of over-simplification.

Specifically, Gordon Rottman, a 26-year veteran of the US Army Special Forces, came up with the plan to take down the bridge. In addition to his military career, he's the author of a number of non-fiction military titles from Osprey Publishing, and the award-winning author of *The Hardest Ride*, a great western novel. If you ever need to blow up a bridge, Gordo's your man.

Continue reading for a preview from the next
Billy Boyle Mystery

THE DEVOURING

CHAPTER ONE

LIGHT IS FASTER than sound.

Strange, the things you think about when you're about to die. Even as tracers lit the night air, their silent silvery phosphorescence clawing at our small aircraft from the ground below, a tiny part of my brain mused on this practical demonstration of that scientific fact. The rest of my brain panicked madly, sending surges of adrenaline coursing through my body, urging me to get the hell out, *now*.

Which was not at all helpful, given that we were flying at five hundred feet, heading directly into heavy antiaircraft fire, making one hundred and eighty miles per hour.

Then came the sound. The chattering of ack-ack fire. Flak exploding in blinding flashes all around us. Shrapnel struck the aircraft, rending the metal, sounding like the devil's own hail storm on a sheet-metal roof.

"Hold tight!" shouted the pilot as he dove the Lysander and put it through twists and turns to evade the lead rising up against us. I looked below as he dipped the airplane and saw the twinkling of automatic fire from along the stretch of river we'd been following.

"They're on the road," I shouted to the pilot in the single front seat. It was a column of German vehicles, moving at night to avoid Allied aircraft, and we'd flown dead at them.

The pilot didn't waste breath answering. He banked left, violently, diving to treetop level at a right angle away from the river. Looking back, I saw tracer fire searching vainly for us, then fade as the Krauts gave up and continued on their way.

The Lysander jolted, loud *thumps* whacking against the aircraft frame.

"Sorry, chaps," the pilot muttered, pulling back on the yoke and gaining altitude. "Almost landed in the pines. She's a bit sluggish, might've caught some shrapnel in the rudder." He banked the Lysander, bringing us around to the river again, the only map to our destination.

"There may be other columns on the road," Kaz said, adjusting his steel-rimmed spectacles. Even after nearly being blown out of the sky and tossed around inside the cramped Lysander, he managed to sound nonchalant, his precise English leavened with the slightest of Polish accents.

"The Saône River is our only landmark," the pilot said. "Jerry's travel plans notwithstanding. If we veer off to the east, we run the risk of entering Swiss airspace. It'd be damned embarrassing to be shot down by the Swiss, after all."

"Why?" Kaz asked.

"You know the Swiss. Chocolate, watches, and sheep, that's what they're famous for. I'd never hear the end of it, if I lived to tell the tale."

"Personally, I'd choose death by chocolatier if I had any say in the matter," Kaz responded. Switzerland was our ultimate destination, and we weren't in the market for wristwatches.

"Don't worry about the Swiss or the Jerries," the pilot said. "I haven't lost a Joe yet, and I don't plan on starting tonight."

We were his Joes. It was what the Special Operations Executive pilots called the agents and commandoes they flew into occupied Europe. No names, nothing to reveal if captured and tortured, just an anonymous one-way ride to some grassy field in the countryside. In a few minutes we were back on course, flying low over dark hills and a glistening waterway, the bright half-moon at our backs providing a tempting target for alert Kraut gunners, the river our only guide.

"What's the next landmark?" I asked the nameless pilot.

"We'll bear left at the Rhône River in Lyon. There's a sharp bend in the river, it'll be easy to spot, even with only a half-moon. Then Lake Gris, a narrow lake about twelve miles long. I set us down outside of Cessens, in a nice open field on a ridge overlooking the lake. A bit tricky, but very secluded."

Tricky I didn't mind, if it meant no Krauts.

We flew on, no sign of movement below us, not a single light visible in the blacked-out countryside. The drone of the engine was mesmerizing, lulling us into a sense of security and safety, the sudden, surprising bright barrage of fire now behind us. The high, clear canopy gave us a majestic view of the sparkling heavens. The half-moon, the stars, and the faint glow from the instrument panel our only illuminations, guiding us as we traveled across a calm sea of inky black.

I almost relaxed.

"What is that?" Kaz asked, leaning forward and pointing at two o'clock. Searchlights flickered in the distance, an orange glow growing at the horizon.

"Bloody Bomber Command most likely," the pilot answered in a low growl. "Hitting the rail yards in Lyon. Or the airfield west of the city. Either way, they've stirred up a hornet's nest for us."

"Can we go around it?" I asked.

"No," he said. "I don't have the fuel. We're at the extreme range as it is. I topped off at a forward airstrip in Normandy, but I've barely enough to make it back."

"We must fly through that?" Kaz asked. As we drew closer, the night sky grew brighter with searchlights, explosions, and burning buildings.

"Unless you Joes want to abort the mission. Say the word and I'll turn around."

"Have you ever had to abort?" I asked.

"No. Thought I'd offer, that's all," he said, turning to smile at us. SOE pilot humor, I guess. "It's not as bad as it looks, mates.

We're under their radar, and the Jerries are looking for high-altitude bombers, not our little Lysander."

"Don't fly under the bomber formation," Kaz said. "Being hit by an RAF bomb would be more embarrassing than being shot down by the Swiss."

"Right you are," the pilot said. "Now all we need to do is catch a glimpse of the Rhône River. It'll be even easier with the sky all lit up. Jerry's doing us a favor!"

That was one way of looking at it.

We drew closer to the city, the searchlights casting wide beams of white light, looking like columns holding up the night sky. Phosphorescent tracer bullets sought out the bombers, dancing against the darkness in graceful, deadly arcs. Bombs exploded in front of us, maybe a quarter of a mile away. The pilot banked the Lysander, moving away from the flames and smoke. The aircraft shook as shock waves from the explosions buffeted us, sending the plane into a sideways dive. The ground looked damned close.

"Hang on," the pilot told us, as if we hadn't already figured that one out. He pulled the small craft up, his voice a nervous quiver he couldn't quite hide. "That's the main rail yard. We should be fine now. Look, there's the river."

It was the Rhône, heading west from the burning city, shimmering with moonlight and mayhem, antiaircraft fire dying down as the bomber stream departed.

"Is the airplane damaged?" Kaz asked. There was a metallic rattle coming from the fuselage.

"She's banged up," the pilot said. "But I can hold her steady, don't worry. The good news is I can cut some time off our trip and make sure you chaps get to Cessens. The Rhône meanders a good bit, so I'll cut across the bends heading ninety degrees west. That'll bring us to Lake Gris all the quicker."

"What's the bad news?" I asked.

"It will bring us close to a Luftwaffe airfield. Sounds worse than it is, really. Any night fighters they have left will be airborne, going after the bombers. We'll scoot right by. You should be on the ground in thirty minutes."

"So the airfield poses no danger?" Kaz asked, his tone skeptical.

"Right. Long as one of the flak batteries doesn't open up on us. So, once again, hang on." He increased speed and lost altitude, skimming the treetops until we found ourselves over open fields. It felt as if he were going in for a landing at two hundred miles an hour. The rattle clanged even faster, the fuselage shuddering as we raced for the next bend in the river.

"Airfield coming up on the right," the pilot informed us through clenched teeth as he held the yoke firmly in his hands.

"There," Kaz said, pointing to black shapes that were probably hangers. The landscape zipped by underneath us, and we were nearly clear, about to leave the blacked-out airfield behind.

Then the sky lit up.

Searchlights, some only a few hundred yards away.

Bright explosions ripped into the blackness ahead, followed by a series of blasts falling across our path. I lifted my hands to shield my eyes as one of the beams caught us, sending blinding white light into the canopy. More explosions sounded as the pilot climbed, seeking to escape the clutches of the searchlight and the antiaircraft fire it would soon bring to bear.

Concussions from the bombs hit us, shaking the Lysander, dragging it through the sky as if it were a kite on a string. We'd guessed wrong. The bombers were targeting both the rail yards and the airfield. We'd flown straight into the second raid.

The light found us again, staying with the Lysander even as the pilot gave up on altitude and put the nose down, hoping to shake the flak. Tracers burned the night sky, hitting us in the wing, shearing metal, and sending us into a spin.

The searchlight lost us. I grabbed onto my seat and Kaz's arm, hoping the pilot could steady the aircraft. I braced for impact.

It didn't come. The sturdy Lysander managed to fly straight, so low we could've been hit by a well-thrown stone. I craned my neck to see behind us, the orange glow of flames and the white search-lights fading in the distance. Wind whistled through a bullet hole in the canopy, the clanging rattle of metal still sounding from within the fuselage.

"The aircraft is damaged," Kaz said, as calmly as he might observe that it may well rain.

"She'll get you there, don't you worry," the pilot said. "Although getting me back home is another thing altogether."

"You are welcome to join us, if you wish," Kaz said.

"Not in the cards, Joe. The Germans would love to get their hands on a Lysander. I'll stay with the plane until you're safely away and then put the torch to her. Maybe I'll get lucky and spend the rest of the war learning French from a farmer's daughter, if Jerry doesn't catch me."

"Sorry," I said. I felt bad for him, but at the same time I was glad he didn't take Kaz up on the invite. Things would be tough enough without an extra man along. If he was lucky, our Resistance contacts would leave somebody with him. But we had places to go, and fast.

"C'est la guerre," he answered, the yoke vibrating violently in his hands.

A harsh knock came from the engine, followed by a metal-on-metal grating. The propeller stopped. Oil sprayed the windscreen.

"Oh shit," the pilot said.

The Lysander dropped from the sky.

CHAPTER TWO

"BILLY! WAKE UP!"

I felt someone push me. It was Kaz, bracing himself against my shoulder and grunting in between shouts for me to wake up. I tried to clear my head, but it hurt like blazes. I wanted nothing more than for him to shut up and get off me so I could go back to sleep.

Then I began to choke.

That got my attention. I tried to focus, wiping my eyes with the back of my hand. It came away wet and sticky with blood. Kaz was kicking at the canopy, using me to steady himself as he hammered away at the latch.

"It's stuck," he announced. Obviously, since otherwise why would we be inside a crashed aircraft filling with smoke?

"Let me," I said, twisting around in the seat to bring my legs up. I smashed both feet against the twisted metal frame, once, twice, and then again. The latch broke as I gasped for air, and Kaz shoved the shattered canopy back. The air drew smoke like a chimney, and my gasps turned to ragged coughs.

"The pilot," I managed to croak.

"Dead," was all Kaz said as he clambered down the ladder on the side of the fuselage. "Hurry!"

I leaned forward as I made for the opening. The pilot was slumped over the yoke, his bloodied head at a terribly wrong angle.

Sparks flashed on his instrument panel, followed by the soft sound of gas fumes igniting. Flames drove me back, licking at my limbs as I made for the open canopy and jumped to the ground. I rolled into Kaz's arms and he dragged me away as fire spread from the engine, half-buried in the damp ground. It filled the rear compartment, roaring and swirling within the Perspex enclosure, the blaze an angry crimson column as it raced out the opening and into the air.

Then the fuel tank went up, a bright, searing fireball lifting the Lysander and slamming it back into the earth in a flurry of broken metal and black smoke. The heat scorched our faces as we scrambled backward, arms linked and eyes fixed on the conflagration.

"Are you badly injured?" Kaz asked.

I didn't know.

"I don't think so," I said, feeling my forehead. I winced as I found a gash on my scalp, hair matted in sticky blood. "We have to move."

"Right. We are not far beyond the airfield. This fire will be visible for miles, and the Germans are sure to investigate." Kaz helped me up, his eyes darting to the horizon. We were in the middle of a field, lush green grass that might have made good grazing for some farmer's herd of sheep. Our pilot picked the crash site well, if he'd had any say in the matter.

"Which way?" I asked. Kaz took a compass from his pocket and waited for the luminous hand to steady. The burning wreckage cast a flickering light against his face, the steel-rimmed glasses reflecting a shimmering yellow glow. His high cheekbones were marred on one side by a scar that split his face from eye to chin. The other side was darkness. Much like Kaz himself.

"East is that way," he said, snapping the compass shut and nodding toward the forested hillside ahead.

I brushed the dirt from my trousers and adjusted the strap of the small rucksack across my shoulder. We each had a few supplies.

K rations, maps, matches, a flashlight, and extra cartridges, not to mention a wad of Swiss francs. We were both armed with a revolver, no real match for a swarm of Krauts looking for downed airmen.

Then it hit me.

The rear canopy was open. They'd know someone made it out, which meant they'd come looking. I stopped, watching the inferno burning itself out. But not fast enough. Kaz caught my eye, nodding his understanding.

We searched the ground for a stick or a branch, anything big enough to push the canopy closed without getting too close to the red-hot fuselage. I came up with a tree limb, probably snapped off by the crash. I tried to push against the canopy, but it was the wrong angle. The canopy opened to the rear, sliding on rails. With the aircraft nose down, it was too high to reach, and besides, the branch gave me nothing to grab on with.

"I could climb the ladder," Kaz said as I threw the useless wood aside. Lysanders had a metal ladder built into the side, to make for quick drop-offs and pickups. From the top, only a few steps up, the canopy would be within easy reach.

"The metal on the canopy is too hot," I said. "Not to mention the ladder itself. How could you grab hold?"

"Give me your overcoat," Kaz said. We were wearing civilian clothes, and I was taller by almost a head. He was going to use the longer sleeves as gloves.

"You sure?" I asked as I shed my wool overcoat.

"It's better than being chased by Germans," he said. He put my coat on over his, giving him more protection from the heat. I emptied my rucksack, putting the strap across his shoulder.

"Use this to snag the handle and pull it shut," I said. He tucked his hands as far inside the sleeves as they'd go and reached for the rung. The flames weren't as ferocious as before, but the fuel was still burning off. The stench of roasted flesh assailed us, and for a second, we both staggered back. I cupped my hands to give Kaz a boost. With one hand on my shoulder, the other grasping hot metal, he started up. I prayed the thick wool would protect him.

Two steps and he was close to the canopy. Still holding on with one hand, he leaned back and tossed the strap at the handle, tantalizingly close.

He missed.

Another toss, another miss. I checked the horizon in the direction of the airfield. Maybe they weren't coming.

Kaz made another throw, this time hitting the mark. He let go of the ladder, pulling on the rucksack with both hands. He grunted, leaning away from the fuselage. He yelled, cursing in Polish as he pulled as hard as he could.

The canopy slid forward. Kaz tumbled from the ladder, falling onto me. We both hit the ground hard.

"Are you okay?" I asked, checking his hand. The fabric was smoking.

"Yes, I think so." He shook his hand and winced. "A small burn, perhaps, but nothing too bad."

I could see a red line in his palm by the light of the fire. Another few seconds and it would have been much worse.

"But we must take care of that," he said, pointing to the canopy. The rucksack hung from the exterior handle. I looked around for the branch, which would now come in handy. As I did, I saw a faint light in the distance. Moving. Bouncing, as if going over a country road.

"Germans!" I whispered, even though I could have shouted without my voice carrying far enough to worry. On the run in civilian clothes behind enemy lines had that kind of effect. I grabbed the rucksack and gathered up the contents I'd emptied from it. The headlights were closer now, coming cross country and making for the burning wreckage. Kaz tossed me my coat and we hightailed it out of there, due east, up a gently rising knoll, until we were safely under cover in the pines.

"Give me your hand," I said, opening the first-aid kit. I squeezed burn ointment into his palm and wrapped it with gauze. Kaz whispered his thanks as we peered into the night, watching two trucks park near the Lysander, headlights illuminating the ground around it. Germans swarmed about the aircraft, dark smoke billowing from the engine as the fire lessened. I could make out shouted orders and saw soldiers fanning out in a methodical search. Nothing unusual about that. If they thought this was a planned landing gone bad, there might be members of the Resistance nearby. Not that any sane SOE pilot would voluntarily set down a few miles from a Luftwaffe airfield.

"We should go," Kaz said.

"Right," I said, stuffing the medical kit back into my rucksack. I rummaged through the contents, looking for the map, hoping it included our current area.

It wasn't there.

"Damn," I said with a hiss. "The map's gone. I thought I put it back."

"They might not find it," Kaz said. "Or they may think it came from the aircraft. The front canopy was fairly smashed." A dog barked. Sharp, mad dog growls.

"If he has a scent from the map—" I said.

"Run," Kaz said, grabbing me by the shoulder. I followed, working to keep Kaz in sight. Moonlight was sparse within the pine forest, the sound of Kaz's feet on the soft ground my best guide. We both took a few tumbles, tripping on roots and rocks invisible in the gloomy dark.

Soon the land began to slope downward, and we sped up, sliding and careening through stands of dead pine, many of the trees snapped in a windstorm like matchsticks.

"Careful," I panted, catching up to Kaz. "We don't need a broken leg."

"That would be inconvenient," he said, gasping for breath. "As would be a German shepherd at my throat." We took a quick rest, heaving in the crisp night air, listening for sounds of the chase. Barks echoed against the hillside, the dog excited at the prospect of a moonlight hunt.

"How fast can a dog run?" Kaz asked.

"Plenty fast," I said. "But his handler won't let him run free. He'll keep a tight leash until he has us in sight."

"And then?"

"Then they shoot us, or unleash the dog. Unless we give up, and then they shoot us later."

"The prospects are quite limited, Billy. Is there anything can we do?"

"Keep running, for one. There's a chance that dog is a plain old guard dog. He'd be dangerous if he saw us, but if he's not trained to follow a scent, all we need to do is stay ahead of him."

"Let's go," Kaz said. "Since we have no way of knowing, we should assume he is tracking us. Although it is *your* scent on the map, Billy." Before I had a chance at a wiseacre comeback, the barking started up again. Too close for comfort, tracker or guard dog.

I wet my finger and held it up. The wind was coming from the east, the direction we were headed.

"We could start a fire," I said. "It's the only thing that could throw him off the scent."

"Burn all traces," Kaz said. "Good."

"The smoke will do most of the work. The wind will blow it right in their faces. Gather some wood."

We were surrounded by dead and weathered limbs, perfect for starting a forest fire. The trick was to get it going fast. They'd spot the fire in no time, so it had to be a blazing inferno with thick, choking smoke before they got too close. We stacked small branches against a fallen tree and I lit a match. The wind blew it out. I tried another, shielding it with my body. The flame took, climbing twigs and brush until it leaped onto larger sticks, the dry pine a tinderbox of roaring, dancing fire in no time. The wind fanned the sparks, sending glowing embers out over the fallen trees.

We had our inferno.

A rapid pace took us to the crest of the next hill, where we stopped to rest and check on our pursuers. Lines of yellow and red blurred by whirling smoke snaked down the slope, obscuring our visions. And theirs. No dog barked, no boots thumped against the ground.

"They've given up?" Kaz said.

"Or wised up," I said. "Why fight your way through smoke and fire when there are other Germans to the east? There have to be patrols along the Swiss border."

"We're not close enough for border patrols," Kaz said. "I prefer to think they've gone back to their warm beds. No reason for all of us to be miserable out here."

"You're a prince, Kaz," I said, slapping him on the shoulder as we leaned into the wind and continued our eastward journey.

"A mere baron, Billy, but thank you."

OTHER TITLES IN THE SOHO CRIME SERIES

Sebastià Alzamora
(Spain)
Blood Crime

Stephanie Barron
(Jane Austen's England)
*Jane and the Twelve Days
of Christmas*
Jane and the Waterloo Map

F.H. Batacan
(Philippines)
Smaller and Smaller Circles

Quentin Bates
(Iceland)
Frozen Assets
Cold Comfort
Chilled to the Bone

James R. Benn
(World War II Europe)
Billy Boyle
The First Wave
Blood Alone
Evil for Evil
Rag & Bone
A Mortal Terror
Death's Door
A Blind Goddess
The Rest Is Silence
The White Ghost
Blue Madonna
The Devouring

Cara Black
(Paris, France)
Murder in the Marais
Murder in Belleville
Murder in the Sentier
Murder in the Bastille
Murder in Clichy
Murder in Montmartre
*Murder on the
Ile Saint-Louis*
*Murder in the
Rue de Paradis*

Cara Black cont.
Murder in the Latin Quarter
Murder in the Palais Royal
Murder in Passy
*Murder at the
Lanterne Rouge*
*Murder Below
Montparnasse*
Murder in Pigalle
*Murder on the
Champ de Mars*
Murder on the Quai
Murder in Saint-Germain

Lisa Brackmann
(China)
Rock Paper Tiger
Hour of the Rat
Dragon Day

Getaway
Go-Between

Henry Chang
(Chinatown)
Chinatown Beat
Year of the Dog
Red Jade
Death Money
Lucky

Barbara Cleverly
(England)
The Last Kashmiri Rose
Strange Images of Death
The Blood Royal
Not My Blood
A Spider in the Cup
Enter Pale Death
Diana's Altar

Gary Corby
(Ancient Greece)
The Pericles Commission
The Ionia Sanction
Sacred Games

Gary Corby cont.
The Marathon Conspiracy
Death Ex Machina
The Singer from Memphis
Death on Delos

Colin Cotterill
(Laos)
The Coroner's Lunch
Thirty-Three Teeth
Disco for the Departed
Anarchy and Old Dogs
Curse of the Pogo Stick
The Merry Misogynist
*Love Songs from
a Shallow Grave*
Slash and Burn
*The Woman Who
Wouldn't Die*
*The Six and a
Half Deadly Sins*
I Shot the Buddha
The Rat Catchers' Olympics

Garry Disher
(Australia)
The Dragon Man
Kittyhawk Down
Snapshot
Chain of Evidence
Blood Moon
Wyatt
Whispering Death
Port Vila Blues
Fallout
Hell to Pay
Signal Loss

David Downing
(World War II Germany)
Zoo Station
Silesian Station
Stettin Station
Potsdam Station
Lehrter Station
Masaryk Station

David Downing cont.
(World War I)
Jack of Spies
One Man's Flag
Lenin's Roller Coaster

Agnete Friis
(Denmark)
What My Body Remembers

Leighton Gage
(Brazil)
Blood of the Wicked
Buried Strangers
Dying Gasp
Every Bitter Thing
A Vine in the Blood
Perfect Hatred
The Ways of Evil Men

Michael Genelin
(Slovakia)
Siren of the Waters
Dark Dreams
The Magician's Accomplice
Requiem for a Gypsy

Timothy Hallinan
(Thailand)
The Fear Artist
For the Dead
The Hot Countries
Fools' River

(Los Angeles)
Crashed
Little Elvises
The Fame Thief
Herbie's Game
King Maybe
Fields Where They Lay

Karo Hämäläinen
(Finland)
Cruel Is the Night

Mette Ivie Harrison
(Mormon Utah)
The Bishop's Wife
His Right Hand
For Time and All Eternities

Mick Herron
(England)
Down Cemetery Road
The Last Voice You Hear
Reconstruction
Smoke and Whispers
Why We Die
Slow Horses
Dead Lions
Nobody Walks
Real Tigers
Spook Street
This Is What Happened

Lene Kaaberbøl &
Agnete Friis
(Denmark)
The Boy in the Suitcase
Invisible Murder
Death of a Nightingale
The Considerate Killer

Heda Margolius Kovály
(1950s Prague)
Innocence

Martin Limón
(South Korea)
Jade Lady Burning
Slicky Boys
Buddha's Money
The Door to Bitterness
The Wandering Ghost
G.I. Bones
Mr. Kill
The Joy Brigade
Nightmare Range
The Iron Sickle
The Ville Rat
Ping-Pong Heart
The Nine-Tailed Fox

Ed Lin
(Taiwan)
Ghost Month
Incensed

Peter Lovesey
(England)
The Circle
The Headhunters

Peter Lovesey cont.
False Inspector Dew
Rough Cider
On the Edge
The Reaper

(Bath, England)
The Last Detective
Diamond Solitaire
The Summons
Bloodhounds
Upon a Dark Night
The Vault
Diamond Dust
The House Sitter
The Secret Hangman
Skeleton Hill
Stagestruck
Cop to Corpse
The Tooth Tattoo
The Stone Wife
Down Among the Dead Men
Another One Goes Tonight

(London, England)
Wobble to Death
*The Detective Wore
Silk Drawers*
Abracadaver
Mad Hatter's Holiday
The Tick of Death
A Case of Spirits
Swing, Swing Together
Waxwork

Jassy Mackenzie
(South Africa)
Random Violence
Stolen Lives
The Fallen
Pale Horses
Bad Seeds

Francine Mathews
(Nantucket)
Death in the Off-Season
Death in Rough Water
Death in a Mood Indigo
Death in a Cold Hard Light
Death on Nantucket

Seichō Matsumoto
(Japan)
*Inspector Imanishi
Investigates*

Magdalen Nabb
(Italy)
*Death of an Englishman
Death of a Dutchman
Death in Springtime
Death in Autumn
The Marshal and
the Murderer
The Marshal and
the Madwoman
The Marshal's Own Case
The Marshal Makes
His Report
The Marshal
at the Villa Torrini
Property of Blood
Some Bitter Taste
The Innocent
Vita Nuova
The Monster of Florence*

Fuminori Nakamura
(Japan)
*The Thief
Evil and the Mask
Last Winter, We Parted
The Kingdom
The Boy in the Earth*

Stuart Neville
(Northern Ireland)
*The Ghosts of Belfast
Collusion
Stolen Souls
The Final Silence
Those We Left Behind
So Say the Fallen*

(Dublin)
Ratlines

Rebecca Pawel
(1930s Spain)
*Death of a Nationalist
Law of Return
The Watcher in the Pine
The Summer Snow*

Kwei Quartey
(Ghana)
*Murder at Cape
Three Points
Gold of Our Fathers
Death by His Grace*

Qiu Xiaolong
(China)
*Death of a Red Heroine
A Loyal Character Dancer
When Red Is Black*

John Straley
(Alaska)
*The Woman Who
Married a Bear
The Curious Eat Themselves
The Big Both Ways
Cold Storage, Alaska*

Akimitsu Takagi
(Japan)
*The Tattoo Murder Case
Honeymoon to Nowhere
The Informer*

Helene Tursten
(Sweden)
*Detective Inspector Huss
The Torso
The Glass Devil
Night Rounds
The Golden Calf
The Fire Dance
The Beige Man
The Treacherous Net
Who Watcheth
Protected by the Shadows*

**Janwillem van de
Wetering**
(Holland)
*Outsider in Amsterdam
Tumbleweed
The Corpse on the Dike
Death of a Hawker
The Japanese Corpse
The Blond Baboon
The Maine Massacre
The Mind-Murders
The Streetbird
The Rattle-Rat
Hard Rain
Just a Corpse at Twilight
Hollow-Eyed Angel
The Perfidious Parrot
The Sergeant's Cat:
Collected Stories*

Timothy Williams
(Guadeloupe)
*Another Sun
The Honest Folk
of Guadeloupe*

(Italy)
*Converging Parallels
The Puppeteer
Persona Non Grata
Black August
Big Italy
The Second Day
of the Renaissance*

Jacqueline Winspear
(1920s England)
*Maisie Dobbs
Birds of a Feather*